T0267513

SEELIE CASTLE

CASTLE

TERRA

THE WITCH EATER'S COTTAGE

FAERY VALLEY

THE NEVERENDING FOREST

ONYX

SIREN'S SEA

ASHWOOD FOREST

JACK'S MANSION

CRYSTAL LAKE

THE MARKETPLACE

CALLA'S APARTMENT

ESTRELLA

STARLIGHT INN

MAP OF ILLUSTROS

HUMAN TERRITORIES

A Reckless Oath

A RECKLESS OATH

KAYLIE SMITH

HYPERION
Los Angeles   New York

Copyright © 2024 Kaylie Smith

All rights reserved. Published by Hyperion, an imprint of Buena Vista Books, Inc. No part of this book may be reproduced or transmitted in any form or by any means, electronic or mechanical, including photocopying, recording, or by any information storage and retrieval system, without written permission from the publisher. For information address Hyperion, 77 West 66th Street, New York, New York 10023.

First Edition, January 2024
10 9 8 7 6 5 4 3 2 1
FAC-004510-23313
Printed in the United States of America

This book is set in Minion Pro, 1726 Real Espanola, and Caslon Antique Pro/Fontspring
Stock images: suns (title page): 1993962125; sun and moons (chapter openers): 1194153976/Shutterstock
Designed by Tyler Nevins
Map © 2022 Sveta Dorosheva

Library of Congress Cataloging-in-Publication Data

Names: Smith, Kaylie, author. • Smith, Kaylie. Ruinous fate.
Title: A reckless oath / by Kaylie Smith.
Description: Los Angeles; New York: Hyperion, 2024. • Series: A ruinous
    fate • Audience: Ages 14–18. • Audience: Grades 10–12. • Summary: "Calla
    and friends must deal with their losses and come to grips with their own
    part to play in the Fates' War ahead"—Provided by publisher.
Identifiers: LCCN 2023017296 • ISBN 9781368081634 (hardcover) •
    ISBN 9781368081849 (ebook)
Subjects: CYAC: Fate and fatalism—Fiction. • Witches—Fiction. •
    Magic—Fiction. • Revenge—Fiction. • Fantasy. • LCGFT: Fantasy fiction. • Novels.
Classification: LCC PZ7.1.S6393 Re 2024 • DDC [Fic]—dc23
LC record available at https://lccn.loc.gov/2023017296

Reinforced binding
Visit www.HyperionTeens.com

SUSTAINABLE FORESTRY INITIATIVE
Certified Sourcing
www.forests.org
SFI-01681

Logo Applies to Text Stock Only

For Isaac—wherever you go, I'll follow. Anywhere. Everywhere.

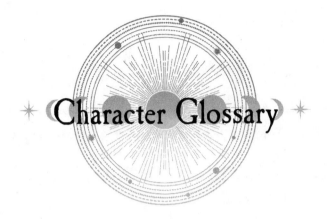

Character Glossary

THE WITCHES

Onyx

Lysandra Black (she/her): The Onyx Queen, mother of Gideon and Ezra.

Gideon Black (he/him): The elder Onyx Prince, son of Lysandra. Gideon is also one of the six fated Blood Warriors and is soul-bonded to Calla Rosewood.

Ezra Black (he/him): The younger Onyx Prince, son of Lysandra.

Caspian "Cass" Ironside (he/him): An Onyx witch and Gideon's best friend. Kestrel's beta in the Onyx Queen's Guild, alongside Gideon.

Kestrel Whitehollow (he/him): Commander in the Onyx Queen's Guild.

Rouge

Myrea (she/her): The Rouge Queen.

Calliope "Calla" Rosewood (she/her): A Blood Siphon and one of the six fated Blood Warriors. She is soul-bonded to Gideon Black.

Hannah Carmine (she/her): Calla's and Delphine's best friend. Trained in necromancy and dark magic.

THE SIRENS

Delphine DeLune (she/her): Calla's and Hannah's best friend. Formerly part of Reniel's Shoal in the Siren's Sea.

Reniel (he/him): Leader of a Shoal in the Siren's Sea.

Celeste (she/her): Member of Reniel's Shoal. Delphine's former roommate and love interest.

Eros (he/him): Member of Reniel's Shoal.

Zephyr (he/him): Member of Reniel's Shoal.

Bellator (he/him): Reniel's brother.

THE VALKYRIES

Ignia (she/her): The Queen of the Valkyries.

Amina (she/her): A once-exiled Valkyrie and Lyra's and Sabine's best friend.

Sabine (she/her): Lyra's and Amina's best friend.

Lyra (they/them): Sabine's and Amina's best friend.

Meli (she/her): Sabine's ex.

OTHERS

The Gods of Fate: Four beings who rule over Illustros.

The Wayfarer: A mysterious magical being who is cursed to roam the planet.

Jack of All Trades (he/him): Calla's former landlord and leader of the largest black-market trading group in Estrella. Human.

Witch Eater (they/them): Ancient immortal being that resides in a cottage within the Neverending Forest and tracks the affairs of the Gods of Fate.

Em (she/they): The Witch Eater's familiar—a soulless, shapeshifter bound to do the Witch Eater's bidding until their debt is paid.

Prologue

The flames devouring the night around the witch cracked like breaking bones. He could feel the call of the Witch's Die thrumming through his veins as he got closer and closer to the spawn site. The pounding of footsteps echoing in the distance and the blazing inferno at his back spurred on his pace until he reached a breakneck speed. This was a race—and the price of losing was death.

A harsh expletive slipped from his lips as his muscles tightened in pain. He wasn't sure how much more his body could take at this rate, the spasms in his calves making his stride wooden. Just as he was about to crash over his breaking point, he finally saw it—the crimson beacon of light emitting from the Witch's Die twinkling through the thicket of the bloodroot field ahead. Luring him closer and closer to his long-awaited fate. A cry of relief fell from his mouth in sync with the shout of someone behind him, but they were too late. He crashed into the field, swiping bloodroot stalks from his path, trampling their thorned vines under his heavy boots.

There it was.

He dove toward the cursed cube, scooping it up and tossing it back down in a blink. The soldiers at his back caught up an instant later, but by the time they hauled him to his feet, the magic die had already settled onto its chosen number.

Five.

A burst of golden light erupted from the witch's left arm, and the soldiers paused in shock. He grinned as he looked down at the black dots that mapped out his Rolls of Fate, nerves humming with anticipation as the sixth, and final, number appeared. An instant later, the fateful marks began turning into a gilded constellation on his arm, each dot shimmering to life one by one.

When the golden light finally faded away, he felt the magic in his core shift into something different, something colder.

He spun to face the band of Rouge soldiers surrounding him in the middle of the bloodroot now, the thorned plants wilting from the growing heat around them. One of the Rouge witches unsheathed a dagger from their belt and lunged forward, jabbing the weapon right into his abdomen. The tip of the blade pierced the material of his shirt without hesitation, but when the sharp point met his skin beneath, the steel bent and curled in on itself. He knew then that the curse was locked into place, that all the rumors were true. His flesh would no longer be able to be penetrated by weapons, his physical being now impervious to any magic or harm.

Someone in the distance shouted a gruff order, but the world around him had faded. In this moment it was just him and his destiny—more tangible than it had ever been before. Relief and fear flooded his body in equal measure as the laughter that bubbled out of his throat became wilder than the encroaching flames.

The fifth Blood Warrior had been chosen.

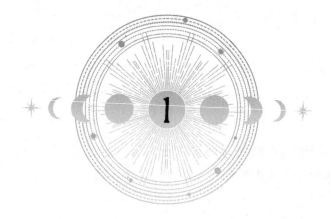

Delphine DeLune was surrounded by darkness.

She was sitting against the rocky wall of her cell, bound in chains, with her head drooping in exhaustion. There was no way to tell exactly how long she had been down here, but it was long enough for the webbing between her fingers and toes to fully grow back in.

A metallic *clang* vibrated through the water, and she lifted her head to see the door of the cell opening, her silver hair floating up around her face with the movement. A tall silhouette hovered in the doorway. Delphine's eyes slowly adjusted to the intruding brightness, a sharp pang shooting through her head as she strained to focus on the details of the person's face. She didn't need to be able to see to know exactly who was before her, however.

The man who strutted forward was a waking nightmare, one that made her entire body clench with the anticipation of pain. He sank down until he was at her eye level, a glint of light bouncing off something around his neck. A key.

A wicked smile slashed across his face. "Ready, moonlight?"

Delphine let out a vicious scream of rage as he gathered her chains and dragged her out of the room.

T hunder rolled through the tempestuous sky above the Neverending Forest as Calla stalked through the woods. Rain was pouring down around her, soaking her hair and saturating her clothes until they clung to her body like a second skin. The ground beneath her shoes had turned to mud, the pungent smell of earth permeating the air as she blinked droplets of water from her eyelashes.

The scream of terror hadn't been too much farther ahead.

Calla wove through the trees, ducking out of reach of the twisted branches that jutted into her path. Her steps made an awful squelching sound as the mud tried to glue her feet in place, but her momentum never slowed. Not until she reached what she was looking for. Or rather *who* she was looking for.

There, a few yards away—caught in a trap Caspian had made out of vines with meticulous expertise—was a very familiar green-haired nymph.

Calla surged forward, the pounding of her steps echoing the onslaught falling from the sky. When she halted in front of the nymph struggling in the makeshift net, a spike of triumphant adrenaline shot through her veins. Every time the nymph tugged against the tangled trap, the vines constricted tighter and tighter.

"*Let me go!*" she cried, panic seeping into her gaze.

"No," Calla answered, her voice nearly drowned out by the rain. "You owe me something, and I'm here to collect."

The roar of the tempest swirling above them was climbing to a crescendo now. The nymph looked as if she were about to respond with something cutting when her eyes flicked over Calla's shoulder, relief replacing the panic.

Before Calla could turn, she felt the cool press of a knife against her throat. She swallowed and the steel blade scraped at her skin, but she didn't so much as flinch.

"Don't make a single move," a voice hissed from behind.

It was the rose-haired nymph—whose name was too buried in a foggy memory to remember—and Calla smiled with satisfaction that she'd managed to lure them both here much faster than she expected.

"Have you forgotten what I am?" Calla tilted her head, letting the knife glide over her wet skin and leave a shallow cut. She felt a hot trickle of blood drip from the wound down her neck.

"I'll spill your blood—" the nymph began, but before she could get the entire threat out, Calla was reaching up to grip her wrist like a vise, causing the knife to dig even deeper for a sharp moment.

Calla focused on the way the nymph's chest heaved against her back in fear as her inner siphon locked on to its mark. The nymph tried to pull away, but Calla spun, mud splattering underfoot, hand shooting out to grip the woman's throat this time. "Whatever impression that the two of you, this forest, or the Gods might have been under before, let me assure you I am no longer someone you want to play your little games with," Calla said in an even tone as her magic fully awakened and stretched in her bones. "You owe my friend and me each a favor, and I'm not leaving until we receive them."

To drive the point home, Calla carefully reached out with her magic and drained a kernel of the nymph's energy. Just enough to make her blood sing with anticipation and the woman's pulse to go into overdrive with fear.

"Please," the nymph choked out, the knife in her hand falling to the ground at their feet. "We'll settle our debt. Just let Gabi go!"

Gabi, Calla's mind parroted as she recognized the trapped nymph's name. Calla's last encounter with the two of them had been too hazy to commit any of the details to memory, but tonight she was prepared for any mind tricks the two of them might attempt. She had ingested a handful of glamour-resistant elderberries Caspian had been collecting during their journey. The same ones Gideon had tied around her wrist before they entered the forest—since the bracelet had been lost during the chaos in their showdown with the hydra. Right before everything went from bad to worse.

"I want a way to bring someone back from the dead," Calla ordered as the worst of those memories threatened to drag themselves out of the dark pit of her mind.

Gabi's emerald eyes bulged at Calla's demand. "We cannot perform that kind of magic—"

"Then you're going to find me someone who can," Calla asserted.

"Darci and I cannot do that sort of magic," Gabi continued, "but *you* can. You're a Rouge witch. Your queen chose the source of her line's magic to be both blood and bones. Life and death."

Calla's eyes narrowed at the suggestion. "Necromancy only reanimates the dead; it doesn't reconnect the *soul*. And I won't use dark magic." She thought of Hannah. After years of being forced to perform necromancy, Hannah's magic had gone dormant, and now her friend became violently sick every time she even attempted to access it.

"If it's a soul you're looking for, the avenues to get a spirit back are not as easy to find," Darci inserted, the tight grip Calla maintained on her neck making the words a bit faint. "Valkyries, for example, can harvest souls and ferry them wherever they'd like, as well as summon them directly from the afterlife, but finding one willing to do such a task wouldn't be easy."

"Out of the question." Calla shook her head. "Next."

"None of the alternatives really matter if the corpse you're trying to reconnect a soul with doesn't have a *heart*," Darci taunted.

Calla sucked in a breath. "How the Hells do you know about that?"

"We know plenty. Whispers of what may have happened at the Witch Eater's cottage have reached every edge of the forest, but most of that is just petty gossip. The real damning truth is in the absence of the Valkyrie. Which can only mean one thing: she's paid her exile's debt." Darci's eyes gleamed with delighted spite. "Quite the ruckus you've caused—even by the Neverending Forest's standards."

"You're lucky I'm not requesting *your* heart to bring him back," Calla snapped, so close to unleashing her body's urge to siphon even more and wipe the smugness from the nymph's face. "I'm not in the mood for your judgmental tone."

The gleam in Darci's eyes dimmed at the silent threat beneath Calla's hold. *Good.*

"Back to the point," Calla pressed on. "Heart aside, how do I get a soul back?"

Hearts were replaceable. Souls were not.

"The Valley of Souls," Gabi blurted out. "If the Valkyrie hadn't reaped his soul, then it would have gone there. You can open a gateway to the Valley of Souls—with the right ingredients and spell—and then bring a soul back here with you."

"What ingredients? What spell?" Calla demanded.

"Summoning gateways requires an unprecedented amount of power and a token from the place you're trying to get to," Darci said. "As for the spell, again—we don't do such magic. You're on your own for that."

"You mean a token from the Valley of Souls specifically?"

Both girls nodded.

"That's what I want from you, then," Calla requested.

Darci smiled wickedly. "Sorry, you used up your favor already. You wanted to know a way to bring someone back from the dead, and we provided you with the directions to do so. You should choose your words more carefully next time you want to demand more than that."

This ought to have brought on Calla's ire, but she felt absolutely nothing. It was as if all her emotions in the last twenty-four hours had been replaced by a glacial apathy that was slowly spreading through her mind and body like poison. Even the torrent of rain pelting down on her skin felt like little more than an inconvenience.

She wondered if the moment Ezra had lost his heart, she had lost hers as well.

Calla finally let Darci go and watched, unmoved, as the woman began coughing. Instead of arguing, Calla stated, "You still owe the Onyx Prince a favor. I'll make sure we choose our words extra carefully for that one."

Darci wrinkled her nose with disdain. "You and that prince better watch your backs. You'll need much more than calling in a favor or two to get you out of the mess you're in. How's that soul-bond treating you so far?"

Calla narrowed her eyes. "What do you know about the soul-bond?"

The gleam in Darci's eyes was back. "Ah, so that rumor *is* true."

Damn it. Calla knew better than to be goaded into revealing her business to a fae, especially with such an easy trap. Since she was already here, though . . .

"Do you know how—" she began, but Darci cut off her words with a mocking giggle.

"Do we know how to break the bond? Sorry. We don't possess magic strong enough to sever a link that ingrained. I wouldn't bother trying to call in that favor." She paused. "*Why?* Tired of the elder Onyx Prince already? I thought he was the one you chose. That's what his brother was surely convinced of after seeing the two of you kiss, at least."

The words should have shattered Calla's heart—Darci looked as if she'd chosen them to do exactly that—but they barely registered.

"Gideon and I didn't *choose* the soul-bond," Calla retorted. "Nothing is going to stop me from—"

Heavy steps splashed through a nearby puddle to their left, and Calla's words died on her lips. Darci and Gabi both paled about three shades at the sight of the six-foot-two silhouette stepping out of the tree line.

"Calliope."

Speak of the devil, Calla thought as the magic in her core hummed at his arrival.

Gideon strode forward, his dripping cobalt-blue hair plastered to his forehead, eyes as dark as the storm, assessing the scene before him. His irises hadn't so much as flickered silver once in the last day.

Calla's body instinctively shifted toward Gideon as he approached, his all-black ensemble making him a shadow in the night. She squinted a bit as she trailed her eyes over his face and down his neck, noting the shallow knife cuts that mirrored her own and the blood from which had yet to be completely washed away by the rain. They hadn't had time to test the limits of their bond yet, but so far it seemed to have two clear effects—every injury one of them suffered the other did as well, and they could sense each other's heightened emotions if they were in close enough proximity. Or, at least Calla could sense Gideon's emotions. Right now, for example, she could feel the anger rolling through him, but all she had to return was indifference.

"You weren't supposed to come here alone," he told her with a hard look.

"I heard the scream and didn't want to risk them getting away." Calla shrugged.

Gideon's gaze roamed down Calla's figure, as if to make sure she was okay despite the fact that the soul-bond would have told him otherwise. She shifted on her feet, becoming very aware of the way she must have looked. Her hair was tangled in an unruly mess, her soggy tunic drooping over her thick curves in what was probably a very unflattering manner—as were the black trousers she'd borrowed from Cass that were much too snug to button and much too long to walk in. The hems had been folded into tight cuffs around her ankles three times in order for her to move without tripping on them. Never had she expected to be in the forest for the better half of a week when she and the girls had hastily left Estrella, and she was grateful she could squeeze into Caspian's pants at all.

Gideon's voice sounded tight as he interrupted her train of thought to ask, "Did you make the request—"

Calla nodded while the nymphs scowled next to them.

Gideon shifted his eyes away from her, with effort, and glanced over to Darci and Gabi. "I'll be keeping my favor in my back pocket for now, if you don't mind. Not that I give a fuck even if you do."

Darci bared her teeth at him. "Damn you to the Hells, *Prince*."

"I'm already there," Gideon riposted as he began walking away, beckoning for Calla to follow with a jerk of his head.

Calla ignored him and dug a knife out of the secret pocket in Caspian's trousers, stepping over to cut through the intricately knotted vines. Darci rushed to her friend, helping Gabi to free herself of the netting before sliding something off one of her fingers and tossing it at Calla's feet. "When he's ready to collect his favor, smash the stone to call on us. We'd prefer not to be trapped like wild animals by any of you ever again."

A heartbeat later both fae were out of sight.

Before Calla could bend over to pick up the ring, Gideon's voice rang out from right behind her.

"What were you saying to them when I walked up?"

She faced him, shifting a step back at his proximity as she racked her brain for the moment he was talking about.

Gideon and I didn't choose *the soul-bond. Nothing is going to stop me from finding a way to break it.* That's what she had been about to say when he walked up.

She shook her head. "Nothing of importance."

The lie might have been more bitter on her tongue if not for the tightrope they were currently walking and her fierce instinct not to push either of them over the edge. Things were too volatile to delve into the topic of their magic link right now. The heavy fog of death still clung to the air around them, and until she was sure there was even anything they could do about their bond, she'd rather focus on the more pressing issues at hand. Like finding Delphine and figuring out how to summon a gateway to the afterlife and find the Valley of Souls.

Gideon watched her for a long moment, a flash of lightning illuminating the solemn expression on his face. His jaw clenched as he finally looked away. If he suspected there was something she wasn't telling him, he didn't press the matter. "Did you get what we needed?"

She winced. "Not exactly. I didn't word my request carefully enough. . . . All I could get out of them was a few bits of information."

"Was the information at least helpful?"

She sighed. "If you mean in the way that now we know our quest isn't *impossible*—sure. It just involves finding a way to get to the Valley of Souls."

Gideon pinched the bridge of his nose. "I suppose I shouldn't have had very high expectations when it came to dealing with the fae. At least Cass remembered where to get the seaweed we'll need to go after Delphine. Anything else before we get the Hells out of this forest?"

Calla muttered, "I sure hope not. Our list of tasks is becoming damn near unmanageable as it is."

Gideon gave her a wary look and said, "Let's go fill in the others."

The prince didn't linger as Calla crouched down to fish the nymph's ring out of the mud, holding it out to let the rain wash the dirt away from the pink-and-green gemstone that adorned the top of its golden band. As she tilted her head to inspect it from the side, she caught a movement out the corner of her eye. Her body tensed and she twisted her head to the right, but nothing was there. Squinting through the downpour to scan the ground and woods around her, she didn't relax until a long minute later when there was still nothing of interest to note. She turned back to the ring—

And a black rabbit snatched it right out of her hand.

3

Amina paused when she reached the barrier at the end of the Neverending Forest. She had tried this many times before. All previous attempts had ended with her writhing on the forest floor in bone-shattering pain.

Thump-thump. Thump-thump. Thump-thump.

She looked down to the bloody heart of the Onyx Prince in her grip. An unfortunate end for the poor witch—but a new beginning for her.

She rolled her shoulders back and summoned her wings, spreading the feathery appendages out to their full span. She tightened her grip on the still-beating heart with one hand and raised her other to hover over the invisible veil before her. She could feel the tickling vibration of the forest's glamour against the delicate skin of her palm. She took a deep breath, then plunged her hand through, waiting for the curse that kept her exiled within these monstrous woods to activate and deny her escape just as it had before.

Except it didn't. This time, her arm passed right through.

Amina let out a sound of elation and lunged forward, moving through the thick, gel-like barrier and into the world outside with lightning speed, worried the magic keeping her trapped might change its mind at any moment. When she came out the other side, she almost cried. Stars, *real* stars, twinkled above her. Not fake ones fabricated by the forest's glamour. The scent of snow and witch hazel hit her nose a second later, and she inhaled deeply, reveling in the frigid breeze that glided across her skin.

Her exile was finally lifted.

Amina had not gotten to soar this high in over two years. She'd missed the wind caressing her curls and running through her feathers. Had she not been so eager to reach her destination, she might have stayed out until the break of dawn.

She flew miles and miles over the Onyx Witch Realm, the thin winter air at her current altitude a welcome burn in her lungs. In between the silver-lit cities scattered across the land below were expansive fields she knew were littered with purple and red witch hazel. About an hour after she flew over the Onyx Queen's gaudy palace, she finally crossed the midway point to her destination—Silver Lake. The mercurial lake looked especially ethereal beneath the moonlight, and Amina could have sobbed at the sight of it. She was almost home.

By the time she shot over the Witch Realm's border into the Land of the Valkyries and broke through the clouds to see the familiar marble-and-gold city of Valor in the distance, her wings felt as if they might give out at any moment. The tendons barely holding her weight begged her to stop, to rest, but the moment she spotted the crest of the expansive estate, she only pushed herself harder. About a half mile out, she tucked her wings together, tight against her back, and fell like an arrow through the night. She shot toward the familiar courtyard in front of a large manor, aiming to land on the checkered marble of the front terrace. As soon as she was mere feet away from the ground, she reopened her wings, letting them catch on the air like a parachute to gently drift the rest of the way down. When her bare feet touched the cool stone in front of the manor's steps, she let herself kneel and admire her surroundings in awe.

She was finally, blessedly, home.

Rising to her feet, she pounded up the marble steps that led to the grand front entry. She raised the knocker on the door and brought it down, hard, three times. Her entire body was poised with adrenaline when the door finally cracked open.

"Prepare to meet the end of my dagger for waking us up this damn early," the Valkyrie who answered the door grumbled.

Amina's breath caught as she stared at the girl before her, irrevocably different from the last time they had seen each other.

"*Amina?*" the girl choked out, stumbling a step outside.

Amina opened her mouth to say the Valkyrie's name, but at first it did not come. Her friend had transitioned, had made the perilous journey to the Veritas Tree—without her—and the old name she had once used for her friend was now dead and gone to the world. Replaced by a True Name.

Sabine, a voice in her head whispered, the magic of the Veritas Tree settling into her mind. A name as sharp and strong as a blade. It suited her friend perfectly.

"Sabine," Amina said, tasting the name in her mouth. Her entire body ached to wrap her arms around the other Valkyrie, but it had been so long since they'd seen each other, and Amina was worried such a sudden move would spook the other girl.

"*Amina,*" Sabine repeated, her pale jade eyes lighting up with emotion. "How are you here?"

"It's a long story," Amina stated. "I'd love to tell it to you . . . if I can come in?"

Sabine stepped aside in the doorway without hesitation and Amina pushed past, taking in the familiar grand foyer of the manor. Not a single detail had changed since she last saw it. It was exactly the way it had existed in her dreams.

"Is Lyra—" Amina began to ask, but as soon as she said Lyra's name it was as if she had summoned them.

Lyra rounded the corner at the end of the grand foyer, stalking through the house with great purpose. "Sabine, who— Dear Gods," Lyra whispered as they froze in their tracks.

"Lyra," Amina breathed.

The sound of their name on Amina's lips had Lyra's feet moving again, sprinting down the hall to meet their friend with a tight embrace. Sabine smiled softly as she joined in. They all stood like that for what felt like an hour, maybe even two, and when the trio finally pulled apart, Amina felt a little more solid than she had in the last two years.

"What happened?" Lyra swallowed thickly. "How did you escape?"

"Funny thing. Our queen must not have realized how common—or foolish—princes are when she set the price of my exile," Amina said, the heart hidden in the pocket of her dress pulsing right on cue.

Lyra and Sabine exchanged a *look*. Amina shifted on her feet.

"All right, we clearly have a lot to catch up on," Lyra told her. "After you've gotten some rest. I'm sure it was a long journey back."

"That sounds ideal," Amina agreed. "Is my old room still available?"

Lyra bit their lip. "Actually . . . Lark moved back in. About three years ago. He needed a place—"

"*Three* years ago?" Amina cut the Valkyrie off. "How long have I been gone?"

Lyra's expression turned melancholy.

"*How long have I been gone?*"

Sabine answered, "Six years, two months, and eighteen days."

Amina reared back. Six years. To her it had only been two, but of course time passed differently in the Neverending Forest—even the waters within the forest had their own measure of time. She had known that, but she still had never imagined that it had stolen four extra years from her. From all three of them. It was cruel, it was earth-shattering, it was . . . precisely why she had been exiled there. The Valkyrie Queen had made no mistake. Had known exactly the punishment she had sentenced Amina to.

"You need some rest," Lyra maintained. "You need to process. I'm sorry about your room. I didn't mean to . . . to upset you."

"No," Amina said, steeling her nerves. She shut out the emotions churning in her belly—the rage, the sadness, the agony—before she broke down in front of them. "It's fine. I can stay in a guest room."

Lyra nodded immediately. "Of course. Pick any one you'd like."

Amina dipped her chin in thanks and began to push past them, ignoring the glances the two of them exchanged as if they had created some secret language she did not know in the time she had been gone.

Six years.

"Amina?" Lyra called.

Amina glanced back over her shoulder but continued walking.

"Welcome home, friend."

Amina didn't answer, just slipped into the shadows of the house, her feet carrying her through the hallways, the memory of the manor's layout still deep within her muscles. When she made it to the first empty guest room she could find, she shut herself inside. Leaning back against the doorframe, she slid down to the floor, the enraged sob breaking out of her chest the only sound in the dark.

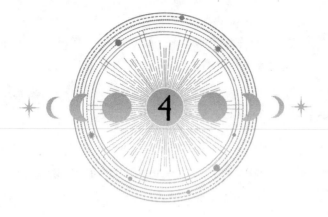

4

"Why are you lugging around a bloody heart?" Sabine asked the next morning as she peeled her orange with a ridiculously large machete.

Amina tapped her black nails on the counter as the orange peel fell in one long spiral to the floor at the other girl's feet. Sabine was dressed in her usual fanfare—and it was comforting to see that at least that had been untouched all these years. Sabine's style had been *hot and lethal* for as long as Amina could remember. Today her friend wore a crisply tailored silk-and-leather bodysuit that was such a rich emerald it made Amina's stomach turn as it brought on images of the forest.

Despite the unpleasant memories the color conjured, Amina had to admit that it complemented Sabine's eyes and fair skin beautifully. Black flying leathers were strapped tightly over the green suit, along with every sort of weapon one could need—regardless of the fact that Sabine often preferred to use her own claws and teeth. The garment accentuated Sabine's lithe, muscled build in a way that Amina knew the other girl used to her advantage when luring in her prey. Whoever, or whatever, that might be. Today, it seemed to be the orange.

"Need a bigger knife?" Amina commented as she shifted her weight to her left hip.

Sabine set down the machete on the marble countertop, broke the newly peeled fruit in half, and unceremoniously stuffed her mouth with one of the two pieces. Juice trickled down the girl's chin.

"I'm good, thanks," she said around the mouthful of fruit. Only it sounded more like *Mmm goof fanks*.

"Honestly, Sabine, must you eat like a slob?" Lyra asked, exasperated.

Lyra was, in a word, the most graceful of the three. Though that gracefulness usually lent itself to being efficiently deadly more than to any sort of social decorum. While Sabine's clothing made her look every inch the warriors they all were, Lyra's elegant silhouettes didn't automatically scream *danger*. Amina knew better, however. Knew that underneath Lyra's long-sleeved sapphire dress, there were just as many weapons hidden.

Lyra had always been the best at making others see only what they wanted them to. They knew what colors would complement their reddish-brown hair and light brown skin perfectly if they wished to be the center of attention—the distraction. They also knew how to blend in and become a wraith in the night. Amina and Sabine were the ones people always kept their eyes on in the light of day—but it was Lyra who would be your demise if you didn't pay attention to the shadows.

The roles they all played had always fit like a glove.

Six years they've managed without you.

Amina's body froze up at the thought. Six years that Sabine and Lyra had to learn to move through the world, just the two of them, making it hard to remember the spaces where Amina used to fit. She wondered if they would ever be able to make room for her again.

Sabine finally swallowed and flicked a strand of her dark blond hair out of her face before cleaning the juice from her chin. "You have a lot of nerve complaining about how messy *I* am when I eat, Lyra, when the last time you tried cooking, you got blood *all over my outfit*."

"*You* were the one who asked for your steak to be *rare*—"

Amina let their argument fade into the background as her mind raced. She could feel the anger that had been brewing in her core the past couple of years bubbling to the surface now, the rage that slowly ate through her every time she thought about another aspect of life here that she'd missed out on. Like the inside jokes she didn't know. The memories she was absent from. Unlike everything else she had missed, however, reapings were the one thing she was grateful to have had a reprieve from.

Valkyries were the harbingers of death—as assigned by the Gods. In centuries past, they had been used as shepherds for incorporeal spirits who got lost between this world and the afterlife—like tour guides to the Valley of Souls. Now their roles were a little more muddled, giving them a certain *reputation* among other immortal beings.

Amina knew it was the direct result of the Valkyrie Queen's tithe—the quota of souls they had to reap and harvest for their ruler every month lest they incur whatever punishments the queen decided to bestow upon them all. Amina had been saying for years that their ruler turned the Valkyries' abilities into something dark and macabre—no one liked being called a souleater or soulstealer. She also knew that sometimes, being the Valkyrie they all assumed she was could be an advantage. Being feared meant poachers had stopped hunting them down for their coveted feathers.

Worst of all, perhaps, was the way the tithe had exacerbated their rivalry with the witches. A rivalry that—with what she knew now—was about to get so much worse. Even though it wasn't their battle, a war was never good for anyone.

"Amina?" Lyra's voice cut through Amina's thoughts. "Why don't you start from the beginning. Before Sabine gets bored and looks for entertainment elsewhere."

"That reminds me!" Sabine exclaimed, pushing off the counter she was leaning on and waving the last half of her fruit around. Her pastel-green eyes lit up in delight, and Amina was instantly wary. "There's a group of Valkyrie fledglings whose wings grew in last week coming to the inner city to start flying lessons today! I was thinking it might be fun to push them off the training roof and—"

"Sabine, *no*," Lyra interrupted, tone serious.

Sabine looked put out, making a soft, indignant noise in the back of her throat.

Amina might have laughed if she wasn't aching inside. She had always been the one to reel Sabine in. She cleared her throat.

"Slayers." The trio's old endearment from their own fledgling days still rolled easily off her tongue. "We have a lot to catch up on, I realize. But first, I have some pressing matters to attend to. I'll only have so much time before word gets back to Her Highness that I am back from exile. What I gathered from the calendar in the grand room—I've come back just in time for the queen's Reverie, is that correct?"

Lyra lifted one elegantly shaped brow, intrigued by where this conversation was going. "Yes, it's next week."

Amina turned to Sabine. "Do you think you'd be able to get us all an invite? Without maiming anyone in the process."

"Well—" Sabine began to protest, but Lyra stepped in.

"Maim people in your free time, Sabine. We need to stay as under the radar as possible right now." Lyra pointed a sharp nail at the girl.

Amina's foot bounced on the ground with impatience. When Sabine pouted and went to grab another piece of fruit, Lyra swung a look of suspicion over to Amina.

"Why do you want to go to the Reverie?" Lyra's eyes narrowed.

"It's the perfect occasion to get what I'm looking for. Everyone will be drunk and distracted, and we can slip in and out with no one the wiser." As Amina spoke, her fingers reflexively twitched toward the heart beating steadily in the canvas bag tied at her hip. Lyra's gaze homed in on the pouch, tracking the movement.

"What exactly are we after, Amina?" Lyra asked, crossing their arms over their chest.

"I had a lot of time to think in that nightmarish forest. About what led me there, about the future I might no longer have when I finally left." Her hand absentmindedly wandered up to grasp the amulet hanging from her neck, the smooth amber stone cool against her palm. "I had a lot of time to think of what I *wanted*. And I want vengeance. Atonement."

Lyra was quiet for a long moment. Something Amina was used to anytime she or Sabine was scheming.

"Vengeance is a dangerous game," Lyra finally said.

Amina dropped her necklace and grinned. "That's the only kind of game that's fun."

5

A colorful curse fell out of Calla's mouth as she lunged for the rabbit. The wicked creature zipped off, ring still in its maw, as she landed on her hands in the mud. She pushed off the ground and back to her feet, paying no mind to Gideon calling her name from somewhere in the distance as she chased after the Witch Eater's familiar. The rabbit darted through the trees like one of the bolts of lightning above, and Calla was barely able to keep up as she wove through the forest, her clothing snagging on the jutting branches.

"Get back here!" she yelled, and to her surprise the creature paused. She lurched forward and snatched the familiar up by its scruff before it could get away again, shaking it in her grip until the ring dropped out of its jaws and into her palm. She raised the rabbit in front of her face to glower into its haunting crimson eyes. "You're a terrible little thing. If you dare screech for your master, I'll—" Calla's eyes suddenly focused behind the rabbit, her words catching in her throat.

The familiar had brought her back to the Witch Eater's cottage.

Her hand went slack, and the creature fell to the ground with a heavy *plop* and a squeak of protest. The cottage was not in the exact same location as before, and Calla wondered if the Witch Eater changed where it appeared whenever a whim struck them. The last time she had seen the quaint house, it had been disappearing into thin air. After everything went disastrously wrong with the Witch Eater's spell to erase Gideon's and Calla's Rolls of Fate, she had hoped she'd never see the cottage—or its ancient keeper—again.

The rabbit righted itself at her feet and skittered away without fanfare, and Calla wrinkled her nose in distaste as the familiar vanished from sight.

Good riddance, she thought, slipping the ring she had retrieved onto her right ring finger for safekeeping. She turned back to the cottage and slowly walked to the large front window, squinting to peer through the glass, but thick curtains obscured her view.

An extra-boisterous gust of wind whipped through the woods, and a soft *click* sounded to her right. She watched as the front door slowly creaked open. Her breath caught, but when no one shut the door from inside, she cautiously shuffled toward it, peeking around the frame to see no lights were on, no candles lit, just shadows upon shadows. For a long moment she stood there, staring into the entrance as water pelted her skin. She knew she shouldn't go in. Knew she should get the Hells out of there and go back to the others . . .

She glanced behind her to see if Gideon had followed her little detour through the woods, but when the prince was nowhere to be seen, she took a deep breath and pushed her way into the cottage. Water rolled off her and pooled on the hardwood floor. A heavy, invisible pressure draped itself over her shoulders as she looked around, and the feeling was so unsettling that she almost turned and ran out then and there. It was only her ever-damning curiosity that kept her feet firmly in place.

I am *already inside. . . .*

The first thing that caught her attention was the fact that the cottage was much less cluttered than before. There were still piles of bits and baubles littering the corners and lining the walls of the room, but the middle of the floor was now clear. No longer were there feathers or papers strewn about, or a makeshift pathway snaking around the grotesque jars of various organs and other unsavory things, making it much easier to walk.

The second thing she noticed was that no one was home.

She took a couple tentative steps forward, shutting the door as she went to block the rain from splattering inside. When her eyes adjusted to the dark, her attention snagged on the giant map of Illustros that expanded across the wall ahead, its chaos of strings untouched in the last day since she and Gideon had been there. She lifted her hand and lightly traced her fingertips over the tangles of red string, wondering what it all meant. Following the string from the Faery Valley to the Witch Realms to the Land of the Valkyries, all the way back down to the right corner of the map, she noticed the paper was curling up—revealing another map beneath.

She smoothed down the corner and realized there were words written along the bottom edge:

Illustros: The Fates ¦ Sixth Realm of the Hells: The Valley of Souls

When she lifted her hand, the thick parchment rolled back in on itself once more and she took in its description as well:

Noctum: The Knights ¦ Second Realm of the Hells: The Shadow Gates

She gently lifted up the corner and found a third map:

Calor: The Infernals ¦ Third Realm of the Hells: The Fires of Salvation

She wondered if the Witch Eater kept track of the ongoings of all the other continents just as much as Illustros. If they—

"Calliope," a voice boomed behind her.

Calla nearly jumped out of her skin, her left hip knocking into one of the precariously balanced piles of objects sitting against the wall beneath the maps. The mound of books and trinkets spilled to the floor with a noisy clatter. She spun to see Gideon's frame now taking up the entire space of the doorway, and all at once she was hit with the sensation of her body recognizing his magic. She'd been so enraptured by the maps, she hadn't noticed the warmth of his familiar energy sneaking up on her.

"What the Hells are you *doing*?" he demanded.

"Help me clean this up!" she hissed as she dropped to the ground and began restacking the books and papers. Gideon crouched down to gather some of the smaller objects that had rolled in his direction—an odd silver coin, a glass marble, a wooden cat figurine.

Calla quickly reassembled the tower as she explained, "The Witch Eater's familiar took off with the ring the nymphs gave us and—"

"And you decided to just pop inside for a visit?" he chided.

"They aren't home." She slammed the final book atop the stack. "I don't know, I just couldn't . . . resist."

He fixed her with an exasperated look as he handed over the first handful of objects before turning to search for the last few that had gotten away. "You're lucky it was me who caught you. You've got to stop running off into the woods without warning anyone. We've been gone long enough already."

He was right. Cass and Hannah were most likely worried to death about where the two of them had disappeared to. When Calla had heard the nymphs trigger their trap, she'd taken off without a word while the others had been going back and forth on what they were going to do with Ezra. Caspian had wanted to give the younger prince a proper burial from the beginning. Gideon hadn't been ready for that conversation. And Calla—well, trapping the nymphs was her plan.

Calla's chest tightened ever so slightly now at the idea of burying Ezra in this forest. She tried to grasp the echo of pain that thought brought on for a moment longer, to revel in the sharpness of it, but it slipped away too quickly, numbness settling into place once more. The only indication that Gideon felt the sudden flash of emotion running through her was the slight clench of his fists by his side.

She delicately balanced the last of the baubles he'd recovered onto her neat stack, one by one. He began to say something else, but before the words could leave his tongue something pulled his attention. Calla followed his gaze toward the large dining table where one of the dislodged knickknacks lay glittering on the floor beneath.

Gideon reached over and picked it up, turning it over in his hands a few times in disbelief. It was an oval amulet. An amber stone nested in the center of intricate bronze metalwork and hung from a matching metal chain.

"What is that?" she asked. "It looks familiar."

"It's an Esprit. And you've definitely seen one before—on the Valkyrie," he answered.

A spark of realization went through her.

Gideon's grip tightened around the necklace. "We need to go."

Calla snorted. "All your fussing about me coming inside and you're going to take something?"

"It could be decades before they bother to notice this is missing—if they ever do at all."

"Why do you even want it?" she prodded.

"Do you know what an Esprit does?" he asked, and when she shook her head, he revealed, "Esprits are able to hold souls. Valkyries wear them so they can harvest and transport multiple spirits at once. For us, however . . ."

She sucked in a breath. "Ezra."

Without any more consideration, Gideon pocketed the necklace. "Now let's get the Hells out of here."

Calla didn't bother to argue any longer, simply slipped past where Gideon held the door open and waited while he used his magic to clean up the rain they had tracked on the floor inside. As they set off to get back to the others, another strike of lightning lit up the sky overhead, making them both pick up their strides. Neither of them looked back.

6

By the time Gideon and Calla got back to the campsite, the storm had dwindled, now barely a light drizzle. They found Caspian sitting in the damp cave they'd stumbled across earlier that morning—after nearly six hours of walking and watching the two men carry Ezra's heartless body through the forest the night before. Now it was about an hour until dusk and Cass was nursing a fire, using his magic to keep the wind away from the flames. Hannah's head was pillowed in his lap as she rested. The blonde had only begun getting her voice back in the last couple of hours and was still feeling the exhausting effects of the magic she had used trying to heal her damaged vocal cords.

"There you are," Cass scolded them, keeping his voice just low enough not to disturb Hannah. "What the Hells? You both disappeared without telling me anything!"

"Sorry, there wasn't time to explain," Calla apologized at the same time that Gideon said, "I didn't want Calliope facing the fae alone."

Calla fought the urge to roll her eyes. She thought she'd handled the situation perfectly fine by herself. Well, not *perfectly*, but the *fine* part was accurate.

"You've got to warn me next time," Cass fussed. "Kestrel vanished after walking away for less than a minute. I was getting worried."

"Your trap worked, Cass," Calla inserted before Caspian could catch the way Gideon winced at the mention of their commander's name. They had zero leads on where to start looking for Kestrel.

Gideon had tried to use his compass the night before, to assess if it could lead them to wherever the commander had gone, but the needle only spun around aimlessly, refusing to land on any specific point.

He might have left voluntarily, Cass had reasoned to them when the compass hadn't worked. *There was no indication that he was attacked, and he couldn't have gotten very far after that fight with Ezra. It wouldn't surprise me if he'd just gotten fed up and deserted us. Especially after that right hook Ezra gave him.*

Calla had asked how the commander could have just left in the middle of the forest. Gideon's answer hadn't sat right with her.

There are a lot of things Kestrel is capable of that I don't even know, Gideon had said. *Maybe he walked just far enough out of range that the forest's glamour blocked Cass from sensing him. If Cass says there were no signs of struggle, I think the most logical thing to do is leave him to his own devices until we've dealt with everything else.*

Calla hadn't objected. She was more than happy to keep their focus on getting Delphine back and dealing with whatever they'd need to deal with for Ezra. Which brought her back to the present.

"Let me get changed and then I'll tell you all what happened with the nymphs," she told them as she scooped up the trousers Cass had set out for her before ducking behind another boulder sitting farther back in the shadows of the cave. After kicking off her worn-out shoes, she peeled the drenched bottoms off her legs and discarded them. She pulled on the clean pair, which took a great deal of effort to get over her hips, then bent down to cuff each of the hems before returning to the others.

Caspian was gently shaking Hannah awake. "Time to get up, little witch."

Hannah blinked up at him groggily. While she stretched and rubbed the sleep from her eyes, Cass leaned back against the wall, arms crossed over his broad chest as he watched Calla with anticipation.

Calla cleared her throat. "Do you all want the good news or bad news first?"

"Good," Cass and Hannah answered in sync at the same time that Gideon said, "Bad."

"Majority rules," Calla acknowledged. "The good news is that there *is* a way for us to get Ezra's soul back. It involves getting an artifact from the afterlife and doing some sort of spell to summon a gateway there."

"You consider that *good* news? Where the Hells do you suppose you'll be able to get an artifact from the beyond? Better yet—where do you think you'll get the money to buy something that rare?" Caspian's brows knitted together in frustration.

"You were the one convinced it wouldn't be possible at all," Gideon reminded him. "And as for the money, we'll just have to figure that out when we get to it."

"Because it *shouldn't* be possible," Caspian said for the millionth time since Calla and Gideon had brought the idea up. "It's unnatural. Don't you think we've all played with fate enough? I went along with your plan to look for the nymphs because I never thought any information they gave you would be convincing enough for you both to think you could actually do this, but it's gone too far. You two have to accept that he's gone."

"*No,*" Calla and Gideon responded.

Calla felt Gideon shift his gaze over to her—whether in surprise at her solidarity or the harshness in her tone, she didn't know—but she didn't take her eyes off Caspian. Caspian, who looked as if he wanted to wring their necks, the closest she had ever seen him come to outright anger. It probably didn't help that they'd been having this same argument for the last twenty-four hours.

"You know what?" Caspian huffed a laugh. "Do whatever you want. But I'm not helping. If you both want to go on another fool's errand, be my guest."

"I suppose the bad news won't be so terrible, then," Calla said. "The only place I have any familiarity with that sells the kind of contraband we'd need access to in order to find such a token is the Starlight Inn. Specifically, Hannah's and my old landlord, Jack. Which means—"

"We're going to have to split up anyway," Gideon finished as he realized where she was headed.

"Even if you *can* manage to get a portal to the afterlife and find Ezra's soul, you still can't put it back in his current body without a heart," Caspian argued. "Where the Hells do you plan to start with that?"

The nymphs had told Calla the same thing, but she was way ahead of them. "Simple. I'm going to track down the Valkyrie."

Gideon tilted his head in contemplation as Caspian scoffed, "*Simple?* The two of you have utterly lost your minds."

"Listen, if we go through the trouble of getting Ezra's soul back, there's no way I'm going to let finding another heart stop us," Calla said. "I'll dig the heart out of one of the Witch Queens myself if I have to. I was already planning to do that anyway."

The conviction with which she said the latter had them all silent for a moment.

Caspian rubbed at his jaw before finally letting out a defeated sigh. "Clearly, I won't be talking you out of this. So, what's the plan? The two of you will go back to Estrella to find the ingredients you need while Hannah and I get Delphine?"

"Pretty much," Calla confirmed. "Except I can go to Estrella alone."

Gideon looked ready to argue with her at that claim, but before he could start anything Hannah questioned, "What will you do if people are still looking for you in Estrella, Calla?"

"Oh, I have no doubt that as long as Ramor and Boone are around, that is surely the case—but I know the inn like the back of my hand. I'll be in and out before anyone even knows I was there." Calla waved off her friend's concern. "I'm just going to have to use whatever glamour

I can manage to disguise myself and hope I don't run into anyone familiar—or too sober."

"Calliope, I'm going with you," Gideon inserted firmly.

That was *not* what Calla had in mind. "You might be even more recognizable than me! Especially with how you quite literally *crashed* that auction. The inn isn't a good place for you."

"Like you said, we'll just have to disguise ourselves well. I have much more experience with using glamour for long periods of time than you," he argued.

Calla was about to protest more, but she saw Caspian was nodding in agreement with the prince. "Gideon's right; he can help you with glamour. And despite the fact that I think this entire quest is asinine, it isn't safe for you to go on it alone. Hannah and I will work to get what we need to go after Delphine, and then Gideon will be able to use his compass to get you both back to us."

If it actually works again, she thought. Then said aloud, "What will the two of you do without anything to navigate you here?"

"The ring," Gideon suggested. "They can use the other favor from the nymphs to get to the Siren's Sea safely if we don't get back before then. Time moves much slower here than it will in Estrella."

"Then it's decided, I suppose," Calla muttered as Gideon gave her an inscrutable look. "At least we have the Esprit now to—"

"*The what?*" Caspian ran a hand back over his short silver hair and scoffed incredulously.

Gideon threw Calla a look that seemed to ask *Why would you mention that right now?* as he reluctantly dug the amulet out of his pocket to show the others.

"When the Hells did you get *that*?" Cass demanded. "*Where* did you get that?"

Before Calla or Gideon could respond, a cold draft blew in from outside, whipping Calla's and Hannah's hair around their faces. As Calla wrangled the long strands out of her eyes, a terrifying silhouette appeared at the cavern's mouth and all the oxygen in the small space was sucked away at the bone-chilling voice that echoed around them.

"I believe I can answer that."

The Witch Eater.

7

Amina was draped across a chaise in Lyra's bedroom, watching her friend pick at a tray of strawberries as they waited for Sabine to return. The silence between them felt strange; not uncomfortable but *charged* since their conversation at breakfast and the mention of vengeance. Lunch was a welcome distraction—especially one as luxurious as this. Made of the freshest fruit, cheese, and meat Lyra's personal chef could find. A far cry from what she'd had to forage for in the forest.

Lyra's family was one of the wealthiest in the entire capital city of Valor. Their parents were often traveling, their business taking them to the farthest corners of Illustros and even some of the other continents. Meanwhile, the twins—Lyra and their brother, Lark—kept up the family home and collected enough souls for the Valkyrie Queen's tithe so their parents could peacefully pursue their other line of work.

Lyra's three-story manor was complete with a full household staff, masterful carvings of the Gods in the moldings, lush oil paintings that stretched all the way across the expansive walls, and lavish, handmade textiles throughout. It wasn't unlike the Valkyrie Queen's own gilded castle, except in size. Lyra themself had a penchant for the luxurious; their room was covered floor to ceiling in rich blue velvet, and shiny trinkets and artifacts that they'd painstakingly collected for the last few decades were carefully scattered over the surfaces of antique armoires and imported, hand-carved vanities. Amina had always found it to be cozy, despite the oddity of most of the enchanted objects lying around.

"Do you think Sabine got sidetracked?" Amina mused, filing her long black nails with a throwing blade.

"Of course she did," Lyra answered as they plucked a berry from its pile. "But she should still be back by now."

Amina opened her mouth to say something else when the door to the bedroom burst open and Sabine sauntered in, a feline grin on her face.

"Gods help us," Amina muttered as she sat up. "What did you do?"

"Exactly as you asked," Sabine said not-so-innocently. "I got some information on where we can get invitations to the Reverie."

"And why do you look like you just stabbed someone for fun?" Lyra quipped.

"Because I did." Sabine waved off the interruption. "But that's not the point. You'll never believe who I was told has the spare invites."

"Who?" Lyra asked, their tone wary.

There was a wicked twinkle in Sabine's eyes as she answered, "The Wayfarer. He's finally come to Valor."

"This is not going to go well," Lyra muttered under their breath as they all landed in front of the Wayfarer's small, temporary shop on the west side of the city.

Valor was broken up into thirteen districts; seven of them were completely residential and the other six were organized by trade. They were currently in the merchant's district, a grid of limestone shops and outdoor markets. Very few carriages roamed Valor, or any of the other cities in their land, since they were only used by fledglings or those unable to fly. This meant their roads were slightly more narrow than other places she had been to in Illustros, leaving room for the sloped sidewalks that lined the streets so the shops were easier to access.

The trio made their way up the mild concrete incline now, and Sabine pushed open the door as if she was the one who owned the place, Amina and Lyra piled inside behind her.

The Wayfarer was, for lack of a better term, a scavenger. From what Amina knew, the man was less interested in being an entrepreneur and more intent on finding very specific items that he could use for leverage in whatever quest he was currently involved in. Which was why the shop was nearly bare, only a single wooden shelf with a few magical artifacts taking up space against the left wall.

Sabine walked up to the counter and reached for the small golden bell that sat atop it, ringing it incessantly until a figure stepped through an open archway on the left that must've led to a back storage room. At the sight of the man, Sabine dropped her hand back to her side and the grin on her face grew five times larger.

Amina had always thought the Wayfarer was one of the prettiest beings she had ever seen. His black hair, with curling tendrils framing his face, was turning silver at the ends—silver that had spread to even more strands since the last time she'd seen him. That time was in the Dragonwoods, many years ago, but aside from the increasing gray of his hair, everything else about him had remained the same. His piercing blue eyes still held an infinite number of secrets, and the fair golden skin of his arms was still decorated with peculiar tattooed maps all the way down to his fingertips.

Amina's eyes traced the ink around his biceps as the maps' dotted lines and curving bands shifted directions every so often—like the tattoos were alive.

He's still not as pretty as that witch from the forest. Caspian. What a lovely name . . . a haunting voice snickered inside her mind, and Amina gritted her teeth at the unwelcome thought.

The Wayfarer took the three of them in as he sidled up to the counter, his deep blue eyes roaming over their figures. Not in a way that was leering, but to assess any possible weapons or other threats they might be hiding. He wasn't one to be fooled by a pretty display of faces or finery.

When he got to Sabine, his eyes narrowed. Once recognition dawned, his lips curled back in a snarl. *"You."*

"Me!" Sabine gave a toothy grin. "Different look, different pronouns—same stabby bitch."

His hands tightened into fists on the countertop. "I ought to—"

"Do you really want to threaten three Valkyries?" Amina tilted her head.

"No, I want to threaten one Valkyrie." He glowered. "The last time we crossed paths she *set me on fire.*"

"It was only a little fire," Sabine protested, as if this detail somehow helped. "And is it really my fault if you got in the way of my aim?"

"Considering you were aiming for *me*," he retorted, "yes!"

"Well, is it my fault someone paid me handsomely to shoot you? Having a bounty on your head seems more like a *you* problem." Sabine crossed her arms and leaned her weight on her left leg.

"Sabine," Lyra warned, before the situation could escalate too much more.

"I want her out of my presence," the Wayfarer told them.

"Oh, come now." Sabine pouted, twisting a strand of her golden hair around one of her fingers. "What about forgive and forget?"

He leaned both hands on the counter in front of him and scowled in her face. "I would love to forget the feeling of my flesh melting from my bones, believe me."

Sabine was unfazed. Lyra had gotten distracted from the entire confrontation and was studying some sort of map in the far corner, and Amina was losing her patience.

"*Enough*," she told them both. "We're here on business. The two of you can battle to the death about this later."

Sabine's interest was piqued by the suggestion, but Amina immediately fixed the other girl with a glare.

"I don't want, or need, your business, Valkyrie," the Wayfarer said, still fuming at Sabine.

"Sure you do." Amina unfurled her most lethal smile. "Unless you'd like Sabine's friend, the one who paid her to shoot you with a flaming arrow, to find out exactly where you'll be hanging out these next few days."

He was unimpressed. "I survived that hit twice already. What's once more?"

"Then how about I relieve you of the heart in your chest?" Amina's tone sharpened now.

His grin was vicious as he taunted, "Come and get it, Valkyrie. You and I both know you won't risk killing me and taking on my curse."

He was right, she wouldn't. Hells, Sabine was lucky she hadn't been successful in killing him all those years ago. His curse forced him to wander the world for eternity, unable to stay in one place more than a week at a time—and never able to return to the same place twice. The world was big, but it wasn't infinite. Lyra once told Amina that the only way out was to collect the elusive pieces of a magic puzzle before there were no places left to go—or death. After her exile, Amina knew better than most the nightmare of being unable to return home when you desperately needed to.

"How about a trade?" Lyra interrupted. "Everyone knows what you're looking for." They gestured to the tattoos on the man's arms as they stepped away from the map they had been studying. "We know you have certain . . . limitations."

His sapphire eyes watched Lyra carefully, but it was clear that his interest spiked.

"What if I told you I have something in my collection that could help with your hunt?" Lyra said.

He didn't say anything for a long moment, contemplating if his grudge against Sabine was worth passing up whatever it was that Lyra was offering. "What is it you all are here for, exactly?"

Before Lyra could answer, Amina stepped up and chimed in, "Invites to the queen's Reverie. Sabine has a friend who claims you may have a few extra."

"Four, to be exact." His smile was cocky. "I was supposed to attend with some old acquaintances, but they became otherwise engaged."

"Give us three and I'll give you a Transvectio Talisman," Lyra told him.

His jaw went slack. "Impossible. There's only two of those in existence and one has been missing for over a century. You're telling me the other—"

"Collects dust in one of my vanities. Yes. Give us the invites and you'll have it tonight."

"Done," he agreed without hesitation. "The invitations will be in your mailbox before dusk. Just leave me with your address."

Once all the details were squared away, the three of them filed out, Sabine turning to blow a farewell kiss to the Wayfarer just before the door swung shut behind them.

8

There was blood all over the front of Delphine's outfit. She knew that wasn't what she should be focusing on at the moment, but she couldn't help it. If Calla and Hannah could see her right now, they wouldn't recognize her.

"What do you think, Delphine?" Reniel looked down at her, the trachea he had just ripped out of her throat still in his hand. "Should I give you a break?" He knew she couldn't answer, of course, which only made the grin on his face widen.

Delphine dug her nails into her thighs as the sharp pain of involuntarily swallowing cut through her open throat. She was shocked to discover that all these years had made her truly forget what Reniel was like. How cruel his steely gaze was when it was turned on you.

The siren twisted her trachea in his slate-blue hands before tossing it away and crouching down to her eye level. "I'll tell you what. I'll show you a little bit of mercy."

She would have rolled her eyes if she weren't in so much pain. Mercy was not something Reniel was familiar with.

"You were always my favorite, you know." He spoke softly as he reached out and gently brushed a finger against her cheek. She tamped down the urge to bite the appendage off and spit it back at him. "So I'll do you a favor. I'll let you have a visitor or two in your cell. Some company in between our daily quality time together."

Delphine shook her head wildly, her mind echoing with the pleas she couldn't voice aloud.

No, no, no.

Reniel's laugh was sharp. He knew. He knew this wasn't a *favor*. He was hoping it wasn't. She was the girl who had embarrassed him by running away from the pedestal he had placed her on. What better way to get back at her than to let the sirens who'd paid the price for her betrayal have unfettered access to her in such a vulnerable state?

Sirens who were once my only family.

Calla's and Hannah's faces flashed in her mind for a moment. Hannah's words were slipping away further and further into the darkest parts of her mind with each day that passed.

Reniel leaned forward and put his lips next to her ear. "You are no one special anymore."

He stood then, bubbles rising around her with the movement. He gestured for someone on the other side of the room to get her up from the marble table he had strapped her to with braided ropes made of seaweed. She couldn't see who it was, didn't really care either, just let them untie her restraints and haul her to her feet without a fight. As she moved, the blood still seeping from the gaping wound in her throat swirled through the water around them.

"Tell Eros and Zephyr they can find a key to her cell in my study," Reniel ordered. "Let the welcome-home celebration begin."

Delphine drifted in and out of consciousness for so long that she couldn't tell what was real and what was a dream. Until her mother showed up. That's when she always knew she had fallen back asleep.

"*Stand up straight,*" *her mother snapped.* "*You'll never be offered a spot in Reniel's Shoal if you don't learn how to present yourself.*"

Delphine rolled her shoulders back and stood a little taller as her mother continued weaving pearls into the strands of her hair. The weight of her hair had begun to give her headaches more and more these days, but now that her silver tresses had grown almost down to her knees, her mother refused to let her cut it. It made her stand out, her mother claimed. And when you were trying to get early admission into one of the most elite groups in society, there was nothing more important than standing out.

"*I was chosen for a Shoal by the time I was your age. Of course, it wasn't nearly as prestigious as being part of Reniel's empire. Which means it's high time you start taking this seriously. To have an opportunity like this—*"

"I'm only ten," Delphine chimed in, defiance coloring her tone. "I have ten more years to be Claimed by a Shoal."

Not that she even had any desire to belong to one of the stuffy ruling factions of their underwater kingdom. If she didn't have to be Claimed by a certain age in order to keep her magic, she didn't think she'd want to live in this place at all, actually.

"Yes, and then you will have to join those at the bottom of the barrel instead of someone with real status like Reniel," her mother spat out. "Or worse—you don't get picked at all and you never get Claimed. Do you know what happens to sirens who aren't Claimed?"

"They lose their ability to use their siren song, and it's harder for them to find a place to live, I know, I know," Delphine huffed. "Seems just as boring to be controlled by a bunch of snobby people for the rest of your life. Besides, I'm not worried. I'll definitely be the prettiest one there."

"Those snobby people make sure you have food to eat and are protected," her mother scolded. "And don't get cocky. You cannot only rely on being pretty. You need to make sure your tongue stays sharp, and your words stay interesting. You'd be surprised how quickly your luster fades once you aren't the newest and shiniest thing in the room anymore."

Delphine looked down at her hands as she soaked in her mother's words. Her perfectly manicured nails were painted an opalescent silver, the two hours her mother spent on them that morning very evident. There was not a single detail on Delphine's person that had been unattended to—as was the case every time another spot in a Shoal opened up. This *time, though, her mother was being more belligerent about appearances than usual.*

Reniel had an opening in his Shoal for the first time in a year, and her mother was determined that the spot go to Delphine. She recalled a couple weeks ago when her mother had been talking to one of her own Shoal members about how horrendous the political climate in the Siren's Sea was becoming—how Shoal leaders were abusing their ability to Claim other sirens in order to make sure only those willing to do their dirty bidding got to keep their magic. When Delphine confronted her mother about the conversation, however, her mother had simply told her it was better to be unhappy from the comfort of the inside than unhappy on the fringes of society, all alone.

"What if he doesn't Claim me?" Delphine spoke up as she looked at her mother's reflection in the mirror.

Her mother dropped the braid she had been working on and reached up to grip Delphine's chin. "That's not an option." Her mother shifted Delphine's head side to side to check that the makeup on her daughter's face was still pristine.

Next, her mother went over to the far side of the room to pick out one of the necklaces that sat atop the marbled vanity. Delphine met her own gaze in the mirror, taking in her starlight eyes and shimmering blue skin. Her sharp, symmetrical features were highlighted with various sparkling dusts and glitters. The cut of her dress was modest but still seemed far too mature for her age.

"What if I wasn't pretty?" Delphine whispered.

Her mother came back over and motioned for Delphine to turn around, unclasping a pearl necklace as her daughter obeyed. Delphine lifted her chin to expose her neck so her mother could slip pearls around her throat.

Her mother stepped back to admire the final result as she recited, "If you aren't pretty, you are nothing."

I t had only been a little over a day since Calla had last seen the Witch Eater, but their harrowing appearance still surprised her. Gray skin stretched over lean muscle with an unnaturally elongated face and soulless glass eyes. Their too-long spine made them hunch over a bit as they lingered in the mouth of the cave, the too-familiar demon rabbit right on their heels. Calla wrinkled her nose at the cursed creature.

"Hells . . . What did you *do*, Gideon?" Caspian whispered as they all took in the ancient being.

The Witch Eater's mouth stretched into a macabre grin. "Hello, fated ones."

Calla took a step forward, lifting her chin. "What are you doing here?" She was usually much better at bluffing, but the sight of the being made her adrenaline kick into overdrive. She knew exactly why they were here.

"That's a mighty tone, girl, considering it was *you* who invaded my space first," the Witch Eater proclaimed.

Caspian and Hannah swung their gazes to Calla, but she ignored them.

The Witch Eater's chest heaved a laugh. "You did not think it would escape my attention, did you? Naivete doesn't suit you, Great Muse."

Calla's lip curled with distaste, the nickname grating on her nerves. "What do you want?"

"You stole something from me. I am here to return the favor. Em?"

At the sound of their name, the rabbit at the Witch Eater's feet transformed into their human form. No, *human* wasn't quite right, considering the familiar's translucent skin and the grotesque webs of protruding black veins pulsing beneath. Other than those few details, however, the familiar had the appearance of a young girl.

Em turned to her liege with anticipation.

"Thank you for leaving the door unlocked," the Witch Eater told her.

The girl dipped her head in a nod, and Calla's stomach dropped.

"It was a trap," Calla accused them.

The Witch Eater's grin turned sharp. "It was an *opportunity.*"

"You knew we would take the Esprit?" Gideon demanded.

"I knew you were on the precipice of the next fork in your destiny, and it was making my vision murky. I knew if I presented you with an opportunity, you would have to make a choice," the Witch Eater stated.

The obsidian in Gideon's eyes sparked with fury. "What if we hadn't made that choice? What if we hadn't taken the amulet?"

"That is not the case, so it does not matter, does it? Balance in all things," the Witch Eater declared. "You had no qualms about stealing what you wanted from me, and I have none about taking what I want from you. Em, if you'd please."

Em blinked from sight, teleporting to somewhere in the back of the cave, before reappearing a long moment later with Ezra's carefully wrapped corpse lying on the ground at their feet.

Though the magic in his veins would keep his body from decomposing—for a few centuries at least—it had felt disrespectful to leave him exposed. Now the familiar pulled back the meticulously woven blanket Calla and Hannah had made out of moss and leaves from the forest and revealed the prince's sleeping face beneath.

Ezra Black was beautiful even in death.

At the sight of his face, the slight coldness that had taken up residence in Calla's veins turned to a soul-chilling ice.

This isn't him. He's not gone yet.

"Don't worry," the Witch Eater reassured her. "I'll take good care of him. And if you would like to come back and barter for his body, you know where to find me."

Gideon snarled, "You set us up so you could make us bargain with you for my brother's *body*?"

"I'm always a thousand steps ahead of you, Prince. You'd do well to remember that." The Witch Eater snapped their fingers, and Ezra's body disappeared. "Nothing is an accident. No one told either of you to go snooping where you didn't belong. The Esprit is yours to keep, though—use it wisely. When you find the Valley of Souls, do tell the Fates hello for me."

A noise of rage ripped from Gideon's throat as he lunged forward and sliced his hand at the ancient one's face. By the time Gideon reached the spot where the Witch Eater had been standing, however, they were already gone. The prince stumbled a step, spinning around with wild eyes as the wind picked up around them.

"Gideon—" Calla held out her hands to calm him. She could feel the maelstrom of emotions clamoring to get to the surface from his end of their bond.

"What the Hells were you two thinking?" Caspian's tone was hollow as he looked at them. "You stole something from the Witch Eater?"

"Cass," Calla warned as the storm inside Gideon continued to brew.

Cass only repeated, "What were you *thinking*?"

Gideon's eyes were pitch-black as he stared back at his friend, blue electricity beginning to spark up from his hands and crawl up his forearms. Calla scrambled to shove herself between the two wound-up witches before either of them did something they would regret.

"Please," Calla implored. "Arguing won't solve anything."

For a moment, Caspian looked as if he wanted to disagree. Instead, he only shook his head and backed away. As he stalked out of the cave, Calla caught the flicker of hurt barely concealed in his steel eyes. Hannah followed after Cass, throwing an empathetic look in Calla's direction before disappearing from view with the other witch.

"Every time I make a decision that I think will help," Gideon said, the blue magic around his arms slowly dissipating as he took a few deep breaths to settle down, "I dig us further and further into the ground. I might as well have dug Ezra a grave with my bare hands."

"Don't give yourself so much credit, Gideon," she told him evenly. "I was right there with you every step of the way. We're going to fix all this, okay? The very slim silver lining here is that at least we know exactly where to find Ezra when we're ready."

"He doesn't deserve this." Gideon closed his eyes. "Any of this."

Calla swallowed. "I know. But all we can do right now is continue forward. We'll go to Estrella and find a way to bring his soul back. I won't accept any other options."

After a minute of soaking in her words, her tone that was much too sure for all the adversity they had already faced, he finally nodded and opened his eyes. The solid black of his irises was shining with grief. "You don't want me to go with you to Estrella."

Calla didn't deny it. "It's going to be difficult enough for me to go back to the inn. It doesn't help that . . ."

"It'll be with me?" Gideon finished.

She pressed her lips together, swallowing the words she wished she were able to say. The ones that were too selfish for her to dare utter.

He changed the subject. "I'm sorry for getting upset. When the Witch Eater disappeared with Ezra, the rage just took over and I couldn't stop it."

"I'm sorry I *didn't*," she admitted. "I should be right there with you, but the fury is . . . unreachable. Everything inside me feels wrong."

Calla looked down at her hands. More to herself than to Gideon, she whispered, "How are we ever going to get through this?"

Gideon brushed a thumb over the constellation of dots embedded in the skin of his left forearm. The ones that had turned crimson to match her own. "Together?"

The word sliced through her mind like a blade. Their fates were intertwined more now than ever before, and yet she had never felt further apart from everything and everyone.

She took a deep breath, not ready to return the sentiment, and said, "Let's go find the others. We need to get going."

A muscle in his jaw ticced, but he only dipped his chin in response, waving a hand for her to lead the way. When they reached the opening of the cave, Calla noted that she could no longer hear the sound of rain, and as they ducked outside and looked around, she realized why.

The sky above them had returned to a calm, depthless midnight. Gone was the canopy of thick, moss-covered oak trees. In the oaks' place stood red crape myrtles, packed together so densely with dripping blooms that Calla could barely see through the branches. The once muddy ground was now blanketed in crimson petals, making everything look as if it were covered in blood.

10

Gideon found Caspian stewing at the edge of the tree line a few yards outside the cave. The moment Hannah spotted him striding toward Cass, she scampered off to find Calliope, probably to avoid whatever confrontation she figured was coming.

Gideon cleared his throat as he paused behind Cass. "I should have known the Witch Eater's cottage was a trap."

Caspian tilted his head up toward the sky, his shoulders rolling back as he stated, "Yes."

When Gideon didn't say anything more, Cass faced him. The two of them had gotten in their fair share of fights over the years—and had the scars to prove it—but the tension between them now felt different, and Gideon couldn't stand it.

"I'm sorry." Gideon shoved a hand through his hair. "I know I took a risk stealing that amulet—"

"I'm not upset that you took a risk, Gideon." Cass raised his brows in disbelief. "I've spent the better part of the last decade by your side taking risks. I'm pissed all this happened because you didn't trust me enough to tell me about the Heartbreak curse and include me in your plans from the beginning."

An overwhelming shot of guilt racked Gideon's body. "I was afraid if I told all of you what I was doing . . . with the Witch Eater and transferring the curse . . . you'd try to stop me."

"Of course I would have tried to stop you!" Cass threw his hands up. "I know how bad things have been with Kestrel for the past couple of years—not to mention the Guild and your mother. I know being at the mercy of your Rolls of Fate has made you feel like you always need to be in control. But I can't continue like this if you aren't one thousand percent honest with me."

Gideon looked Cass dead in the eyes and acknowledged, "You're right."

Caspian's entire body relaxed with relief, and the witch clapped Gideon on the shoulder and squeezed in reassurance, though the glint in his eyes was not as bright as it usually was. "You're my best friend, Gid. Don't make me get that close to strangling you again."

Gideon snorted.

"Still friends?" Calliope asked, tone carefully even as she approached.

Caspian sighed good-naturedly. "Always. Where's Han?"

"Gathering our things." Calliope hooked a thumb over her shoulder. "It's time for us to get going."

"Agreed," Caspian said. "Drop us off at Crystal Lake, and we'll get what we need to head to the Siren's Sea. How long do you think it'll take you to get through Estrella?"

"We'll need rest, but it shouldn't take us more than a day to get back to the inn," Gideon said. "Finding what we need, however, will be a whole other story."

Hannah appeared an instant later with the few belongings they had left, and as the four them went on their way, Gideon begged the Gods to let them catch a break and leave the forest without any more surprises.

)·)·)·●·(·(·(

Leaving the Neverending Forest was not nearly as much of a relief as Gideon thought it would be. Someone in the universe must have heard his plea, because they managed to make it to the end of the woods without any other delays. As they passed through the dense wall of magic, Gideon couldn't help but think of how the last time they crossed through the glamoured barrier there had been five of them.

The tension between him and Calliope was thick as they stepped back into Estrella. Neither of them had said a word since leaving Caspian and Hannah at Crystal Lake with heavy good-byes. He was desperate to know what was going through her mind. Even if it meant facing her fury. Because despite the new mask of indifference she wore, he couldn't imagine that she wasn't furious. After what had transpired over the last twenty-four hours, there was little room in his own body for anything but self-loathing. Every breath he took that Ezra didn't burned in his lungs, and now that the Witch Eater was holding Ezra over their heads . . .

Calliope cleared her throat, the sound cutting through his thoughts. "I know this village is more aware of glamour than other places in Estrella, but we have to get some sleep if we're going to make it back to the inn by tomorrow."

"We can stop at the next town; it shouldn't be more than a mile or two if I remember correctly." He looked up to assess the triple moons in the night sky. "It's just before dawn. Hopefully, that means there won't be too many people to run into on our way, but we should cover ourselves just in case."

"I've only ever glamoured my eyes," she admitted. "I'm not sure how long I can keep it up on other features."

"Stick with your eyes and hair for now. If it starts to slip, I can assist."

She nodded and closed her eyes. Using glamour as a witch was like stretching out a muscle. Unlike the fae, they didn't have that type of magic stored on tap. Witches had to work on converting their inherent power into something akin to a fae's glamour—though those trained well enough could easily tell the differences in the energies apart. Gideon had spent a great deal of time learning how to keep his disguises in place when he was with the Guild to make sure no one accidentally caught a glimpse of his numbers. Calliope clearly didn't have as much experience.

It began with her hair. The length started to shorten, and her loose waves straightened themselves out until they hit just at her shoulders. If he looked closely enough, he could see the hazy, transparent film of magic hovering around her disguised tresses. But that would be overlooked by most. The real issue was the color.

He smirked. "If you were going for the color of a banana, you nailed it."

She opened her eyes and reached up to sift the bright yellow strands through her fingers, making a face at the ostentatious shade. "I meant to make it blond."

"It's best if you picture a reference in your head—Hannah's hair, for example. And don't forget your eyebrows," he said, realizing her brows were still dark brown.

She tried again. This time the strands turned a flaxen shade nearly identical to Hannah's, just as he had suggested. When she blinked her eyes back open, he saw that the colors of her mismatched irises had also changed—to a pale shade of green that was not nearly as enchanting. After her glamour was settled, he focused on his own, making his cobalt hair a bright white and transforming his eyes to a solid shade of brown. He focused on the tips of his ears and willed them to sharpen, taking on the details of a fae. Regular fae were not only the closest in appearance to witches, but were commonly regarded to be wanderers wherever they went—especially in Estrella. Therefore, they shouldn't raise any red flags if they came and went without a trace.

"Good?" he asked.

She gave him a nod of approval and adorned her own ears with points before they set off without another word.

They passed through the first village like ghosts in the shadows. They kept their eyes and ears alert as they moved down the cobblestone road toward the next town. The journey was a lot less eventful when the forest around them wasn't trying to kill them anytime it had a whim. The familiar scent of crisp winter pine still clung to the air, but the lack of bite in the wind tipped Gideon off that spring was creeping in—which meant much more time had passed here than in the forest. He wondered if his mother had grown suspicious of his absence yet. Another clock they were racing against that he was trying to forget.

A mile later, he noticed Calliope's energy slowly wane. Though she never complained, he knew they would have to find food soon if they were going to make it. The sky above them was growing brighter and brighter as the morning washed in, the chatter of birds overhead a welcome sound after the days of eerie silence in the forest. Not a single soul was out during their trek, but Gideon knew the streets would awaken soon enough with couriers and other travelers. He could already see an approaching cluster of buildings just over the horizon. Hopefully, there would be an open inn for them to rest for a few hours.

When they were just a half mile from their destination, she finally broke the silence. "What will we do for money? We don't have much left."

"We'll have to find a pawnbroker or bartering shop. I have a spare knife or two that should get us more than a decent amount."

"Do you think they will be open this early?" she wondered.

"If not, I'm sure we can find a tavern and wait it out."

She didn't say anything else, and though he yearned to keep her talking, he didn't press. They made it into the city a few minutes later and found a few people had already awoken and started their day. The first person they spotted was a young troll woman. Trolls looked like any other fae being, but it was easy to recognize them due to one key identifier—they all wore a little vial of dirt somewhere on their person. Every sort of fae had their own traditions and superstitions. For trolls it was said that if they traveled too far from the land on which they were born, or stayed away for too long, they could lose their magic. So they took that soil with them wherever they went.

Gideon was sure this was a rumor started by the beings who resided in the inner fae courts in order to scare their brethren into never leaving their manipulative clutches, but, regardless, the superstition had stuck. The woman in front of them wore her bottle of dirt on a hardy silver chain around her wrist, and the glass bottle clanged noisily against the metal bracelet as she juggled a large, linen-covered basket in one hand. She used her other hand to fiddle with a key ring and unlock the front entrance of what appeared to be a bakery.

Calliope stepped over and offered to hold the basket so the woman could open the door, and Gideon had to swallow the urge to protest as the woman threw Calliope a grateful look.

"If you wouldn't mind me asking . . ." Calliope said as the woman inserted her key into the lock and clicked it open. "We were hoping to get an audience with whoever buys or trades goods here. Would you happen to know who that might be?"

"What kind of goods?" the woman wondered, briefly glancing over Calliope's shoulder at Gideon with uncertainty. "If you're looking for the produce or fish market, they're on the north side—though good luck negotiating with the fishermen. They'll hassle every last spéctral out of you with the winter shortage still going strong. If you're looking for other supplies, Gerard's pawnshop is a few streets over. If it's anything in the magical artifacts realm, you'll have to wait until later tonight when the night market opens."

"Thank you so much . . ." Calliope prompted.

"Lina," the woman told them sheepishly.

He watched as Calliope gave the woman a smile, and something in him ached that the gesture seemed to take a great deal of effort. The woman didn't notice the strain behind Calla's mask, though, and simply took the basket back from Calliope's hands as her warm brown cheeks grew rosy.

"Thank you, Lina," Calliope said. "Do you know if the pawnshop is open yet?"

Lina shook her head. "Won't be for another hour. But I'm about to put everything out here, if either of you wants some breakfast?"

He stepped in before Calliope could answer. "It's appreciated, but we have to be going."

Lina nodded politely before glancing back at Calliope and blushing once more. "Well, Gerard's is just four blocks up and three to the right. You can't miss it."

"Thank you," Gideon repeated before turning to Calliope and tilting his head in a way that said *Let's go.*

It wasn't until a block later that she pointed out how brisk his pace had become.

"What's the rush?" she questioned with a raised brow. "We have an hour to kill. We could have at least taken her up on breakfast."

He didn't bother to look back as he answered, "We shouldn't be hanging around anyone long enough for them to familiarize themselves with us. We needed to get out of her sight before she committed us to memory."

"We spoke for three seconds," she reasoned. "I doubt she'll be giving either of us a second thought."

This time he did look back, scoffing, "I think you seriously underestimate how memorable you are—even with the glamour."

She rolled her eyes but otherwise didn't argue, and this time he couldn't take her silence.

He stopped walking.

"Calliope."

She continued past him a few steps before twisting around to face him, a wary look in her eyes. When he tried to take a step toward her, she flinched back. He froze.

She shook her head. "Don't."

He tugged on one of his earrings as he searched her face. "I know you must loathe me, but—"

"What? Gideon, I don't *loathe* you," she said, cutting him off. "I don't . . ." She sighed while she tried to find the exact words she was looking for. "I don't feel much of anything right now."

He stared at her for a moment. She had said something similar after the Witch Eater disappeared, about her fury being unreachable, but he hadn't understood. Not when he'd felt like he was drowning. Coming back to Estrella was hard for her, he knew that. There were so many memories of those they had lost here. It was probably the last place she had seen Delphine truly happy. And now the siren was gone. It was also probably the place she had thought of as the closest thing to freedom she'd ever find, and since the auction—and the fact that she was a wanted fugitive by the Witch Queen—that comfort was gone as well.

He didn't want to push her over the edge. Not here, where so much weight was sitting on her shoulders. Not when he knew she had meant her words to be comforting.

He wasn't going to tell her that they weren't, not in the least, or that he'd rather she hate him than feel nothing about him at all.

So he nodded and said, "Okay."

With that, she turned away and continued on. Another small piece inside him cracked, but he ignored it, and followed her.

By the time the pawnshop was about to open, Calla's stomach was growling as if she hadn't eaten in weeks. They had posted up at a tavern across the street from the shop while they waited, but much to her disappointment, the kitchen was closed. Now she was sitting in a dark corner of the bar, watching as Gideon ordered them each a glass of water. The bartender was doing everything in their power to engage the prince in flirtatious conversation, but he was completely oblivious. She might have been amused at the scene under different circumstances.

When Gideon returned a moment later and handed her a glass, she drained it in three gulps.

"We should head over now," he told her as he took the empty glass back to the bar. "I want to make sure we can snag a room at the inn before they fill up for the night."

She let him lead her back out, weaving through the old wooden tables and chairs, pausing only to set their glasses back on the bar. The bartender gave them a *look*, but neither of them acknowledged it. They were little more than phantoms, haunting every place they went.

They wove their way across the newly awakened street, toward a little store with a sign that read GERARD'S SHOP in blue letters. The sign's paint was cracked and peeling, and the front window looked like it hadn't been washed in years, a thick layer of dust and grime smudged across it. Gideon pushed the door open, sending the tinkle of a bell through the quaint space. The air inside the shop was a bit stifling without the breeze, and it smelled like mothballs and wood. The store had an array of different-sized shelves and cupboards that held a plethora of miscellaneous items from dinnerware to clothing. Several couches and chairs were pushed together in a far corner with boxes of knickknacks piled on top. The center of the shop was taken up by a large, ornate desk covered in stacks of papers and small piles of spéctrals. Behind the desk sat a man—Gerard, she presumed—with thick sage-colored hair and a full beard, square-framed glasses sliding down his nose as he recorded something on one of the documents he was working on, the scratch of his pen the only sound in the shop after the bell settled.

"Can I help you?" he questioned without looking up. Calla deferred to Gideon with an expectant look.

The prince pulled a dagger from his pocket. The blade was on the shorter side, nothing particularly noteworthy—except for the hilt. A gold inlay in white marble glistened beneath the yellow lighting from the chandelier above. The five jewels that lined each side of the grip sent a scatter of rainbows across the desk's surface.

"How much would you give for this?" Gideon asked.

Gerard glanced up, expression uninterested until it snagged on the gem-encrusted piece. He pushed his glasses up the bridge of his nose as he set his pen down and stood.

"May I?" He lifted a hand, and Gideon placed the weapon in his palm hilt first.

They were quiet as the man ran his fingers over the smooth marble, inspecting every detail and weighing the piece in his hand. He reached down to open one of the desk's drawers on his left, fishing out a small jeweler's loupe to get a better look at the gems. When he looked back up at them, there was something twinkling in his eyes.

"I haven't seen a piece like this in years," he told the prince, an undertone of excitement in his words. "Black diamonds have been scarce these days."

Gideon looked as if he was very aware of that fact. "How much?"

"I can offer six thousand spéctrals, but I only have about half on hand. You'll have to wait for the rest until tomorrow," the man informed them.

Gideon shook his head. "We'll take the half now. Keep the rest and don't mention where you got it."

Gerard narrowed his eyes and Calla worried for a moment that he would accuse them of stealing the weapon or question them further, but a second later he simply nodded.

"I'm assuming you don't wish to fill out any paperwork, then."

"You assume correctly," Gideon said.

The man took the hint. "Wait just a moment while I get your payment."

He took the dagger with him to the far corner of the room, where a large steel safe sat. Calla glanced around, bored, stomach tightening with hunger more and more. She walked over to one of the charming little cupboards as they waited for the man to unlock the safe. The cabinet was filled with all sorts of sparkling treasures: a heart-shaped locket, a ring with a small switchblade built in, and a gilded fox brooch. The item that held her attention, however, was a pair of golden earrings shaped like violet blossoms with clusters of pearls in the centers of their petals. She reached out to brush a finger over one of the pieces, which was about a third of the size of a spéctral, longing to just be a normal girl who came to a shop to buy something pretty.

You will never be a normal girl, an insidious voice in her mind whispered.

She snatched her hand back from the earrings and returned to Gideon's side, ignoring the way the prince was observing her out of his peripheral vision. When Gerard finally unlocked the door to his safe, he placed Gideon's blade inside and traded it for three canvas bags that made a metallic jingling sound as they were shuffled around. When the safe was resecured, the man walked back over and handed the bags to Gideon.

"Pleasure doing business with you."

Gideon placed the money deep into the satchel he wore across his chest and nodded his thanks before ushering Calla out of the shop and back into the crowded street.

"Where to now?" she asked. "Preferably somewhere with food."

"I saw an inn a couple blocks back. The sign said they served meals."

"Thank the Gods."

They retraced their steps to the inn Gideon had scouted. When they made it inside, Calla's stomach growled for the millionth time as she caught a savory whiff of whatever was cooking in the back, her mouth watering at the idea of a hot meal for the first time in a week. Gideon stepped out from behind her and approached the small reception desk that sat across from the entrance. A bored-looking girl with a thick lavender bob was filing her nails and leaning on the countertop with her elbows.

"Hello," Gideon greeted her.

The girl glanced up but otherwise said nothing.

Calla stepped forward. "We'd like a room for the night—or day, rather."

The girl refocused on her nails as she informed them, "We book by the hour as well, if you need."

Calla's brow furrowed. "Oh, I suppose—"

"Calliope," Gideon murmured, cutting her off, and if she didn't know better, she'd say he almost looked *amused*. He turned back to the receptionist and asserted, "We'll book a full night in a room with *two* beds. And the room comes with meals, correct?"

The girl gave a nod and said, "A single night includes two meals and bath tokens for the showers out back."

"Perfect," Gideon confirmed. "Will this cover it?"

The girl set aside her nail file and looked down at the small pile of spéctrals he placed on the counter. She plucked a single one out of the pile and handed it back before scraping the rest noisily off the edge of the desk and into her other palm. She lifted the creaking lid off a large wooden box sitting to her right and dumped the money inside before procuring what looked to be a large pad of paper from somewhere beneath the countertop. A room log, Calla quickly realized.

The girl began scanning the list of numbers with a column of check marks next to it. "It looks like we only have single-bed rooms left."

Calla's heart thudded in her chest. There was no way they were sharing a bed—

"That's fine," Gideon answered.

Calla swung her gaze over to him. "What—"

"I'll nap on the floor," he told her, his voice low.

"Mhmm," the receptionist hummed to herself, a smirk playing on her lips as she recorded a check next to room number forty-six and then pulled out a drawer full of keys. She lifted out the one with the correct number and set it in front of them. "Up the stairs, fourth floor to the right. If you are unable to access the stairs, there's a ramp just around the corner. Have a great stay."

Calla snatched up the key and took off for the staircase on their right, refusing to look at Gideon. Instead, she focused on making it up the four flights of stairs, a bead of sweat at each of her temples by the time she arrived at their room and shoved open the door. She was surprised to find that the room was quite spacious. A small bed took up space on one side with a nightstand next to it and a large chair in the opposite corner. A dresser with an old mirror sat against the wall across from the bed, and everything looked to be well kept and clean enough for her not to question sleeping there.

Gideon came in behind her, and she spun on him once she heard the door click shut.

"Why would you agree to a single bed?" she demanded.

"Because it was this or nothing, and at least one of us should get decent rest before we walk for another thirteen miles," he told her, tone even. "If you really can't stand sharing a room, I can go down and request another."

She made an incoherent, unsure sound in the back of her throat.

"I mean it," he reiterated. "I can easily go get a separate room. Just say the word."

She gave a deep sigh. "No. No, it's fine. I'd feel safer if both of us were in one place. I just feel terrible that you'll have to be on the floor."

"I've slept on much worse," he deadpanned. "Go get some food downstairs and rest. I'm going to see what I can gather in town. We both need a change of clothes and some food for the road."

"I need new shoes." She bit her lip as she looked down at the worn-out ones on her feet. "These are terrible."

"All right, new shoes. Anything else?"

Her eyes lit up. "A brush would be amazing. And if they have any-thing for menstruation, it probably wouldn't hurt to have on hand. Just in case."

He nodded as he moved to unload the pack he was carrying onto the chair in the corner. He took a few coins out and shoved them into his front pocket before heading out with a soft "I'll be back."

Once she was alone, Calla sat down on the bed and lay back, thank-ful to find it was soft. She wasn't sure how long she stayed like that, fighting the urge to drift asleep, but eventually her stomach growled and made her sit back up. By the time she hauled herself off the bed and grabbed one of the bath tokens off the dresser, the light filtering through the small window was golden like the afternoon.

12

Hannah had been surprised to find that Crystal Lake was wildly different from the Siren's Sea even though both were located in the Neverending Forest. To start, this water was a calm, clear blue, unlike the sea's glassy black surface. She wanted to believe that might mean there were fewer haunting creatures below, but she knew not to get her hopes up about anything in this forest. She was still feeling the loss of Calla splitting up from them, and something inside her was becoming increasingly more unsettled. Worrying about the unknown was not helping.

"Respiroot grows in the dark," Cass informed her as he dipped the toe of his boot into the water, sending a ripple through the serene surface. "You'll usually find it in small caverns or in patches at the very bottom of the lake where the sun doesn't reach."

"How much do we need to get?" Hannah wondered.

"Well, first of all, *you* won't be going to get anything." Cass gave the blonde a pointed look. "You're still not fully healed."

Hannah's hands twitched at her sides as she fought the urge to tighten them into fists of frustration. "I want to *help*. I don't want to just watch while you all do the work it takes to fix everything. Standing by and doing nothing is why Delphine . . . She . . ."

When Hannah's bottom lip began to wobble, Caspian walked over to her. He placed both hands on her shoulders and waited until she looked up at him. Cass had started to become the older sibling she'd never had—fiercely, and sometimes annoyingly, protective. The old Hannah might have been surprised that she was able to warm to another person outside of Delphine and Calla so quickly, but Caspian made her feel safe. And even though she didn't like being told not to help, she deeply appreciated the sentiment.

"It wasn't your fault, Han. It wasn't as if you had a choice and made a bad one. You fought for her. We all know you fought for her. *She* knows you fought for her."

"I want to help," she repeated.

After a moment of deliberation, Cass conceded with a sigh, "All right, just stay close, okay? We need to gather as much as we can possibly hold. It's imperative to make sure we have enough to get Delphine back. Worst-case scenario is getting captured in the Siren's Sea and they hold us long enough that we run out of the respiroot and drown."

Hannah confirmed that she understood, and when Caspian kicked off his shoes and emptied his pockets, she followed suit. They both placed themselves at the very edge of the lake and looked down at the tranquil surface, their reflections staring back.

"Ready?" Cass asked her.

She nodded. They waded into the lake together, the water lapping at Hannah's waist where it only hit Caspian midthigh. The farther they moved, the deeper the water became, and just as it hit Hannah's neck, she felt the ground beneath their feet reach the edge of a drop-off point.

"This is where the trench begins. It should be a straight shot down to where the seaweed grows," Cass explained. "Deep breath. One . . . two . . . *three*."

They dove beneath the surface in sync. The water rushed in her ears as she plummeted into the depths of the lake, a tornado of bubbles tickling her skin, and she tried to get her bearings. Caspian was right beside her, reaching out his hand in offering, and when she accepted, it didn't take as long as she would have thought for the other witch to drag her down into the shadows at the floor.

When they reached the bottom, they came upon the respiroot, the slippery green plant slithering over Hannah's skin and tangling in her hair. She watched as Cass yanked one of the tendrils of the magic plant and shoved the piece that broke off into his mouth, gesturing for her to do the same. She stuffed the dark green seaweed into her mouth as quickly as possible, trying to swallow as little lake water with it as she could manage. The bitterness of the respiroot nearly made her gag, but when she finally gulped it down the magic effects began almost instantly.

It started in her chest. One moment her lungs were burning with the lack of oxygen, and the next a warming sensation slowly crept through her torso until the pressure was completely gone. She inhaled hesitantly, a smile breaking onto her face when she found that she could breathe.

The two of them began gathering up the respiroot by the fistful, stuffing the slimy chunks of the plant deep into their pockets. Hannah wriggled through the underwater jungle, imagining that this must be what Delphine experienced. For a moment she got lost in that thought, daydreaming about the two of them exploring the sea together, letting Delphine show her the magic of the ocean. The last few days she had felt so adrift, the better half of her heart so far away, but here, surrounded by the cool water, she allowed herself to pretend Delphine was nearby. That the siren was playing somewhere in the seaweed, hiding as she waited for Hannah to find her.

Before she could stop herself, Hannah brushed back a curtain of the respiroot in front of her, stomach sinking when she found nothing behind it but more of the slimy plant. She dropped her arm and forced herself back to reality. It wasn't until too late that she realized she'd lost track of Caspian in the thick of the weeds. She twisted around in alarm, searching for any sign of him, but the strands of green were too thick to see through. She pushed herself off the lake floor and swam up, out of the tangle of plants.

The first thing she spotted in the open water was Cass, thrashing in pain. The second was a flurry of green-and-purple fins. She barely had time to suck in another breath when a shadowy figure struck from her left.

When Calla woke, it felt like she was rising from a century-long slumber. She supposed that was what happened when she finally got some rest that wasn't on the cold floor of a demonic forest.

She cracked her eyes open, fighting through the foggy haze in her mind to push herself up from the mattress. All she remembered was going downstairs and scarfing down a bowl of whatever sort of stew they had been serving, nearly boiling her skin off in the steaming showers, and then passing out on top of the mattress with Gideon still nowhere in sight. She had zero recollection of climbing the four flights of stairs back to the room or having the forethought to remove her shoes before getting into bed.

"Gideon?" she whispered into the dark, noticing the curtains on the window had been pulled tightly shut.

"I'm here," his deep voice answered from the chair in the corner.

She rubbed at her eyes until they adjusted and she could make out the prince's silhouette in the corner, his glamoured hair and eyes still perfectly intact. "Did you sleep at all?"

"Some. I got you some new clothes if you'd like to change. I didn't want to wake you too soon, but we should probably get going before it gets much later."

Calla stretched out her limbs as Gideon stood and moved to light the gas lamp on the nightstand. She squinted a bit when the fire ignited, small white spots darting across her vision. When she looked down, she noticed that the glamour on her own hair had disappeared. She frowned.

"I'm surprised you held it as long as you did," he reassured her when he noticed what she was looking at.

"I'll have to get better at that," she muttered as she walked over to the neatly folded pile of garments atop the dresser.

"I'll let you change; I'm going to go fill up our canteens downstairs. I set up your own pack over there as well."

With that, he left, and she began to strip off the old clothes she'd put back on after her shower. The material on the inner thighs of Caspian's trousers had been rubbed raw from all the walking, and she was grateful she would no longer have to deal with the chafing. Unsurprisingly, the prince had impeccable taste in clothing. She unfolded the sleeveless, high-neck top he'd gotten her and slid the buttery-soft knit material over her head. The top was just the right size, hugging the thick curves of her body in all the right places, and she reveled in finally wearing something that fit. The woven cotton trousers he'd bought slid over her hips just as easily and were a length that she'd actually be able to walk in. The pants were equipped with multiple pockets down the side and some sort of utility belt around the hips. Both articles of clothing were in shades of purple so dark they could have been black. Last were the leather boots.

Calla's breath hitched a little when she saw the care that had been taken with the shoes. The leather had been oiled and stretched, making it less stiff for her to walk in. The insides had been padded with bits of cotton—by hand—in all the places that new boots might give her blisters. A pang of emotion reverberated through her chest, but it was gone before she could grasp it. She knelt down to lace up the boots, and by the time she was done there was a soft knock at the door.

"Come in," she said.

Gideon stepped back inside, the refilled canteens in his hands. "Ready?"

She nodded as he handed her one of the water bottles.

"I got each of us a backpack," he told her as he walked over to pick up one of the bags. "It has extra clothes, food for the road, anything I thought we might need. There're also a couple knives for you to keep on your belt. You just button the sheaths on and you're good to go."

Calla took the backpack from him, a hollow feeling inside her. "You barely slept," she accused him.

"I'm fine, Calliope," he told her, his eyes unreadable.

"Don't lie to me."

"What else do you want me to say?" he asked, his tone sounding almost defeated. "That I can't sleep because of the nightmares? Because every second I'm here and *he's* not is slowly killing me? That being useful is the only thing keeping me together? And how you . . ." He shook his head as his words trailed off.

They hadn't *really* spoken about Ezra—or anything else that had happened between them, for that matter—other than to scheme how to get the other prince back. Whatever was happening with her emotions had made it easier to lock away the all-consuming pain and grief that loomed in the shadows at the back of her mind. The place she stored everything she wasn't able to face. She wondered, however, if it was worse for Gideon to keep it all bottled up. He'd always had such tight control of his emotions before, but that clearly hadn't been a benefit to anyone.

"If you need to talk about it, we can," she offered.

"We don't have to." He tugged on one of his earrings.

"I know we don't *have* to."

He dropped his hand and narrowed his eyes at her. "Would it help?"

"Would what help?" she questioned.

"Whatever's broken between us. I want to fix it. Tell me what you need, and I'll do it."

"I don't *know*," she confessed, her tone colored with frustration.

"Calliope . . ." Gideon's voice was low, strained.

"There's so much grief inside me," she continued. "I can feel it crawling beneath my skin, but it won't come to the surface. I feel like I should be shedding tears for him every second of every day. It makes me feel more broken now than before." She was digging her nails into her palms, leaving angry red indentions in her skin, trying desperately to feel the ache, but it faded too quickly.

Gideon took a step toward her, but she recoiled, almost involuntarily.

"You were never broken before," he implored as he halted his movement. "And if you're broken now, so am I. Together, remember?"

There was that sentiment again.

Before she could come up with a way to respond he gave a cruel, sharp laugh. "Do you ever find it impossible not to wonder if all this effort is useless? Even if we did the impossible by bringing Ezra back, at the end of the day all of us ending up dead at the hands of the Witch Queens is nearly inevitable anyway. Maybe it would be less cruel to let him rest in peace. At least then it would only be me who has to suffer with the guilt of being the cause of his death."

Something about his words angered her. She felt it in her core—the quick strike of a match trying to catch fire despite the cold. "No."

"No?" His expression turned wary as he crossed his arms over his bare chest.

"You don't get to shoulder all the blame in some misguided attempt to punish yourself. And you definitely don't get to say the queens' win is inevitable. Not until I've gotten my chance on the battlefield, at least. If they are left standing at the end, it will be among the ashes of the power that I drain from them with my last breath if I must. I will *never* just let them win."

His brows shot up at the conviction in her voice as it thundered through the small space, the silver and obsidian of his eyes swirling like a tempest now.

"You punish yourself for everything so no one else has to take the blame. And maybe some of the blame does fall on you—and me. We *both* made these decisions. But what we don't need right now is to wallow in guilt until we fade away or give up this fight before it's truly begun. That's how the queens get away with what they've done. And the Fates. They're just as much to blame as you and me for what has happened."

"And what about taking responsibility for what I've done to you?" he murmured. "Am I at least allowed to do that? You claim you don't hate me—yet—but how long before you start resenting me for giving you the Heartbreak curse and taking away your ability to fall in love?"

"You say that as if the Heartbreak curse isn't something terrible that also affects *you*, Gideon. It's not as if either one of us could have predicted what the spell was going to do—we both took the same risk."

His jaw clenched, but he didn't get a chance to argue any longer when a loud knock sounded through the room and made them both jump.

"Housekeeping," someone called, their voice muffled.

"Fix your glamour," Gideon reminded her.

She worked on returning her hair to the silky blond disguise as she watched him let the housekeeper in. It was an older fae woman with warm ivory skin and long white hair who smiled at them politely as she placed a stack of fresh bed linens onto the dresser.

"I hope I'm not interrupting anything," the fae said, glancing between them. "I was told you were checking out?"

"Yes, we were just packing up," Gideon confirmed. He lifted one of the bags and handed it to Calla. As she fixed the pack over her shoulders, she caught him slipping something from the front pocket of his trousers—a tiny black box—and into the front pouch of his own bag. When all his own gear was settled in place, he told the fae, "We'll be going now."

"I hope you both had a lovely stay," the woman told them.

Gideon's smile was tight as he said, "Thank you."

The two of them didn't linger a second more. They made their way downstairs and slipped out of the inn, back into the city. Calla was grateful for the timing of the fae's interruption. She wasn't ready to delve deeper into the topic of the Heartbreak curse. Of all the things they currently had to be worried about, she was sure that was at the bottom of both of their lists.

14

For a moment, Hannah's world was blurry. Something had tackled her from the side, sending her flying through the water before a pair of clawed hands gripped her biceps and drove her down to the sea floor. Her back slammed against the sandy ground, and the force of the hit made everything around her hazy for a split second. She looked up at the being hovering over her and took in their forest-green hair, the shimmering patches of purple scales all over their upper body that matched the shade of the tail flicking behind them.

A nereid.

Hannah struggled against the seawoman's hold, thrashing her legs to try and wiggle away. The grip on her shoulders only tightened. From somewhere in the distance she heard a yelp of pain, and she froze.

Caspian.

This couldn't be happening again. Her blood boiled with a fury she hadn't felt in a very long time. A tornado of bubbles raced to the surface from her mouth as she unleashed a scream stifled by the water around her. She willed her magic to come to her, to be able to fight back and get to Caspian like she hadn't been able to for Delphine.

Delphine, who had protected her for years. Who had been the most tangible form of happiness Hannah had ever known—and let slip through her fingers. Hannah thought about how she had failed the siren every waking second. Delphine's face as she was dragged away was burned into Hannah's memory, a constant loop of torture reminding her of her shortcomings.

Now Caspian needed help. Caspian, who always made sure to check in on her while the others dealt with their own grief. Cass, who had become her *friend* in such a short amount of time, but whom she now couldn't imagine not knowing.

Hannah gnashed her teeth with effort as she pulled and pulled and pulled at the magic in her core. The nereid smiled down at Hannah, pupilless blue eyes shining with anticipation.

I can do this, she told herself. *I will not let another person down. I will be stronger. For Delphine. For myself.*

When the seawoman lunged forward, wide-open jaws angled toward Hannah's throat, everything slid into focus inside Hannah's mind with a *click*.

A hard pulse emanated from Hannah's chest and reverberated through the water, causing a circular ripple to spread out around her. Her eyes ached as colors became too bright and saturated. She cringed as an earsplitting screech ripped from the seawoman's mouth above her. A familiar vibration of power began slowly crawling through her veins, and when she lifted her hands to inspect them, she saw pulsing black veins slowly spreading from her fingertips and all the way up her arms.

She dug her fingers into the seafloor at her sides and opened her mouth in a wordless battle cry as dark energy ripped through her. The sand beneath the lake bed began to kick up and swirl in the water as the magic she expelled sent a shock wave through the lake. She didn't know what happened to the nereid, or how long she lay there, writhing in pain as her magic leaked out of every pore in her skin—as if her body was detoxing the old, dead power from her system. Her consciousness began to fade in and out.

Just before her eyes fluttered all the way shut, someone pulled her away. Gentle hands wedged themselves beneath her arms and tugged her up and up and up until her head broke the surface and cool air hit her skin. The person dragged her out of the water and onto the grassy bank, calling her name over and over again.

She was too tired to respond, though, too drained. She simply turned to her side, curled up, and passed out.

15

"How long has she been out?" a familiar feminine voice asked. *Celeste.*

"A day this time."

"A day?" Celeste repeated in shock.

"Her healing is getting slower and slower each time. Having to regrow the same body part over and over is messing with her magic. If it continues, she'll stop regenerating that part altogether."

The second voice was just as familiar as Celeste's, and Delphine knew she must be imagining the edge of concern in its tone. She slowly pried her eyes open, ignoring the raw aching in her throat as she looked around.

Eros realized Delphine was conscious before Celeste and pressed Delphine down by her shoulder before she could sit up.

"You're—"

Delphine didn't wait to hear the end of his sentence. She simply reached up to dig her nails into his wrists and focused on every ounce of water around her, sending a stream directly into his face. She scrambled off the bed and backed herself against the wall, teeth bared, ready to fight.

"Delphine." Celeste held up her hands as Eros recovered. "We—"

"Get the Hells away from me," she tried to say, but the sound that came out was worse than nails scratching over glass. They all cringed.

"If you ever want to sing again," Eros advised, crossing his arms over his chest, "I would save your voice for a little while. The repeated damage could be permanent if you don't rest."

"And why would I listen to *you*?" Delphine hissed.

"Do whatever the Hells you want, moonlight." Eros rolled his eyes. "I'm just telling you what they said. It would also behoove you not to alert the guard down the hall with any ruckus you may be itching to cause."

"Don't call me that," Delphine snapped.

It was the nickname Reniel had called her since she was ten, the fellow members of her Shoal having adopted the endearment as their own. When she was younger, it had made her feel special, like she was loved. As she grew older, however, she realized nothing she had experienced here was really love. Just manipulation.

Eros glanced over to Celeste. "She is officially your problem. Get her on board, or don't, I couldn't care less. She's always been too much trouble for me."

With that, he left. Delphine counted every footstep he took down the hall and out of sight. She could hear the sounds of him saying something to the guard who was posted at the door but couldn't make out any words.

Delphine locked eyes with Celeste.

"Why are you here?" Delphine demanded. "I was sure Zephyr would be the first one to come torture me."

In the years since she'd seen Celeste, the other girl hadn't changed a bit. Celeste's neat silver coils still hung halfway down her back, her mouth painted a shimmering metallic that complemented the siren's midnight-blue complexion and the silver freckles splashed across her skin like stars. It was as if Celeste had been frozen in time, an exact replica of how she existed in Delphine's memories. Meanwhile, Delphine knew she must look like an entirely different person—hair chopped above her shoulders, her deep blue nails unpolished, lips cracked, and blood staining the front of her top.

There was a time when Delphine considered Celeste one of the only people who truly knew her. A time when she daydreamed about breaking free of the Siren's oath binding her to Reniel. It was one thing to be in his Shoal—something she'd willingly entered into—but being forced into a magic oath with him was a different kind of cruelty altogether. So, while Celeste and Eros made plans for their futures that they never followed through with, she made plans to get out and never set foot in the watery depths of the Siren's Sea again. The day she'd begged Celeste to leave with her, Celeste had been shocked that Delphine was truly that unhappy in Reniel's Shoal.

That's the day Delphine realized Celeste didn't know her at all.

"Unlike some of the others, Eros and I don't want to torture you," Celeste said, brushing a curl out of her face. "You're more paranoid than I remember."

Delphine's throat wasn't the only thing on fire now. Four years' worth of anger burned through her body, and the words were out of her mouth before she could stop them. "As if you have any reason to accuse me of being unjustly paranoid after you *betrayed*—"

"You have no idea what you're talking about, Delphine." Celeste cut her off with a pointed finger. "I know you're angry, but *Hells*, have you never stopped to think once in all the time you've been gone that you aren't the only one who regrets what happened between us? You wanted me to make a life-altering decision in an instant—what was I supposed to do?"

"Not tell *Zephyr* so he could go to Reniel, for starters." Delphine laughed cruelly.

"I thought I could trust him," Celeste gritted out. "I didn't know—"

"That he has only ever looked out for himself? I've *always* told you I hated him—since the moment he was Claimed."

"You hated everyone, Delphine." Celeste threw up her hands. "You never wanted to make friends here. Did you never think that's why you were miserable?"

"Did *you* ever think it's because I knew no one could be trusted? Especially Zephyr! Common sense, Cel. After Reniel made Zephyr swear a Siren's oath for having an affair with one of his lovers, Zephyr became desperate to climb back to the top. You can't trust someone like that!"

"I thought because he knew what it was like to be punished with the Siren's oath, he would understand why we'd want out," Celeste whispered.

"I may have been jaded," Delphine admitted, "but my mother taught me better than to trust any of them and get burned. Except by you, of course. I never saw you coming. And look where that lapse in judgment led me."

Celeste strode across the room until she was standing chest to chest with Delphine, their faces only inches apart. Delphine froze. Celeste was breathing heavily, the gills on both sides of her neck filtering water in and out at a rapid pace. The last time they had been this close together, she had been begging Celeste to leave with her.

"I never thought you would really go," Celeste told her. "You *left me.*"

"You didn't even try to come after me," Delphine returned.

"I was too scared before."

Delphine tilted her chin up, looking down her nose at Celeste as she said, "And now?"

"Eros and I"—Celeste swallowed—"we've been making plans. We want your help."

Too little, too late, Delphine thought. There was no way in Hells she'd ever trust them again. She'd rather rot in this cell than help them after what they'd done to sabotage her. "Since when did you and Eros get so close? If I remember correctly, Eros was just as much Reniel's lapdog as Zephyr was when I left. He was leading the pack back in the forest!"

"You have no idea what the rest of us went through once you left. Reniel locked everything down for *months*. He tortured us for weeks, convinced the rest of us were planning to defect just as you had. Zephyr turned all his anger into desire to get revenge on you. Eros and I . . . we realized, together, that you were right to leave. You had seen what Reniel was capable of long before so many others."

"You have no idea the things I've seen him do."

"Because you never told me," Celeste retorted. "You kept so many things to yourself."

"To protect you!" Delphine yelled. "To protect myself!"

Because even as much as Delphine had loved Celeste, she would always have chosen herself over anyone else. Then she'd met Hannah. And Calla. Trusting them had been a long process. Luckily for Delphine, Hannah and Calla both had much more patience than she ever did. The two of them never pushed her, never made her question her boundaries, and that made it easier to trust them unconditionally.

Maybe in a different environment she could have learned to trust Celeste like she did Hannah and Calla. But then she probably would have never met the other girls, and this version of herself wouldn't even exist. The version of herself she finally loved.

"We've finally seen it for ourselves." Celeste's words brought Delphine back to the present. "And we're ready to leave it all behind now. With you. You got out once and can do it again. Only this time, I won't let you do it alone."

Delphine laughed, a quick, harsh sound. "You're right. I can do it again. So what makes you think I'll let the two of you hold me back again?"

"At least hear us out," Celeste insisted, her voice dropping lower. "You're our best chance to make our plans work and get out of here. You're a wild card. Something Reniel won't be able to predict anymore. Unlike Eros and me. Eros was leading us that day in the forest as a test—Reniel told Zephyr to report back on every single move he made. His obedience was to convince Reniel that he could be trusted. It was an act, I promise."

Delphine was about to tell the siren to eat glass, that their promises meant nothing, and she didn't care if it had been an act or not. She would never help either of them escape after they dragged her back here. A voice in the back of her mind stopped her, though. Belonging to Ezra Black, of all people, from some random night months ago when he'd been at the girls' apartment teaching Calla the rules of Bourrée.

You always play your opponents. Never the cards.

If Celeste and Eros were willing to give up their plans to her, why should she refuse? More information was always an asset, and when it was time to carry out whatever scheme they had come up with, she would do so—alone. She hoped the bitter taste of betrayal choked them like it had her for years.

So Delphine said, "What is it the two of you had in mind?"

Celeste's eyes narrowed. "You'll hear us out. Truly?"

It took all Delphine's effort to keep the bite out of her tone as she answered, "I just asked, didn't I?"

Celeste searched for something in Delphine's face, and she must have found whatever she was looking for because she closed her eyes for a moment and leaned closer. "Delphine, I . . ."

Delphine froze at their proximity, at the way Celeste lifted her arms and circled them around Delphine's neck.

Play the game, a voice whispered in the back of Delphine's mind. *If she needs to believe you still could have feelings for her . . .*

Delphine allowed Celeste to embrace her for a few seconds, and when Celeste opened her eyes again, they were full of hope. Hope Delphine planned to crush.

16

Even with all the miles they had walked over the past several hours, it was stepping into the Starlight Inn that knocked the breath from Calla's lungs. Memories of the times she had been in and out of the buzzing lobby—the smell of charred magic that would cling to her clothes days after she left, the burn of alcohol pouring down her throat—almost buckled her knees. A fracture began to split through the glacial barriers erected in her mind.

The memory of waking up, disoriented, in a stone cell after being kidnapped by Ramor and Boone came roaring back to her. She could still feel the sickening churn of her stomach as she was dressed up like a doll to be sold.

"Hey." Gideon's deep voice jostled her from her thoughts. "Are you going to be all right?"

It was the first time she'd heard him speak in hours, both of them having been too much in their own heads during most of their trek through Estrella's countryside to make casual conversation. Calla couldn't make her mouth work to answer him, though, and when he tried to reach for her hand, to ground her back in the present, she flinched away.

A flicker of something went through his glamoured eyes, but he simply dropped his hands and told her, "We don't have to do this. We can leave."

"And then what?" she whispered. "Waste more time trying to figure out an alternative place to get what we need? Leave the others to fend for themselves for even longer because I'm overreacting?"

"Calliope, this is not overreacting."

"Ezra would have told me it is." She squeezed her nails into her palms. "I've been here a million times, what's once more?"

Gideon pressed his lips together in a hard line for a moment before telling her, firmly, "The last time you were here you were almost *auctioned*. If your mind is having a hard time processing that, then we can leave."

"You would forfeit our best chance to get him back if I asked you to?"

"I could find another way," he responded immediately. Instinctively.

She resisted the urge to roll her eyes. "I'll be fine. Just go ask if there will be any vendors we can meet with tonight."

"Will you be okay waiting here?"

She nodded. She could collect herself enough to do this. Especially considering this would probably be the easiest part of the night. "I can hold on to your things while you wait in line."

Gideon handed off his backpack to her and went to join the long queue at the check-in desk while she propped herself against the wall. She tracked every movement of those around him from her vantage point, on edge that someone would remember him from the auction or recognize him as the Onyx Prince even with the disguise. She swore she'd be able to pick out his careful movements, his poised demeanor—not to mention his *voice*—anywhere. But with all the hubbub no one bothered to even spare him a second glance, making her shoulders relax a bit as he continued to move up in the line.

As she shifted her weight, her ankles knocked against the sides of his bag at her feet and a brief memory ran through her mind from when they'd left the last inn.

I shouldn't . . . she thought, but a moment later she was lifting the bag back up into her arms, tentatively glancing at where the prince was standing in line to make sure he hadn't turned around.

Calla knew she had no right to snoop through his things—didn't know what was possessing her to lift the flap of the front pouch and dig around for the small black box she knew she'd caught him sneaking in there. Until she pulled the lid off the tiny package, and every ounce of oxygen rushed out of her lungs, that is.

It was the gold flower earrings from the pawnshop.

She hurried to replace the lid, shoving the box as deep down into the bag's pocket as it would go, and then dropped the entire pack back on the floor. When the flood of adrenaline suddenly going through her body made Gideon twist around to check on her, she knew she had to pull herself together.

She waved his look of concern off, and he narrowed his eyes, but before he could step out of line and come back to her, the receptionist called, "Next!"

He was back less than two minutes later with a small silver key and a suspicious set to his mouth.

"What's that?" she blurted.

"I used the name you gave me. They handed me this and told me to go to the fourth floor," Gideon explained. "Are you okay?"

She ignored the latter question, leaning in to peer at the small object in his palm with skepticism. "I've never been to the fourth floor. I have no idea what we might be about to walk into. Maybe we shouldn't have used Jack's name."

"It'll lead us somewhere, regardless," Gideon told her. "You said your landlord was well connected, right?"

"An understatement." She snorted.

"Then this is our best lead." Gideon folded the key in his fist. "Are you okay to go?"

Calla took a deep breath and nodded. At least they weren't going down to the gambling room in the basement. She most definitely wasn't prepared for that.

She led Gideon to the staircase next to the pulley elevator, and the two of them took the steps two at a time. The smell was the first thing that hit them when they made it to the landing. Calla choked on the putrid scent of dark magic, and if it weren't for Gideon standing by her side, she would have lost her nerve immediately.

"What room is it?" she questioned, pulling the high neck of her sweater up over her face as she glanced down the long corridor of doors.

The hideous carpet and wallpaper were the exact same patterns as those in the rest of the inn. A small shiver ran down her spine at the claw marks on the walls and a few suspicious burns on the bottoms of some of the doors.

"Third on the left, they said." Gideon gestured with his chin. "What are our names again?"

"I'm Lily," she told him as they made their way to the door. "And you're Blue."

Gideon quirked a brow. "Those are terrible undercover names."

"It's not like I had a ton of time to workshop them," Calla huffed.

Gideon resisted the smirk that was trying to unfurl on his face and slid the key into the door. When they pushed their way inside, she saw a group of people crowded around a long table, and every one of their heads snapped up from whatever they were huddled over to look in their direction. The door slammed shut behind them.

Calla swallowed when she noticed that in the middle of the room was a long table. In the center of that table lay a vaguely familiar, shirtless fae. The man's body was covered in awful burns, splotchy red patches marring his porcelain skin. She hoped he was only unconscious, but the knives protruding from multiple places on his body made her doubt that was the case.

None of that was what made Calla's jaw drop.

Her landlord, Jack, was here in the flesh, brandishing a knife over the scarred fae on the table. And on either side of him stood Ramor and Boone.

A loud noise clanged through the dungeon's corridor and snapped Celeste out of whatever trance she'd been in. When they didn't hear anyone coming down the hall, she let out a breath, though her expression remained wary.

"We should talk more about . . . that . . . later," Celeste said. "I have to be somewhere."

Delphine put on her best look of innocence. "We need to be careful about whatever *that* was, before things get messier than they already are. Nothing can happen between us—not until this is all over and we're free."

Delphine needed to string Celeste along as far as she possibly could, but she had no desire to trap herself into any more displays of affection.

Celeste nodded. "I'm sorry, I don't know what just came over me. I know you're still angry. The way Eros and I had to act—"

"I get it." *No, I don't.* "You did what you had to do." *And I'll do the same.*

"I just want you to know that Eros and I only assisted in bringing you back because it would have been highly suspicious if we hadn't."

Delphine forced herself to shrug as she combed her fingers through her hair and pushed the strands out of her face. When she saw how Celeste's eyes were tracking every movement, she knew she had her right where she wanted her.

Celeste cleared her throat. "When you used your magic in the Siren's Sea, it was like kelpies getting their first taste of blood. Reniel sensed it right away—through your Siren's oath. Eros convinced Zephyr to let us go with him to find you, saying we wanted revenge even more than Zephyr did, and our plan was to turn on Zephyr the moment we found you—but then Mariana somehow weaseled her way into coming with us."

"And? Then there still would have been only two of them and all of us—"

"Mariana had a tracking ring on her," Celeste said, cutting her off.

Delphine's breath hitched in surprise. Reniel's tracking rings were infamous throughout his Shoal. Forged with dark magic, the rings allowed Reniel to track the wearer anywhere in the world. Though that wasn't the most insidious part.

Whoever wore the ring couldn't just slip it off. They would have to remove the finger the ring was on altogether in order to be rid of it, and the magic in the cursed band would stop the appendage from ever growing back. And if you killed someone who wore one of the rings, the band's dark magic would not only mark you as the killer—it would make you horribly sick and keep your magic from healing you correctly.

"Reniel put it on her a few months after you left," Celeste continued. "Another thing to add to the list of things they blame you for. If we had turned on the two of them and she got killed . . ."

"*Gods*," Delphine spat. "He sent her with you all on purpose."

Celeste nodded. "Eros suspected the same thing. We don't know which of us he didn't fully trust, but we've had to be more careful than ever now. Mariana's reward for helping to bring you back was getting the ring removed. She's been scarce around here trying to lie low and avoid catching Reniel's attention again."

"And yet she'll remain loyal to him despite what he did to her."

"Probably. But there are a lot of other Shoal members who have become unsatisfied with Reniel's reign of terror. Not just Reniel—the other Shoal leaders, too. They're keeping the ability to Claim sirens to themselves and letting our people's magic be snuffed out. It's their way to stay in control, but it's causing so many to leave the Siren's Sea—or not join Shoals at all."

"It only took four centuries." Delphine's tone dripped with sarcasm as she shook her head. "Are the Shoal leaders not worried what will happen if they continue like this?"

"The opposite, actually. Reniel has started new traditions since you've been gone." Celeste's voice was tight. "Instead of the traditional Claiming ceremonies, he's begun to let those who wish to be Claimed challenge his Shoal members in combat. If the winner is the Shoal member, they get a promotion. If the winner is the rookie, they are

Claimed and receive their spot in the Shoal—at the cost of the old Shoal member's life."

Delphine looked at the girl in disbelief. The Claiming ceremonies had always had an edge of competition, but *this* was on a whole other level. Killing off Shoal members? It was dramatic even for Reniel. No wonder the Shoals were becoming restless. Most were used to being Claimed and living the rest of their lives attending Reniel's lavish parties without a care in the world. Reniel was the most well-connected siren in the Siren's Sea outside the Sea King himself, and most of his Shoal members shared in his vast wealth as long as they remained on his good side.

"I know you're upset with the part Eros and I played in your capture—and I know after seeing us in those roles, it's probably hard for you to separate us from Zephyr," Celeste said. "But you being back can be to all of our advantages. The next Claiming is on the Blood Moon in two weeks."

Delphine swallowed, desperately trying to tamp down the venomous replies aching to crawl out of her mouth. She wasn't sure how she was going to be able to fake pleasantries with Celeste and Eros long enough to work with them—she couldn't care less about whatever reasons Celeste went along with Zephyr's plans. She had offered Celeste an opportunity all those years ago, and she hadn't taken it; it was Celeste's own damn problem to find a way out now.

When Delphine didn't say anything for another long minute, Celeste reached out and gently tucked a short strand of Delph's hair behind her ear. The last time someone had done something so tender was . . . Hannah. At the thought of Hannah, Delphine let her eyes flutter shut and pressed her cheek into Celeste's palm, imagining it was her friend. Just for a moment. That's who she needed to keep in mind.

Getting back to Hannah and Calla.

"I'll get you out of here," Celeste swore.

Unlike the warm thoughts of Hannah and Calla, Celeste's empty promises didn't get anywhere close to touching her ice-cold heart.

"And this time I'm coming with you," Celeste finished.

We'll see.

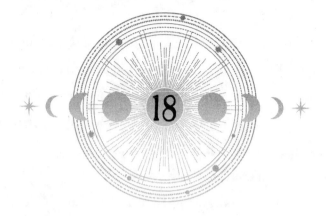

18

The last people Calla had expected to see tonight were Ramor and Boone. She thanked the Gods she was quick enough on her feet to fix her poker face in place before she let them see her surprise.

She tucked a strand of her glamoured blond hair behind her ear as a fake smile unfurled on her lips. "We aren't interrupting, are we?"

"Who the Hells are *you*?" Ramor demanded, ever brash. "This is a private room."

Calla lazily scanned the room. "Clearly. We do apologize; they must have given us the wrong information downstairs."

Calla twisted to give Gideon a *We need to get out of here* look over her shoulder, but before either of them could turn to leave she heard, "Wait."

Calla had only met Jack a handful of times. She knew using his name would carry some weight with the inn's patrons—enough to get them connected to someone who could help with their task. She never considered that Jack himself would be here tonight of all nights. The man had a reputation for constantly being out of town and letting his network of lackeys run most of his businesses. When the girls had to pay their rent, it was one of those many employees who collected it from them. Every now and then, however, Jack himself would be at his home waiting for the money, and Calla would make as little conversation as she could manage without being rude. On those occasions, he had never been anything other than pleasant. On the surface, at least.

Jack moved around from the head of the table to get a better look at Calla and Gideon. His appearance was so at odds with everyone else's in the room. He was just so very . . . mortal. And yet he somehow managed to make himself stand out no matter whose presence he was in. He was about five foot ten and had perfectly swept-back chestnut hair and piercing honey eyes. His ivory skin was usually warmed by the sun until it was a light golden color. His outfits reminded Calla of something she would see Kestrel wear, and his ears and fingers were always adorned with glittering jewels and rings.

Calla recalled Delphine saying he was dreamy a few different times, but there was a darkness in his eyes that always kept Calla from agreeing. That wicked glint was very much present now as he demanded they stay, and she could feel Gideon's body tense behind her at the man's tone.

"Have we met before?" Jack asked, a small smile playing on his lips. It was a dangerous question, and he knew it.

Calla shrugged. "We've met a lot of people. It's hard to keep track."

Jack's smile turned knowing. "What's your name, sweetheart?"

"Lily," she lied evenly.

"Lily," he repeated. "What brings you here?"

She didn't hesitate as she said, "We were told there was someone here by the name of Jack who had a collection we might be interested in. Our source said we might be able to deal with one of their vendors if we came by tonight."

"Ah, then you're in the right place after all," Jack said, turning the knife he held over in his hands. "*I'm* the Jack of All Trades."

Calla made a show of letting her mouth drop into a small O shape before recovering and saying, "It's nice to make your acquaintance. We must be in luck tonight."

The second the word *luck* left her mouth, the dimple in the left side of his face popped out. "I'm curious. . . . If you don't mind me asking, who sent you to me?"

Shit, Calla thought. She didn't have a single name to connect back to Jack that wasn't hers or the girls' or Ezra's.

"Axle Savis," Gideon inserted. "A friend of mine."

The wicked gleam in Jack's eyes shifted almost imperceptibly, the name clearly piquing his interest, but Calla wasn't sure whether it was in a good way or bad.

Jack turned to Ramor now. "Axle Savis . . . When's the last time you've seen him around here?"

Ramor looked thoughtful. "About a month ago. The night of the auction." His hand waved over the body on the table. "A couple hours before the fire—"

"Enough." Jack cut Ramor off. "No need to scare off our guests with that nonsense."

As if the man on the table with knives sticking out of him wouldn't be enough to terrify us? Calla thought an instant before it clicked why the man was so familiar. He was one of the fae who had burned her apartment down.

Calla hoped he wasn't just unconscious after all.

Jack flicked his gaze back over to Calla and Gideon in curiosity before turning to Boone. "Take this." Boone scrambled to take the hilt of the blade Jack was thrusting toward him. "If the fae wakes up again, carve out his liver this time," Jack ordered before snapping his fingers at two other giants hanging against the wall behind him.

The giants immediately stood at attention. Jack whispered something to one of them, who nodded and stayed in place while Jack and the second made their way over to Calla and Gideon.

"Why don't we do business somewhere more private?" Jack suggested, waving a hand toward the door for them to exit.

Gideon pulled the door open and waited for Calla to duck out first, following close on her heels. Jack and the giant who was clearly his bodyguard stepped around them and strutted ahead down the hall.

Calla turned to Gideon and discreetly mouthed, *Axle Savis?*

Gideon leaned down to her ear and whispered, "My contact who got us the siren's tongue for the Witch Eater's spell."

Calla filed that information away for later as they got closer to where Jack was unlocking another one of the rooms that had the exact same setup as the one before. Jack waved for them to take a seat in the uncomfortable-looking chairs on one side of the table as he took up a spot across from them. His guard stood at alert over his shoulder, and Calla tried not to let the giant's cold stare unnerve her.

"Tell me," Jack started, folding his hands on the table in front of him. "How did you come to know Axle?"

Gideon answered with a shrug, "The gambling circuit. He was always a good one for a wild night."

"The two of you are in the gambling rings? I've never seen any fae who weren't courtless join any of the groups around here."

Calla flicked her eyes over to Gideon and took in his extra-sharp chin and cheekbones, the points of his ears and the way his nose now tilted up at the end. She wasn't sure what detail in their glamour was missing—or added—that had caused Jack to assume they weren't one of the many courtless fae that made Estrella their home, but at least their glamour was convincing.

Gideon explained, "We mostly stay up north when we're not back in the fae courts. We've only come this far south for . . . you."

"I'm honored," Jack said with a healthy dose of sarcasm as he leaned back in his chair. "Now, before we talk about anything, we need to go over a few preliminary measures."

"*What* measures?" Calla narrowed her eyes.

Jack shifted to rest his elbows on the table once more. "Due to the little display you just witnessed and the nature of things we will be dealing with, both of you surely wouldn't mind cooperating with a few contingencies to guarantee that none of it is repeated before we do business?"

"Exactly what contingencies do you mean?" Calla pressed.

Jack snapped his fingers, and within seconds the guard placed something on the table in front of them. Two small glass vials filled with blue liquid.

"Forgetting potions. Always handy," Jack explained with a sleazy grin. "Don't worry—it will only make you forget up to three hours. I'll allow you each to write a note to yourselves explaining that you agreed to take the potion after our dealings were done to protect my operation and employees."

"No way." Calla shook her head instantly.

"Oh, I apologize." Jack laughed. "I didn't intend to make it seem like you actually had a choice—though I *do* have a game we can play if it makes the medicine go down easier."

Calla bristled at the man's amusement. "What game?"

Jack snapped his fingers again, and the giant produced three more bottles, all with identical liquids as the first two.

"Have you ever played roulette?" Jack asked. "It's one of my favorite games. You can agree to take the first two potions and be assured only three hours are wiped from your memories—and you get to write the letters to yourselves as promised. *Or*, I can add these three vials to the mix. One of them is mixed with a drop of my blood and enchanted to only erase memories with me in them. One is a placebo and will do nothing to you whatsoever."

Calla braced herself as she waited for the last shoe to drop.

"The last vial," Jack murmured as he picked up one of the glasses of blue liquid, "will lock down your magic for exactly seventy-two hours."

Calla whipped her head in Gideon's direction to gauge his reaction, half-relieved to see that he was already shaking his head. "Absolutely not. We'll just agree to take the original forgetting potions."

"Are you sure?" Jack coaxed. "One of you could get the placebo and not forget anything at all."

Calla chewed her lip as she kept her eyes on Gideon.

Gideon shook his head. "It's not worth the risk." Then he looked at Calla and vowed, "We'll be okay. I promise."

Jack sighed deeply. "Fine, be boring. Do we have a deal to proceed, then?"

"After we drink the potion, how long will we have before the effects set in?" Gideon countered.

Jack shrugged. "Five to ten minutes, give or take."

"I want to be allowed to write down exactly the items we received and what we paid for them in our notes," Gideon negotiated.

Jack rolled his eyes before nodding. "Deal. Now, tell me—what is it the two of you are after?"

19

Amina swung open the door to Maven's Dress Shop, Lyra and Sabine on her heels.

"Do you think they have anything with pockets?" Sabine asked no one in particular as she walked off to look through one of the rows of gowns while Amina and Lyra headed in the opposite direction.

"What exactly is your plan?" Lyra crossed their arms as Amina sifted through the racks. "Get to the Reverie and corner the queen about your exile? Set one of her butlers on fire to make a point? I know you had a lot of time in that forest to think, but I'm starting to wonder if any of the thinking was critical."

Amina threw an unamused look over her shoulder as she ran the tips of her sharp nails over the fabric of one of the hanging garments in front of her. "Since when do I need to spell out every little detail for you?"

Lyra's brows rose in disbelief as Amina pulled the dress she had been admiring from its hanger. "Since the last time something went a little wrong and we didn't see you for six years. I don't think caution is such a bad place to develop personal growth."

"Why are you worried about caution? Everything leading up to my exile was a fluke—it wasn't as if we planned out an entire operation and it crashed and burned." Amina knew her tone was harsh, but Lyra was poking her where it was still sore. "This is *my* revenge to sort out. All I'm asking is for you to back me up."

"How can I possibly do that if I don't know what I'm backing you up *for*?" Lyra pushed.

Amina lowered her voice so none of the other patrons in the shop would be able to hear her. "I simply need to collect something from the queen in order to get the justice I deserve for all the trouble she put me through. If you trusted me like you used to, that would be enough for now."

Lyra narrowed their eyes as they decided how to respond, trying to determine if Amina's words were meant to be some sort of test. Eventually, they settled on: "And if she sends a wrath of soldiers after you for whatever you plan to do to get this justice?"

"My dear Lyra. Is six years all it took for you to forget who I am?" Amina flicked her eyes to her friend, hoping her tone masked the disappointment underneath. "When have I ever not had a contingency plan?"

"Contingency plans only work if everyone is in on them," Lyra said bluntly.

Amina's hand clutched the fabric of the dress in a white-knuckle grip—the only indication of how upset she was. Lyra was right—they had been right the night Amina had gotten exiled, too—but that wasn't the point. Amina fully intended to share everything . . . once she actually finished sorting out the details. What hurt was the lack of trust. Before her exile Amina could have asked the two of them to help her bury a body and the grave would have been dug before they even asked whose body it was.

"Do you trust me?" Amina's words were low, a challenge.

Lyra's amber eyes met Amina's evenly. "It's not that I don't trust you, Amina. But things have changed."

It took everything in Amina not to flinch. "Like the fact that I no longer have a room at the manor? Or do you mean more tangible things? Like Sabine going to the Veritas Tree without me? Is there no space for me anymore? Has too much happened that I will never be able to make up for?"

Lyra's jaw dropped a bit before they quickly sobered. "Some bonds are harder to replicate when they've become tighter than others."

The hurt that slammed through Amina at those words made the breath rush out of her lungs. Lyra didn't stop.

"But do *not* act like Sabine's trip to the Veritas Tree was a slight against *you*. Sabine did not deserve to suffer in a form that was not true for her because you couldn't be present. It almost *shattered her heart* to go without you."

Amina swallowed thickly, shutting her eyes. "I didn't mean to imply that I was upset with *Sabine*. I would *never* be upset that she finally received her True Name. I know very well the queen is the reason I didn't get to be there. My rage lies with Her Highness alone. But . . . it was supposed to be us by her side. *Both* of us. I cannot bear that I was not present, and now I worry that no matter how much I make up for my absence, the two of you will forever be on a different playing field. It makes me want to burn the queen's entire empire down, until there is nothing left but ash."

Lyra's face softened. "Amina . . . Sabine doesn't hold it against you. You should ask her about it. . . . She would love to share that story with you. We still love you—that much will never change. But you cannot expect things to snap back overnight."

Amina only gave a single nod of acknowledgment as she turned away, heading to the dressing stalls in the back with the gown she had picked. Lyra followed, waiting outside the room as Amina changed.

Amina rushed to strip her current dress off, removing all her accessories except the leather utility belt she kept permanently buckled around her waist and the pulsing pouch attached. She nimbly unbuttoned the back of the crimson bodice before stepping in and shimmying the silk over the flare of her hips. She smoothed a hand across the crinkles in the fabric where she had clutched it too tightly during her tense conversation with Lyra and hoped steam would be able to get the wrinkles out. Sweeping back the dressing room curtain, she stepped out and strutted over to the pedestal that rested before an enormous gilded mirror.

When she was atop the pedestal, she reached around to her back and tried to begin fastening the small buttons, but after watching her struggle for a while Lyra finally rolled their eyes and asked, "Would you like some help?"

She opened her mouth to decline, but Lyra, now joined by Sabine, was already there, shoving Amina's hands away. Lyra buttoned the bodice all the way up her back.

Amina flattened her hand over the front of the dress. The boning around the strapless bodice's cups and down the torso was a slightly darker red than the rest of the dress's material, designed to stand out and accentuate her shape. The silk skirts were draped asymmetrically on the left side of her body, a long slit revealing her right leg. It had a devastating effect.

"That's the one." Lyra nodded.

"Agreed." Amina twirled to inspect every angle. "What did you pick out, Sabine?"

Sabine held up a gauzy black jumpsuit with a structured, corset-like bodice wrapped in tulle. "It'll match my daggers."

Amina snorted and turned back to the mirror. Before she could begin trying to unfasten the corset herself, Lyra slid in to assist once again, getting all the way down to the bottom before they froze.

"Amina." A statement. An accusation.

"You're not thinking . . ." Lyra reached out and placed their hand over the pulsing bump disguised beneath the draping of the dress. "The heart."

"Yes."

"You chose a dress that could hide the heart. . . ." Lyra's eyes dilated as the realization hit them. "You said you needed to collect something from the queen."

"Yes." Amina met their gaze in the mirror.

"What the Hells is going on?" Sabine griped, her gaze flicking between her two friends locked in a stare-down.

"You can't do this," Lyra gritted out. "I never would have bargained with the Wayfarer for those invitations if I knew—"

"Don't tell me what I can't do when you don't know what I went through," Amina said harshly.

"Then tell us what you went through!" Lyra said. "*Talk* to us! I know time is of the essence; I get it, Amina. But, again, you cannot expect to walk back into our lives like this and act as if we should pick up like *six years* didn't happen with no explanations! Going after the queen won't heal this, Amina. It won't magically mend everything among the three of us. Only we can do that with one another. I'm asking you to let us do that."

"And I'm asking you to let me be angry," Amina said. "We were never anything but loyal to her—carrying on a rivalry with the witches that serves no one. How many unready souls have our people had to reap because of her? How many souls have you and Sabine taken that have made you sick to your stomach, just to pay a tithe *she* owes? The next soul I reap will be *his*, right in front of her, do you understand?"

"Amina." Lyra's voice was desperate. "What if she exiles you again? What are we going to do? You're lucky you made it out this time! What are the odds that you even found a prince's heart to break the spell in the first place?"

"How *did* you meet a prince?" Sabine interjected in a tone that suggested she was trying to alleviate some of the tension. "And were they hot?"

Amina ignored Sabine, answering Lyra with, "The odds are greater than you think."

"What do you mean?" Lyra demanded.

"I *mean*," Amina said as she turned away to head back into the dressing room, "nothing happens by chance. Something I quickly learned in that forest."

"What else did you learn in the forest?" Lyra continued to push as Amina quickly changed.

"What do either of you know about the Witch Eater?" Amina asked as she reemerged from the dressing room.

The two Valkyries exchanged a look. Amina gritted her teeth.

It was Sabine who answered. "Aren't they a God or something?"

"More like . . . the referee of the Gods. They aren't bound by any higher beings or force of nature."

"You met them, then, in the forest," Lyra deduced as the three of them paid for the two ensembles at the front and left the shop.

"Yes," Amina confirmed. "They're the reason I ended up in that witch prince's path. They aren't technically allowed to get involved with the Fates or the Gods, but they can bend the rules. And I can't help but feel they guided me while I was there."

"Witch prince?" Lyra paused in the middle of the street. "*Witch prince?*"

"Did I not mention that part?" Amina tilted her head as she combed through her memory, the long coils of her hair falling off her bare shoulders and down her back.

"You're telling me," Lyra said slowly, deliberately, "that you stole the heart from one of the Onyx Queen's sons?"

"I stole *nothing*. I accepted what I was promised when the elder prince made an ill-advised bargain."

"I'm done. Unless you want to spill every single detail about every single second you spent in that forest, I am not helping you."

Amina was about to tell Lyra they were overreacting when she caught Sabine shuffling closer to the other Valkyrie. It was subtle, but it gutted her.

So instead she said, "Fine. I can do it by myself. I don't want to endanger either of you anyway."

There was a long pause as the three of them stood there, an electric current in the sticky, humid air that told them all a storm was coming. Both literally and figuratively. Every decision they made from here on out would change the course of their futures forever, and they had to decide if they were going to continue as a trio.

Lyra was the first to begin unfurling their wings, the mottled brown-and-gray feathers fluttering as they prepared to take off. Sabine bit her lip as she looked back at Amina for a moment longer before following suit.

Amina watched them become dark specks in the sky above her. Wondering if this was them leaving her behind for now—or forever.

20

At no point in time had Gideon expected to find himself standing in a trove of extraordinary artifacts that belonged to Calliope's former landlord. The two of them had been reluctant when Jack arranged for a carriage to take them back to his home, the idea never crossing their minds that that's where the rarities would be kept. According to Jack, it was safest to have his collection right under his nose. Gideon was surprised, if not suspicious, at how forthcoming Jack was being, but he supposed the fact that he and Calliope would be forgetting everything that transpired meant the man didn't need to be as tight-lipped as he might otherwise have been.

Gideon was standing on high alert, examining some sort of fang Jack claimed had come from a rare species of dragon. He turned away from the tooth—which was the size of his forearm—and headed over to see what strange item Calliope was gawking at as they waited for their host to return from answering a knock at the door. He left them to be chaperoned by the hulking giant, who hadn't said a single word but had been watching Calliope in a way that made Gideon want to shove a dagger between the bastard's ribs.

"The label says these cuffs make you *disappear*," Calliope said in a hushed tone as Gideon approached over her shoulder, angling his body to block her from the guard's view. "How in the Hells do you think a *human* has managed to collect all this?"

"I'd imagine the answer must include him selling his soul to some sadistic God," he murmured back. "I've seen immortal collectors who don't have nearly as rare a cache and they've been hunting things down for centuries."

Calliope shuddered, whether from the draft in the oversized mansion or the idea of Jack having sold his soul, Gideon wasn't sure.

Less than a minute later, Jack finally returned. "My apologies, I had a floral delivery to attend to."

Calliope watched skeptically as the man walked over to a shelf in the far corner of the room and began digging out a large wooden box buried beneath a few jars and books, collecting dust. He brought the box over to them and placed it atop a small oak writing desk in the center of the packed space and clicked the gilded latches open. She moved closer to get a better look at whatever was nestled in the plush green velvet lining inside, but Gideon remained in place.

"These are stones from the Valley of Souls. Each one contains a lifetime of memories from a single soul who's crossed the valley into their final resting place. They carry the stone with them to remember who they were, and at the end of their journey through the valley, they leave the stone behind. Very few beings are capable of collecting them and bringing them over to our world. Fortunately, I've come across a couple of those rare beings, and they've owed me enough favors for me to get these."

"How much would it cost us for one?" Gideon eyed the smooth opalescent stones from where he stood.

"Twenty thousand spéctrals."

This was the part they hadn't really planned for, and now they would have to wing it—just like he had told Cass.

"And if we don't have that sort of money?" Calliope asked nonchalantly, but Gideon could see the calculations behind her eyes. She must figure that the man would have a backup offer.

Gideon watched as Jack smiled like he was hoping that would be the case. "Luckily for both of you"—Jack tilted his head—"I don't just deal in money."

"Spit it out," Gideon demanded. "Whatever it is you want."

Jack's amber eyes flickered over Calliope. "I want a single favor from each of you. My choice of favor and my choice when I collect it."

Gideon exchanged a loaded look with Calliope. When she dipped her chin in a nod, he turned back to Jack and said, "Fine."

"Excellent. I'll need a drop of each of your blood, to summon you when I please."

Gideon tensed. This was a terrible idea.

"What about a spell to use with the stone? To summon a gateway like you promised," Calliope reminded him.

Jack nodded easily. "There's a grimoire here that has such spells—though I cannot guarantee how it will perform. I'll write it down on the notes you leave for yourselves."

"All right," she allowed. "And one more thing . . ."

Gideon gave her an incredulous look, wondering what else she could possibly request—

"Is there anything you might have that could break a very powerful bond?" she asked.

Gideon's stomach dropped. He knew Calliope must have felt the sudden wave of dread that rolled through him at her words, but she didn't spare him a glance. Jack, however, watched them both with a wild sort of glee in his amber eyes.

Gideon couldn't understand why she hadn't expressed to him that she was so desperate to get rid of their bond that she'd ask a snake like Jack for help. He didn't want to break the link between them. If it wasn't for her tethering him here, he might not have survived losing Ezra long enough to be on this quest in the first place.

"I'm unsure what sort of bond you might be speaking of," Jack said, "but I have things that will break even the most permanent of ties. Most cost an enormous personal sacrifice, however, and the outcomes are often unpredictable."

"*No*," Gideon declared, to Calliope, to Jack, to the universe. "No more sacrifices. No more uncontrollable outcomes. We need the stone and the spell, and that's it."

Calliope looked at him now, her expression unreadable, but after a few agonizing seconds she blessedly conceded with a nod. Yet the fire burning in his veins remained.

Was her recent apathy his fault? Did she think he didn't want to hear how she was feeling? That her thoughts would be a burden on him? He wished he had been more open with her since the day they met. He wished he had done so many things differently.

"Then let us conclude this evening, I have other matters to attend to." Jack gestured at his guard. "Retrieve us something to write with."

As the guard stepped out to complete the task, Jack plucked one of the stones out of its case and snapped the lid shut. He handed the artifact over to Calliope, and she tucked it deep into her pocket. Next, Jack turned his attention to searching for the tomb of spells he had mentioned before, Gideon let the background around him blur as he watched Calliope. Silently begging for her to look at him. She didn't.

After Jack jotted down something from one of his books, he passed a pen and paper over to Calliope and then to Gideon. Gideon took a deep breath as he looked down at the parchment and began recording the important details of what occurred. How they retrieved the stone and the spell, what it cost them, as well as an explanation of the forgetting potion. Then he scribbled down one last note to himself before passing it back to the other man to inspect. Jack smirked as he looked over Gideon's handwriting. Finally, Jack procured a pin to prick their fingers with, and a sudden realization hit Gideon. The soul-bond.

Calliope glanced over to him with wide eyes as if the same thought had just occurred to her.

"Who's first?" Jack asked.

Gideon cleared his throat. "Me."

Jack approached him with the pin and a small glass vial. Gideon offered up his left hand and observed carefully as Jack pressed the sharp tip of the needle into the skin of his forefinger and slid a single drop of blood into the little glass container before Gideon's magic healed the wound. Gideon's eyes flicked over to Calliope, who was nonchalantly biting the tip of her finger, as if she were nervously chewing at her nail, in order to lick her own blood away.

Jack walked back to repeat the process on Calliope and Gideon simply tucked his hands into the pockets of his trousers, wiping the bead of blood he felt well up as her finger was pricked inside and out of sight. When Jack finished putting away their blood, the guard was already waiting with the forgetting potions.

Jack passed each of them one of the blue concoctions and said, "The effects will be quick. Once you've swallowed them fully, you are both free to go."

Gideon uncorked his vial and waited for Calliope to do the same.

"Hopefully, it's not poison," she muttered just loud enough for him to hear. "What a useless way to go."

That's when he made a decision. He was going to tell her everything. Because she was right—if it was poison, their deaths would be useless. There was too much left unfinished.

They both tipped the contents of the vials into their mouths in sync, and Gideon felt a rush of adrenaline. The thick liquid tasted sickly sweet, like raw honey or cane syrup. It slid down the back of his throat, leaving a tingling feeling in its path. When they had both swallowed every last drop to Jack's approval, the man waved a hand toward the exit.

"Until we meet again."

Calla watched as Gideon strode across the mansion toward the front door. Before she could catch up with the prince's strides, someone caught her arm from behind and tugged her to a halt. She spun around to see Jack, his dark silhouette haloed by the soft glow of light coming from the treasure cove, something clutched in the hand that wasn't holding on to her.

She squinted in the dark to make out the stem of a single purple flower.

"Do you know what I find so interesting?" he wondered to her as he dropped her arm and twirled the stem in between his fingers. "How immortals have all the magic and abilities in the world and still manage to be the easiest beings to manipulate."

"What—" she began, and then she froze as she suddenly recognized the flower he was holding.

A calla lily.

"Lily was a clever choice of name," he said ruefully. "And don't worry, that's not what gave you away. Nor was it the very well-executed disguises." He snapped the purple bloom from its stalk and slowly reached out to place it behind her ear, leaning in to whisper, "I have eyes and ears everywhere."

Calla swallowed. Her mind was becoming more and more hazy with every second she stood there, the room around her beginning to blur at the edges.

"That fool Ramor has no idea that all that time he and his friend spent playing cards with an Onyx witch, it was really a prince in their midst. But *I* knew the second that Queen Lysandra's sons took a single step in this town. I also know what happened in that forest and what you're trying to do."

"Why didn't you call our bluff, then? Why assist us at all?"

"Simple. I wanted your favors." He grinned. "I knew you wouldn't agree to hand over your blood if you suspected I knew who you were—and what you were worth. The final Blood Warrior and the Onyx Prince she's soul-bonded to. I wonder what price that's going to fetch for me one day."

She gaped at him as he reached out to spin her around by her shoulders, roughly guiding her toward the open front door.

"I own you," he whispered into her ear. Then he shoved her out the door and slammed it behind her.

"*Gideon,*" she called as she hit the first marble step outside, her mind beginning to feel increasingly fuzzy as she headed for the road. She spotted the prince waiting for her, his haunted gaze tracing every inch of her face as she bounded toward him. "Gideon—"

"I want to keep the bond."

Calla's words died on her tongue. It took her foggy brain a moment to fully grasp what he had just said, and when it did she managed to choke out, "Why are you telling me this right *now*? When we are going to forget—"

"Because if you want to get rid of it, I don't want to affect your decision. And also because I cannot bear you hearing what I'm about to say and still deciding to sever it."

She held her breath.

He took a step toward her, his face more open than she had ever seen it before. "I have wanted you since the first time Ezra told me stories about the wild girl he met in a gambling den, who could hold her own against him. I know that makes me the very worst kind of person, but I knew with my Rolls of Fate I could never risk wanting someone *real*. So I fell for the girl who only existed in his stories, the one that he was supposed to betray. Knowing you could never be more than a dream. A wish. Whether or not he was ever able to go through with his mission from Myrea, the moment he moved on I knew my wishing would come to an end, and I swore I'd never think of you again. I never thought I'd actually meet you."

Her breathing came out ragged now.

"Letting people know me has only ever put them in harm's way. I left for the Guild at thirteen to distract my mother with my training so she wouldn't focus on Ezra. I broke up with Kestrel when he started to get attached so he wouldn't draw my mother's attention. The only reason I haven't left Caspian behind is because we have bigger plans for the Guild, and I promised I'd help him see them through. But with you . . . the moment I saw your numbers, I knew I had finally found someone I could be on equal ground with."

His words were becoming more rushed with each sentence, the glamour over his eyes flickering in and out, giving her glimpses of the whirlpools of silver that lay beneath.

"I had been lost for so long trying to find purpose. It's why I couldn't . . . why I *can't* let go of control. I just wanted to make a future where my friends could be happy, because I've always known such a future was never my destiny with this war looming over us. I never once imagined I would find something that made me feel like I was alive and not just going through the motions. But with you . . ."

"*Gideon.*" The sound of his name on her lips was a plea, but she didn't know for what. Unable to tell if she wanted him to stop or keep going.

"You're so determined to forge your own path and be your own person—even when you refused to acknowledge the incredible power you have within yourself. You care about your friends with the same fierceness that I care about mine. You challenge everyone around you and make them want to grow into someone better. I never wanted anything to do with this war, but I'll fight by your side to the end if it means there's a life after it with you in it. In whatever way. Just to stand by someone who understands what all of this has been like."

He reached up and cupped her cheek with his left hand. She felt the potion's magic at the edges of her mind, slowly creeping in, but she fought against the torrent. Shoved it away, begging to hold on to this moment for a little longer. To see what came next.

"I want to keep the bond. And I realize that's selfish. Hells, just telling you all of this right now, when I know you won't remember it, is the most selfish thing I've ever done, but I finally feel tethered to something so much greater than a curse. And I realize this whole quest has been fucked. Things have gone so wrong, but *Gods* . . ."

"Gideon," she whispered as the darkness in her mind finally took over, beginning to eat holes in the delicate web of her memory.

"Every wish I've ever had has been granted in you."

For a moment the entire world was clearer than it had ever been.

Then there was nothing.

21

Caspian resisted the urge to pound his fist into the ground with frustration as he worked to wring out another shirt full of water to lay over Hannah's burning forehead. The little witch had been unconscious for nearly fifteen minutes after he hauled her out of the lake. Now the scary black veins that had spread over every inch of her skin were finally beginning to recede, but he couldn't get her damn fever to break.

"Cass?" she whispered.

"Yes?" he answered, his voice as soothing as he could make it.

"I'm scared," she whimpered.

As he wiped the cool material over her cheeks in comfort, he lied, "It's going to be all right."

The moment the words were out of his mouth, a tremor shook the ground beneath him. The smell of charred magic filled the air, singeing his nose as he sucked in a breath. The forest around them shriveled in on itself. The leaves on the trees drying up and crumbling away, the grass beneath them turning from a vibrant green hue to a dull grayish brown. A chill slithered through the air and up his spine.

This can't be good.

22

"Is there a bed shortage or something?" Calla muttered as she took in the single mattress and bedframe that sat in the center of the far wall.

Her head was still murky from the effects of the potion they had woken up from, still fully glamoured, in the middle of the street in front of *Jack's* house. That latter detail was the most unsettling of all, though the holes in both their recollections were also quite disturbing. They made her feel like a stranger in her own body. The only silver lining was finding the ingredients and the spell they had been seeking shoved in their pockets.

Now they were at the cheapest hostel they could find, and Calla was more than ready to get this whole thing over with.

She'd barely had a second to drop her bag onto the bed when Gideon locked them inside the room and declared, "We need to talk."

Her brows rose at his tone as she plucked the strange stone and the crumpled note scribbled with the spell from her pockets. She placed the items onto the colorful quilt draped across the bed and answered, "I'm not sure how much there is to say. Whatever we agreed to with Jack, at least we have what we need—"

"No," he interrupted, finally dropping his glamour now that they were alone. It was both a relief to be able to read the swirling silver of emotion in his irises again, and a shock to see what was reflected there currently. Anger. At her. "I want to talk about what you're hiding from me."

"What do you mean?"

"The note I wrote to myself," he told her slowly, his eyes darkening with each word. "It says you want to break the soul-bond."

Calla's breath caught a bit in surprise. Gideon watched her expression carefully and for a second she thought about denying it. For leaving this discussion for later. Instead she let him read the truth plainly on her face.

"So, it's true. And the nymphs—you *were* asking them about it. Were you thinking of using our second favor on that? Were you ever going to tell me you were hoping to get rid of it?"

"Eventually. It just wasn't the very first priority—"

"I didn't realize it was a priority at all," he told her. "Or that it was something you'd want so desperately that you'd bring it up in front of that asshole."

Calla fixed him with a disbelieving look. "*Of course* I want to break the bond. It's not something we *chose*. I'm so tired of things happening *to* me. Aren't you?" She took a deep breath. "Just when I was starting to find my footing on how to feel about myself, my magic—my entire being—was tied to another person. I just want to be able to know how I feel about everything without all these other influences constantly intruding in my mind. Not to mention when we get Ezra back . . . What then, Gideon? This is a *mess*."

He shook his head at her words, combing the disheveled tendrils of blue hair that fell onto his forehead back with a hand as he huffed, "You're right."

Something about the way he said those last words made her chest tight, but she decided not to pull at the seam slowly coming undone between them any more tonight.

Instead, she took a deep breath and said, "Okay, then. Are you ready to do this?"

His answering tone was grim. "As I'll ever be."

They had been sitting cross-legged on the floor, trying to make the spell work, for the last two hours. Calla could see exhaustion taking its toll on Gideon and wondered if the prince would crash if they pushed themselves any more tonight. She said as much aloud.

"I'm fine," he insisted, as if she couldn't see his eyelids growing heavier by the second or feel the fatigue through their magic link. "I just don't understand why it's not working. If that asshole gave us a defective spell—"

"I think we just need more energy," she chimed in with a sigh. "The nymphs said it took an unprecedented amount of power to summon a gateway like this."

Gideon didn't hesitate to rip back the sleeve of his jacket and undershirt, revealing the marks of his Rolls of Fate. "Here. Siphon."

"*No,*" she argued. "You're about to pass out as it is. I'm not taking anything from you."

"You don't need to drain me," he asserted. "Just take a little of my magic and see if combining it with yours does . . . something. We should try everything we can think of at least once."

"Gideon." She fixed him with a skeptical look.

"Calliope." He lifted a pierced brow, and she could tell his patience was slowly waning.

She huffed in frustration as she rolled up her sleeve, slowly unveiling her own crimson constellation. She checked one last time. "Are you sure?"

He nodded, and she tentatively reached out to clasp his wrist. She felt her inner Siphon roar to life, the sleepy magic in her core unfurling as it stretched like a cat. As the wisps of her energy reached out toward Gideon's, she felt something else awaken inside her as well. Something new.

Before she understood what was happening, the barriers in her mind began to slowly defrost, hints of the emotions that had been cir-cling out of her reach for days slipping though. Rage, grief, *hope*. She felt her eyes prick as the intensity of the feelings washed over her. A part of her wanted her to shove them away and slam the barriers back into place. The other part of her urged her to latch on to them before they slipped away again. She missed the warmth.

The sound of her name was frantic on Gideon's lips as a bright burst of light filled the room. Her eyes burned from the scarlet radiance flooding everything in sight. She looked down in awe when she realized it was coming from her. From *them*.

Their numbers were gleaming.

She snatched her hand away from his skin, and the light extin-guished just as quickly as it had ignited.

"What just happened?" She gaped.

Gideon didn't answer as he flexed the muscles in his arm, and she wondered for a horrifying moment if she had hurt him. Then he looked up at her, jaw slack in awe.

"You restored my energy."

"*What?*" she exclaimed.

Gideon's eyes narrowed as he examined his Rolls of Fate with new-found interest. "The soul-bond . . . when we aren't touching, we get glimpses of how the other one is feeling—emotionally and physically. When we do touch . . . That's it." He had a newfound determination in his voice. "Repeat exactly what you just did and use the rechargeable energy we exchange as a conduit for the spell. I don't know how much power the bond is capable of giving us, but if we push it as much as we can, maybe it will work this time."

Calla nodded numbly as she followed his directions. She picked up the opalescent stone resting between them in her right hand and took a deep breath before clutching his wrist once more. She let her Siphon reach out again and grasp his energy, and when the red beam of light flashed to life again, she could feel the shot of relief that zipped through Gideon's body. With a shaky voice she recited the spell on the paper Jack had written out for them for the millionth time, and there was a charged moment after she finished where nothing happened.

Then a ripple of fire tore through her body and she bit down a scream of pain.

Gideon's hold on her own wrist tightened as a tremor of pain went through his own body. Calla worried that whatever was happening would rip the very sinew from their bones. The magic was overloading their systems, leaving behind what felt like electricity in her veins. Just when she couldn't tamp down the groans of agony any longer, the bright crimson light around them dimmed to a soft glow. Out of the corner of her eye something dark began to form.

A gateway.

"It's working," she whispered, still holding on to Gideon's arm, worried that breaking their connection would make the portal disappear.

Before they could celebrate, however, something in her chest tightened.

She looked down in confusion, and the movement caused the room to start spinning.

"Calliope," Gideon choked out as her light-headedness grew. "Our heart rates—"

His words died out as the temperature of their skin dropped dangerously low, as if the circulation of their blood had been suddenly cut off. She could feel it then, the steady thudding of their pulses slowing more and more, getting dangerously close to stopping altogether. They pulled each other up to their feet, their stances shaky, and Gideon's hand loosened a bit around her wrist. His ice-cold fingers slowly slid down until he was barely even clutching her hand, and the portal in front of them shifted in and out of focus.

It took all her effort to tighten her hold on him, and she watched as the gateway solidified once more.

"We can't let go," she told him. "We have to hold on."

"Our hearts are going to stop," he warned as he swayed on his feet.

Calla held out her free hand to the gateway, gently brushing the tips of her fingers over the glassy black surface. A ripple moved over it, distorting her reflection. For a fleeting instant, she didn't recognize herself. She was surprised to find that fact didn't bother her in the slightest.

She plunged her hand through the magic portal and held her breath as she watched her arm disappear. She felt something wrap around her wrist on the other side and before the sound of alarm fully left her lips, whatever had latched on yanked her through.

23

The past several days were a blur in Delphine's mind. Celeste would show up every few hours, pockets stuffed with fruits, cheeses, and other bits of food that was leaps and bounds better than the gruel the guard shoved into her cell each morning. It was the only thing that made the visits tolerable to Delphine these days. Sometimes she would pretend she was asleep, because Celeste's small talk made her wish her trachea was still gone just to not have to carry on the conversation. The visits did offer one advantage, however: tracking Celeste's schedule.

Learning the siren's routine meant being able to commit the guards' shift rotation to memory as well. She recorded the hours that Reniel granted Celeste access to a key and the ones when she had to rely on the guard. Delphine etched her notes into the stone wall behind the mattress of seaweed in her cell with her nails.

The hours when Delphine wasn't faking unconsciousness, Celeste would get comfortable enough to fall back into her old gossiping habits. The little details no one else might think twice about, Delphine clung to, filing every single one away in the back of her mind. She knew from Celeste's ramblings that Reniel had thrown a rowdy party three days prior, which was most likely why he hadn't bothered with Delphine recently. That—or the man had finally grown bored of ripping her to shreds. Three days ago, she would have been relieved that Reniel had such a fickle attention span, but now that the kernel of a plan had begun taking root, she wished she knew how to summon a visit.

A heavy set of footsteps suddenly echoed down the hall, making her sit up from where she was hanging off her bed, upside down, counting the stone bricks on the ceiling. She had been waiting for Celeste to come by with Eros and lunch.

Unfortunately, the person who appeared before her cell was not Celeste.

"Hello, moonlight."

Zephyr's voice was smooth as velvet, his pearly-white irises sparkling with the promise of pain. His inky-black hair was slicked back, not a single strand out of place.

She scrambled to her feet. "What the Hells do you want?" she gritted out.

Zephyr laughed as he held something up in front of him between the bars of the cell. A flash of silver glinted in the bluish light of the neon jellyfish that lined the walls of the corridor.

A key.

"I told Celeste to take an afternoon off from torturing you." He shoved the key into the lock with a metallic *clang*. "It's my turn."

"Fuck off, Zephyr," she told him, planting her feet firmly in place.

"What's wrong, Delphine? Don't want to play? I thought you'd be bored down here all alone." He grinned as he stepped inside.

"If you touch me, I'll make you regret it."

"I'd like to see you try," he sneered.

Delphine's eyes darted to the wide-open exit over his shoulder. She didn't think twice. She smashed a fist right into Zephyr's core, slipping out from between him and the wall as he doubled forward. She slithered through the water, like a serpent, toward the corridor outside the cell. She made it halfway before Zephyr grabbed a fistful of her shirt and yanked her back.

"You little bitch," he spat as he slammed her against the wall. "I'm going to—"

Delphine swiped out with her magic, sending a violent jet of water directly into his mouth, effectively shutting him up. She raked her claws down his face, making his hold on her loosen as he let out a strangled shout. She took off for the cell's exit again, and this time she got through. She stroked as fast as she could down the dungeon's hallway, never bothering to look back.

She got all the way to the prison's exit, close enough to see there was no guard posted outside through the small glass window. But it didn't matter.

A second later Zephyr caught up to her. She wasn't even sure which side the blow came from. All she knew was an explosion of pain followed by the dark.

)·)·)·●·(·(·(

Delphine hated Claiming ceremonies. This was her third—the previous two her mother had considered strictly practice.

Reniel's crystal palace was buzzing with people, all in elegant formal wear, eager to get a front-row seat to the drama. Her mother pushed her through the tight crowd, and the closer they got to the main room, the more Delphine's stomach churned. She didn't want to be a part of Reniel's Shoal. She didn't want to be a part of anyone's Shoal. She just wanted . . . freedom.

She sucked in a breath and swiftly locked those feelings back up inside her.

Her heart was a vault, and no one would ever find the key.

"Opal," a deep, masculine voice said, causing her mother to halt in her tracks and turn.

Delphine had to tip her head all the way back to take in the man's impressive height. Even if he didn't tower over most of the guests, he would have stuck out among the crowd in the odd ensemble he was dressed in. Unlike the other sirens, who were wearing expensive suits and opulent gowns, this man had on some sort of leather fighting gear. A utility belt was fastened around his waist with various weapons and other tools—daggers, throwing stars, a compass, a spool of rope. . . .

"What are you doing here?" Her mother's eyes narrowed at the man, a scowl settling on her face. "I didn't think you bothered to return here anymore."

"I don't. Usually," the man said as he flicked his eyes around the room, seeming bored. "I had a bit of business to attend to. It's nice to see you as well, though, Opal. This must be your daughter?"

Opal clamped her hands down on her daughter's shoulders. "Yes. Delphine."

"Your spitting image," he noted as he looked Delphine over from head to toe, something like disapproval in his obsidian eyes.

Delphine swallowed, her nerves pricking a bit under his stare. She looked better than moonlight tonight. She had to. How dare this man look at her as if he were entirely unimpressed?

Delphine lifted her chin a bit and declared, "I'm going to be picked at the Claiming tonight."

Her mother preened behind her. The man only frowned.

"Is that so?" he murmured.

Before he could say anything more, someone else approached. This person Delphine recognized immediately.

"Reniel." Her mother sighed dreamily.

"Opal, you made it." Reniel's smirk was slightly crooked. "I was just about to show a few guests one of my new collectibles. Care to join?"

"Of course," Opal answered, patting Delphine on the shoulder. "I need to speak with Reniel alone. Behave until I'm back."

Delphine didn't want her mother to leave her alone in the swarming hallway, but the protest on her lips died as her mother slipped away without a backward glance.

"You seem a bit young to be joining a Shoal."

Delphine startled. For a second she had forgotten the other man was still standing there.

"You seem a bit old not to know how to mind your own business," she quipped back.

He snorted, raising an amused brow. "Aren't you . . . precocious."

"Mhmm," she hummed, already looking for an exit from this conversation. Perhaps she could sneak a goblet of wine before her mother came back—

"You don't want to be a part of Reniel's Shoal," he warned, interrupting her internal schemes.

"And how would you know what I do or do not want?" She curled a lip at him in disdain.

"I know Reniel. His choices aren't always . . . morally upstanding. Or predictable."

"Beings like him are always predictable," she recited automatically. "He's a collector, isn't he? He likes pretty things, and by my calculations, I'm the prettiest thing in this room."

Her words were plain, no hint of arrogance beneath. She was the prettiest thing in the room. She had to be.

"He likes pretty things, yes," the man told her, his words deliberate. "He also likes to break them."

She only answered with "Good thing I'm not made of glass."

With that, Delphine pushed past the man, out of the hallway, and snuck behind a waitress with a tray full of wine. She snagged one of the goblets and drained its contents in one gulp. She thought about what the man had said, his warning.

You don't want to be a part of Reniel's Shoal.

She shook off the words and snuck a second cup off another tray. She was already here. Her mother had worked so hard to make sure every detail leading up to tonight was perfectly in place. It didn't matter what she wanted anymore.

If it ever did.

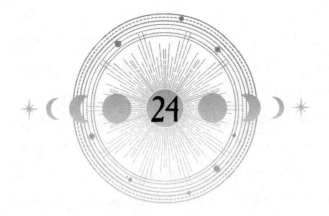

24

*H*ello? Calla tried to call out, but no sound came from her lips. She was standing in the middle of an unending ether, unable to see anything in the pitch-black emptiness around her except for a trail of golden light stretching up above her. No, not a light—a thread.

She followed the gilded thread from the sky all the way down to herself in awe as she realized that her entire body was dripping in the glittering string. It twined up her arms to her neck, draping down around her shoulders before wrapping around her torso. She took a cautious step forward, and a bit of the thread unraveled into the atmosphere above. She strode farther into the inky abyss, the thread pulling taught with each step. She wondered what would happen when she made it to the end of the string.

Come find us, Calliope Rosewood.

Calla jumped at the musical voice that reverberated through her mind. She looked back up at the gilded string as it gleamed a little brighter. She continued through the dark for minutes, hours, days, until she caught a glimpse of something coming into view. A peal of laughter rang through the air, and she urged her feet forward faster.

When she finally reached the scene ahead of her, she froze.

Before her—was herself. Not her present self, but herself at thirteen.

The vision was of younger Calla surrounded by her old coven members, all standing before an ornate clock. It was the scene of her Initial Roll ceremony. Thirteen-year-old Calla was laughing as her friend Kai tugged on the sleeve of her shirt to lean closer so he could whisper something in her ear. Kai had been the only person brave enough to touch her so casually back then, even through clothing.

The second person she recognized was her first guardian—the witch who took over her care after her mother had died—and watched as they shushed the two witches, gesturing for them to pay attention to the hands on the clock as they slowly ticked around, inching closer and closer to midnight. Young Calla's eyes sparkled with anticipation at the sound of the tolling bells that announced she was officially thirteen.

Calla let out a gasp of wonder as a red glow appeared and began to grow in the air in front of her—a Witch's Die was spawning. Unlike other dice that could spawn anytime around any witch who hadn't yet completed their rolls, this die was meant only for her—to ensure she would receive her magic. As soon as the die was finished forming, it dropped from the air, and Calla reached out and caught it before it could hit the table. She noticed everyone around her holding their breath, waiting to see what number she would roll and how much magic she was destined to receive.

Calla took a deep breath as she shook the magic cube in her hand, and when she released it onto the table in front of her, she went still with concentration. The crimson die bounced, once, twice, three times before clattering to a stop.

Six.

"Oh my Gods," her guardian whispered from over her shoulder.

Calla was frozen in utter shock at what she was looking at. Six. Six. Six. It couldn't be. It was the most power any witch could receive, and yet she knew no one in her coven who had it as their Initial Roll. Before she could insist it must be a mistake, a burning sensation began in her left arm, and she looked down to watch as six black dots began to appear on her skin. Then the flood of magic came.

The vision blinked away, and Calla came roaring back to the present.

Hello? She tried to speak again, still to no avail. What's going on?

Come closer, the same voice from before answered.

This time Calla didn't hesitate, her pace turning brisk as she moved through the inky abyss. When she spotted another vision approaching in the distance, she hurried toward it. This time, she was unsurprised at the memory she found waiting for her.

"Oh, you did not." Calla rolled her eyes at Kai, but the boy ignored it and pressed on.

"I did!" he exclaimed, running a hand through his silky black hair to move it out of his eyes. "In the marketplace! He must have snuck away from the palace or something."

"There's no way one of the Onyx Princes was just roaming around unsupervised, Kai. It had to have been someone else."

"I'm telling you, Cal," Kai insisted. "It had to have been one of them. Why else would there be an Onyx witch here?"

"It could've just been one of the Onyx Queen's guards," she reasoned.

"A guard that young? He looked to be our age."

"There are plenty of witches who become lackeys for the queens at our age. We're almost fifteen, it's not like we're ten."

"Okay, but—" Kai began before something abruptly cut his words off. Calla furrowed her brow at the boy, opening her mouth to ask what the problem was, when she felt it, too. It was the call of a Witch's Die.

"Cal, do you—"

"Yes," she whispered as they both spun in the direction the magical pull was coming from. They were standing outside Kai's house, gathering bunches of witch hazel for their lesson that evening. There was a small river just north of the main road that ran through their neighborhood, and when Calla squinted, she could see a crimson glow just over the horizon in that direction.

"Maybe someone else will go to it," Calla told Kai, but as the words left her mouth, she took an involuntary step forward. Kai followed.

They both exchanged loaded looks. Kai broke their stare first, glancing down at his left arm where three numbers were already marked in his skin.

Three, two, five.

Calla glanced down at her own arm. There was a single six. Her feet were moving before she could even think about what she was doing. She heard Kai scream her name from behind her, but she paid him no mind. By the time she reached the die, she was nearly out of breath and Kai was catching up.

She spotted the little cube in the middle of the riverbed, quite an inconvenient place for it to have spawned, and she sloshed through the ankle-deep water in order to scoop it out. The magic pull in her core immediately disappeared, and when she turned to face an equally out-of-breath Kai, she watched as his face twisted in anger.

"Why would you do that, Calla?" he demanded. "We could have just raced for it fair and square."

"Don't be dense," she chided him. "You already have three rolls, and I only have one. It's no big deal."

Kai looked like he wanted to argue with her some more, his lavender eyes narrowing a bit as she stepped out of the river. He must have thought better of it, however, because he simply took a deep breath and shook his head. He knew how stubborn she could be.

She gave him a triumphant smile. It was his turn to roll his eyes.

"All right, then," he huffed. "Go ahead and roll."

Calla nodded and unceremoniously tossed the die to the ground. It skipped over the grass once, twice, before settling on a number. Kai sucked in a sharp breath, and as Calla stared down at the number in shock, she realized how wrong she had been. This was a very big deal.

It was another six.

When the scene evaporated this time, Calla could feel her chest heaving. Seeing Kai again was like a shock to her system.

What's happening? Who are you? Why are you doing this?

The voice didn't answer this time. So she walked forward, on and on, until another scene faded into view. This time it was her at sixteen, her last guardian standing before her.

"Listen to me, Calla," her guardian implored. "When I leave and you roll that die . . . if it's a six, you have to disappear. Don't tell a soul where you go. Take your share of the coven's stash from the cupboard and run."

Calla was slumped over the dining table, staring at the cursed artifact resting in the center of her palm. She lifted her gaze to her guardian, noting the terror that shone in their eyes. They had taken her in after her third home had decided they couldn't handle the pressure that came with caring for a witch who had rolled the same number twice. Not once in the last five months had Calla ever seen a hint of fear from her current caretaker, and when Calla didn't respond, they simply slipped out of the house without another word, leaving their ward to deal with this heavy burden alone.

So much had changed after that fateful day she took the die instead of Kai. Including their friendship. Their coven started to whisper when they found out, some of them were unsettled enough by the Siphon girl with an Initial Roll that gave her an unprecedented amount of raw power to isolate her, but to find out she also was at risk to be marked as a Blood

Warrior? Kai's parents had banned him from seeing her after that, and it seemed like her life had been unraveling ever since.

Her eyes pricked as she folded the die in her fist. She could do this. It wouldn't be a six. It couldn't be. She was cursed enough.

She released the small cube onto the table in front of her, and it clacked across the marble until it bounced all the way over the edge. She stood from her chair, its legs scraping noisily against the ground, rushing over to find out what her destiny would be.

Her knees hit the ground as a sob racked her whole body.

As she disappeared into the shadows of the starless night, she wondered what she had done not to deserve even a twinkle of guiding light in her darkest hour.

25

alla was boiling from the inside out. The rage in her belly felt like a relief as she plunged her way past that last aching memory.

Show yourself, cowards! she yelled internally. She was practically running, determined to get her hands on whoever was at the end of this trail of torture. The only thing that stopped her in her tracks was the sight of *him*.

Because of course he would be here, too.

Ezra was crouched in front of her on the street outside the inn as she clutched her throat in pain. She needed air.

"You are going to take this from me—"

Calla slashed her hands wildly through the vision, making the scene disappear into the air. She couldn't bear the weight of emotions that came with that particular moment of her past just yet. Instead, she continued through the nothingness, the golden thread slowly thinning out over her body. The darkness around her began to change, tiny embers of light that reminded her of lightning pixies winking in and out. The glowing blips grew thicker and thicker until it looked like she was walking among the stars.

Calliope!

Calla skidded to a halt as *that* voice reverberated through her mind. When she whipped around, she found Gideon striding toward her, dressed in his own spool of thread, each one of their backpacks slung on a different shoulder. She rushed back to him, and for a moment she had the urge to fling her arms around his neck, grateful that he hadn't left her in the dark alone, but she resisted.

I didn't know if you had come through with me. She tried to speak to him, but her words didn't come out of her mouth.

It didn't seem to matter, though, as he answered in her mind, *I will always follow after you.*

She swallowed thickly as she held out her hands for her bag. She wondered if he had seen any visions of his own.

I didn't want to leave any of our things behind in case someone checked our room while we were gone, he explained. *I saved the Esprit in the front pocket of your bag.*

She nodded in approval before turning back to the endless void in front of them. *Where are we? Where do you think we're supposed to go to find the Valley of Souls?*

Gideon stepped up beside her, brushing her shoulder with his own as they gazed at the twinkling embers around them.

I think we're in limbo—the waiting place for souls while they decide if they are going to hang on or pass over. It was something Ezra and I were taught growing up.

Is the Valley of Souls after this? How do we find it? She reached up to try to touch one of the floating lights, but it evaporated into thin air.

Gideon had opened his mouth to answer her questions when a golden light engulfed her vision, and for a moment her eyes burned so badly tears welled up and spilled onto her cheeks. As her vision slowly returned, she found the blackness around them had dissolved and they now stood before an enormous stone staircase, the steps looking as if they went on infinitely toward the starless sky that now appeared above them. On either side of the staircase were identical stone pillars made up of four intertwined beings.

The beings carved into the stone wore no clothing, their bodies covered only in the same threads currently wrapped around her own body. The strings dripped from every one of their limbs and twined around their torsos. Each of their faces was covered in masks with a single eye adorning the center of their foreheads. One of the mask's mouths was smiling, one was frowning, and a third was twisted by anger. The fourth, however, had no expression at all, but they were the only one holding something in each of their hands. Balancing scales.

The Fates.

Down the staircase dripped millions, maybe billions, of severed gilded threads just like the ones wrapped around them currently.

Come meet us, Calliope Rosewood.

Calla made to climb the first step, but Gideon grabbed her shoulder.

We cannot go to them, Calliope, he told her.

Why not? Her mouth twisted with disdain.

The lifethread, Gideon said, gesturing to the string wrapped around them. *Once it runs out . . . I believe we'll be stuck here. And I am not sure we could survive trekking up such a long way, regardless.*

Her hands balled into fists at her side before she looked back up at the sky. *Why don't you come down and face me, you gutless bastards?*

You are the one who challenged us, girl. They laughed.

Why did you show me those memories? she hissed.

We thought you might need some proper motivation, they taunted. *You have so much potential and yet you waste your vengeance. Save it for the war.*

Is that why you've done all this? she spat. *Taken everything from me? You've made me into your unwilling weapon and expect me to still do your bidding in this war?*

The weapon you've become was sharpened by your own hand, Calliope Rosewood, the Fates continued. *Being born the daughter of the woman who spurned a Witch Queen made you a convenient choice, we will admit, but you are the one who proved to be worthy of your destiny.*

Calla reared back in shock. *What the Hells are you talking about?*

Gideon silently pressed his shoulder against hers as he observed the entire exchange, an ever-steady presence at her side.

Indra didn't know that leaving the Rouge Queen to have a daughter with someone else would provide us a Great Muse, of course, but alas your mother made her own decisions as well, the Fates told her.

Queen Myrea and my mother— You're lying! Calla accused them. *Neither of my mothers ever mentioned—*

Everyone has secrets.

Calla swallowed the bitter taste in her mouth. *Is this just petty entertainment for you? My mothers had history with Myrea and you made me the target of the queen for your little puppet show? Cursing me with my Rolls of Fate, the Siphon curse—*

Giving you an Initial Roll of six was simply a test of power, the Fates corrected her. *The second test, actually. The Siphon curse was the first. What a curious combination, don't you think? All that volatile, raw power in the wrong hands could raze the world, but in your hands, it has been dormant. Your second roll is what confirmed what we already suspected.*

The memory of Calla racing toward the Witch's Die so Kai wouldn't have to make another roll flashed in her mind.

You chose your own path when you took that die over your friend, the Fates confirmed. *You chose it again when you decided to leave your coven, your home, instead of putting them in danger. You chose it when you stayed in that game of cards with the younger prince. And again when you chose to follow your prince into the woods.*

No, she screamed.

Though we've bestowed certain gifts upon you, you have always had a choice to decide what to do with those gifts, Calliope Rosewood. Remember that power comes with choice. Wield it. Unleash yourself on the world.

That was it. Calla took off for the stairs.

The Fates laughed at her fury.

Calliope. Gideon slid himself next to her, wrapping an arm around her waist to tug her back down a step. *We either attempt to reach the Gods—and most likely fail—or find Ezra and make it back to the gateway.*

A shot in the dark at her vengeance or . . . Ezra.

She lifted her chin to Gideon. *Fine. Take me to the Valley of Souls. I'll get my audience with them soon enough.*

As Gideon guided her to the left of the staircase, toward the rolling hills in the distance, she heard one last whisper in her mind.

See you on the battlefield, Great Muse.

26

The Valley of Souls was a wasteland of haunted memories. Gideon wasn't paying the sea of gray any mind as he traced his eyes over the girl in front of him. He was so unsure what she was going to do after everything that had just happened.

Calliope stood atop the hill looking down on the valley like a divine entity. There was no wind in the afterlife, no sound or temperature to be heard or felt, but Gideon could feel the energy of her presence around him in his bones, his *soul*. This quest had been changing him slowly. Breaking and twisting him into something new.

She was changing, too. He didn't know how she was going to cope with everything the Fates had told her. The truth about her parents and their history with the Rouge Queen would be a brutal blow—he knew all too well what it was like to realize the version of your parents in your head does not always match who they actually were. The shift happening inside her now was subtle, but he could feel it all the same. The first glimpse he'd gotten of her emotions since the bond between him was forged. He was enamored.

She peered over her shoulder at him then. As if she could hear his thoughts. He found himself wishing she could.

Coming with me? she asked.

Anywhere. Everywhere.

Calla and Gideon descended the steep hill slowly, careful to watch their footing lest they went tumbling down into the throng of meandering souls. Each soul looked like a regular person who had been drained of every ounce of color until they were only different shades of gray and slightly transparent. As they got closer and closer, Calla could begin to make out the individual faces of the spirits while they trailed forward together in the massive crowd.

Each being held one of the same opalescent stones Jack had given to Calla and Gideon for the spell, their eyes glazed over in a trance as they clutched the iridescent rocks and headed toward their final resting place. Calla wondered what the significance of it was and if Jack's explanation of it was lost to the forgetting potion, or if the man had bothered to explain it at all.

When Calla and Gideon reached the bank on the side of the recessed pathway through the valley, the prince cautioned, *Make sure not to step into the fray unless we find him. I'm not sure how the souls will react.*

How long is this valley? she asked. *How far could he be?*

I've heard some say it's almost infinite, but there is most definitely an end. When souls reach it, they are allowed to pass over into their final resting place. But we are at the beginning now, where the newest souls that have died will be. Which hopefully means he has not gone too far for us to reach.

Calla nodded and they began their walk along the grassy edge, scanning the bland horde for Ezra's face as she moved. The souls' pace beside her was agonizingly slow, but Calla still worried she wouldn't be able to cover enough ground to find Ezra in the throng of dead before he got too far for her thread to reach. Gideon followed closely on her heels, his eyes examining the crowd just as intently, his swirling irises never settling as they darted over each individual's face.

Ezra! she called, but not a single soul responded with so much as a twitch.

After half an hour, Calla looked down to see how much of her life-thread was left, and her stomach dropped. The thread was nearly all gone. She stopped.

She wanted to scream. Frustration was making her fists clench at her sides. She was sure the Fates must be laughing. She'd come all this way just to be defeated by another one of their obstacles.

No.

She was going to go in.

Without a second thought, she dove into the fray, the frantic sound of her name echoing through the valley, but she paid Gideon no mind. The souls around her paused as she jostled past them, but they continued to shuffle forward seconds later, moving her with them as if she were no heavier than air. Adrenaline rushed through her as she began to weave her way forcibly through the spirits, checking every face as she shoved past. When they began to squeeze in on her tighter and tighter, she thrust her elbow into one soul's back with all her strength. There was a momentary shift in the spirit's gaze before they shook it off and the glassy expression returned.

That's it, she realized.

She pushed the spirit again, as hard as she could, and woke them back out of their stupor.

Ezra! she shouted in their face when they twisted around to observe her with newfound clarity.

Ezra? the soul repeated. *That's not my name.*

No, she told them. *It isn't. But we have to find Ezra.*

The soul blinked at Calla in confusion for a second before turning to their neighbor and reaching out to tap them on the shoulder. In the middle of the action, she could see the fogginess begin to creep into their gaze once more. Calla nudged them again.

Find Ezra, she repeated when they woke back up. *Shake them harder.*

The spirit jolted the other spirit more aggressively this time, and a shot of triumph went through Calla when she saw them come to as well.

Find Ezra, the first soul told them.

Calla darted through the lines of spirits, repeating the process, and soon the chain reaction was in full effect.

Find Ezra. Find Ezra. Find Ezra. Find Ezra. Find Ezra.

Soon Ezra's name was ringing through the valley. The beat of her heart thundered almost as loud when she realized the sea had begun to part. She squinted into the distance as the souls began to curve around something—someone—whose features she couldn't quite make out.

But she knew. Her feet sprang into action, first one step, then another. Soon she was flying, her lifethread unraveling almost to the end of its line, but she didn't stop.

And there, at the end of the cleared path, he stood.

As he came toward her, the look on his face went from confusion to recognition to shock. When she was only a few feet away he spread his arms as wide as he could, and she leaped into them. He rocked back on his heels as he caught her, and she buried her face in his neck, winding her arms around him as tightly as she could.

Ezra.

Gideon's knees slammed to the ground as Calliope pulled his
brother from the crowd. Ezra looked just as he had before the
fateful moment he lost his heart, only slightly more transparent, his complexion and clothing graywashed. But even in death
Ezra's midnight eyes shined with vitality.

Brother, Gideon choked out, a sob rising in his throat.

Get up, Ezra demanded. *Get up, Gideon.*

Gideon slowly rose back to his feet, ready for every devastating blow
Ezra was about to give him. None ever came. Instead, Ezra lunged forward and wrapped Gideon in a hug—the first one they had shared since
they were children. Gideon shattered completely then. Tears were shining in his eyes.

I'm sorry, Gideon told him. *I'm sorry it was you and not me.*

I'm not, Ezra assured him, his voice equally gruff. *The world needs
you, Gideon.*

Gideon pulled back, chest heaving with a tight breath. *I love you,*

Ezra. I'm sorry we were divided for so long, and I never really told you that. His words were rushed, desperate as he was not to go a second longer without Ezra hearing them.

Ezra's lips lifted in a sad smile. *I love you, too. Thank you for coming for me—you didn't have to.*

Of course I did, Gideon said with conviction. *This was my fault. I screwed up completely. On so many levels.*

Ezra sighed. *We all screwed up. Yours was just a little more . . . permanent than the rest of ours.* Ezra laughed good-naturedly. *But it wasn't only your fault. I made the deal with Myrea that I did. . . . None of this would've happened without that decision in the first place. And you cannot waste so much potential by letting yourself be held back by your guilt. You have something I could never seem to find—a purpose.*

Not without you. Gideon shook his head.

Ezra glanced over to Calliope, who had been lingering several yards away, half turned around to give them some privacy. *Don't say that. We both know you do.*

She's— Gideon began, but Ezra cut him off with a shake of his head.

She's her own person. Not someone for us to claim for ourselves because one of us met her first or screwed up worse or is magically bound to her. She doesn't need anyone fighting over her; she needs support—to be the force of nature she was destined to be. And if my death was the catalyst that unlocked the potential—which we both know she's always had—then I will not have died in vain. And if she chooses you to be by her side . . . I want you to be happy. Both of you. You deserve that.

Gideon stared at his brother. He didn't have the words to express what exactly he was feeling as they stood there, on solid ground together for once. Then something clicked in his mind.

You will not have died in vain. . . . Are you saying . . . Ezra—

There's only enough lifethread for two people to go back, Ezra told him. *Souls that are brought back from here—by whatever means—require a great sacrifice. I could return to the earth, but one of you would have to sacrifice yourselves and remain here. The world requires balance.*

Gideon shook his head. *No. I'll stay. Let me stay.*

I'm already here, Gideon. I'll find peace on the other side. You've already brought me peace here, now. Ezra's expression turned sympathetic. *If it was a different sacrifice, I might be selfish enough to let you make it. You've already sacrificed so much for me, though. Every time you protected me from our mother . . . I know it cost you. I will never take your life. From you . . . or her. Her heart has been broken enough by my hand.*

Gideon knew there was no more arguing. Even in death Ezra was a stubborn fool. *Death has made you pragmatic. I didn't see that coming.*

Ezra smiled ruefully. *Death is oddly freeing. There's nothing more to lose—it makes you think of things differently.*

With that, Gideon stepped aside and let Ezra move past him to go to Calliope.

Calla?

Calla spun to find Ezra coming up behind her. For a long moment they just stood there, staring at each other in disbelief.

How did we get here? she finally asked.

He smirked. *I believe it started with a bottle of bourbon and a—*

She rolled her eyes. *Don't make me regret coming all the way over here to get you.*

The twinkle in his eyes dulled a bit.

What? She narrowed her eyes.

Calla.

An alarm went off in her mind. *No.*

Calla . . .

No. I'm not leaving you here. I refuse.

It's going to be okay, Calla.

No. I did not come all the way here for nothing. She shook her head wildly. *You are coming with us whether you like it or not.*

Calla, watch, he told her as he scooped up her hand and pulled her farther away from the valley.

At first, she had no idea what he was trying to show her, but when she looked down at their joined hands, she stared in horror. With every step they took together, a bit of her lifethread began to transfer to him. The color of his skin became a shade less gray the farther and farther they wandered, and hers . . . was losing its vibrancy.

No, she repeated with devastation as he pulled her to a stop.

I want you to know, he told her slowly, making her face him completely, *that I don't regret anything. Not one thing.*

The barriers holding back the emotions in her mind began crumbling.

It's unfortunate that our time together was cut short. But it's okay to realize we weren't going to work out even if it hadn't been.

What? She felt her lip tremble. *There's no way for you to know—*

Calla. He fixed her with a hard look. *The foundation we were trying to build on was cracked beyond repair—by my hand. I never wanted to see it, but it didn't matter what we built together after that; the crack would always have been there. You deserve to love someone who would never shatter the foundation in the first place.*

I know things got complicated . . . that they still are . . . but time heals things, Ezra.

Time heals things. He nodded in agreement. *And so do the right people.*

She furrowed her brow in confusion, but when his eyes flickered briefly over her shoulder, her expression hardened.

I can't. I won't. Not after this.

He shrugged. *Do what you want. But stop using me as an excuse to not acknowledge the things you clearly feel.*

She shook her head in denial.

Ezra stepped forward and grabbed her face in his hands. *Let go of me, Calla. You were ready to move on before I died, and we both know it. Guilt is such a stupid reason not to let yourself be happy.*

Why are you doing this? Why won't you come back with us? she pleaded. *We came all this way—we can't do this without you. You're a part of us.*

That will never change whether I'm physically with you or not. I spent too much time making a mess of things when I was alive. But now it's time for me to untangle a few things before I go.

Calla pushed past the prince and stomped up to Gideon. *You're just going to let him do this?*

Gideon looked at her evenly. *I've never really let Ezra do anything. You've argued with him before—I'm sure you know how that usually ends.*

The two of you are going to drive me absolutely mad, she growled, looking back and forth between them. *Why did the Witch Eater make us think we could use the Esprit to bring Ezra back before they stole his body? And the nymphs—they aren't able to lie, and they also said if we could summon a gateway here, we'd be able to bring you back.*

The Esprit is for once you pass through the gate—Ezra is not tied to a physical body like we are. Once he passed through, it would be only the essence of his spirit on the other side, so, as usual, the Witch Eater wasn't lying, but they weren't going to bother warning us of this outcome either. Same with the nymphs. Gideon crossed his arms over his chest. *We can technically bring him back—they just omitted the part where one of us would have to get trapped here in order to do so.*

This can't be it. Calla shook her head. *This isn't fair.*

I know. Ezra smiled sadly. *It's going to be okay. You're going to be okay.*

Calla walked back to him until they were standing chest to chest, gaze unwavering though she could feel the tears welling in her eyes. *I once told myself that one day I would forget to think of you. I was angry then.*

He snorted softly.

But I want you to know I take that back now. I will never forget you, she vowed.

Ezra smiled, and this time it was hopeful. He leaned down and kissed her on the forehead.

Gideon came closer then, and Calla stepped back to let the brothers share one last hug before Ezra turned back to the sea of spirits behind him.

Ezra paused. *Oh, and, Calla?*

She lifted her chin.

A slow grin spread across his face. *Tear the queens to shreds.*

And then he stepped back into the fray.

Calla and Gideon retraced their steps as the gilded string around them became thinner and thinner. When they reached the stairway to the Gods once more, they stopped.

How do we do this? Calla asked.

I'm not sure, Gideon told her. *We were walking through limbo before but I'm unsure how to return there to get back to the portal—*

I meant, she corrected him, *how do we go back without him? What are we going to tell the others?*

I don't know, he admitted.

He left too soon. He left too . . . understanding. He was never like that before.

Death changes people. It clarifies things. Gideon rubbed the back of his neck, his face drawn in contemplation. *I once told you that Ezra needed to be the one who saves everyone—because he thought he needed to be more like me. But the truth is—carrying the weight of everything and never allowing anyone to help is my greatest flaw. His greatest flaw was ever thinking he needed to be like me to deserve love. I hope he real- ized that when he crossed over.*

Calla swallowed at the heaviness of those words, letting them soak in for a moment before squaring her shoulders. *Let's figure out how to get back to the portal.*

As she spoke, a small orange ember floated down from above. Calla lifted her hand and caught it in her palm, where it sizzled out and dis- appeared. A few feet ahead of her another ember winked in and out, almost as if it were a lightning pixie.

It's a trail, she realized. The two of them followed the sparks of light and soon they became more and more clustered together, until they were so thick the luminescence made her eyes squeeze shut, just like before.

Calliope, look.

When her eyes opened again, they were standing back in the dark nothingness.

The gateway is just ahead, Gideon pointed out.

I wonder what Hannah and Caspian will think, she speculated. *If we will sound mad to them.*

Gideon gave her a considering look. *As long as that means we get back to them safe and sound, I'll take it.*

There's no other place I want to be right now, she concurred.

When they reached the portal once more, they paused. Only a few inches of string were left hanging around their wrists. As Gideon lifted his hand in offering, the lifethread went completely taut, but she didn't reach for it. Not yet.

Instead, she said, *Together?*

His eyes flashed silver. *Together.*

They stepped through.

28

"Hannah," Caspian warned. "You have to get control over yourself! You don't want whatever your magic is calling in these woods to answer."

"I'm not doing it on purpose!" Hannah swore in a voice that belonged to a creature of the Hells, her hands shaking at her sides. "I don't know how to stop it."

A wisp of wind howled through the bare trees, snapping off thin twigs and throwing them to the ground. Hannah's hair began to whip around her face, and Caspian knew whatever was about to happen could easily become catastrophic.

"Hannah," Cass said again as he tried to soothe the witch, but before he could say anything more a bright spark of light appeared before them, and he had to shield his eyes.

When he was able to see again, his jaw dropped.

"Calla? Gideon?" he exclaimed, eyes widening incredulously.

Calla and Gideon, for their part, looked just as shocked.

"What the Hells?" Calla's jaw dropped as she looked around the forest, letting her backpack fall to the ground.

"Did you both just *teleport* here?" Caspian asked.

"Something like that." Gideon shoved a hand through his hair as he unloaded his own bag from his shoulders. "I guess when we said we needed to be with Caspian and Hannah, the portal . . . listened."

"Portal—" Cass began, but he was quickly distracted by the way Hannah began thrashing on the ground next to him. "Later! I need help! She's been like this for the last half hour."

"Don't touch her!" Calla warned as she knelt beside Cass and let a small tendril of her Rouge magic reach out to assess Hannah's. "*Shit.* This is very dark magic."

"What do we do?" Caspian questioned with concern.

The distress in Caspian's eyes clearly surprised Calla, though it shouldn't have. While Calla and Gideon had been so wrapped up in their own grief, Caspian and Hannah had only had each other these last couple of excruciating days.

"Hannah, you have to stop," Gideon beseeched her, his voice firm. Not a request, but an order.

Something flashed out the corner of Caspian's left eye, and he realized what had Gideon's concern rising. There, sprouting out of the red petals littering the forest floor, was an arm. An arm with decaying grayish skin and hands that ended in razor-sharp talons. A moment later, a second arm popped up from the ground, and soon both limbs were clawing their way out of the earth.

"Hannah," Calla whispered.

A head and torso sprang up next, a creature of nightmares. A viperidae.

"Hannah!" Calla screeched this time.

"I can't stop," Hannah sobbed. "I don't know how to stop!"

Gideon cursed and quickly turned to his fellow beta. "It's undead—you have to remove their heads!"

Caspian didn't hesitate to follow Gideon's order, taking off toward the serpent-like figure in an instant.

"Calliope, make her stop!" Gideon yelled as he followed Caspian.

Cass blithely passed a throwing dagger to Gideon with barely a glance in the prince's direction. Years of training together had them moving perfectly in sync, like a choreographed routine. Gideon speared the dagger right through the creature's neck, splattering black blood through the air, and Cass caught the blade one-handed as it came through the other side, the sickening sound making Cass cringe.

"Hannah!" he heard Calla scream somewhere behind them.

"I don't know," Hannah cried, tears streaming down her face. "I don't know how to turn it off. I don't know, I don't know, *I don't know.*"

"Calliope!"

Cass whipped his head in the Siphon's direction, worried she had gotten hurt. What he found was so much worse. Another reanimated viperidae had managed to pry itself all the way out of the ground and now towered over both the girls. Worse still, three new pairs of arms had just thrust up behind it.

Caspian was the first to spring into action, barreling headfirst toward one of the beasts, unsheathing a dagger from his belt and going right for its neck.

"Calla, *watch it!*" Gideon yelled in warning.

Calla spun in time to dodge one of the other viperidae's strikes as Gideon leaped over the serpent's swinging tail to make his way over to the girls. Calla hovered above her friend, and as her eyes traced over where the blond was trying to push herself up from the ground, she noticed that Hannah's nails had turned nearly blue—as if from hypothermia. There had been only one time in Calla's life that she had seen such a thing happen to a Rouge witch.

Necromancy itself wasn't illegal, but the unnatural way it was used for bone brothels *was*—and Hannah had been raised in one. Bone brothels brutally trained Rouge witches until their magic was molded into something perverse, monstrous. Queen Myrea had banned them long ago. Not to spare the poor witches who were tortured for them, of course, but because Myrea feared how the transformation in those witches would affect her hold over her subjects. Hannah had been on the verge of no return when she had escaped her mother's clutches and run to Estrella, but Calla had never seen this side of the other girl before.

Hannah's black pupils were dilating and contracting as the telltale smell of dark magic began to waft into the air. A shiver ran down Calla's spine.

"I'll distract it; you find a way to get close enough to siphon," Gideon told Calla.

As Gideon taunted the creature to follow him, Calla snuck toward its backside. She was within inches of grasping at the dull, flaking scales of the serpent half's tail when she was tackled from her left and thrown to the ground. She grunted in pain, Gideon's own sound of surprise echoing a few feet away. One of the other viperidae pinned her to the ground, the grotesque humanoid half hovering above her, baring its sharp rows of teeth in a ferocious smile.

Before the creature could rip out her throat with its canines, Calla locked her inner Siphon onto the stagnant blood in its body where the beast's hands were gripping into her shoulders, her stomach roiling from the rotten essence of it. Her Rouge magic could immediately tell how unnatural the energy flowing through the reanimated monster was.

As the viperidae dove forward, she squeezed her eyes shut and pulled as hard as she could with both her Siphon and her Rouge magic. A sick, wet popping sound rang out above her, followed by a cascade of warm liquid. She wiped at her eyes until she could reopen them, blinking down at the foul black blood that was now covering her head to toe, along with bits and pieces of the viperidae's flesh.

She leaned to the side and retched onto the ground.

Gideon yelled something in the distance, and she weakly wiped a hand across her mouth as she searched for him. The wind around them began to grow stronger, and it took her magic less than a second to recognize it as Gideon's power. She spotted him an instant later, though her vision was starting to become noticeably blurry, her head a bit faint as her Rouge magic continued to react to the blood covering her skin. Gideon looked noticeably uncomfortable, and she knew he was probably feeling the same effects from the viperidae's rancid blood through their bond, but there was nothing she could do about it as she bent over to heave once more.

The prince finally managed to get behind the creature he was opposing, and she caught a glimpse of him ripping the spine straight from its back, causing the entire serpent to drop and writhe on the ground. He threw the spine to the side and immediately turned to lose the contents of his own stomach. Luckily, he recovered much quicker than she was. He rushed over, dropping to his knees by her side and gathering her hair out of her face and off her neck, expertly twisting the long strands into a bun at the crown of her head. She didn't bother to pull away from his doting—she was too sick and exhausted—and admittedly craved the touch of his cold hands on her feverish skin as her stomach churned again.

"What's going on?" he asked, looking equally nauseous but infinitely more composed.

"The viperidae blood is toxic." She gagged. "My magic is trying to purge it from my system, but I'm drenched in it."

He immediately reached down to tear a strip of material from the bottom of his shirt and began wiping the blood from her face. It wasn't enough.

"We have to wash it off. Now. How do I stop Hannah?"

Calla tried to answer, but when she opened her mouth, nothing came out—and then the world began to tilt.

"*Shit,*" Gideon said as he caught her just before she crashed back into the ground.

Her eyes were barely open as she watched Gideon jump back to his feet and head toward where Hannah was still grappling for control over her magic. He ducked his face until his eyes were level with the blond's.

"Stop, Hannah," he demanded, his voice clearer to Calla's ears despite the fact that he had gotten farther away. "Stop. *Now.*"

Gideon's wind picked up, whipping through the clearing so violently the petals that littered the ground started to form small twisters. Which, unfortunately, caught Caspian just as he tried to land the killing blow on the last viperidae. His knife missed its mark, and the beast whipped its tail around, hitting the Onyx witch directly in the gut and sending him flying back to the ground. When the creature twisted to find its next victim, its depthless eyes locked right on Calla. Caspian rolled easily back to his feet, but it was too late.

Calla tried to call out to Gideon, but the prince's attention was still trained on Hannah, and before she could get the words out of her mouth the viperidae descended upon her and gripped her throat with one of its taloned hands.

Calla didn't know if she should be concerned or grateful that the pain of the viperidae's sharp claws piercing her neck faded as quickly as it came on. She caught a glimpse of Gideon spinning around as he realized what was happening. The prince took a staggering step toward her, terror igniting in his eyes. She tried to wave him off. He didn't listen.

The prince ran straight for the viperidae, leaping onto the monster's back and blasting a crackling ripple of electricity through the creature, making it loosen its grip on her throat so it could toss the Onyx witch away. Gideon slammed into the ground with a groan, and Calla felt the impact through her own body. She exhaled as she pushed through the pain, not wanting to miss the opportunity of the beast's distraction. She lurched up with her hand to make contact once again and latched on with her Siphon until it caused the viperidae to combust from the inside out like the one before.

Cass was approaching just as a second onslaught of blood fell from above.

"Damn it, Gideon, are you out of your mind?" Cass yelled as he made his way toward Calla. "You're lucky that move didn't break your necks!"

"I'm fine," she choked out to Cass as he crouched down to inspect her for any major injuries. "For the love of the Hells, just make her stop!"

Cass wrapped an arm around Calla's waist to help her stand up straight, asserting to Gideon, "I've got her; go help Hannah."

Gideon hesitated for a moment but nodded at Caspian, his trust for his friend clear on his face as he returned to Hannah once more.

"Are you hurt?" Calla asked Cass, trying to focus on anything except the way the world was spinning around her.

Cass gave her a dim smile. "Not even close. I've faced much worse than a few undead viperidae."

Calla squeezed her eyes shut as she muttered, "It's hard for me to say the same at the moment."

"I know you're a Rouge witch, but I'm not sure if blood is really your color," Cass agreed, reaching out to wipe his sleeve over her forehead to clear away some of the gore. "No offense."

Calla started to laugh, but it quickly turned into a heave, and Cass leaned out of her way as she began to retch once more.

The Onyx witch looked back over his shoulder and called, "Any luck?"

Calla managed a glance in Gideon's and Hannah's direction. The two witches were staring each other down, the crape myrtle blossoms tumbling through the air around them.

"Hannah." The prince voice, the one that came out anytime Gideon reached his limit of patience, echoed through the clearing. Something about that tone that emerged during the most intense situations had always been different, but the edge it had now was unsettling.

"*Stop,*" he thundered.

Hannah did.

One moment the energy in the forest was tumultuous, the uneasy feeling of corrupted magic swirling around them. The next—everything froze. Gideon's own wind went stagnant, letting the airborne petals drift to the ground. A moment later, the viperidae's corpses began to decompose. It was so fast Calla nearly missed it, but the two viperidae corpses that she hadn't exploded simply *dissolved*—right back into the earth where they came from. Hannah, on the other hand, looked no different—like she was on the verge of another episode, the girl's arms still covered in black veins.

Cass stood, shaking his head at Gideon. "I'll never understand how you do that."

"Do what?" Gideon questioned as he left the blond to decompress, the inky lines on her arms finally beginning to fade, and headed back over to Calla.

"Nothing." Cass waved a hand as he moved aside so Gideon could scoop Calla up into his arms. She couldn't even protest as her head lolled into the crook of his neck. Everything was becoming more and more dizzying by the second. She wasn't sure how Gideon was pushing through it.

"I have to get her cleaned off," Gideon told the others, his throat vibrating against her forehead as he spoke.

"You can't put her in Crystal Lake—there're nereids. That's how this whole ordeal started in the first place," Cass informed them.

Gideon cursed. "All right, we'll be back. Once the magic has fully left Hannah's system, she'll probably be too tired to go on anytime soon. Which means we should set up camp and get as much rest as possible."

"Maybe we should head out a little farther," Cass suggested. "You know, so we don't have to sleep on viperidae guts."

Calla didn't know if Gideon responded to that. Their voices had begun to grow softer and softer—though she hoped he agreed. She never wanted to see a viperidae again for the rest of her life.

Now Gideon was moving, and she wanted to ask how long he thought it might be before they found a source of water that wasn't Crystal Lake, but her mouth wouldn't open. Instead, she took a deep breath and closed her eyes, letting herself curl into him.

29

abine quietly re-dressed and laced up her boots, careful not to wake up the Valkyrie currently tangled in the shredded sheets. She hoped they hadn't been too expensive.

Mika? Michael? Whatever his name was—he had not been nearly memorable enough for her to offer to replace them. She'd only do that if she planned to be in them again and that was not likely.

As she slid her last knife back into place beneath her satin trousers, she tiptoed toward the bedroom's exit. She slowly twisted the doorknob and cracked open the door ever so slightly, trying to mitigate how much light flooded in from the apartment building's hallway. Before she wedged her way out, the beam of light that pushed into the room through the small sliver she had opened caught on something shiny sitting on the dresser.

Sabine knew she really should leave before she was caught sneaking out, but she hardly ever did anything she really should. So she moved toward the dresser, where the golden shimmer was calling her name with a stronger pull than the song of a siren.

She peered down into the small trinket dish Matthew clearly used to collect random bits and pieces. There was only one in particular that stood out: a small gold pin shaped like a dragon's head, two onyx jewels for eyes. She plucked it out of the bowl, carefully placing it in the center of her palm. It was no bigger than the size of a spéctral.

There was a rustle of noise from the bed, and Sabine held her breath as she turned to see if Milo had woken, exhaling with relief when she saw he had just shifted positions in his sleep. She pocketed the dragon pin and walked back to the door, slipping out into the hallway and never looking back as she made her way out of the building and summoned her wings.

She stretched out the mottled brown-and-white feathers before launching herself into the sky, reveling in the way the wind caressed her skin and combed through her golden hair. Her hair was finally at a length that she could braid and fix it with the glitzy pins she pilfered from Lyra's collection. It had been nearly four years since she received her True Name from the Veritas Tree, but the first few years she had kept her hair cropped like she'd been used to before her transition, worried that not knowing how to secure it properly would mean it'd be in her way during combat or reaping. With Lyra's tutelage, however, she had picked up quickly on how to pin it up in neat buns or plait it so it would stay secured.

Weaving her way through the sky, she peered down at the citizens of Valor as they made their way home for the evening. She could see the Miroir Mountains in the distance, their silvery peaks glistening with the last bit of sun. As she passed over the queen's marble palace, she braced herself for landing, Lyra's equally impressive abode just a few roads over now. She tucked her wings in as she dropped, heading straight for the manor's roof, letting the adrenaline of the free fall seep through her veins. At the last moment, she parachuted her wings out behind her and floated down until her feet hit the gilded tiles of the expansive gable with a light *thud*.

"Sabine!" a voice hollered from below. "What have I told you about landing on the roof?"

Sabine grinned at where Lyra was standing with their hands on their hips, foot tapping in annoyance. Sabine slid herself down to one of the house's awnings before kicking off the slanted surface and finally landing on the ground in front of her friend.

"Good evening to you, too, Ly." Sabine smoothed her hair over her shoulders.

"I'm going to carve your liver out and feed it to the harpy eagles the next time you use our roof as your landing pad." Lyra pointed a threatening finger, smoothing away a strand of their reddish-brown hair with their other hand.

Sabine rolled her eyes. "No offense, Ly, but your threats are getting stale."

Lyra did, in fact, look mildly offended. "All right. How about I'll gut you and use your intestines as my ensemble's statement piece for the Reverie, then?"

"That's more like it. What an honor." Sabine winked before striding past the exasperated Valkyrie and up the steps to the front door.

"The invitations from the Wayfarer arrived," Lyra commented from behind Sabine as they shouldered the heavy entrance door open. "Amina's ready inside."

"Amina? Early?" Sabine asked with slight surprise.

"The forest changed a lot, apparently," Lyra murmured.

It had taken exactly twenty-four hours for Amina to show back up at the manor after Lyra's ultimatum. Part of it could have been the fact that she had no other ties in Valor, and therefore no other place to stay, but Sabine knew with every fiber of her being that wasn't it. If Amina didn't care enough to make some sort of effort to untangle whatever was going on between the three of them, Sabine knew her friend's pride would have made her sleep on the cold street before giving in. Instead, she had told them to meet her tonight to finally discuss whatever the Hells was going on with her revenge schemes.

Lyra had struggled with Amina's disappearance most, and no matter how much Sabine had tried to pick up the pieces, things had never quite healed from when their friend, their once leader, had been sent away. The entire ordeal had happened during the year Sabine began traveling more, disappearing from Valor for weeks at a time, and sometimes Sabine wondered if, had she been there with Lyra and Amina *that* night, things would've gone down the way they did. She knew wondering about what-ifs was useless, though. The circumstances were what they were, and now the three of them were at a crossroads.

"She's still our Amina, Ly." Sabine slid her gaze sideways.

"Is she?" Lyra worried at their lip. "This vengeance . . . She was always the steady one. Nothing rocked her like this—before."

Sabine paused. "I know she's keeping us in the dark, but give her time. Let her work up to telling us about the forest. It was hard for us here, but we have no idea what she endured in that hellscape. I can't imagine . . . I can't imagine having had to go away and then return wondering if I fit with the two of you anymore."

"I know." Lyra nodded, squaring their shoulders and lifting their chin as if they were preparing to go into battle. "I'm just worried she's been so used to fending for herself that maybe she doesn't understand how to collaborate anymore. Or worse—maybe I'm worried she doesn't need us anymore altogether."

Sabine scoffed. "Did you see that ball gown that she picked out today? If we weren't around, who'd have done all those buttons up for her?"

Lyra rolled their eyes to the ceiling and shook their head as they rounded the corner, but Sabine swore she saw a small smile on their lips. The two of them made it back to Lyra's bedroom a couple minutes later, Sabine swiping an entire tray of snacks from one of the butlers heading out of the kitchen to serve dinner to Lark. Sabine hadn't seen Lyra's twin in a few days, but if there was a copious amount of food being prepared, it was always almost certainly for him. The butler was quite put out that they had to trek all the way back for more, but as Sabine speared a grape with one of her nails and popped it on her tongue, letting the sweet juice flood her tastebuds, she couldn't be bothered to care.

"I've secured the heathen," Lyra announced to Amina as they both strode into the room.

"The heathen has secured the provisions," Sabine said around a mouthful of cheese and apple slices.

Amina, who was sitting on the sapphire velvet settee with one leg crossed over the other, lifted a single brow at Sabine's manners. Or lack thereof. Sabine swallowed and set the tray down on the small table in the middle of the sitting area Amina was occupying.

"Settle in." Amina waved a hand at the two chairs across from her. "We've got a lot to get into."

Lyra chose the chair to the right, so Sabine claimed the other, kicking her feet up on the empty space next to Amina.

"I'm honestly not sure where to begin," Amina admitted.

"Let's start with the witch princes and end with whatever it is you plan to do at the Reverie," Lyra suggested. "That seems most pressing."

Sabine nodded eagerly. "I must agree. The witch princes are very pressing to me. On a scale of one to ten, how—"

"They weren't *that* hot, Sabine," Amina interrupted with a pointed look.

"Please, I've heard the rumors."

"Sabine, focus," Lyra scolded.

Sabine sighed. "Fine. You're right. How about you start with how you found the princes and how you managed to get one of them to bargain away their heart."

Amina nodded. "All right. It started with the Witch Eater. Like I mentioned before, I had come across their cottage while I was wandering through the forest, and they invited me inside. At first, it was just a way to satisfy my curiosity, and boredom, but I quickly realized if I was going to get out of there, they were a good ally to have. So I made it a habit to visit.

"And they told you the witch princes were coming? Can they predict the future?" Sabine asked.

"*Omnipotent* is one word for the Witch Eater, I suppose," Amina said thoughtfully. "*Infuriating* is another. From what I gathered, they aren't allowed to mess with the course of fate unless it's already been derailed—like if a being has already veered off their original destined path. Which meant they couldn't give me any certainties. What they did give me, however, was the gift of sight."

"What do you mean?" Sabine wondered, leaning forward with piqued interest.

"The Witch Eater is a collector, a cross between Lyra and the Wayfarer if I had to try and describe it. They have all sorts of enchanted items in their hoard, and their cottage was often unsupervised. Which is how I got my hands on *this*."

Amina dug into the pocket of her dress and pulled out a small compact mirror. It wasn't much to look at, just a simple gold compact with filigree embossing on the top. Amina pried it open, and Sabine was disappointed to see it was just as unimpressive inside.

"A mirror?"

"An enchanted mirror," Amina corrected. "It let me see anyone, or anything, I wished. It hasn't worked since I left, though."

"Its magic must be bound to the parameters of the Neverending Forest," Lyra concluded. "I have a magic looking-glass in my own collection that only works in the fae courts."

"How did you get that?" Sabine asked.

"Stole it from an ex," Lyra answered flippantly. "Back to the subject—so you saw the prince coming with the mirror?"

"Precisely," Amina continued. "I made it a point to keep track of every newcomer who entered the forest the entire time that I was there. I wasn't going to let any opportunities slip through the cracks—and I didn't."

"So, where does the bargain come in? Why didn't you just rip out one of their hearts?" Sabine prodded.

"Two words." Amina's brown eyes flicked between her and Lyra. "Blood Warrior."

30

When Calliope slowly blinked her eyes open, Gideon saw her gaze snag on the clusters of lightning pixies swirling through the moss that dripped from the branches above. She lifted her head from his shoulder to take in how the forest had changed from the haunting gray woods to the enchanting foliage of the angel's oak trees. The Terra Witch Realm was one of the few places the angel's oak grew naturally—without the help of the heavy glamour the Neverending Forest used. Gideon remembered loving the trees every time he saw them during his trips to the Terra Realm and how the branches twisted down and spilled over the ground, making it easy to climb all the way to the top when he was a kid. He wondered now why such magical trees would appear in these nightmarish woods.

"We're almost there," Gideon assured her when her eyes flicked over to him questioningly, adjusting her weight in his arms as he continued to tread forward and maneuver around the tangles of tree limbs.

"How long have I been out?" she asked as she twisted her head to look around them.

"Barely ten minutes," he answered, spotting a break in the trees a few yards ahead and what looked to be a shallow river sparkling in the distance. Thank the Gods. "I'm surprised it wasn't longer."

She mumbled something he couldn't make out as she stuffed her face back into the crook of his neck.

They made it to the river a few moments later, the sound of the running stream music to his ears. "Do you think you can stand?" he asked, stopping on the edge of the bank.

She nodded and he gently set her down on her feet, slowly unwrapping his arms from around her waist to make sure she didn't collapse to the ground. She tested the pressure of her full weight on her feet before she untangled her arms from his neck and took a hesitant step toward the water. She was still a bit wobbly but, luckily, didn't fall.

"Here," he told her as he rolled up the sleeve of his shirt, his jacket long discarded during the fight with the viperidae. "Try recharging yourself—or siphoning if it helps."

He was pleasantly surprised when she didn't argue, simply rolled up her own sleeve and reached out to grab on to him. Their numbers lit up just as they had before, and when she released her hold a minute later, the color had returned to her cheeks.

"That is helpful," she said softly.

He watched as she turned and stepped into the flowing ravine, not bothering to remove her bloody boots. The crystal-clear liquid began to turn a brownish gray from the mixture of the viperidae blood and her own. As the water became murky, he spotted something moving below the surface, popping out from beneath the rocks. A water sprite.

The sprite flew out of the water and right into Calliope's face, the tiny being's opalescent wings beating rapidly with fury. The little fae being shook their fist in her face, and Calliope looked back to Gideon with alarm. He was already walking off, however, and as she spun to find where he had gone, she accidentally sent the sprite flying to the left with the whip of her hair.

"Sorry!" she called after the tiny being as they buzzed away in anger.

Gideon pressed his lips together to keep from laughing as he approached one of the oak trees. He snagged a bit of the moss drooping down from one of its limbs and brought it back to the river where Calliope stood, curious.

"Here." Gideon showed her the angel's moss.

He crouched down to begin spreading the spongy gray tangles in a large circle beneath the water around where she stood, placing rocks from the riverbed on top of the tendrils so they wouldn't float away. Calliope watched as the blood running off her was quickly absorbed into the moss, the ichor no longer polluting the river.

Gideon stepped through the river to the other side and continued his ministrations as he explained, "Angel's moss purifies almost anything. We wouldn't want a horde of water sprites after us."

Calliope waited patiently as he meticulously created a ring out of the spongy material, biting her lip when he finally finished and looked back at her.

"What?" he asked.

"I need to . . ." She gestured awkwardly at her filthy clothes. "Strip?"

Hells. Not what I need to be thinking about right now.

He cleared his throat. "Right."

He turned all the way around and sat only a few feet in front of the riverbank. Close enough that if the forest thought to throw something else at them, he'd be right there to help.

He listened intently to the sound of her unlacing and kicking off her boots, to the water sloshing as she moved through it, and tried to keep his imagination from picturing the scene in his mind. He could swear the temperature in the forest rose a hundred degrees as he made an effort to busy himself with observing their surroundings for any threats.

After a few minutes, she asked, "How did you not get as nauseous as me? I could barely stand it."

Gideon gave a shrug. "You said your Rouge magic was reacting poorly to the spoiled viperidae blood, right? That may be why your reaction was drawn out longer."

"You can look now, I'm dressed again," she told him. "Do you mind helping me dry off?"

He turned to find her stepping out of the river, sopping wet, but at least the gore was all gone. Her long hair had been scrupulously detangled, and the top half had been braided and secured out of her face. He obliged her request with a flick of his magic.

"Thanks," she offered as she plunked herself on the ground and began shoving her boots back on. She tied the laces in a messy knot on the first and moved to do the other in an equally haphazard manner.

Gideon tried not to cringe. "You're horrible at tying knots, did you know that?"

"Sorry I've never had knot-tying lessons," she commented sarcastically. "Would you like to do it, then?"

He took the opportunity before she could rescind it, crouching down and pulling apart the sloppy laces to rework the strings into uniform bows.

She rolled her eyes as they both got back to their feet when he was finished. "You're being a busybody."

"I didn't realize offering my help caused you pain," he said dryly.

She fixed him with an unreadable look. "I saw the way you jumped onto that viperidae. If it had thrown you any harder—"

"I get it," he interrupted. "You could've gotten hurt, too."

She sighed. "When we finally get this bond severed, you can go back to risking your life and I promise to only complain a little."

The world around Gideon tilted.

"What?" he whispered.

Calla furrowed her brow. "What?"

"You still want to cut the bond?" he asked, voice drenched in disbelief.

"Gideon." She looked helpless. "We've been through this. Nothing has changed—"

"*Everything has changed,*" he insisted.

"I want to cut the bond because it's *hurting* us," she reasoned.

"Look what it just did for you," he argued back. "And what it did for me back in Estrella when I thought I would collapse from the exhaustion. I thought after that you'd . . ."

"Do you really think the small ways it's been helpful are worth the risk it poses to us both?" she asked.

"Small? It gave us enough power to open that gateway. Think of what it could do when we have to fight in this war! It could be an advantage."

"It could also be a detriment, Gideon. I'm trying to be rational about this."

Gideon shook his head. "It's more than that. You locked away your emotions after Ezra died, and you're refusing to let them in again. I thought the coldness coming from your side of the soul-bond was because you were angry with me—something I more than deserved. But now I see you're just scared of facing the truth of what accepting the bond might mean."

Something in her facade cracked at those last words, and for a moment Gideon hated himself for pushing her so hard, but he needed her to free herself from the shackles of her own mind. He needed her to *fight*.

"If I could feel the full force of my guilt right now," she whispered,

"I fear it would be incapacitating. I'm afraid it would burn me from the inside out until I turned to ashes. I want to be able to grieve, properly, but the only time I get a clear grasp on anything is when you and I are near each other." Her cheeks warmed a bit at her confession. "And that is not something I can be dependent on. I've already lost so much. I can't . . ."

"You aren't going to lose me, Calliope." He didn't know what he needed to do to convince her of that, but he had a feeling that after she'd just watched Ezra walk away from her, for good, it wouldn't be an easy task. "That's the one thing the bond guarantees—what happens to you happens to me."

"And what about losing our hearts if we continue on like this? That's why I don't want to fight whatever is keeping my feelings at bay. The numbness helps us keep from fulfilling the Heartbreak curse, too."

Gideon stared at her for a long moment, unable to argue with that last point. He shook his head and stepped back from her, huffing out a laugh. "It's a sick joke, isn't it? The fact that the Gods gave us a soul-bond that strengthens with physical touch at the same time as a curse that requires us to keep each other at arm's length at the risk of losing our hearts."

"It feels like a losing game." She took a shaky breath.

"It *is* a losing game." His jaw clenched. "We've both already lost more than we ever thought it was possible to survive. And now we'll lose the soul-bond, too."

"I don't think we have a choice at this point."

"Like the Fates told us—there is always a choice to be made. So, if this is what you're choosing, fine. I'll find a way to break it." Every single word singed his tongue. He meant them all, though. If she wanted the bond gone, he would hack it to pieces himself.

"Since when are we listening to the same Gods who have cursed us? I'm not doing this because I want to cut *you* out of my life," she asserted. "Please tell me you understand that."

He closed his eyes and murmured, "I get it."

"You won't hate me after all this, right?"

He looked her dead in the eye as he said, "That's never been the danger between us."

With that, he pulled away and headed back to the others.

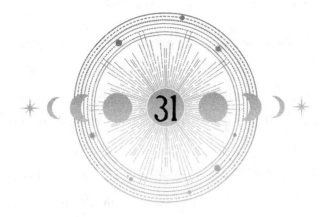

31

"*Blood Warrior?*" Sabine choked out at the same time that Lyra said, "So, the rumors are true, then."

Amina eyed Lyra with unpleasant surprise. "Rumors have spread?"

"Where in the Gods' names are *you* hearing rumors that I'm not?" Sabine threw at Lyra. "Are you going out without me?"

Lyra rolled their eyes. "Meli told me when she got in last night from the border. Meli has a not-very-secret lover in the Onyx Queen's Guild and apparently there have been whispers that the final Blood Warrior has been found and that the war is going to begin any day now. So many Valkyrie circles have been buzzing about it nonstop. They think it means we will finally be able to stop the tithe."

"I don't know about *any day now*," Amina said. "But I do know the final Blood Warrior has been found. Or should I say *warriors.*"

"*What?*" the two Valkyries exclaimed in sync.

"There's a girl. A Siphon. She and the elder prince got themselves soul-bonded thanks to some convoluted deal with the Witch Eater—they almost sabotaged my chances of coming home—and now both bear the final Blood Warrior numbers."

"I assume that isn't the prince whose heart you have, then?" Lyra questioned.

"No. That's what I meant by *sabotage*." Amina gritted her teeth and crossed her arms. "The elder prince promised me his heart, and then the bastard managed to get ahold of a pair of Fates' Dice when his ordeal with the Witch Eater backfired. Luckily, where there's a bargain, there's almost always a loophole."

"Fates' Dice." Sabine whistled. "You don't come across those every day."

While Witch's Dice were the burden of witches alone, Fates' Dice were a different sort of beast. *Any* being who intentionally rolled a pair of Fates' Dice not meant for them, or interfered with a roll, invited dangerous consequences into their life.

"And naturally his brother's heart was that loophole," Lyra concluded.

"I tried to be fair." Amina played with one of her curls, nonchalant. "The moment they entered the forest I knew who they were—the Witch Eater had been keeping an eye on them, too, that much I gathered. It didn't take long to find out that while the Witch Eater may have been keeping tabs on the elder prince, they were most focused on mapping out every move the *Siphon* made. *She* was the true Blood Warrior. So, I made the elder prince a bargain, figuring if I took his heart fairly, then I could avoid the wrath of the Onyx Queen, and I wasn't risking killing the Blood Warrior."

"And then they got themselves soul-bonded." Sabine cackled as she bent forward to spear another grape. "I don't know whose luck in this story is worse."

"Well, I got the heart and left exile. The rest is the witches' problem now." Amina dropped the curl she had been playing with.

Sabine had to agree. Amina hadn't deserved her exile in the first place, and the witches had been lucky that Amina was as honorable as she was to offer them a bargain instead of just taking the heart she needed to leave. If it had been Sabine, there would've been a lot less talking and a lot more blood, that was for certain.

Nothing made Sabine see red more than thinking about the night she had gotten word from Lyra that Amina had been taken by the queen's guards. Sabine had flown for hours back to Valor, until her wings ached and her feathers had begun to molt. By the time she had arrived at the palace, however, Amina was already being sentenced.

The accusation was that Amina had interfered in a jealousy-driven altercation that subsequently got Rovin—a dragon-shifter who had become the Valkyrie Queen's favorite lover—killed. Rovin had gone down to the border to confront a Valkyrie named Lex who had also been warming the queen's bed. Lex had been in the process of reaping a witch's soul, and when Rovin got between Lex and the witch, it was

Rovin's soul that was reaped instead. The witch hadn't hesitated to take the opportunity to make sure both Lex and Rovin met their untimely ends and the only person there to witness it all? Amina.

Since no one else had been around to blame, it was *Amina* who had to pay for the men's ridiculous feud. Exiled to the Neverending Forest until she acquired the beating heart of a prince as a payment to break the magic enchantment that had sealed her there. It was the harshest punishment Sabine had ever heard their queen order. Usually, exiled Valkyries were only banished from their lands. Keeping Amina contained in that nightmarish forest was a vicious ostracism born of pure spite.

Sabine was of the opinion that perhaps the queen should have just picked a lover who was smart enough not to start a fight while witches were present in the first place, but unfortunately no one had asked for her input at the trial. Though she had given it anyway—in the form of about a thousand filthy curses. She hadn't stopped until Lyra forcibly dragged her back home after the queen threatened to exile them along with Amina. The two of them had been ready to go, but Amina vowed never to forgive them if they did. So Sabine and Lyra went home and waited. For six years.

"Do you think the witches are going to come for the prince's heart?" Sabine wondered as she forced her thoughts back to the present.

"By the time they attempt to come for it, it will already be in someone else's chest," Amina answered.

"I had a feeling that's where this was heading," Lyra stated.

"Wait a minute." Sabine paused the grape she had halfway to her mouth, lifting her feet from where they rested next to Amina and leaning forward with excitement. "You mean—"

"When everything went down that day, I knew having the forethought to store Rovin's soul in my Esprit would come in handy," Amina explained. "Not only because it meant the Queen wouldn't be able to summon him back to life herself, but because I knew it would eventually give me the upper hand. My original intention was to use it to get out of the banishment, but I knew there was a chance that even if I gave it to her she would still banish me anyway. So I kept it as my little secret, and now all I need is the key to unlock Rovin's coffin. It's been less than a decade, so his body should not have started to decay yet—which means I'm going to bring him back and make a little bargain with our Queen."

"And since a Valkyrie that restores someone's soul gets the ability to have influence over them . . ." Lyra put together. "You're going to be able to have real leverage against her."

"Leverage for what?" Sabine asked.

Amina lifted her chin. "Getting every single one of us out of the tithe. And not even that feels like enough after what she's made me endure. For what she took from me—the years, your trust, missing Sabine's journey to the Veritas Tree."

Sabine sucked in a breath. "Amina. I need you to know it's the hardest decision I ever made—going without you. I wanted you there with me more than anything."

Amina looked down at her hands. "I don't want to make such an important thing in your life about me. I just . . ."

Sabine leaned forward and grabbed the other girl's hands. "I know what you mean. I always imagined you'd be there, too—it was about being my True Self, and I'm not my True Self without *you*, Amina."

Amina swallowed as she looked back at her friend, reverence shining in her eyes.

"After we figure things out," Sabine continued, "I'd still like to take you there someday—to the Isle of the Veritas Tree. It's . . . it's like nothing you've ever experienced before. I imagine it's the one pure gift that any of the Gods has ever granted us."

"Was it everything you wanted?" Amina leaned forward, lacing her fingers through Sabine's and squeezing with affection. "The True Name ceremony, I mean."

"It was more." Sabine grinned. "When I carved my old name in the bark, when the tree erased it from existence forever, it was an instant weight off my shoulders. I just felt . . . lighter."

The magic of the Veritas Tree was something of exquisite beauty. The moment Sabine had released her old name to the tree's magic, every person she'd ever met instantly forgot it. No one would ever be able to speak it again. The tree's magic replaced it in everyone's mind with her True Name instead—the second name she carved into the tree. The one that unleashed the transitioning magic on her being. Even Sabine did not know the Dead Name she once bore. She only knew her True Name, the one *she* had given power to.

"I would love to go with you someday," Amina whispered. "Make up for what I missed."

Sabine untangled their hands and threw her arms around her friend. When she pulled back, she looked at Lyra. "I think it's worth the risk."

Lyra watched them both with an intense look on her face. "I know."

Sabine turned back to Amina. "I know what it's like to need something so badly for yourself—no matter what it might cost. You need vengeance. You need to burn away the anger inside you so you can rise like a phoenix from the ashes. Start over. With us."

32

When Calla and Gideon made it back to the others, Calla darted straight to Hannah. The witch was sitting with her back against a tree trunk, steadily sipping from one of the canteens, the dark veins that had taken over her body before nowhere to be seen.

"Are you all right?" Calla's voice was earnest as she reached out to grab her friend's hand in comfort.

Hannah squeezed Calla's hand back. "I should be asking *you* that. I'm so sorry, Calla. I don't know how that happened; my magic has never just reacted like that before."

"Hannah." Calla said the witch's name with a heavy dose of exasperation. "I am the last thing you should concern yourself with right now. I just got a little nauseous. As soon as the blood was washed off, it went away."

Hannah nodded like she knew exactly what Calla meant.

"What on earth happened?" Gideon asked.

"After the two of you left, Caspian and I dove down to gather the respi-root. We were down there for maybe two or three minutes—max—when a nereid attacked us."

"The nereid got to me first," Caspian inserted. "But when she was unable to drag me down, she set her sights on Hannah."

Hannah told them about how she had gotten pinned to the bottom of the lake and then heard Caspian's scream.

Caspian's eyes softened with guilt. "I was yelling for you. I didn't realize you thought—"

"No, it's all right," Hannah said, cutting him off. "I'm sorry about the viperidae, but . . ."

Everyone waited patiently for the witch to find the words.

"My magic has been dormant since I came to Estrella after I left my mother." Hannah squeezed her eyes shut as she spoke, like she was hoping that doing so would make the memories disappear. Calla tightened her grip on the girl's hand. "I left the bone brothel the night after the biggest ritual my mother had ever had us attempt. It was me and another Rouge witch—Gods, I can't even remember their name. The ritual nearly ripped the flesh from our bones—the magic was too powerful to contain. It was trying to tear itself out of us. The other witch . . . They died before the sun rose the next day."

Hannah's voice sounded like there were tears in her throat, but her eyes were clear, and Calla's heart ached for her friend. People always presumed Hannah to be the soft one, but that never meant that she was weak. Calla knew Hannah's gentleness came from having to shed her scar tissue, from having the strength to start over.

"I knew then that my mother would let me destroy myself if it meant she got what she wanted." Hannah swallowed. "So I left. And I haven't been able to use any of my magic since. It's like the summoning that night took it all away from me. I've felt empty for so long, and then today, the thought of not being able to help Cass like I couldn't help Delphine—it's like it unlocked a vault of magic inside me I didn't know I still had."

The two men took in her words, Caspian trying hard to keep his jaw from dropping in utter disbelief that Hannah, *Hannah*, had experienced such dark magic in her life, and yet she was still a source of light for all of them. She had always been the person Calla and Delph looked to when they were feeling so lost in Estrella.

It was Gideon who broke the silence. "Maybe your magic has finally healed. If it almost destroyed you like you said, maybe it's just taken this long to replenish."

"*Healed* doesn't seem right," Hannah said as she looked down at her hands. "It felt more like destruction to me."

"Only because that's how you had to use it before," Caspian said. "But that's not who you are. If you learned how to control it yourself, it doesn't have to be dark."

Hannah perked up a bit as she met Caspian's eyes, and Calla could see the bond the two witches had built over the last few days in that one look.

"Do you think so?" Hannah asked.

"You're powerful," Cass told her. "But *powerful* does not have to mean *unfettered*. You should never have to be afraid of yourself. If your magic is going to slowly come back, then we're going to retrain it to be something good—like you. We can start training a little bit each day. You deserve to feel like your magic is yours again, not your mother's."

Hannah dropped Calla's hand and lunged forward to wrap her arms around Caspian's neck, whispering, "Thank you."

Cass returned her hug with a large grin before pulling back a moment later and switching to look at Calla and Gideon. "All right, now why don't you two explain how the Hells you *appeared out of thin air*. How long were you even gone?"

"Nearly two days." Gideon ran a hand through his hair.

Hannah sputtered. "It wasn't even an hour for us."

"Start from the beginning," Cass urged.

So they did. Calla explained how they'd lost their memories after making a deal with Jack and getting the ingredients they needed to summon a gateway to the afterlife. How they'd spoken to the Fates themselves—and Ezra.

Cass was quiet for a long minute. Then he said, "That's it? He's just . . . gone?"

Calla swallowed. "He said he was at peace. I just hate feeling like it was such a waste going all that way and failing. . . ."

"It wasn't a waste." Caspian shook his head after her words trailed off. "You got the closure you needed. I'm not sure how you, or any of us, would have gone on without that. Now we know he's okay. But are you?"

Calla and Gideon exchanged a loaded look.

It was Gideon who said, "No. But now I think we might have a better chance of getting there."

"I'm sorry for your loss," Cass whispered, his expression painted with sincerity. "Both of you. I know what I said about bringing him back before you left. But I truly am sorry that you weren't able to do so."

Calla reached out to squeeze one of the witch's hands. "I'm sorry for your loss, too, Cass."

They all sat there with each other in silence for a long while. Finally letting the grief fully wash over them. A scar they would all share forever.

"What's our plan now?" Hannah whispered eventually.

"I've been thinking," Calla told them. "After we get Delphine and Kestrel back, we need to find the other Blood Warriors."

Caspian and Gideon raised their brows in sync. Gideon asked, "How would we find them?"

"No idea." She shrugged. "But there's enough of us to split up and track them down. The more Blood Warriors we can get in one place, the better chance we have to start mapping out what starting this war will look like."

Gideon nodded at her suggestion with fervor. "You're right. We need to get them all on our side and strategize exactly how to begin—and end—it as efficiently as possible. Witches who have already completed their Rolls of Fate are most likely not going to be of help to us, but that's where Caspian's work with the Guild comes in."

Calla bit her lip and looked to Hannah. Hannah smiled at her sadly.

"Oh . . ." Gideon sucked in a breath. "I'm sorry, Hannah, I didn't mean—"

"I know." Hannah took a deep breath. "If my power is what has to be sacrificed to take down the queens, though, it's worth it."

"I'm not sure other witches will feel that way," Calla muttered, before glancing back at the men. "And what work with the Guild do you mean?"

"*That* is a story for another time." Cass pushed himself up to his feet. "It's my turn to bathe now. Gideon, if you don't mind pointing me in the right direction?"

"I'll take you there," Gideon offered, and a minute later both men were trailing off, heads bent together, discussing something Calla couldn't make out.

As soon as they were out of sight, Calla and Hannah both changed into clean sleeping clothes before building a makeshift bed for the night. When they were both finally settled in side by side, staring up at the stars, Calla whispered, "You'll find your way back to your magic, Han. I've never seen you falter down any path you've taken before."

"I've never been this lost before," Hannah whispered back. "Not since I first arrived in Estrella."

"And yet I've always wished I could do what you do—look forward instead of trying to chase something in my past that's always been just out of my reach," Calla confessed. "My future is murkier than ever. It's hard to feel tethered to anything when everything is constantly changing."

Except Gideon, she thought, but she couldn't say that out loud. Couldn't look too closely at what that meant and risk opening the floodgate.

"There's nothing in my past worth looking back at, so I might as well look forward," Hannah said as she glanced at Calla, the forest's silver stars reflecting in her large violet eyes. "I found my home. You and Delph are my home. It's easy not to falter when you're walking along with the only destination you ever care to reach. Without Delphine, though, I feel like it's made me realize there are so many things I've been putting off for so long."

Calla had always thought of the girls the same way, like the closest thing to home she would ever feel, and until she had started facing her power, she'd never understood why that hadn't been enough for her. "I understand. I wish I had done so many things differently. I wish I hadn't been so scared to use my own magic against that siren when I had the chance. Gideon's right—no one should ever have to be afraid of themselves—and I've spent so long with my head in the sand that I let my friend get taken instead of stopping it. I'm just . . . I'm sorry. For all of it."

"I know you are. We're all learning as we go," Hannah said sincerely. "We've all tried to use each other and those around us to make ourselves complete, but that doesn't work. I never thought I needed anything as long as I had you both, but now I see I shouldn't have waited so long to face my magic again. Now that it could become a threat."

"I get it." Calla took a deep breath. "I should've learned how to control my Siphon a long time ago. Maybe then I'd make less of a mess of the monsters I splatter everywhere."

Hannah let out a surprised laugh, and the sound made Calla's lips tilt up a bit at the corners. She missed the sound of laughter.

Hannah sobered a moment later and after another beat softly added, "I'm sorry about Ezra. I can't imagine how hard it was to say good-bye. I don't think I could have done it if it was *her*."

"Can I confess something?" Calla whispered.

Hannah turned to face Calla. "Always."

"I had imagined it might be impossible to let him go." Calla closed her eyes. "But then it wasn't."

Hannah waited patiently.

"He told me that we were never going to work out." Calla swallowed. "He implied the only reason I was holding on was because of my guilt."

"Yes." Hannah nodded.

Calla widened her eyes at the instant agreement.

Hannah sighed. "Calla, the two of you were like mixing oil and water. Sometimes the people we have history with and passion for are not the right person for us *forever*. Sometimes they're just right *for now*. And when you met Ezra, you needed someone to bring you out of your shell and to make you feel alive again—and he did. But the two of you were too similar. And if what happened hadn't happened, I think you would've come to realize that."

Calla pushed herself up on her elbows and looked over to her friend in utter shock. "Why didn't you tell me any of this before?"

"In the last two days, you mean?" Hannah asked. "When we were all still processing it? Or months ago? Because Delphine *absolutely* told you that fifty thousand times and you refused to listen."

"Yes, but Delphine never thinks anyone is good enough for either of us. I thought it was just Delph being Delph."

Hannah snorted. "Well, now you know. I am sorry, though. This has to be the worst way to move on from someone."

"An understatement," Calla agreed.

They were both silent for a long while. Then Calla said, "You, me, and Delphine are forever."

"Yes," Hannah whispered. "I should've told her I loved her every single day since the moment I realized it."

The two of them didn't say anything after that, and a minute later

Calla looked over to see the blond had drifted off to sleep, the sounds of the other girl's steady breathing the only noise besides the soft breeze moving through the trees around them. Calla felt her own eyes become heavy soon enough, and it wasn't long before she followed her friend into unconsciousness.

When Delphine woke, she found herself on the floor of her cell, Zephyr nowhere to be seen, agony shooting through her body. She let out a mewl of pain as she raised her arms to inspect them, biting back a gut-wrenching sob when she found the delicate fins that had just begun to grow back in were now ripped away. With a shaking hand she reached over to brush a finger over the torn, uneven edges of the delicate membranes protruding from her left forearm. A sharp, shooting ache ran through her body, and it took everything in her not to be sick to her stomach. She could feel the familiar sensation of her body trying to repair the damage but knew after the trauma of the past week and the lack of well-rounded meals, it would take longer than usual.

"I have to get out of here." She heaved, her breathing becoming shallow as panic began infiltrating the edges of her mind. "I can't do this. I can't do this. I can't do this."

For a moment she didn't know if she was going to be able to peel herself off the ground. She felt violated. She felt hopeless. Worst of all, she felt trapped.

Concentrate on something else, a voice in her mind told her. *Your safe place.*

Delphine searched her mind for the last moment she remembered feeling truly safe. It was with Hannah. That fateful night Calla had gone to meet Ezra at the Starlight Inn before everything became so complicated. She and Hannah had been out on a walk together, going nowhere in particular—just taking in Estrella and the stars. Delphine remembered feeling like something in the air was shifting as she and Hannah meandered through the town in the cool winter night. She had felt so at peace, though, that she had asked Hannah to stay out in the cold just a little longer. Then they had returned to their apartment and found Calla with a Witch's Die.

You're okay. Just stay angry. Keep going. You're okay.

Delphine pushed herself up from the floor and carefully moved over to the mattress. Her brow furrowed as she realized there was something hard beneath where she sat, and she lifted herself to find a small silver hand mirror had been left on the bed. She wasn't sure if this had been a gift from Zephyr or Reniel, but whoever it was knew where to hit her the deepest. When she held the reflective surface up to her face, she barely recognized the person who stared back at her.

The girl in the mirror hadn't had a haircut in weeks, the silver strands brushing the tops of her shoulders now. Her gills had fully grown back in, and dark blue scales decorated her skin in random patches at her temples and on her shoulders. The soft webbing between her fingers and toes was becoming thicker by the day. None of those details were what made her pause, however. Those changes she had expected. It was her eyes that made her want to smash the mirror into a million pieces.

Her once bright silver irises were now a dull gray.

Reniel likes to break pretty things.

She let out a shriek of rage as she stood from the bed. The mirror, faceup atop the mattress, shattered at the earsplitting sound. She balled her hand into a fist and slammed it into the stone wall over and over again, until her knuckles were split open, blue-black blood spilling into the water around her.

"Is this a bad time?"

Delphine whipped her head toward the front of her cell. Eros.

She charged up to the bars, teeth bared. *"What the Hells do you want?"*

Even in the dull light she could see the lavender strands that were woven into his bright silver hair, nearly the exact same color as his periwinkle complexion. She could tell the slits cut through each of his eyebrows had been freshly touched up—his signature look.

"Keeping up a ruse means following orders." His voice was little more than a whisper. A guard must be on duty. "The mirror was Zephyr's idea, if you were wondering. He said it would get a rise out of you. I'm surprised to find he was right."

"He ripped off my fins! Don't you *dare* fucking tell me I'm being dramatic," she snarled.

Before Eros could respond, a pair of footsteps echoing down the hall caught both of their attention.

"I told you not to come visit her without me," Celeste scolded Eros as she approached.

"I didn't know where you were," Eros replied.

Celeste held up a bunch of sea berries to Delphine in offering. Delphine didn't hesitate to snatch the fruit from the girl's hand and crush them in her grip.

"Did you know Zephyr was going to pay me a visit today?" Delphine accused. "That he was going to tear my fins to shreds?"

"*What?*" Celeste reared back in shock as she saw the damage that had been done to Delphine's arms and calves, and though the surprise on her face looked genuine, Delphine's eyes still narrowed. "Delphine, I had no idea; I swear I would have tried to intercept his visit."

"Zephyr and Mariana said they wanted to celebrate this morning, but I didn't think they meant *this*," Eros inserted, and both girls snapped their gazes over to him.

"Celebrate *what?*" Delphine inquired.

"Reniel removed Mariana's tracking ring today. As a reward for helping get you back," Eros explained.

The laugh that came out of Delphine at his words was half-wild. "You all are so lucky I am locked in here. Using me to win favors from Reniel—I should carve out your intestines and wear them as—"

"That's *them*, Delphine. The two of us want to call a truce." Celeste cut off Delphine's threat before it got any more graphic. "We need to work together."

"*A truce?*"

Eros opened his mouth to retort, but Celeste held up her hand. "We are in just as vulnerable a spot as you, Delphine."

"Oh really?" Delphine's tone was dripping with sarcasm. She knew she should keep her facade bolted firmly in place, but the shock of waking up with her body torn apart hadn't yet worn off. "Is watching my demise incredibly hard for you both? Zephyr came down here and attacked me, Celeste."

"It isn't like I could have stopped it without making Reniel or Zephyr suspicious," Eros argued. "Not to mention we're already putting our necks on the chopping block enough to get this plan together to help *you* out. Because everything always has to be about you, right, Delphine?"

"Eros." Celeste shot him a hard look. "Don't start a fight."

"Why not?" he asked, tone bland. "Seems to me that's exactly what she's looking for."

"Maybe I am," Delphine sneered. "My ego could use an easy win."

"We don't have time for this," Celeste hissed, her hands balling into fists at her sides. "If you two start fighting we're never going to get through this. We only have two weeks to make this plan work before the Blood Moon."

"Sorry if some of us don't have your grace, Celeste," Eros gritted out, flicking his eyes from Delphine to the other girl and back. "I've been waiting for years to give her a piece of my mind."

Delphine gripped the bars in front of her. "Let's have it, then. I'm the reason Reniel tortured you, right? It's all my fault for taking an opportunity to save myself. Or maybe you're just upset you didn't have the guts to—"

"*Stop*," Celeste said again. "Save the low blows for when we're free. Try to kill each other for all I care—*after* we get out of here. Zephyr's up to something. I don't know what exactly, but he has a vendetta and I'm afraid he's going to make a move before we can."

"I will gouge Zephyr's eyes out before I ever let him near me again," Delphine spat.

The pitying frown Celeste gave her made her nerves prick with fury.

Delphine rattled the bars. "I swear on my blood, I will *never*—"

"*Delphine.*" Celeste looked aghast. "Watch what you're saying."

Delphine drew up short, realizing what words had been coming out of her mouth. Her breathing was hard, her knuckles on the bars almost white with the strength of her grip, and it took a moment for the magic she had just begun to activate to settle back down in her core. She had been close to making the magic-binding vow—their Siren's oath—she wouldn't have been able to take back.

"Delphine." It was Eros who spoke now, and she looked back at him, expecting to find a smug look in his eyes, but the only thing she saw was determination. "We all have a long way to go with repairing everything that's happened here. I promise we want our freedom just as much as you do."

"I *had* freedom," she asserted.

"Did you?" He looked back at her evenly. "As long as you are bound by that oath to him, you'll be looking over your shoulder everywhere you go."

He was right. "And you're not worried about that being your own destiny if you ever manage to run away yourself?"

"Eros knows someone in Estrella who can help us out with that. But our top priority right now is figuring out a way to have you present at the Claiming ceremony," Celeste broke in. "That's when we will strike—when everyone is caught up in the chaos."

Delphine was ten steps ahead. She had already assessed that there was only one angle for her to take in order to escape this cell—getting back on Reniel's good side. Celeste had let it slip a few times that his other Shoal members were becoming increasingly anxious about the upcoming Claiming, going as far as making plans to not be there—an offense that did not come without consequence. If Shoal members were willing to incur Reniel's wrath, Delphine knew it would take something truly grand to make them reconsider. That's when a glimmer of an idea crept into her mind. There was nothing Reniel loved more than an audience, and to get an audience you needed an attraction.

"We can't disparage Reniel's pride," Eros said. "The reason he's so pissed at Delphine is because she made him look bad. It won't be easy to undo that damage in such a short period of time."

She loved it when people underestimated her.

"When you have a plan"—Delphine pushed away from the bars—"get back to me."

Delphine made a show of clearing the broken mirror from her bed and curling up on her side as Eros and Celeste bent their heads together and disappeared down the hallway, Celeste looking back at least twice as they walked out of sight. Delphine waited for the telltale signs that they were gone—the creaking sound of the exit door opening and then the back-to-back *click* and *thud* of it shutting behind them. She waited a few minutes before she climbed out of bed again, when she knew they were truly gone, and then she yelled for the guard she suspected had come back sometime when she was unconscious.

The guard approached her cell, face wrinkled with disdain at being called over like a dog.

Delphine grinned. "Please tell our humble leader that I would like for him to pay me a visit."

34

Gideon was up well before the sun the next day. While he waited for the others to rise, he decided to gather breakfast, unable to stand still for too long. He had never been one to sleep well, but his restlessness was worse than ever.

The few memories he had of his childhood with Ezra wouldn't stop looping through his mind. Worse was remembering all the moments without Ezra, when their mother had forcibly kept them apart.

Now he pulled himself onto a tree branch above his head, trying to reach a green apple dangling from one of the higher limbs. When he landed back on his feet, he placed the fruit in his satchel with the others and turned to make his way back to the camp, pulling his compass out to make sure he was going the right direction. By the time he got back, the sun was just starting to peek through the clouds above, and he watched as Calliope began to stir from where she was entangled with a lightly snoring Hannah. He immediately looked away, gritting his teeth at the way his magic warmed at the sight of her.

He couldn't allow himself to get used to that feeling.

The only people his magic had ever gotten used to were Kestrel, Cass, and Ezra—and that was after *years* of being around one another. The sensation with Calliope started out the same way, he hadn't really noticed it at first, not until the fight they had gotten into with the sirens, when the girls got separated from the rest of them and he felt the tightening in his chest the farther she had gotten from him. Since the Witch Eater's cottage, though, it had been twenty times stronger.

"Gideon?" Calliope whispered as she sat up, blinking sleepily.

"Breakfast?" he murmured as he approached, holding out an apple in offering.

She nodded in thanks as she accepted the fruit before standing up and stretching out her limbs.

"I filled up the canteens last night, too, if you need any water," he informed her as he turned to set the heavy satchel down.

"Thanks. I don't even remember falling asleep."

"I'm not surprised. You and Hannah were dead to the world by the time we came back." He faced her once again and shrugged. "But aside from Cass and me getting bitten by a couple of angry water sprites, it was pretty quiet."

"I was exhausted. I'm surprised I stayed awake at all after all the magic I expelled fighting the viperidae."

"Are you feeling all right after that?" he asked. "No other side effects?"

"Not that I can tell."

Since their conversation at the river, Gideon suddenly felt like the two of them were walking a tightrope, trying to keep their balance before they accidentally fell into the widening chasm that always seemed to be waiting beneath them.

"What?" she asked, her mismatched eyes narrowing.

"Nothing," he murmured. He pulled another one of the fruits from his pocket and fixed it between his two palms to split it in half and then into four quarters. Calliope raised her brows at the impressive feat as he bit the core out of one of the pieces and then turned to spit it to the ground. "I've been thinking."

"About?" she asked around a bite of her own breakfast.

Before he could respond, a sudden vibration slithered through the ground beneath their feet.

"What the Hells?" Cass shouted as he jolted awake, his volume prying Hannah out of her own slumber.

"Huh?" Hannah blinked her eyes open.

"You both felt that, too, right?" Caspian said as he scrambled to his feet.

The ground began to rumble again as if to confirm that they had in fact felt it.

"You've got to be kidding," Calliope griped as she tossed the core of her half-eaten apple to the side. "It's too early in the morning for this!"

Hannah pushed herself up from the tangle of makeshift blankets as all of them braced for whatever was about to happen. The ground continued to vibrate, and Calliope choked on a sound of surprise as the earth began to split open at her feet. Everyone stumbled back as the chasm grew larger, but when Gideon slipped on the crumbling edge, his grip on the compass he was still holding loosened, and he watched in horror as it tumbled into the pit. He reached out with his wind magic, but the artifact was already too far down.

Everything that happened next took place within two heartbeats.

One.

Caspian met Gideon's eyes and pleaded, "Gideon, *don't.*"

Two.

Gideon jumped in after the compass.

Calla gaped down into the black abyss where Gideon disappeared. When the two witches on the other side of the pit didn't move, jaws equally slack with shock, she yelled, "We can't leave him down there alone!"

"Unlike Gideon, I have a rule about not jumping into *random holes in the ground,*" Caspian shouted back, throwing his arms in the air with exasperation.

Calla knelt and tried to peer into the darkness, but she couldn't see a thing.

"Gideon!" she yelled, her voice echoing down. "Gid—"

The ground beneath her crumbled, and Calla tumbled forward, Hannah shouting her name above her as she fell.

Hannah slid her gaze over to Caspian. "I want to say I can't believe they both just did that, but, well, it would be a lie."

"I don't know what the Hells Gideon is thinking half the time these days," Cass started, but the moment the words were out he shook his head and sighed again. "That's not true. I know *exactly* what he's thinking. The only way he feels like he can be in control is being the damn hero all the time."

Hannah threw him an empathetic look.

"I just wish Gideon coped like the rest of us—shaving off all his hair or getting a new tattoo." Cass ran a hand over his shaved head in frustration. "Instead, he dives into situations that could get him killed. I can't lose him, too."

"I'm sorry about Ezra and Kestrel," she told him. "I know all this has been just as hard on you as the rest of us even though you don't show it as much. I wanted to tell you that earlier."

Cass gave her a sad, warm smile. "Thank you. I have full confidence that Kestrel can take care of himself—wherever he may be—but losing Ezra . . . He was like my little brother, too, you know? We didn't get to spend as much time together, since Gideon and I would only really see him back home on our annual breaks from the Guild, but I've known him for a decade. It's hard to wrap my head around the fact that everything has changed so fast."

Hannah nodded again. Then she whispered, "Cass?"

"Yes?"

"Are you scared? About what's to come? Calla started talking about the war last night and I realized it's all . . . real. She's never talked about it as if she were going to be part of it before."

He nodded. "Yes, I suppose it's hard not to be scared. Though my fear isn't really for myself."

"Even after the dream the demon's oak gave you?"

Cass raised his brows in surprise that she had remembered what he'd told her about that—it had been an attempt to distract her and Ezra on their trek to find Gideon and Calla after the witches disappeared to go to the Witch Eater. "The glimpses of the future those dreams gave us aren't set in stone. And even if they were—it's hard to be scared of something you can see coming."

A wave of emotions went over Hannah's face, and he worried that he had just said the wrong thing until she told him, "I'm scared all the time. For Delphine and Calla and you and Gideon. The war that I'm going to be on the opposite side of from all of you . . ."

Caspian had the urge to hide Hannah on the other side of the world, where the Witch Queens would never be able to find her or cause her harm. He wasn't sure exactly when he'd become so protective over the little witch, but in the last few days something between them had grown. He was more than grateful for her warmth and camaraderie among the chaos.

"But I'm mostly scared of myself," she finished in a whisper, bringing him out of his thoughts.

He reached out to gently squeeze her hand in comfort. He wanted to be able to tell her it was going to be all right, but that would be a lie.

So instead he told her, "Whatever happens, we'll deal with it. You're stronger than you think, Hannah."

Hannah sniffed a bit, looking down at her hands. "What if I'm not?"

"You are. You've made it this far. You might bend, but you won't break."

She gave him an unconvinced smile but didn't argue as she carefully peered back over into the pitch-black pit in front of them. "Do you think they're okay?"

"There aren't any screams of agony yet," Cass muttered. "Gideon should be able to slow their momentum with his magic anyway. Not that he doesn't deserve a broken bone—or ten. Let's just hope the hole doesn't close and bury them alive before I get a chance to strangle Gideon myself."

35

C alla let out a shriek as she plummeted through the darkness. She fell for what felt like an eternity, eyes squeezed shut with fear. A giant gust of wind blasted upward as she finally reached the bottom, slowing her momentum greatly. She was surprised to find it wasn't the ground she landed on but a pair of muscular arms.

"*Oof,*" she grunted as Gideon caught her, his arms braced so tightly that it felt like her ribs had slammed into concrete bricks.

"What in the *Hells*, Calliope?" His voice rang out in the dark as he placed her on her feet.

"I fell in," she deadpanned.

"I can see that," he admonished her, and though they couldn't see each other's faces in the dark, she still gave him an annoyed look.

"*You're* the one who jumped into a giant hole for a compass." She crossed her arms over her chest. "Speaking of, please tell me you at least got it before it shattered on the ground?"

"Luckily, if my magic is good for anything, it's cushioning a fall."

"How the Hells are we going to get back up?" she asked, a bit of panic settling into her core as she realized the gravity of the situation.

"We might be able to climb out. . . . It'd help if we could see," Gideon said, his voice not as close as it was a second ago.

"You know"—Calla laughed nervously—"I was never afraid of small dark spaces before, but after this and the Valley of Souls I'm starting to think maybe they aren't for me."

"Hey," he said softly. "I'm here. We're going to find a way to climb out."

"I just hate not being able to see where I am or what's in front of me."

"Take a deep breath and close your eyes," he said soothingly. "Picture your hands in front of you. Picture that little scar you have on your left wrist. Think of the way you'd see the tendrils of your hair that always fall into your eyes until you tuck them behind your ears."

Her heart pounded at how intimate his descriptions were. She knew his words were supposed to be helping her focus, but her mind was still stuck on the fact that he had somehow noticed that tiny scar on her wrist, a small thin line from where a broken perfume bottle, one of Delphine's, had once sliced her and left a shard of glass she hadn't noticed until her magic expelled it from her skin a week later.

"What next?" she whispered.

"Picture me. Right in front of you," he said just as quietly. "My hands."

And suddenly he was there brushing the strand of hair he had described a moment ago off her cheek exactly where he said it would be. Then he softly placed his fingertips on her warm skin.

"My face."

Here, in the dark, she let herself revel in his touch. When he leaned his forehead right against hers, his fingertips sliding down her face, her neck, her arm, until his hand finally came to rest at her waist. A rush of emotions came flooding through her: grief, hope . . . lust. And this time, without the guilt, she ran toward it all. A sob began to build in her throat, and the pace of their heartbeats was at an all-time high. It was like a rush of adrenaline had been injected directly into her bloodstream just from his skin grazing hers; her senses were sharpened, the fog completely lifted, and this time she knew it was for good.

A red burst of light cut between them. Gideon stumbled back, and Calla gasped at the soft crimson glow. When their eyes met, she swore every nerve in her body was on fire.

"I don't think I'll ever get used to that," she whispered.

"Calliope." He spoke her name like a secret.

She was utterly frozen as he closed the distance between them again, brushing his hand down over her glowing numbers, never breaking their stare. He searched for something in her gaze she couldn't name. She couldn't speak, afraid she would cry if she did with all the growing pressure in her chest.

"Tell me to stop," he whispered.

She didn't.

"This could ruin us," he said.

"I know," she choked out, looking down at where his hand was brushing over her skin. He moved to place two fingers under her chin and tilted her face back up to his.

"I know we're going to get rid of the bond. I'm accepting that. And I know getting used to this, how it feels, is the opposite of wise. But . . ."

"But?" she prompted.

"I just want to feel everything. Just for a moment."

"Gideon," she whispered, wished, hoped. "We keep playing with fire."

"I know," he said, letting his eyes fall shut for a moment before straightening himself up and taking a deliberate step away from her. "I hate this."

"Which part?" She huffed a bitter laugh as she felt a wave of disappointment at the loss of his contact.

He didn't answer, but the intensity in his eyes, highlighted by the red glow, made a shiver run down her spine.

We are so unbelievably screwed.

Gideon finally turned away from her and began to inspect the walls, raising his arm to cast the light over the jutting rocks and vines in the dirt.

"I think we'll be able to climb out," he told her, waving her over to inspect for herself.

Calla nodded, grateful he was the one to pull back this time, not sure if she had the strength at the moment. She approached the wall beside him, reaching to grab onto a thicket of roots and hauling herself up onto one of the protruding rocks. She began a steady ascent, careful to evenly distribute her weight between steps in order to not dislodge any of the debris and slip. Gideon followed her path below, and they both made it almost ten feet off the ground before they heard, and felt, a shift below.

Calla peered down, past Gideon, and squinted into the dark. It was nearly impossible to see anything outside the reach of the crimson light, but there was no mistaking the movement or the shape of the figures that had just stepped out from the wall.

Terrachnids.

Gideon cursed before telling her, "Climb!"

Calla didn't have to be told twice. She began moving at a relentless pace, clawing her hands into the earth when there wasn't a sufficient object for her to grasp, gritting her teeth at the uncomfortable feeling of dirt and pebbles getting caked beneath her nails. Her biceps were screaming as she continued to heave her way up faster and faster. Sweat began to bead at her temples as she felt the force of the terrachnids crawling up after them, their many spearlike legs plunging into the walls as they scurried up. Dirt crumbled down into her eyes, and she slipped a few feet, hands desperately scrabbling to find purchase until she felt a wave of Gideon's magic envelop her. The pressure of his wind kept her afloat long enough to regain her hold.

"You're okay," he assured her, his voice strained with effort but firm. "Just keep going."

Calla took a deep breath and continued, and when she could finally make out the opening above them, when there was enough light from the forest to drown out the red beam still emanating from Gideon's arm, she almost sobbed. Caspian's face suddenly appeared overhead, and he reached down to help her up when she was close enough. She clasped his hand, and he dragged her all the way out before leaning back in for Gideon.

Calla crawled a few feet away from the pit before pushing herself to her feet, arms shaking a bit from the exertion of using muscles she rarely exercised.

"What the Hells is happening with your numbers?" Cass asked just as the light coming from Gideon's arm blinked out.

"No time." The prince waved off his friend's concern. "We need to move—we've got company."

Cass opened his mouth to question Gideon further, but it was too late. Three terrachnids crawled out of the abyss.

36

Delphine felt the moment Reniel entered the dungeon. The water dropped ten degrees, and she braced herself for what was about to happen. Who she was about to become.

When Reniel stepped into view, she was already waiting for him, leaning her shoulders back against the wall, picking at her nails.

"What's this I hear about a request to see me?" he questioned, a sardonic smile playing at the corners of his lips. "A few days with your old pals and you've already decided getting your throat ripped out was more appealing than talking to them?"

Delphine fixed a sultry smile on her face as she pushed off the wall and strutted forward, leaning a hip against the bars. Slipping back into the girl she used to be wasn't necessarily easy, was a little too suffocating, honestly, but it was familiar. She purred, "You mean that wasn't just your version of foreplay?"

Anyone who hadn't studied the siren in front of her for years wouldn't have been able to pick up the trace amount of shock, and thrill, that flitted through his silver eyes. When he bared his sharpened canines at her in a sharklike grin, she knew that, for now at least, she had piqued his interest.

Delphine got straight to the point. "I'm bored. And I've been thinking . . ." She reached between the gaps in the bars and trailed the nail of her index finger down the siren's chest. "Wouldn't we both have more fun if you let me out of here?"

Reniel pressed himself closer to the posts so his face was only inches from hers. "If you think I'm foolish enough to let you seduce me, you've really lost your mind since you've been gone."

It took everything in Delphine not to gag. She simply smiled sweetly and told him, "I'm afraid you've got the wrong idea."

Reniel lifted a brow.

"I *meant*—we both know you well enough to know you lose thrill in things quite easily. Ripping out my throat is only going to entertain you for a couple more days, if you haven't *already* completely lost interest, am I right?"

There was an intrigued glint in the man's eyes, but he didn't bother to answer.

She continued. "I know that my leaving disappointed you."

Now his demeanor shifted, his jaw clenching a bit as he spoke. "Disappointed? Your little stunt almost obliterated my entire reputation. People began to question how firm my hand was. Those who have sworn a Siren's oath to me began to get ideas in their heads they have no business having. *You* are to blame for that."

"You didn't exactly give me a choice." Her smile tightened now. "You refused to promote me from being a gossip collector—"

"Because I had something *better*! But you left before you could even find that out," he spat at her.

"What do you mean?"

"Oh, moonlight." He shook his head. "I know how much you lost during your Claiming."

No, you don't.

"You know that wasn't about you—it was about your conniving mother. And I must say, despite the circumstances that led to you swearing your Siren's oath to me, you've always proven yourself. It's why I was going to finally release you from your oath and promote you to my inner circle. I was going to take you on my trips outside the Siren's Sea so you could finally travel like you always talked about. But then you ran away." His voice tightened as he said those last words.

"Why didn't you just tell me that was your plan?"

"Where's the entertainment in that? The drama you caused on the night you thought you weren't chosen for my inner circle was infinitely more fun, didn't you think?"

"No, I *didn't*," she seethed.

"Clearly," he commented as he pushed himself away from the cell, smoothing down the front of his shirt. "Alas, you made your bed. And now you must lie in it—instead of mine."

Her stomach churned with what she was about to do. "Give me one more chance," she hurried to say. "I know better now. I understand that I should've trusted you more." She swallowed, trying to clear away the acidic taste of the lies. "After what happened with my mother, I'm sure you can understand why trust was never easy for me. Allow me to repent."

Reniel paused, tilting his head at the desperation in her tone. "Why should I do that?"

This was it, where she needed to twist the knife.

"You said I made you look bad to everyone in your circle, but I cannot imagine you ever told anyone that I ran away from *you*." She watched as he shifted on his feet ever so slightly and smiled. "That's what I thought. So, what story did you tell them, then?"

"You and Zephyr had a sordid affair that ended badly when he refused to choose you over me. So you left."

Delphine's mask almost slipped at his admission. Instead, she snorted. "I'm sure Zephyr loved toting that narrative around. But how about I do you one better?"

"I'm listening, moonlight." He smiled languidly.

"Tell everyone I've returned for *you*. Say I couldn't make it on my own out there, that I was desperate to get back to you. That I was a fool. Tell them all that Zephyr drove away your shining star, but I'm so loyal I came back. Use me as an example that there's no better out there for them."

Lies, lies, lies, but she could tell the wheels were turning in Reniel's head as a spark of excitement crossed his face. This was what she had been betting on—with unrest growing in the Shoal, he needed something to reel them back in, and she was handing him the perfect story on a silver platter. Not to mention, those who were trying to get out of the next Claiming ceremony would surely return to get a glimpse of the only girl who had ever managed to escape from Reniel's clutches.

"Why don't we go somewhere more comfortable to finish this conversation, hmm?" Reniel fished a key out of his pocket as he spoke, inserting it in the lock of her cell's door with a metallic *clang.* "This doesn't mean I won't be sending you right back here if you take even one step out of line. It just means you have my attention—for now." He swung the cell door open with a creak and bent down until their gazes were level. "If you try to run again, the pain of the last few days will pale in comparison to the wrath I will bring down upon you."

Delphine's stare didn't falter as she dipped her chin in a nod, though a shot of adrenaline did rush through her body. Time and time again, Reniel had proven that his ego would be his death blow one day. And as Delphine followed Reniel out of the prison, she prayed that she would get to be the one to land it.

37

Delphine pretended to take a sip from the crystal goblet Reniel had placed on the table in front of her. Though getting inebriated took a lot more than a glass of wine for an immortal, she still wasn't going to risk it. Not when she was playing chess and one wrong move could mean game over.

She and Reniel were sitting across from each other in the living area of his grand suite, a place he had never invited her into before. It was her first sign that he was trying to gain the upper hand, putting her in a space he knew intimately and she was totally unfamiliar with. As expected, the suite was decorated in lavish furniture and textiles, all magically spelled to sustain being underwater like the rest of the goods sirens imported into their submerged kingdoms. Delphine wondered what continents some of the unfamiliar materials had come from, if Reniel had them custom-made or pilfered them from some poor merchant or family.

"Tell me, now that you have managed to finagle your way out of your prison, what is it you want from me, moonlight?"

She forced herself not to grind her teeth at the nickname. "I want to start over. I'm a much different person than I was when I left."

"Start over," he repeated, tasting the words as he smiled behind his glass. "And why do you think you should get to start over? I've killed people for even attempting to run away. You abandoned me for almost a decade."

Delphine couldn't help her sudden intake of breath. She had known the time would be much greater here. The depths of the Siren's Sea were outside the influence of the Neverending Forest's magic and glamour, which meant time moved differently between the two. But having it stated aloud was still shocking. Reniel set his glass down at her reaction, a bit more malice in his eyes than a moment ago. As he leaned forward, the ornate Obsidian Key that he always kept around his neck swung out from beneath the collar of his shirt. Delphine's eyes couldn't help but follow the movement, the rare sight of the key making her heart almost stop. The literal key to her freedom.

"Alarming to hear, isn't it?" Reniel's words snapped her attention back to his face. "A decade. Such an insignificant amount of time to us, and yet I could tell you exactly how many seconds you were gone."

Delphine forced a laugh. "I'm sure you had plenty of shiny new things to occupy your time with."

"None as lively as you," he told her, but something about his tone made it sound like a threat.

This time she did take a sip from her glass.

"Would you like to dance?" he asked, holding out a hand to her.

She stared at it for a beat before setting down her wine and placing her slender hand in his. He pulled her from her chair and swept her into his arms, spinning her around in a slow waltz in the middle of the room, though there was no music playing. She used to love to dance at the parties he would throw, and he clearly remembered. It was the only time she got a bit of reprieve from the monotonous routine those in his Shoal experienced.

Once Reniel Claimed a siren and their magic fully settled in, there were a few roles he could assign them to. The most common was being a runner in his bartering empire, transporting goods all over Illustros, and even some of the other continents, in order to earn your stay at the enormous crystal palace. It was the lowest-ranking role you could have in the Shoal—unless you were one of the sirens who were marked by a Siren's oath. Those with Siren's oaths staffed the manor, working in the kitchens and as waitstaff for parties until Reniel decided they had paid him back for whatever betrayal they'd committed, and he released them from their magic hold. Which could take decades.

Other roles in the Shoal included Reniel's guards and advisory board members and, finally, the elites. Not quite part of his inner circle of confidants but certainly the best positioned to be promoted out of everyone else, the elites were not meant to work like the other roles. They were made to be glittering fixtures at all Reniel's social events as well as play nice with other high-ranking, politically involved Shoals in the Siren's Sea. Constant sources of intel and harbingers of salacious gossip, the elites kept Reniel in the loop of other social circles as well as enticed sirens to join Reniel's ranks of brainwashed Shoal members. They were selling the fantasy of being in Reniel's Shoal even if they knew behind the scenes it was often a nightmare.

Delphine had been one of the best elites Reniel ever had—until she woke up.

Reniel spun her in a circle, bringing her back to the present. He was barely two inches taller than her, and she could feel his gaze burning into her as she looked everywhere but his face. There was a large silver mirror that lined the left wall of the suite, and he turned his head to catch her stare in the reflection. His five o'clock shadow scratched against her face as he pressed himself closer, and she resisted the urge to rip herself out of his embrace.

"We could have been so powerful, you know."

She froze. *Could have been.* She tried to lean back, but his arms tightened painfully, not letting her budge.

"You say you want to start over," he muttered.

Her chest heaved as she gulped a deep breath.

He placed his lips right at her ear. "But I don't think I believe you."

She set both her hands flat against his chest and shoved him away.

"Of course you don't believe me. I didn't expect you to. I didn't even expect you to actually let me out of that dungeon."

He watched her carefully, curiously. She was a decent actress; they both knew that. Tonight would prove if she was a great one.

"I didn't leave just because I didn't move up in the ranks," she explained. "I left because of all of *them*. If you had paid more attention—"

"I paid *plenty* of attention," he countered.

She laughed darkly. "When? You were gone for weeks at a time gathering things for your *collection* while I was here, miserable. Party after party, surrounded by hundreds of faces that all blurred together, day in and day out. And then when you didn't give me that spot in your inner circle . . . it was like all I had done to repay you for my *one* indiscretion would never be enough."

"Your one indiscretion was seeing that traitor after I explicitly banned you—"

"She's my *mother*," Delphine snapped. "You already got her kicked out of her own Shoal; she had nowhere to live! What was I supposed to do?"

"It was the least she deserved after her schemes against me. And I was more than lenient with you for disobeying my direct orders—"

"*Lenient?* You made me swear an oath that magically bound my magic to yours." She looked at him in disbelief.

"Considering you got to keep your magic because I Claimed you in the first place, it doesn't seem all that unreasonable of a punishment."

There it was. The reason Reniel believed he owned everyone. He had long corrupted his place as a Shoal leader. There was a time, once, in which Claiming ceremonies were performed on the sixteenth birthday of every siren, when the ability to Claim their people was graciously passed down in turn without hesitation. Back then, it was only a benefit—a way of choosing your own family for life and not having to default to the one you were involuntarily born into.

There were still siren empires in other parts of the world that practiced the old traditions, and Delphine asked the Gods every day why she hadn't been born there instead. In the Siren's Sea, under the anarchist rule of the Sea King, the sacred ability to perform Claiming ceremonies had become amoral. Claimings were now a way to extort the young into signing their lives away so the Shoal leaders could keep their power, forcing the sirens in their society to become pawns in the political agenda of those at the top.

Delphine didn't know of a single Shoal leader who hadn't become a monster over the last few centuries, giving in to the game before they were left out of it. Since the ability to Claim new sirens and lock in their magic had to be passed down *willingly* by those who already possessed it, the rest of them could do nothing more than watch a once-great kingdom crumble before their eyes.

"I was only ten when I joined your Shoal. And only *thirteen* when you made me swear that oath," she told him. "A *child*."

"You had been around for three years. Do not pretend you didn't understand the ramifications of your decisions. Your mother raised you to understand what you were getting yourself into here."

Delphine ached to lash out at him. To tell him how much she hated him for manipulating her into the role she had played the six years she was under his thumb. Too young to understand the political games were more than just laughing at the jokes of adults she didn't understand and batting her eyes to get people to give up their secrets. She knew unequivocally those games had led to the deaths of other sirens. While she danced at parties, those whose secrets she had coaxed from their wine-stained lips were tortured in the dungeons below her feet and used as stepping-stones for Reniel to climb to the top of his dictatorship.

What she hated most was that, back then, Reniel had always been a reprieve from the others when he wasn't traveling—his attention had made her feel special, his disappointment had made her feel devastated. In the last two years before she ran away, however, the weight of his gaze had become unbearable. Celeste had been Delphine's most consistent safety net at that point, after the other girl had screwed up an important bit of intel and ended up swearing an oath to Reniel as well. The two of them had been relegated to sharing a room, isolated from the other elites as a punishment, but gaining the best gift Reniel had ever granted either of them.

But in her last few months, not even Celeste had felt safe for Delphine. This place was safe.

Reniel stopped their movements, grabbing her chin and tilting her face up to his. "What are you thinking of so deeply?"

"I didn't think you'd be counting every second I was gone," she finally answered, hoping the thickness in her voice could be played off as regret.

It was a long minute before he moved again. Dropping her face, he walked over to the dresser on the far wall and yanked open one of its drawers. She could hear the objects inside clinking against each other before he found what he was looking for. He plucked out two pieces. The first was something too small to make out from a distance. The second she could clearly see was a necklace.

Her *mother's* necklace.

Delphine's hands curled into fists at her sides to keep from shaking as he brought the delicate strands of pearls closer. It had been the only thing she truly regretted leaving behind, and the fact that he had it meant he had gone through her things intimately after she was gone. Not that such a realization was shocking.

Reniel stopped in front of her and gestured for her to turn and face the mirror fully, bringing the necklace to the front of her throat and clasping it at the nape of her neck. It settled against her skin like it had finally returned home.

Delphine's expression remained even.

"The night of your Claiming you did the unexpected. You surprised me. And I'm glad, because it would have truly been such a waste for you to be collateral damage in your mother's desperate attempts at climbing to the top."

"What happened to me wasn't all her fault," she bit out.

It was yours.

"She knew exactly the game she was playing, and the risks involved. She didn't care. And when she broke the rules and came to you for help after she was banished, *you* were the one who swore your life away as a consequence. And how did she repay you?"

Delphine shivered as he brushed aside the strands of her hair on the back of her neck to touch the Siren's oath tattoo etched into the skin there. The one that allowed him access to her magic for the amount of time she swore to him while in the sea—or until he voluntarily broke it. Even when you were immortal, three centuries did not pass by quickly, and she had never had any faith that he'd dissolve it earlier.

"I would think her betrayal would make this next part relatively easy for you, so consider this me playing nice," Reniel murmured.

Delphine braced herself for whatever came next. Reniel didn't play nice. He wasn't kind or sweet or gentle. She had spent the last four wonderful years being loved and surrounded by friends who would never hurt her. She had grown new skin over these old scars. It was hard for her not to think that maybe those four years with Hannah and Calla were the only peace the Gods would ever grant her.

As Reniel spoke again, she wondered if they had been worth it.

"Destroy it."

Delphine closed her eyes. The necklace had been passed down to the women in her family for centuries, her mother had always told her. Each time one of them joined their own Shoal. The night of the Claiming was the first time Delphine had ever been allowed to wear it after a decade of admiring it in her mother's jewelry box. When Delphine ran, she hadn't been able to go back for it, had thought it lost to her forever, but knew that at the very least it still existed somewhere in these depths.

She held her breath as she reached up to her neck and tugged at the delicate strands until they snapped, sending a few of the pearls bouncing noisily across the floor. She dropped the necklace to the ground and began crushing it beneath her heel, trying not to flinch at the sound of them breaking, her heart shattering with them. When the last pearl was nothing but dust, Reniel smiled, satisfied.

"Now give me your hand."

Alarm sounded through Delphine's head. "Why—"

That's when he showed her the other piece he was holding. A black steel band with a single sapphire gem embedded in its center. Her heart began to thunder in her.

A tracking ring.

"Put this on"—he watched her like a viper who had a bird caught in its stare—"and I won't make you return to your cell. You can stay in my home for the next three centuries, and when your Siren's oath is paid off, you can have the spot in my inner circle I always intended for you."

The acrid taste of blood filled her mouth as she bit her tongue. No, she couldn't.

"Your other option is to rot in that cell for the next three centuries," he said. "Pick your poison, moonlight."

She began to think about what her mother would tell her to do in this situation before shaking off that train of thought. Her mother would tell her to cut off all the pieces of herself she valued most and sell them if it meant pleasing Reniel. Instead, she wondered what someone who cared about *her* well-being would tell her to do. Someone who would take the same advice that they gave.

Calliope Rosewood was the single most determined person she'd ever met in her life. She couldn't remember a time when Calla refused to do something if it meant they could get what they needed and stay safe. It's why Delphine had followed the witch into this forest in the first place—she wanted to do something for Calla for once.

Ironically, trying to help change Calla's destiny was what led Delphine to this fateful moment, but Calla could hardly be blamed for Delphine never finishing what she'd started here so long ago. Eros had been right when he said she would never truly be free as long as her Siren's oath was intact. Perhaps it was always inevitable that Delphine would end up at this crossroads, and at least now there were people who cared enough to follow her into the darkness. Celeste had never bothered to go after her—but Calla and Hannah would.

High risk, high reward, her friend's voice echoed in her mind. Delphine was either getting out of here once and for all or she was burning the entire place down, herself with it.

"Tick-tock," Reniel said, cutting through her thoughts, face growing impatient.

"Put it on," she gritted out, chin held high as she thrust her hand out toward the man.

The man looked all too pleased to oblige. He hurried to slide the cursed band onto her left ring finger, her stomach roiling as she felt the dark magic infiltrate her body and settle into her core. The ring sized itself to her finger until it was so snug, she worried it would cut off her circulation.

"You've always been so good at surprising me." He dropped her hand. "I'll have someone bring up some things for you. Make yourself at home, moonlight—you won't be going anywhere anytime soon."

When Reniel was gone, Delphine slowly walked across the suite to the open door of the large bathing room, the weight of the ring on her hand too great to move any faster. As she stepped inside, the jellyfish orbs that sat in the sconces on either side of the giant vanity mirror began to glow, illuminating the room in a soft green. She stared at the ragged-looking girl in front of her.

"If you're not pretty," she whispered to her reflection, "you are nothing."

Delphine reached for the steel straight razor that sat atop the counter before her, its mother-of-pearl handle glittering in the neon light. She fingered the strands of her silvery hair for a second, measuring how much she wanted to get rid of. Then she began chopping.

She dug around in Reniel's cabinets and drawers, knowing good and well the man kept an array of concoctions for his hair and skin.

Delphine lathered different potions onto her scalp and face to soak in while she fixed up her nails. After she finished in the bathroom, she searched his room for any clothes that might fit her, finding an entire chest in his wardrobe filled with sparkly dresses and silky garments. By the time she crawled onto the large chaise in the sitting area and curled up to sleep, she felt like there wasn't an ounce of energy left in her body.

As she drifted further and further into unconsciousness, a scene lingered in her mind. An image of her sitting between two girls on a dingy couch, both of them wrapping their arms around her to keep warm. And for just a moment she felt like she was home. Then she slipped away into the dark.

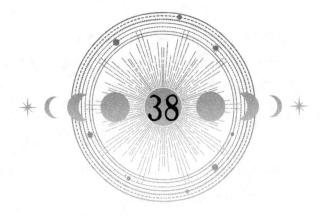

38

Sabine adored a good party.

The Reverie was a grand affair and one of the few attractions she had never been able to weasel her way into. Mostly because during the Reverie, the queen's palace was enchanted not to let anyone through the door who didn't have one of the magic invitations. Now, as she walked up the golden marble staircase that led to the grand entrance, the satin hem of her black jumpsuit a smidge too long and shuffling against the ground, she felt an intense wave of satisfaction when the magic barrier let her through rather than zapping her as it had in the past.

The last several days with Lyra and Amina had been spent going over their plans for tonight in the kind of excruciating detail that gave Sabine a migraine. She was built more for execution than strategizing. Lyra and Amina, however, had pored over stolen blueprints of the palace in order to commit the layout to their memories.

Sabine searched for Amina inside the ballroom. It didn't take very long to spot her friend's stunning silhouette leaning against one of the marble pillars that stretched all the way to the impossibly high, gold-painted ceilings. The ballroom was decorated with intricate tapestries that depicted different parts of the Valkyries' history and were the only bit of color in the room that broke up the white marble and gold details the Valkyrie queen tended to favor. Which was exactly why almost every building in Valor looked exactly the same. Opulent and boring.

A little blood would be such a great addition to the decor, she thought to herself.

Someone on Sabine's right jostled her, trying to pass through the thickening crowd.

"I'm so sorry," a server with a mask in the shape of a fox said as he steadied the tray of drinks precariously balanced in one of his hands before fixing his face covering back into its proper place.

Sabine adjusted her own mask—an expensive piece made of feathers that Lyra had let her borrow—as she grabbed a flute of ambrosia off the platter.

"No worries," she told him as she drained the entire flute in one gulp, returning the empty glassware back to the tray and then strutting off in Amina's direction. Lyra was nowhere to be seen, as planned.

"You should be careful with the ambrosia," a feminine voice warned to her left. "It's potent."

Meli. Fantastic. Sabine *would* run into the one person who not only could recognize her but had a penchant for not knowing when to shut up about things Sabine would rather be kept quiet.

"And yet, it's still not strong enough to make me block out the grating sound of your voice," Sabine quipped back as she turned to meet Meli's wine-colored eyes.

"Oh, Sabine, your mouth is as sharp as ever, I see." Meli propped a gloved hand on her hip.

"Not as sharp as my daggers," Sabine retorted.

"How in the Gods' names did you get in here? These parties are really starting to go downhill." Meli clicked her tongue in disappointment.

"If I were you, I'd worry less about other people's business and more about your own sordid affairs." Sabine flipped her blond hair in the girl's face and moved to step past her.

Meli quickly blocked Sabine's way, narrowing her eyes. "What in the Hells are you implying?"

"Oh, nothing." Sabine tilted her head innocently. "I just think maybe your hands are too full juggling *witches* these days to be sticking them in places they don't belong."

Meli stepped forward until her chest was flush with Sabine's, lowering her voice so only the two of them could hear as she spoke. "I'm growing tired of your bitterness, Sabine. *You're* the one who broke up with *me*, remember? And you took Amina and Lyra away from me, too. What have I ever done to you that was so bad?"

Sabine's hands itched to push the other girl away, but she didn't move. This was a conversation she did not have time to have tonight. Or ever, if it were up to her.

Sabine had broken up with Meli just before her True Name ceremony, and everyone had always just assumed it was because she needed time by herself after her transition. While that reason wasn't necessarily incorrect, it also wasn't exactly why she had made the decision to part ways with the other girl.

That reason was something she'd take to her grave.

"All I wanted was to support you, be there for the most important day of your life," Meli continued. "And you shut me out."

Sabine tried not to conjure the image of Meli's face the day before they were supposed to set off for the Isle of the Veritas Tree. Sabine knew she had been too ruthless that day, but she hadn't had a choice. Not unless she wanted to risk Meli still following her, considering the girl was possibly more stubborn than even herself.

She knew she had done the right thing, though. The True Name ceremony was the sort of thing only the people who mattered most to you should be at. People you intended to be in your life forever, considering they would bear witness to one of the most sacred, magical events any being could ever go through. Unfortunately, at the end, Meli was just not someone Sabine trusted with such a valuable part of herself.

"Let it go, Meli," Sabine finally said dryly, her party mood officially soured by the unexpected run-in. "You seem to have much more exciting options these days anyway."

"Of course Lyra would spill everything to you." Meli scowled, though Sabine could see the hurt in her eyes. "You took everything away from me that day."

"I didn't take Lyra or Amina away from you, Meli." Sabine shook her head as she stepped back and began to move along. "They were never *yours* to begin with."

With that, Sabine wove her way into the crowd, peeking back only once to see Meli pilfering two glasses of ambrosia from one of the other servers and tipping her head back to swallow each of them in seconds. That wasn't going to end well.

"Not my problem," Sabine muttered to herself, though she did find herself feeling a *bit* guilty for the interaction.

"What's not your problem?" Amina asked as Sabine finally reached her.

"Meli," Sabine explained.

Amina looked over Sabine's shoulder to where Meli was now swallowing a third glass of the ambrosia.

"I'm assuming the reason she's currently trying to drown herself, is you?"

Sabine tapped the tip of her nose in a gesture that made it clear Amina's guess was spot on.

"Well, luckily, we have bigger problems to worry about tonight," Amina told her. "Lyra insisted they could be in place after the toast. Which I tried to tell them was . . . never mind. We have fifteen minutes, max, once the distraction begins."

"Does that mean we actually have to listen to the toast? *Blah*." Sabine scrunched her nose at the thought.

"Focus. We have to keep ourselves sharp. There shouldn't be any time for you to grow bored. We all know how that ends." Amina muttered the last bit under her breath.

Sabine grinned, but before she could respond, the echo of clinking glass filled the room. Things were about to get fun.

Amina wasn't particularly fond of parties.

Thankfully, this one was masked, which came in handy as the queen entered the room. Without the phoenix mask—a glittering, ruby-encrusted masterpiece, loaned to her by Lyra—and the feathers woven into the curls that had been fixed into an elegant crest atop her head, Amina would have surely been recognized by Her Highness the moment she stepped into the room. The queen was led through the crowd to the center of the ballroom by her royal guards, making everyone take a large step back and clearing a space large enough for her ball gown. Amina almost cackled at the theme of the queen's Reverie ensemble this year—a dragon.

Fate had such a sense of humor sometimes.

The queen's mask was molded into the shape of one of the reptilian beast's heads. The intricate piece covered the top half of the woman's face and was integrated into her fawn-colored hair, which was braided and adorned with jeweled scales as if it were the dragon's tail. The gown was equally breathtaking. The bodice was shaped like fire and gave way to layers and layers of ruby-encrusted silk that made it look like the flames were engulfing the queen's entire body. Amina wished she wasn't impressed, but she was. Whoever made this had really outdone themselves this year. Before tonight, each year Amina would have to see the queen's Reverie dress as everyone else who wasn't usually invited did—on display in the middle of Valor's royal district the day after.

"There is no way the Fates are being this kind," Sabine said, a terrifying grin stretching across her face, making Amina's own lips turn up.

"I'm not usually a fan of irony, but a person can change," Amina agreed.

A horn sounded overhead, and everyone in the room became still. This was the part of the evening in which the queen announced the number of souls still needed for the tithe and then invited everyone to drink themselves unconscious to forget about the burden the remaining soul count put on everyone's shoulders.

"Welcome, honored guests," the queen said, her painted red lips curling up in a smile that was less than genuine. "Tonight's Reverie marks a very special milestone for our people. This past year was one of the most fruitful in the last century. Over eight thousand souls were reaped for the Gods."

The temperature in the room plummeted at this news, people

shifting on their feet as they were faced with the uncomfortable fact that so many souls were now gone—and the blood was on *their* hands.

"This year will be a pivotal year for our tithe," the queen continued. "There are only five hundred thousand souls left—we've made it halfway."

Only, Amina almost scoffed. Half a million souls would be reaped—some needlessly, some naturally, all tragically—for the Valkyrie tithe, and this poisonous woman thought it was a positive milestone. The fear the Valkyries inspired in the beings of Illustros was justified, as far as Amina was concerned. As harbingers of souls, it was always going to be the hand they were dealt, but the tithe made it so much worse. Without the tithe perhaps the distrust other beings had for them wouldn't be so potent. Perhaps it would be more of a comfort, knowing that your soul was being properly carried to the afterlife only when it was time.

"It is crucial now, more than ever, to keep our goal in mind. We must be unified in our purpose. We must not stray from our path."

Everyone waited with bated breath as the queen snapped her fingers and a server skittered over to place a crystal goblet of ambrosia in her hand.

"To that, we drink! Let the Reverie begin!" Her voice echoed over the room, and a ripple of voices murmuring toasts followed as people tipped their own glasses back and drained them.

The room began to thaw slowly as the queen made her way to the far back, where her throne of gilded feathers had been brought in so she could leisurely watch the debauchery of the Reverie unfold from her pedestal. A symphony of strings began to play, and people started to pull their partners onto the dance floor. Acrobats atop platforms lining the east and west walls of the room were now flipping and twisting in the air, and several enchanted performers with flying metal hoops appeared to float above the crowd.

"Lyra should be ready any minute now," Amina said in Sabine's ear. "Watch for—"

"May I have this dance?" a smooth, deep voice asked from her right.

Amina twisted to find a man dressed in an impeccable crimson suit that almost matched her own gown. His face was covered with an obsidian mask that was molded perfectly to his features, but unfortunately for him, no mask would ever be able to hide his impossibly blue eyes or his silver-tipped hair.

"I'll dance with you," Sabine proposed, a wicked glint in her pastel gaze.

The Wayfarer didn't deign to acknowledge Sabine, deciding to keep his well-earned grudge against his almost-assassin intact as he lifted a hand in offer to Amina. Amina didn't hesitate to accept. Partly because she was worried if Sabine and he were in each other's presence for too long, things could easily get out of hand, and partly because if the Wayfarer was here and asking for a moment with her, then he had something important to say.

He spun her out onto the dance floor, stepping her into an elegant waltz, his form impressive. For someone as tall and muscular as he was, she hadn't expected him to be so lithe.

"I'm here to thank your friend for the Transvectio Talisman. It was worth much more than a few invites to a party," he told her, his voice too low for any of the others swirling around them to here.

"I'll be sure to give them the message," Amina told him.

"No need." The Wayfarer shook his head. "I've already taken care of that myself. Which is how I know what the three of you have planned tonight."

Amina tensed in his arms, and he huffed a laugh, his lips curling in amusement.

"Relax," he murmured. "I'm here to help, as an extra thank-you for such a priceless artifact. I figured assisting with a distraction was the least I could do."

A kernel of irritation unfurled in Amina's stomach. Lyra had been scheming without her. After all the drama of telling Amina that she needed to be honest . . . No. This was not the time to become irritated with them. She would deal with that later.

"As long as that distraction doesn't consist of you and Sabine sword fighting in the middle of the dance floor." Amina returned her attention to their conversation, her tone somewhat serious.

"If only that were an option." He sighed.

Something about the playful look in his eyes and the natural sensualness of his voice made Amina wish that she could revel in this moment. She wished she could pretend that she was at this ball not to perform a risky heist but to meet a handsome suitor who would dance with her all night before whisking her away to a moonlit garden or dark corner to kiss her until she forgot her own name. There had, unfortunately, been no one of interest for her to kiss in the forest. Except . . .

"What's your plan, then?" Amina pressed, shaking off the direction of her thoughts.

"You'll know it when it happens," he told her, finally bringing them both to a halt. "I can't guarantee more than twenty minutes, so you three will need to get in and get out. I already told your friend this, but just for good measure: Make sure you burn your invitations when you get home. Don't leave any trace that you were ever here tonight or we'll all be in deep trouble. You more than me, for obvious reasons."

"You're leaving already?"

He dipped his chin in a nod of confirmation before untangling himself from her and bringing her hand up to his lips. "In case this is the last time we get to meet—good luck, Valkyrie."

With that parting line, he dropped her hand and turned away, leaving her to watch him disappear into the crowd before gathering her skirts and making her way back to where Sabine had been raptly watching them from the sidelines.

"It's a shame he's so damn pretty," Sabine said matter-of-factly as Amina approached, "and yet hates me so much. What a wasted opportunity—a travesty really."

"I think the real travesty would be getting used to someone like that only for them to have to leave over and over again."

"I don't know, that arrangement doesn't sound too horrible to me." Sabine snorted and then waved a hand in front of her. "Well? Anything interesting come up?"

"Brace yourself," Amina told the girl, and just as the words left her lips an explosion sounded from across the room.

39

The thing about terrachnids was that they were even harder to bring down than viperidae—a lesson Calla and the others were learning very quickly. Made of earth and rocks, the spiderlike creatures had the unusual ability to merge together to form one giant eight-legged beast that none of the witches' magic or swords seemed to be able to penetrate.

"Can you feel any of its magic at all when you touch it? Anything you can use?" Gideon asked her now as he smeared a line of blood across his forehead from an already healed cut she had accidentally gotten after getting a little too close to one of the earth-spider's arms.

"Nothing." Calla shook her head. "It doesn't have blood, and its magic feels almost *heavy*. It would take too long for me to siphon."

The prince cursed. "The only thing we can do is run. It should be too bulky to get through the trees fast enough—"

The ground rumbled beneath their feet and the trees began to move, cutting off Gideon's words as the two of them gaped in disbelief. The trees were sinking into the ground. The forest was clearing the area so the four of them couldn't use the oaks as a shield.

"I *hate* this place!" Caspian shouted in frustration on the other side of the boulder creature.

"What are we going to do?" Hannah spoke in turn. "Nothing is working against it!"

"*Damn you.*" Calla looked to the sky angrily.

The terrachnids' giant front leg speared down overhead a second later, and Gideon and Calla both jumped out of the way, splitting in opposite directions. When the rocky appendage hit the ground, it sent a tremor through the earth, and Calla saw Hannah lose her balance out of the corner of her eye. She ran over to help her friend up before the spider slammed down another leg. That's when she caught something glittering out of the corner of her eye.

It was the ring the nymph had given them on Caspian's index finger.

"The ring!" she yelled. "The favor! Use it, Cass!"

Caspian looked down at his hand as her words clicked. He wiggled the small band off and dropped it to the ground before stomping on it with the heel of his boot and crushing the small stone. A pink-and-green wisp of smoke unfurled from the broken gem, and Calla watched rapturously as it zipped out into the forest like an arrow.

Hannah yelled, "Hey! A little help here?"

All of them twisted just in time to see Hannah dodging another stab of the terrachnid's leg.

"I'll help Han with a distraction," Cass threw over his shoulder as he took off.

"Did the ring even work?" Calla questioned.

And that's when she heard the high-pitched voice.

"There's a joke about being between a rock and a hard place in here somewhere." Darci snorted as she and Gabi appeared before them. Gone were the nymphs' usual giggling demeanors now that the pretenses between all of them were gone.

Gideon stepped forward. "We need—"

"Save your request," Darci said, cutting him off. "We brought you something we think will settle the debt between us."

With that, the nymph tossed something at the prince. Gideon plucked the object right out of the air, and when he looked down at what it was, he almost stopped breathing.

It was a gilded dagger with a large heart-shaped ruby nestled in the center of its hilt.

Heart Reaver.

))) ● (((

The world around Gideon was silent and colorless as he stared down at the dagger in his hands. He couldn't believe the nymphs had actually found it. Someone said something, his name maybe, but the sound was muffled to his ears. He didn't know how long he stood like that until he felt a pressure wrap around his wrist, and everything instantly blared back to life.

"Gideon," Calliope repeated, her voice much clearer as she gave him another small squeeze, waiting for him to meet her mismatched gaze. The violet and gold colors of her irises were so vibrant he almost flinched. "Cass and Hannah are getting tired. We need to help them."

Gideon's mouth was dry as he looked around, finding that the nymphs were already gone. He told Calliope, "I can't."

"Gideon," she said seriously, moving to fold her hands over his around the dagger. "He'd want it to be yours—for you to use it. We *have* to use it. Nothing else is working."

Gideon looked back at her evenly. "Do you know how Heart Reaver works?"

"We don't have time for a lesson!"

Gideon unwrapped their hands from the dagger and flipped the blade in his hands until the hilt was reaching toward Calliope. She didn't take it.

"I don't understand," she told him.

"When I hold the dagger, the heartstone doesn't light up. With Ezra gone"—Gideon winced a bit, still not quite ready to accept those words—"the dagger chooses its new wielder. And it has not chosen me. I can wield it, but its magic will not work for me."

"You mean . . ." She looked down at it in astonishment as her words trailed off.

"Take it."

Calliope hesitated for another second before taking a deep breath and reaching out to wrap her hand around the hilt. Gideon watched without surprise as the heartstone instantly began to glow, eliciting a gasp from her lips.

"Why?" she asked, holding the dagger away from her as if it were a venomous snake.

"You know how to collect the hearts of those you meet," Gideon told her. "You and he were similar in that way."

Calliope went to say something when Hannah let out a yelp of pain, bringing them both back to the present. They twisted around to see Hannah rolling her shoulders back a couple times, panting a bit as she and Caspian continued circling the giant rock creature. Calliope adjusted her grip on the handle, a determined look fixing itself on her face.

"Ezra tried teaching me how to throw this once," she said to him as she readied her shot. "When it was just an ordinary knife to me."

"And how did that go?" Gideon murmured as he watched the way her unruly hair blew wildly around her face.

"Horribly," she admitted just as she launched the dagger through the air.

They both watched as the blade speared toward the spiderlike beast, Calliope making a sound of disbelief as it hit its mark. Right through the center of the once-impervious rock.

40

The terrachnid crumbled to the ground piece by piece like an avalanche. The four witches watched in awe as the giant beast once again separated into three individual forms, their rocky limbs curling inward as the life drained out of them. The ground began absorbing the creatures one by one, and a minute later Calla could have sworn nothing had happened there. The only thing left from the ordeal was Heart Reaver, lying on the ground.

"Hannah." Calla ran to her friend, scooping up the dagger and sheathing it in her belt on her way over. "Are you all right?"

Hannah began to nod, but it was Caspian who answered, "Of course not! She almost got flattened by a giant spider boulder!"

Calla winced as she looked at Hannah, ready to apologize, but the blond simply whispered, "It's fine. This isn't about you and me."

Calla was going to ask what Hannah meant, but as she watched Caspian's fists tighten when Gideon approached, she had a feeling she was about to get the answer.

"Cass—"

"No, Gideon." Cass pointed a finger at his friend. "It's my turn to talk first. What in the Hells were you thinking jumping straight into a dark pit in the middle of the *Neverending Fucking Forest* for a *compass*? We *just* went over this! Do you have any idea how absolutely out of your mind you are?"

"And what would we have done without the compass?" Gideon demanded, though his tone did have a hint of apology in it. "I couldn't just lose it."

"And we can't just lose *you*!" Cass shouted, his chest heaving with exertion as his anger boiled over. "How many times will I have to tell you that?! You aren't the only one who lost him, Gideon. And I know maybe that's not fair to say—but how dare you not stop and think for one damn minute what it would be like for the rest of us if we lost you, too?"

Hannah reached out to grab Calla's hand as they watched the exchange. Calla had never seen Caspian so upset.

Gideon swallowed. "I'm not *trying* to be impulsive."

"Yes. You are." Cass laughed without humor. "I have spent more than a decade fighting by your side, Gid. I have watched you calculate the risks of climbing the wrong tree to get a good vantage point. I've watched you mull over the decision on what armor to wear or which weapons to use for an hour. I once watched you go back and forth about how many shirts to pack on a trip for three *days*."

Gideon shoved a hand through his hair in frustration.

Caspian's steel eyes softened a bit. "I don't mean to be an asshole. But when you have people who are risking everything to help you, you don't have the luxury of throwing yourself into danger whenever you want. Getting yourself maimed or killed will only devastate those who love you. And it will hurt *her*."

"Don't." Gideon's eyes flashed bright silver. "Don't bring her into this—"

"I'm not bringing her into anything she isn't already in." Caspian threw his hands up. "*You* brought her into this when you invited her to this forest and didn't tell anyone what you were going to do with the Witch Eater. You two are *soul-bonded*." Caspian swung his gaze to Calla now. "And I'm not going to pretend I understand the stakes of what that means for a second or the toll it's clearly taking on you both, but what I do know," he continued as he refocused his gaze on the Onyx Prince, "is that whatever you do affects her now, too. Think about that the next time you go after a damn compass."

Gideon said nothing.

"I'm going to go with Hannah to find somewhere to clean off the blood." Cass spoke more calmly now, looking to Hannah in question. The blond nodded and squeezed Calla's palm one last time before heading after Cass.

Gideon and Calla stared at each other until the witches were barely more than specks in the distance.

"I'm sorry." She tucked a strand of hair behind her ear.

"For what? He's right." Gideon regarded her intensely. "That could've been much worse. I could've gotten you hurt. Again."

"Caspian is right—we *could* lose anyone at any moment. He's upset because he's grieving just like we are, except we got closure. He deserves to be upset. But I *promise*, I'm fine."

His expression looked pained as she took another step forward.

"I am," she insisted. "In fact . . ."

Another step. He turned wary now.

"What just happened, it made me realize I've been so ungrateful for the fact that I'm even *alive*. So many others . . . Ezra . . . have their time cut short. And I've been here, running away my whole life," she told him. "I'm always holding myself back. I ignored my magic for so long, ignored my Siphon half. I'm tired of refusing to see all the potential I have right in front of me. All the potential *we*—"

"Calliope," he warned before she could finish that last sentence. "Earlier, in the dark, you said that we were playing with fire. If you come any closer . . . I don't know if I can keep pretending that I'm okay with not being near you."

"Maybe that's what it's going to take," she said now.

"What do you mean?" he asked.

The sensation she had felt in the abyss came rushing back to her now, and a shiver went down her spine as she relished it. It was like she had gotten a taste of an addictive poison and would not be satisfied until she had more—even when she knew it was a deadly thing to indulge.

"I want to play with fire," she whispered.

He opened his mouth, but before he could speak, something to their right burst out of the ground. A redwood trunk climbed toward the sky, branches with crimson, gold, and orange leaves unfurling above them. Another trunk shot up to their left, then another, and another, until the clearing was no longer empty, and they were standing in the middle of a forest once again.

She tilted her head back in shock. The sun began to dip lower and lower in the sky, and the way the colors of the leaves bled into each other and swayed in the chilling wind made it look like . . .

"It looks like flames," Gideon commented. "Before, when the pit opened up, I was thinking about how it felt like we've been walking a tightrope and how any day now we risked falling into the unknown and then—"

"A giant abyss opened up and you fell in," she finished, brows lifted. "This forest doesn't just listen, it *responds*."

Gideon gazed around slowly. "I can't believe I never realized it before. Delphine never warned us how astute it is, either."

"Perhaps she never realized," Calla said. "She's never spent much time out of the Siren's Sea—and then she went straight to Estrella."

At the mention of Estrella, the sun fully sank and the stars above them blinked to life. Calla almost couldn't believe it.

"Do you think we could control it, completely, if we tried?" she asked.

A surprised smile slowly curled over Gideon's lips. "How should we try?"

"Well, it happens when we're manifesting something intensely, right?"

"Right," he murmured as he slowly inched forward, giving her plenty of time to back away if she wanted. She didn't. He reached out and placed his fingertips on the side of her throat, searching for her pulse, and the touch seared every nerve in her body.

She felt his fingers trail up her neck, lightly brushing her nape, heat chasing the path over her skin. He plunged that same hand into the thick tendrils of her hair and cupped the back of her head, tilting her face up gently. The tips of their noses were less than a centimeter apart. A fluttering sensation shot directly to her stomach.

Gideon leaned down until his lips were hovering just above hers, his silver eyes half-shut as he brought his other hand up to grip her waist, and another giddy sensation fluttered in her abdomen when a crescendo of noise rustled above them. Gideon tightened his hold slightly to keep her in place as they both looked up.

Thousands and thousands of orange-and-black monarch butterflies burst out of the trees and scattered across the sky.

"I can't believe it," she gasped.

"Me neither." He looked back down to her, moving to untangle his hand from her hair.

Calla took in the swirling color of his eyes, realizing how much she had missed him looking at her with hope. Before she could stop herself, she pressed herself closer to him, letting her lips skim his jawline with a featherlight kiss.

For a beat Gideon was completely frozen. Luckily, she didn't have too much time to rethink what she had done, because an instant later Gideon was cupping the backs of her thighs and lifting her up into his arms. She instinctively wrapped her legs around his waist as his lips crashed down on hers in an electrifying kiss. Every inch of her body lit up with sparks.

This kiss was so different from the first hazy kiss they had shared under the influence of the nymphs. If that first kiss was like a new flame right after you struck a match, then this one felt like the explosion that happened once the fuse burned away.

Gideon bit down on her lip, and she couldn't help the small moan that unleashed itself from her throat. She twisted her hands into his hair, and though she was getting dangerously close to running out of oxygen, she didn't pull away. She tugged on the soft blue strands that her fingers were tangled in and was rewarded with a satisfied groan from his own throat.

He *had* told her he liked a little hair pulling once.

Gideon adjusted his grip beneath her thighs as he deepened their kiss, and an overwhelming sensation of hunger took over her as they pulled each other further and further into the fire. She was insatiable in a way that she had never experienced before. Neither of them came up for air until they heard the first firework soar through the sky.

41

The night around them was glittering with magic, but Gideon was staring only at her.

42

Amina dashed down the dark corridor, Sabine on her heels as they fled the chaos in the ballroom. Amina wasn't quite sure what the Wayfarer had destroyed, but whatever it was did its job. Between his distraction and the three throwing knives Sabine had swiftly, and discreetly, embedded in a few unlucky guests' shoulders, not a single soul had noticed the two girls slip from the room through an exit marked PALACE STAFF ONLY.

"If the blueprints Lyra had were correct, the queen's private study should be in the west wing," Amina told Sabine as they turned a corner to the right—and ground to a halt.

The two of them quickly flattened themselves against the wall, blanketed by the shadows, as a palace guard stepped out of one of the many rooms lining the right side of the hallway. The left side was drowning in milky moonlight shining in from the great expanse of uncovered windows. The guard pulled the door tightly shut behind them before turning in the girls' direction. Amina held her breath until the guard passed and turned the corner to head down the corridor they'd just come from.

"Thank the Gods," Sabine whispered. They cautiously peeled themselves off the wall. "I did not want to have to hide a dead body on top of everything else tonight."

Amina threw a grin over her shoulder as she led the other girl forward once more. When they finally got to the enormous double-door entrance at the end of the hallway, they paused, Sabine keeping a vigilant eye trained behind them just in case there were any more guards. Amina reached out and pushed on the gilded door handle. Locked.

"Of course." Amina sighed. "This better not break my nail."

Amina inserted the long, sharp nail of her right index finger into the keyhole, jiggling it around a bit and twisting until she heard a satisfying *click*.

"Not even a chip," she boasted, and pushed the doors open just enough so they could both squeeze through.

Sabine stopped in her tracks on the other side. "Whoa."

Amina nodded in agreement. The decor of the west wing was no more ornate than any of the other grand rooms in the palace, with one exception—the ceiling was made entirely of glass. The two Valkyries gawked at the stars twinkling above them, and for just a moment, Amina reveled in the sight. She had gone so long without seeing these stars that every time she caught a glimpse of them these days, they stopped her in her tracks.

"Slayers," a voice in the dark whispered.

Amina snapped out of her trance and searched in the shadows for the person that voice belonged to.

"Here!" Lyra directed.

Amina and Sabine rushed over to where Lyra's head was poking out of the sixth door on the left. Lyra stepped back to let both girls in the room before quickly shutting the door and locking it behind them.

"How did you get in here?" Sabine asked before spinning around to assess the small, quaint study. Unlike Amina, Sabine, and most Valkyries, Lyra liked to keep their nails filed down into short points. Not quite as effective for picking locks, though they were excellent for gouging out eyes.

"Window," Lyra answered while they moved to the back of the room toward the dingy old bookshelves behind the large oak executive desk that took up most of the space in the center of the office.

"Uh . . ." Sabine and Amina shared a brief look. "There aren't any windows in here, Ly."

Lyra smiled a bit at that as they ran their hands over the old books on the shelf. "Who said anything about in here?"

Amina and Sabine watched intently as Lyra tilted a book down on one of the shelves and made the entire bookcase swing forward, revealing an opening to another room on the other side. The three of them ducked through, and Amina knew immediately they had found exactly what they were looking for.

Unlike the other study—the decoy—this room was massive. Shelves and shelves of books and scrolls lined every wall. Stacks of loose papers and maps sat atop an intricately carved desk, sticks of wax and an unlit gas lamp next to them.

"Nice," Sabine complimented Lyra, impressed with their work. "But I still don't see a window."

"There's another hidden exit that leads to a tunnel that takes you directly to the queen's private chambers. There's a window in there," Lyra explained. "Which is where we will be escaping from, if anyone was wondering."

"That's quite risky," Amina noted, circling around the desk to begin carefully shuffling through some of the papers there.

"Riskier than the rest of this plan?" Lyra threw her friend a pointed look.

"How about you not warning us that you had cooked something up with the Wayfarer?" Amina countered. "Bold of you to assume we were just going to trust him."

Lyra's lips pressed into a hard line for a second before they reasoned, "Coming up with a distraction on my own was proving difficult, and he had written me to offer his thanks again anyway, so excuse me for enlisting help. You're just upset because you didn't get to control the entire situation as much as you wanted to."

"I cannot believe I'm saying this," Sabine inserted. "But I'm begging you both to save the drama for later."

"Fine. You're right," Amina muttered. She squinted down at one of the documents in her hand. It was some sort of plan for a new building on the outskirts of Valor's market district. Amina rolled her eyes and set the paper back exactly the way she found it. Useless.

Next, she dug through the desk's drawers, trying her best not to move too much around and make it obvious someone had rifled through here.

"If I were a sadistic bitch . . ." Amina began to contemplate aloud.

"If?" Sabine grinned to herself.

"Where would I keep the key to my dead lover?" Amina continued as if Sabine hadn't spoken.

"Do we really think she would let it out of her sight?" Lyra asked. They were currently inspecting a shiny object on one of the shelves. The glittery knickknack immediately snagged Sabine's attention, and the blond flitted over to Lyra with an outstretched hand, silently demanding to see what they had found.

"One of the things I asked the Witch Eater's mirror to show me was Rovin's grave. The queen has him buried in her private garden— in the most intricately locked coffin I've ever seen." Amina tapped her nails against the desk in turn. "When I asked it to show me where the key to his coffin's lock was, it revealed some sort of puzzle box atop what looked to be the surface of a desk exactly like this. It's clearly been moved since."

As they all continued to poke around, Sabine still grasping on to whatever shiny new toy she had found, Amina knew their time was running out. She stepped back from the desk, ready to just start tearing every nook and cranny apart, when the floorboard beneath her shoe creaked.

"Did you—" She looked at Lyra, who was already nodding.

Amina immediately knelt, shoving her skirts out of her way as she pried up the loose plank. Beneath it was a small dial, twelve tick marks circling it.

"It needs some sort of code," Lyra stated. "How in the Hells are we going to find that?"

"What about the date?" Sabine suggested, casually leaning back against one of the shelves.

"*Today's* date?" Amina asked skeptically. "Why would that work?"

"As in the date of the *Reverie*," Sabine explained. "It's the same date every year. Second month, sixteenth day. There has to be some significance there."

"Sixteen couldn't work. There's only twelve marks," Lyra noted.

"Or . . . zero, two, one, six," Amina inferred, clicking the dial to each number in turn.

When the tip of the dial ended on six, a low scraping noise echoed from the right side of the room. One of the stones was now jutting out of the wall.

"Sabine, I could kiss you." Amina grinned at her friend.

"Okay," Sabine said casually.

Amina threw her friend a bemused look as the three of them rushed over to the protruding stone. Amina pulled the large brick all the way out before passing it off to Lyra's waiting hands. When Amina peered inside the hole, her heart began racing as she reached in and fished out a weighty wooden box. Her smile only grew when she felt a small pulse emanate from the contents inside.

"How does it open?" Sabine asked.

Amina turned and walked over to the desk, pushing a few papers out of the way so she could set the box down on the cleared surface. She ran her fingertips along the bottom edge of the left side of the piece until she felt a small indentation and curled her finger into the notch and pulled outward. A small rectangular piece of wood slid out with a *click*, and a moment later the box's lid popped open—just like the mirror had shown her. The others stepped up behind her and leaned over her shoulder, watching raptly as Amina pushed the lid all the way back, revealing the key as well as Rovin's beating heart inside.

43

alla's head was swimming as Gideon began to press a line of kisses to the underside of her jaw. The fireworks were still shooting across the sky above them. The blazing sparks that crackled down from each burst echoed the small explosions of pleasure the prince's kisses were leaving on her skin. He had set her back on her feet—one hand still gripping her waist, the other weaving further into her hair—and she was standing on the very tips of her toes, lightly holding on to the fabric of his shirt for balance.

"Calliope," he murmured against her skin.

She hummed a bit as she tilted her head back to give him better access to the pressure point his mouth was currently pushed against. She couldn't help it—everything was finally in color instead of dull, monotonous gray. She felt grounded, her magic stretching in her bones and swimming in her veins as if it had just been let out after decades of being locked away. The longer Gideon touched her, the stronger she felt, the clearer her mind became. When his mouth captured hers once more, she sank into it completely.

Just as Gideon deepened the kiss, the sound of a branch snapping pulled them apart.

Both of them jerked their gazes to the right—

Just in time to see Caspian and Hannah emerge from the woods.

And they weren't alone.

A group of witches stepped out of the tree line, dressed in black-and-red leather fighting gear, several chestnut stallions in tow. The Rouge Queen's guards.

"Don't tell me," a familiar voice remarked, "that we just missed the show?"

Gideon untangled himself from Calla, lips pulled back in a seething expression as he took in the scene in front of them. Hannah and Cass were gagged, with their hands bound behind their backs, knives pressed between their shoulder blades by two of the guards. And it was strikingly clear who was leading them.

Gideon's fists clenched at his sides. "Kestrel."

44

Amina scooped out the heart into her hand. Its pulsing rhythm nearly matched the one at her hip.

"Did the Queen seriously cut out her lover's heart to keep in her study?" Sabine questioned.

"Are you sure you want to do this?" Lyra asked. "There's no going back once we leave this room."

Amina looked up into Lyra's amber eyes. They exchanged a loaded look, but before Amina could say anything, Sabine pointed to something at the bottom of the box and exclaimed, "Look!"

Amina shifted the heart to her other hand and reached in to grab the key as well as the other contents. Letters, at least ten of them, each with broken wax seals. All the sigils stamped into the wax matched—an intricate crest of four interlocking swords—except for one. The last letter's seal was marked by a mask with a third, open eye in the center of its forehead.

Amina knew exactly who that seal belonged to, had seen it in the corner of the ancient map that spanned an entire wall in the Witch Eater's cottage.

"The Fates," she whispered.

"What?" Sabine asked.

"This is something from the Fates." Amina passed the key and heart into Sabine's hands, who looked a little too thrilled to get her hands on the organ, and pulled out the papers stuffed inside the torn envelope. She scanned the document. Once. Twice. Three times. Her brain refused to compute what she was seeing.

"Amina?" Lyra prompted.

Amina held out the papers for Lyra to take, still unable to say anything. Lyra looked skeptical as they began reading through and Sabine leaned over to get a peek as well.

"What. The. *Hells*," Lyra said.

"It's a contract." Sabine furrowed her brow.

"I knew there was more to the tithe," Amina growled. *"I knew it."*

"We all suspected, but not *this*." Lyra gestured to the contract wildly.

"This changes *everything*," Amina told them after a long minute of heavy silence. Then she snatched the document back and tucked it into the bodice of her dress.

She placed the rest of the letters back into the box and then reached under the folds of her skirts to pull out the bag with the witch prince's heart. She carefully extracted the heart and set it gently atop the letters where the other heart had previously rested. The two hearts were damn near identical. Someone who was better versed in anatomy might note the way the dragon-shifter's heart had a slightly more purple tint to it than the witch's, or how the beats were an eighth of a second off-count. To the mundane eye, such things were hardly noticeable.

"You're switching the hearts?" Lyra raised their brows. "Why?"

"I have a feeling it will end up being a hot commodity to the witches—either to his friends or his mother. Better to not carry around such a liability if we have a replacement, right?" Amina said, then closed the box before handing it off to Lyra to return it to where they'd found it. She shoved Rovin's heart into her pouch and refastened it to her hip.

When the stone in the wall was back in place and the floorboard readjusted, Lyra finally looked to Amina and said, "Stealing that document is a bad idea. She could easily notice."

Amina didn't disagree; she simply said, "We're going to need some sort of proof. Now, how do we get out of here?"

Lyra made their way to one of the bookshelves and pulled on a book like she had in the first room so that another hidden door opened in the same manner. The Valkyrie ducked into the secret tunnel first, followed by Sabine, but before she could get too far, Amina gently grabbed her by the shoulder.

"Hmm?" Sabine twisted around to see Amina holding up an expectant hand.

"Hand it over, Sabine." Amina tapped her foot.

"Hand what over?" Sabine feigned innocence.

Amina glared. "*Sab.*"

"You get to steal an irreplaceable document and an organ, but I can't take *one* tiny souvenir that she probably would never even notice was missing?" Sabine grumbled as she dug in her pocket for the shiny trinket she had taken.

Sabine deposited the small item, a silver rabbit with eyes made of opalescent jewels, into the center of Amina's palm before huffing off after Lyra. Amina hurried to arrange the item back in its place on the shelf and then slipped out of the study after them, pulling the door shut behind her.

))))•(((

When it came to traveling through a secret underground tunnel system in the palace, there was good news and bad news. The good news was that they wouldn't have to worry about running into anyone down here, if the cobwebs were any indication of usage. The bad news was that meant they would all probably be skeletons by the time anyone found them.

Sabine had complained one too many times about how lost they were, and she knew Lyra would rip her throat out if she made another comment, but Sabine couldn't help it. They had been lost for damn near an hour.

"I just don't understand how you found it the first time, but now—"

"Sabine, I swear to the Gods, if you say that *one* more time I will—" Lyra started.

"Wait, hush," Amina ordered, and the two of them went silent.

Sabine strained her ears but didn't hear a sound, not even a rat or bug skittering on the floor, until—*there*. Ahead and to the right was the buzz of a conversation. They crept quietly toward the hum, careful not to let their heels click too loudly on the stone steps.

"We need another crate of wine from the cellar. The red," someone barked.

"Right away," a chorus of voices answered.

"The kitchens," Lyra whispered. "I got it."

Sabine sighed in relief and quickly followed Lyra back up the stairs. They went up two more flights in silence, letting Lyra concentrate as they retraced their steps until, finally, blessedly, they stopped in front of what looked to be the outline of a doorway.

"This should be it," Lyra told them, skimming the wall with their hands until they found a loose stone and pushed.

The door slid open and the three of them piled into the most erotic bedroom Sabine had ever seen. The walls were decorated with red velvet wallpaper; the molding was brushed with gold leaf and had carvings of bones and feathers that bordered the entire room. The bed was laughably big—large enough for eight people to fit comfortably—and the gilded canopy was draped in rich jewel-toned silks. The floor, like the rest of the palace, was white marble, the gold veins running throughout glittering in the light of the enormous crystal chandelier.

"This is even more over-the-top than Lyra's room," Sabine noted.

Lyra elbowed Sabine in the side.

"We need to get out. Now," Amina prompted before the two of them could start giving jabs back and forth.

"The window." Lyra pointed.

"This is where I regret the dress," Amina muttered as Lyra slid the window open and wedged themself out onto the roof, barely squeezing through the tight space. Amina took a deep breath and followed, gathering as much of her billowing skirts as she could to shove out first, but halfway through it was apparent that the Valkyrie was stuck.

Sabine began pushing the fabric, trying to find if it was snagged on something, when she heard a noise coming from the other side of the bedroom door. She cursed. Someone was coming.

"Damn it." Amina pulled at her dress, desperately trying to wiggle her hips out of the tight space.

The doorknob jiggled.

"Fuck it," Sabine said, sliding out a knife from beneath her corset.

Before Amina could protest, Sabine nimbly began slicing away fabric, ripping the seams until she could pull the fabric away and push the girl all the way out. Once Amina was in the clear, Sabine shoved the shredded pieces of the dress into the other Valkyrie's arms and hurried to get herself out.

The doorknob turned.

Sabine dove through the frame with slightly less fuss, and when she made it onto the roof, she slammed the window shut just before the door to the bedchamber burst wide open.

The three of them immediately summoned their wings and launched into the sky. Sabine dared look down only once, when she was sure the lights of the palace as the Reverie roared on could not reach her. The others kept their eyes straight ahead as they flew, and Sabine knew they had not looked back. Knew they had not spotted the figure leaning out of the queen's window to look for who had just escaped.

45

The look on Kestrel's face was the look of a man who knew he had made a bad bet but doubled down anyway because he had nothing more to lose. Calla had seen that exact look on her opponents' faces countless times before when she and Ezra pulled their cons at the inn.

"What the Hells is going on?" Gideon growled at the commander.

"I came back for you," Kestrel told the prince, his gray eyes colder than ice as he took in the way Gideon angled himself toward Calla protectively.

"Came back? Then you *did* desert the group," Gideon told him. "We were worried—"

"Worried enough to come looking for me, I see." Kestrel raised a brow.

"Sorry, we've been a bit preoccupied," Gideon said, fuming.

"So have I," the commander retorted, waving at the Rouge witches.

"What did you do, Kestrel?" the Onyx Prince demanded.

"I've ensured that you, Cass, and Ezra get to come home. Safely. All you must do is hand over the girl."

There was a pregnant pause at the mention of Ezra's name. Cass, Hannah, and Calla collectively darted their gazes to Gideon.

Gideon laughed darkly. "You have *no idea* what you've done."

A flicker of doubt went through Kestrel's eyes at the tension that now hung in the air, but a second later it was gone. "Just let us take her back and we can be done with this, Gideon. We will go home and—"

Calla gave a sharp laugh. "You're a Godsdamned *fool*."

Every head turned in Calla's direction, varying degrees of surprise on all their faces. Even Calla was slightly surprised those words had come out of her mouth soaked with such venom.

Kestrel's lips curled back from his teeth as he said, "Shut your mouth."

Gideon stepped forward, a surge of wind beginning to rustle the trees with the advance, but when Calla held out her hand for him to stop, he did.

"You have no idea what you've done, Kestrel," she said, condemning the commander. "Your jealousy has made you betray your friends, and at what cost? Do you really think Myrea is going to let any of us go—including you?"

"The Rouge Queen made me a bargain." Kestrel scowled.

"She made you a *fool*," Calla repeated. "She would never—"

"Now!" one of the Rouge guards shouted, and Kestrel whipped around to see half the Rouge witches advance on him while the rest headed straight for Calla and Gideon.

Gideon immediately sent a gust of wind into the first two witches, knocking them back several steps as he turned to Calla and yelled, "Untie Cass and Hannah!"

Calla didn't hesitate; she darted straight for Cass. As she ran, she felt the prodding of the Rouge guards' magic trying to seize the blood in her veins, but Calla fought through the sensation, focusing her own magic on making sure she stayed in control of herself rather than fight back. She made it to Cass and ripped through his bonds when her entire body went stiff, and she could barely turn her head to see what was happening.

In the moments it had taken her to reach Caspian's side, Kestrel and Gideon had three guards suffocating on the ground, one with a throwing knife lodged in his left eye, and another missing a hand. If Calla could move any of the muscles in her face, she would look quite impressed. Unfortunately, no matter how well trained the two Onyx witches were, they were no match for fifteen Rouge guards. Calla tried to use her magic to loosen the hold the Rouge witches had on Gideon's blood, but it was no use.

"You're lucky I wouldn't risk the queen's wrath by ending you myself," one of the guards spat in Kestrel's face. "You've been a pain in the ass this entire trip."

Kestrel couldn't move his mouth, but the glint in his eyes told Calla that he'd have some pretty colorful curses for the guard if he could.

"Make the bastards let go!" one of the guards said as they knelt next to the witches still fighting to breathe on the ground.

"Cut it out," the first guard snarled at the two Onyx witches. Calla thought maybe he was the one in charge.

When it was clear that neither Gideon nor Kestrel was going to let go of their hold, the leader unsheathed the cutlass on his hip and sliced it through the prince's side. A muted scream vibrated through Calla's throat, and she felt a rush of blood soak through her shirt before her skin wove itself back together. Gideon didn't even flinch at his own wound, but at the sound of her muffled cry he broke the Rouge witches' hold just long enough to trudge a step in her direction before they doubled their magic on him once more.

Everyone looked between Calla and the prince in confusion, eyes widening in almost perfect sync as they all realized the bloodstain at her side matched Gideon's perfectly.

"What in the Hells?" one of the guards asked at the same time that another questioned, "What kind of freaky magic is that?"

"Test it again," another of the guards suggested.

As the head guard approached Gideon again, Calla could see the way the prince's veins were bulging beneath his skin with effort as he tried to shake the magic hold and move away. She could feel how hard he was fighting as her own magic strained in her core, but it was fruitless.

The guard smiled at Gideon as he lifted his crimson-painted blade and slowly dragged it across the prince's left clavicle, just above the open collar of Gideon's shirt.

Everyone watched in stunned silence as the wound appeared on Calla as well.

"Well, this just got more complicated." The leader narrowed his eyes at Calla before turning to bark orders at the others. "All right, load them all up. Her Highness is going to want an audience with each of them. And make sure to separate those two." The guard gestured between Calla and Gideon. "Where's the second prince?"

"Gone," Gideon said in a clipped tone. "He won't be back here any time soon."

"Do we trust that?" another guard leaned in to ask his leader, eyes narrowing in suspicion.

"His blood pressure didn't change, so I suspect he's telling the truth." The leader looked Gideon up and down.

"That's a problem for the queen to solve later, then, if she chooses," the first guard said, nodding in agreement. "We've got the girl, and that's the most important part."

"All right, move!" the leader shouted, causing the rest of his subordinates to split up in all directions as they followed their orders. "And remember—the girl's a Siphon. Be mindful of where you put your hands."

"How chivalrous," Calla bit out.

The guards let just enough slack out of their magic to push Calla and the others toward the horse, awkwardly throwing Cass and Hannah on the first stallion—loosely retying the restraints on Cass that Calla had managed to rip apart—before forcing Kestrel on the second beast and Gideon on the last. It took a beat before she realized she was meant to ride behind Kestrel, and she dug her heels into the ground. The thought of being stabbed in the side again was preferable, if she were honest.

"Move it, girl." The guard leading her to the horses poked her in the back with their scabbard.

She shifted forward a step, her limbs stiff from the magic still clinging to her body, poised to render her immobile again if she made any sudden movements. Another poke. Another inch forward. Calla used all her might to make the process of moving ten feet forward as agonizingly slow as possible, the temper of the guard behind her rising with every second until the pokes in her back had become shallow slices. She flicked her eyes to Gideon, feeling rather guilty that her defiant display was causing him pain as well, but the look in his swirling silver eyes was almost . . . amused.

"Get on the horse," the guard gritted out when they had finally reached the side of the beast that Kestrel was perched on.

Calla was ready to tell the Rouge guard where he could stick his sword, but before she even opened her mouth, the horse gave a shrill whinny, rearing up as if it had spotted a serpent in its path. A couple of the guards rushed over to settle the horse down, grabbing its reins, but the creature wouldn't settle. It whipped its head to the side, and Calla swore she saw fear in its eyes as it looked back at her. Of course.

"It's the girl." One of the guards curled back his lips. "He can sense what she is. He's spooked."

"Then she can walk." The head guard stepped in, his dark violet eyes regarding her with disdain. Calla stared him down with the satisfaction of knowing that if this wasn't fifteen against one, none of them would last a single second in her presence.

If they had seen what I did to the viperidae, they would be shaking in their boots.

The guard broke first, and Calla's lips curled up as she watched him bark orders for them to start moving. She was forced into place behind the leader and his two betas, in front of the three stallions that had been allotted for the prisoners, while two guards marched on her heels. Her movements were still stiff, but quicker, her magic a bit tired from so much friction. She knew it was no use resisting anymore anyway. Kestrel had screwed them all beyond repair.

Rage built in her core with every step she took farther away from Delphine and closer to her version of the Hells.

The Witch Realms.

46

A mina softly closed the door to Lyra's room and leaned back against it until it clicked all the way shut. Sabine was in the center of the room, ripping at the zipper of her jumpsuit with her sharp claws, impatient to finally get the heavy garment off. Amina's dress was already in shreds, making it easy for her to toss aside before swiftly pulling on a borrowed nightgown from Lyra's closet.

"The game has changed," Amina declared to them both as she began to pace.

Sabine had finished changing and now crossed her arms over her chest as she tracked Amina's path, rhythmically tapping the fingers of her left hand atop her bicep. Lyra was at one of their vanities, brushing out the thick russet waves of their hair, watching the others through the reflection in the mirror.

"So, is revenge off the table?" Sabine complained. "I cleared my whole schedule for this."

"Revenge is the least of our worries now." Amina went back over to her ripped-up dress, digging beneath the bodice and pulling out the folded document they had stolen before bringing it over to Sabine.

The contract was nothing short of catastrophic. Amina wasn't sure if they could fully comprehend the implications of what they were looking at, and worse—she wasn't sure if the three of them truly knew what they were going up against anymore.

When she pried the two folded pieces of paper apart, something slipped out from between them and drifted down to the floor. Amina snatched up the small square of parchment and held it up between her and Sabine, stomach flipping a bit when her eyes scanned over the messy ink scrawled across it.

"Lyra, you have to see this," Sabine called, tone serious. Serious Sabine was never a good omen.

Lyra had gathered their shoulder-length strands and elegantly piled them atop their head. They secured their tresses with a swan-shaped comb before grabbing the letter from Sabine's outstretched hand. The parchment was yellowed, delicate, and Amina knew this letter hadn't been written recently. She guessed it was at least a century or two old by the material alone—laid paper, its ribbed texture a sure sign that it was written before the last one hundred years. It was the same sort of paper that was used in Lyra's priceless collection of the Old Texts of Aetherius.

Amina had spent years helping Lyra collect a few volumes of the Old Texts in their search for the history of Illustros. The Old Texts were one of the most astonishing magic artifacts Amina had ever been in the presence of. The priceless tomes didn't just have the history of each continent they covered, but they had thousands of blank pages in the back where *current* events would appear as they happened. Volumes one, two, and four were about Aetherius's northern continents, and volumes eight, nine, and ten only covered half the southern continents and islands—Illustros not included.

Considering each volume cost a small fortune and the risk of being hunted down by others who wished to get their hands on them, it had been a rather slow pursuit to find them all. Amina couldn't help but wonder whether, if they had been able to get their hands on the one that included Illustros, maybe the information they were currently learning wouldn't be as shocking. Or if even the Old Texts wouldn't know about this. This undid every single bit of lore any of them had ever learned about the history of their people, and Amina's stomach churned to think of how fabricated their entire society must be—how many lies they had all swallowed directly from the Valkyrie Queen's hand.

Lyra looked up from the letter with a solemn face. "The contract was truth, then. And the rivalry with the witches . . ."

Amina took the parchment back from Lyra's hand, reading the words once more. The letter wasn't long, but it certainly said enough.

Ignia,

I find it quite amusing that in your endeavor to get your way you have signed yourself up for such an egregious debt. Your newly gifted subjects may believe this is the decision of a benevolent ruler, but I wonder how they would feel if they knew that once the Fates' War is done and there are no witches left to reap, it will be their own souls that will have to pay the price you've agreed to?

I look forward to that day.

L

"Some things are making so much more sense." Sabine nodded. "The witches have never truly been the issue, have they? They were a means to an end. *We* always felt that."

"Only it doesn't end with them." Amina held up the contract she was still gripping in her other hand. "That selfish *bitch*. She has had Valkyries prematurely reaping souls to pay off her own debt—the damn tithe—all while knowing that the Fates' War will decimate at least half of the witches and there won't be enough to sustain her soul quotas going forward. The witches' proximity to our land is the only reason we've been able to sustain the quotas so far!"

"Look, there's a line in here about how Queen Ignia's people would have to 'bear their new role as Reapers' in order to keep their gifted magic.'" Lyra pointed at the second page of the contract with the Fates.

"*New* role? What does that mean? Valkyries have been Reapers of souls since the beginning of time," Sabine reasoned.

"Or so we've been taught." Lyra shook their head. "The Old Texts suggest it used to be the Fates who sorted souls in the afterlife—and considering they rule over the Valley of Souls, that would make sense. So, when did Valkyries become involved? Something deeper is going on here. Something that has to do with this war and the Witch Queens."

"If the war begins and the witches are devastated, it'll be reap or be reaped among the Valkyries," Sabine predicted, stretching her claws out subconsciously at the thought. "And all the Valkyries at the border are just preening every time a new rumor about the last Blood Warrior comes in. Little do they know."

"Speaking of rumors." Amina narrowed her eyes at Sabine. "Did Meli have anything of substance to say at the Reverie?"

"No," Sabine said flatly, picking at her nails, clearly not interested in the subject of her gossipmongering ex-girlfriend.

"Well, I hope you didn't piss her off too much," Amina commented nonchalantly.

Sabine dropped her hand and scowled at her friend. "And why would that matter?"

"Because Meli's network of gossip is the most notorious in Valor. Which means I need her to be pleasant when we visit her at the border tomorrow morning."

"When is Meli ever pleasant?" Sabine grumbled.

"Glass houses, Sab," Amina said at the same time that Lyra chimed in, "No."

Amina narrowed her eyes. "What do you mean *no*?"

"Amina, we are in way over our heads now. This . . . It changes *everything*. We need to lie as low as possible until we know if anyone saw us at the ball or what other information we could be missing here." Lyra's tone was firm. "If not a single one of us has ever known the truth about the origins of the tithe, imagine what else we don't know."

"Which is exactly why we need to move as quickly as possible,"

Amina threw at them. "We should visit the border and find out what they may know about the Blood Warrior and how much time we may have to warn everybody before the war starts."

"And if someone catches wind that we're snooping around for such information? Someone who maybe saw something suspicious at the Reverie? How long before they put two and two together?" Lyra countered.

"So we should do *nothing*?"

"I didn't say that." Lyra threw their hands up. "I just said we should wait, feel things out first before we start involving anyone else!"

"Maybe Lyra is right," Sabine inserted. "We should wait things out a bit, get our plans together. The scale of this is too enormous for just three people to handle."

"You're only siding with them because you don't like that I brought up Meli," Amina accused.

"It's not *just* that, Amina." Sabine's jade eyes sparked with offense. "We need to be rational about this. You started one scheme and uncovered an entire other beast; we need to regroup."

"Since when do *you* want to be rational?" Amina looked at Sabine like the girl had suddenly grown a second, more responsible head. "While the two of you *lie low*, I'll be doing something about all this."

Amina turned to leave, but Lyra put a hand on her shoulder to stop her. "Why can't you just trust *my* decisions for once?"

"Why can't you just trust me *at all* anymore?" Amina argued.

Lyra snatched their hand back and waved it in the air. "You know, what? If that's how you see it . . . good luck at the border. Good luck with resurrecting Rovin—or whatever else it is that you want to get yourself into. We aren't going."

"Fine," Amina told Lyra.

With that, Amina stormed off to shut herself in her room and wait until she could move on with her plan in the morning. She didn't understand Lyra's priorities, but even more she didn't understand how her friends had gone from jumping into everything with her, no safety net, to questioning every single motive she had. It made her feel like in the years they had been separated they'd lost the bond that connected them equally. The way things used to be, if Amina flew into a storm, the other two would be right behind her, no questions asked. Now it felt like the two of them would just turn back and leave her to weather it alone.

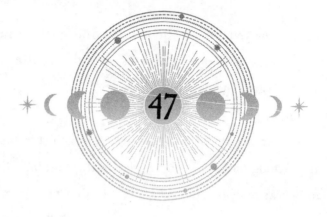

47

A mina lost no time the next day in heading to the largest reaping post on the border, a hub for all the Valkyries who needed to collect souls for their share of the quota each month. The first thing that surprised her when she arrived was how small the group of Valkyries on duty was. When she used to hang around the border there would be almost a hundred Reapers buzzing around, drinking and making boisterous conversation while they waited to for Valkyrie scouts to alert them of souls to reap nearby.

The second thing that surprised her was Sabine and Lyra.

The two Valkyries were currently standing a few yards from where she just landed, observing a couple who were either kissing or trying to see who could swallow the other one first. It was currently a draw.

"Gods help us all," Amina muttered to herself as she approached where Lyra and Sabine were now watching *her* warily. She crossed her arms when she halted in front of them. "What are you doing here?"

Sabine bit her lip and looked at Lyra, nudging the other Valkyrie with her elbow when they didn't say anything for a few long seconds.

"I don't agree with this course of action, for the record," Lyra bit out. "But we didn't want you to come alone."

"Don't think I can take care of myself?" Amina questioned. "I did it for two years without either of you in the forest."

"Oh no." Sabine heaved a sigh.

Lyra snapped at Sabine, "Oh *yes*. I told you this was going to happen." Then, turning back to Amina, they said, "You know what I think your problem is?"

"What's that?" Amina fixed a smirk on her mouth she knew would infuriate Lyra.

It did. "You think your exile only happened to *you*. You were alone for so long you only had yourself to make decisions for and you didn't have to consider anyone else. And I get that, Amina, I really do. But your exile was not just your burden—you have *no idea* what it was like adjusting here without you."

Amina was stunned. It took her a long moment to recover before she could say, "It seems you've adjusted just fine without me. You don't want me to make decisions without telling you every single thought in my mind first—but the two of you will look to each other every time I bring something up. There's no space for me between you anymore."

"Because I'm worried you're going to do something that gets you taken from us again, and if we got used to you being here only for that to happen—I don't think even *we* would survive that a second time!" Lyra exploded.

Now all three of them stood there, startled.

Perhaps unsurprisingly, Sabine collected herself first. "I think we're all afraid to admit that we changed so much, separately, that we are scared we won't fit exactly how we used to anymore. And we *won't*. We're different people now, which is maybe painful to realize, but that doesn't mean we can't be something new. We keep telling each other we'll start over, but that concept hasn't seemed to stick quite yet."

"I just"—Amina sighed—"I want to matter to you both as much as I did before."

"Amina, we sabotaged a royal event and stole highly classified documents from the Queen for you," Lyra deadpanned. "You've never for a second stopped mattering. I know you struggle with not being able to lead, but our roles with one another have had to change, and if we're going to start over . . . we need to trust all our instincts. We need this to be a true collaboration."

Amina took a deep breath. Lyra was right, she *did* struggle with not being able to lead, and maybe that's what led to her getting exiled in the first place—refusing to collaborate and throwing herself in hot water with no one around to help.

"Okay." Amina nodded. "This is our new beginning."

Lyra's body relaxed, and they reached out a hand in offering to Amina. Amina clasped it, a vow of acceptance. Sabine grinned beside them as they dropped their hands, and she threw her arms around both of their necks to force them into a brief group hug.

"Get a grip, Sabine," Lyra grumbled.

Sabine ignored Lyra as she released them, saying, "All right, enough of all that emotional crap. I'm craving violence."

Amina flicked a glance around them, wondering if anyone had noticed that whole exchange, but the couple was oblivious to the entire world, and the only other people around them were several yards away playing a rowdy game of cards.

Amina gestured her chin at the dozen or so Valkyries jostling one another around the makeshift card table they had made out of a large tree stump. "Let's see if any of them know where Meli is. I don't think these two are coming up for air anytime soon."

Sabine's mood instantly soured at the sound of Meli's name, but she followed after Amina nonetheless, hooking her arm into the crook of Amina's as they walked.

"Excuse me," Amina said, when they approached the group. Not a single person glanced her way.

One of the Valkyries flipped a card into the center of the table, and a collective groan rang through the air. A man with long black hair and two steel bars through his left ear threw his hand of cards down on the table with a curse before standing and kicking the log he had been sitting on and stomping away. Another Valkyrie, this one a strawberry blond with freckles scattered across their cheeks, greedily scooped up their winnings from the center of the tree stump as someone to their left punched them in the shoulder.

"*Hello*," Amina growled, her nerves prickling at being ignored.

Still, no one paused. If anything, they only got louder, someone shouting curses over something that happened during the game, while two others were nearly about to throw punches were it not for the Valkyrie in the middle holding them away from each other. A crash echoed as someone shattered a glass mug of brown liquid against the trunk of a nearby elm tree.

"That's enough," Sabine huffed, dropping Amina's arm to unsheathe two unusually long throwing daggers.

Before Amina could blink again, the daggers left Sabine's hands, a second pair already out and ready as the first set pinned a Valkyrie to a tree by his shoulders. The forest around them went deadly silent except for the man's scream of agony.

"Now that we have your attention," Amina said, a tight grin unfurling as she spoke, "we need to know where Meli is."

"*Amina?*" someone asked in disbelief to her left.

Amina's eyebrows rose when she spotted who had spoken. "Sydni. You're a Reaper now?"

Sydni had trained with their trio when they were younger. She was a quiet girl who made custom weapons in a little shop in the technical district. Baden, the girl's husband, had been a close childhood friend of Lyra's.

"For about a year now," the former bladesmith said as she got up from her spot in the circle and came over to them. Her voice lowered as she commented, "I hadn't heard you were back from . . ."

"I haven't been back long," Amina lied. "And I'd like to keep my return as quiet as I can for a while. No need to alert the gossip network."

Sydni smiled slightly. "Well, there's been enough exciting gossip going around that I doubt you'd have to worry too much."

"Oh yeah?" Sabine asked. "Like what?"

"The final Blood Warrior has apparently been located," the girl shared, louder now. "There hasn't been a witch in sight for two weeks. Apparently, Lysandra has pulled them back in preparation. Our reaping numbers have gone down drastically. The only souls anyone has collected recently were a few courtless fae who died passing through the Miroir Mountains."

"Which is not good, considering the queen raised the monthly reaping quota last night at the end of the Reverie," the man with the steel bars in his ear chimed in from where he was eavesdropping, his words tight.

Most Valkyries had a specific season in which they reaped, alternating shifts throughout the year so the responsibility could be shared. Some Valkyries never reaped—and as long as the queen's numbers were met each month for the tithe, they weren't usually hassled about it. At every Reverie, however, the season of Reapers who had collected the most souls each year would receive a large payout from the queen, which meant most families had at least one Reaper in hopes that they would be in the running for such a fortune.

Amina prodded, "What's the new monthly quota?"

"Five hundred souls," Sydni declared.

Amina and the others gaped. For the last century it had only been one hundred souls a month.

"Five hundred?" Sabine nearly choked. "Where the Hells does she think you're going to find five hundred souls to reap every month? Even if the witches were out here in droves, there's no way you could collect that many souls. That would be committing mass murder."

"It already nearly is," Sydni said, expression grave. "The witches have believed Valkyries are lawless, anarchist creatures who survive on bloodlust for centuries. The queen apparently figures there's no harm in perpetuating that notion now—as long as we meet our numbers. Something is shifting."

Amina nodded. Indeed, it was.

Lyra cleared their throat and asked Sydni, "Would you know where Meli is?"

"Meli didn't show up this morning," said the Valkyrie pinned to the tree. Everyone whipped their head toward him in surprise. They'd all forgotten he was there. "Now, would someone mind *helping me*?"

When no one rushed to help him, he cursed at them all colorfully. Sabine took her time heading over and collecting her knives, pulling each from his shoulders as he glared. She grinned the entire time.

"Fine, we'll track her down at her house. Are we good, slayers?" Amina looked to the others, making sure they were on board before she summoned her wings. Collaborating.

The three of them were just about to take off when a rustle of leaves sounded above them, followed by the heavy *thud* of someone dropping to the ground.

"Baden." Sydni's tone was surprised as she went to her husband's side.

"An entire horde of fae was just wiped out by a dragon in the Miroir Mountains," he told her, his hand absentmindedly reaching up to touch the Esprit hanging around his neck, the glow of its stone signaling that there were souls inside. "I collected as many as I could hold, but we need to—" His words cut off abruptly as his gaze caught on Amina.

"Amina?" he asked, tone puzzled. "When did you get back?"

Amina waved away his question. "Not important. What were you saying?"

"We need to get moving if we want to collect those souls before they pass over," he told the group of spectators scattered around them. "Half of you can come with me and the rest can head to the east base of the mountainside and check for any other casualties."

The Valkyries began leaping into the air, sending gusts of wind swirling through the clearing as their wings carried them away. Sydni and Baden lingered behind.

"If you hear anything else about the Blood Warrior rumors," Amina told Sydni, "could you let us know?"

Sydni nodded. "No problem. Good luck with . . . whatever you're up to."

With that, Sydni and Baden bid the trio good-bye and took off after the rest of the Reapers.

"Let's go find Meli," Amina prompted the others.

"And if she doesn't have any answers?" Lyra asked.

"If she can't give us any answers, we may have to resort to finding a witch—"

Amina's words stopped abruptly as something to the group's right suddenly flashed a bright, vibrant red. When the light dimmed, the three Valkyries blinked the spots out of their vision and peered at the ground in disbelief.

A single red Witch's Die had spawned two feet away.

Amina walked over and bent down to pluck the magical cube off the forest floor.

A grin slowly stretched across her face as she looked back to her friends, rolling the die between her thumb and index finger. "Looks like we won't have to find ourselves a witch after all, slayers. They're going to find us."

48

R eniel clinked a butter knife against a crystal goblet. "Ladies and gentlebeings, the Claiming is about to begin!"

Delphine was half-drunk, standing in line with the other candidates for Reniel's Shoal: a pair of twins with a kelpie-hunting success rate that had apparently set records; a young man rumored to be related to one of the Sea King's own familial branches; and another young girl, barely a year or two older than Delphine, who was wearing a dress made completely of diamonds and pearls.

Delphine's mother leaned down to hiss in her daughter's ear, "Stop picking at your nails. Stand up taller."

Delphine dropped her hands and stiffened her spine. Reniel continued his speech at the head of the room.

"Tonight, we have some incredible candidates for my Shoal. And I want to thank each and every one of you for showing up for such a special occasion. As you may know, openings in my Shoal are a rare, priceless position. The members of my court have the responsibility of upholding the quality of our long-celebrated traditions."

Everyone in the Siren's Sea knew this already, of course. Reniel just liked to reiterate it anytime he had access to an audience who would tolerate his boasting.

Delphine stole a glance back at her mother, the woman's perfect heart-shaped face exactly what Delphine imagined her own would mature into soon. When Delphine grew up, they might have even looked like twins if not for her mother's left eye, once a bright silver, now a milky-white color.

"Now, before we begin," Reniel said, his booming voice cutting through Delphine's thoughts. "I'm afraid I have some terrible news. It is with a heavy heart that I must reveal that one of our candidates has committed an egregious offense against my rules."

A low murmur settled over the room as everyone began to whisper to one another. Delphine felt her mother stiffen at her back as she looked over the other candidates in shock, wondering which of them Reniel could be talking about. They were all staring back at her.

"Mother?" Delphine whispered. "Who do you think . . ."

Her words trailed off. Deep in her gut she already knew who Reniel was about to publicly accuse.

"Opal DeLune," Reniel said with a mocking smile. "You and your daughter can step forward."

Delphine was frozen as her mother pushed around her and strode toward Reniel. Before she could reach him, two of his guards blocked his path. Reniel's smile grew vicious.

"What is the meaning of this, Reniel?" her mother hissed at the siren as his lackeys pushed her back. "What are you talking about?"

"You're a great actress, Opal," Reniel complimented her. "One of the best I've seen, in fact. Unfortunately for you, you're not very stealthy."

"Mom?" Delphine whispered as she took a step forward.

Reniel's eyes swung in Delphine's direction. "Come here, girl."

"No!" Her mother whipped around. "Get back in line, Delphine. This has nothing to do with her, Reniel."

"Then why is she wearing a hexed necklace around her neck? I have spies across the entirety of this sea and the Neverending Forest. Did you really think you were going to get away with purchasing a persuasion spell without my knowledge?"

The rapt onlookers gasped as their eyes all shifted to Delphine's pearl choker. Delphine reached up to grasp the necklace in protest.

"No, this is a family heirloom!" she said. "My mother would never—"

"She would and she did." Reniel's tone had turned harsh now, his expression souring with each passing second. "She bought an illegal potion in order to charm the necklace so that it would sway my decision to Claim you for my Shoal. And now she will pay the price."

Delphine's mother was seized by the two members of Reniel's circle. They slammed Opal's knees to the ground as Reniel pulled something from around his neck. An Obsidian Key. Delphine screamed, rushing forward, but someone wrapped their arms around her from behind. It was the man in the odd leather uniform who had warned her earlier in the hallway.

"Let me go!" She beat her fists against his hold. He didn't budge.

"Sorry, moonlight," he whispered, and she was surprised to find that he did sound apologetic. "I promise you don't want to get in the middle of what's about to happen."

Delphine felt a sob bubbling up in her throat as she watched Reniel palm the key he held.

"You're not the only one who has access to hexed items," Reniel declared. "An Obsidian Key is possibly one of the rarest artifacts from Noctum, the second continent. There are only ten that have been forged, and they cost a small fortune—if you can track one down in the first place."

"What are you going to do to her?" Delphine screamed at Reniel, still struggling against her captor's clutches. "Leave her alone!"

Reniel continued as if Delphine had never spoken. "The best thing about an Obsidian Key is that it can unlock anything. It's why everyone covets them so much. What some people may not know, however, is that they can also lock certain things—including magic."

Her mother let out a rageful scream as she yanked against the sirens restraining her. "You cannot do this! You have no right to sentence me to something like this without—"

"You bought an illegal item, which means whatever punishment I see *fit goes. You made a gamble—you lost. Now, hold still, I've heard this hurts a bit."*

Delphine watched in utter horror as Reniel moved behind her mother and jabbed the magic key right into the back of the woman's neck. Her mother let out a scream so piercing that a few of the guests' wineglasses shattered in their grasp. The sirens holding on to her mother let her slump forward as she writhed and twisted in pain. A foreboding, sickly glow began to emanate from where the key was inserted in her mother's skin as it began to slowly seal away her magic.

Delphine had enough. She plunged her sharp teeth into the arm of the man holding her back, ripping through his leather shirt with a ferocity she didn't realize she was capable of. His viselike grip instantly loosened, and she shoved him away, darting to where her mother was still screaming on the ground. Reniel watched the entire ordeal with a cold expression.

Delphine bared her teeth. "Make it stop!"

Reniel met her gaze evenly. "No."

"What do you want?" Delphine begged. "I'll give you anything!"

"I want people in this room to remember what happens when you try to manipulate me. Your mother deserves to pay the price for trying to use dark magic to gain my favor and infiltrate something as precious as a Claiming. Being sworn into a Shoal is sacred. She violated that."

Delphine could feel that she was on the verge of tears as she watched two men haul her thrashing mother up from the floor and drag her from the room. She didn't let any tears fall, however. She only lifted her chin and hurried after the men. Following them through two sets of doors until they were in a small, empty room, Delphine knelt by her mother's side the second the guards let her go.

"Keep her here until after the ceremony," one of the guards told the other before leaving. Delphine paid them no mind.

"Mom," she whispered as her mother's thrashing finally slowed. "What can I do?"

"He can't do this," her mother wept.

"We'll find a way to get your magic back—"

Her mother's head shook vigorously. "I don't care about my magic. But now you will never get into his Shoal. It's over."

"Why is it so important?" Delphine demanded. "Why does that matter so much to you?"

Her mother's sad eyes shifted to her daughter's face. "When your father left, my mother told me I was a disgrace to our family. That I had never deserved that heirloom around your neck."

Delphine reached up to brush her fingertips over the pearls at her throat.

"Your father had an affair with one of Reniel's elites." Her mother made a face as the bitter words left her tongue. "I knew he didn't care about staying for me, but I hated that he left you. I wanted to show them all that I may not deserve that necklace, but you do. You will be my legacy. Never his."

Delphine grasped her mother's hand and squeezed it a single time.

Before her mother could ask what she was doing, Delphine was storming out of the room, pushing past the guard and making her way back to the crowded ballroom. She slammed through the doors just as Reniel was about to perform the Claiming ritual on one of the other candidates—the one who was related to the Sea King.

Every head snapped to her as she rolled back her shoulders and strutted across the room.

"What do you think you're doing?" Reniel sneered.

Delphine smirked. "Offering you an opportunity not to be the most predictable person I've ever met."

Reniel stepped away from the boy he was about to Claim for his Shoal and faced her fully, mouth set in a sharp line, waiting for her next move.

Delphine gave them both a daring smile. "I'm a better bet than any other candidate in this room."

Reniel huffed a laugh, and a few of the audience members followed suit. "That's quite a bold claim."

"Not a claim. A fact." Delphine reached up to take off the hexed necklace she was wearing.

Reniel watched with rapt curiosity as she stuffed the necklace into a secret pocket in her dress, making sure it was not touching her skin so its magic could not work. Then Delphine began.

"You're about to initiate someone into your Shoal who's been spoon-fed luxury all his life and doesn't know the difference between a yell and a whisper. And I'd say he could just do grunt work, but I suspect

he's never done manual labor a day in his life, given the lack of tone in his muscles."

The candidate standing next to Reniel curled his lip at her in disdain, a retort on the tip of his tongue, but Reniel held up a silencing hand. The glint in the Shoal leader's eyes told her he wanted her to continue.

Delphine pointed at the twins next. "They're spies. If one of them had been Claimed, the other was going to take whatever intel they gained back to their other Shoal. I overheard them at another Claiming a couple months ago while I was hiding out in the powder room. I didn't recognize them at first with their new hair color—which by the way, is ghastly." Delphine snorted. "Bright red does absolutely nothing for your complexions."

Reniel took a step toward her now. "Go on."

Delphine slid her gaze to the horrified girl dressed in diamonds next to the twins—who were now both rotating between a string of colorful curses and fearful pleas for mercy as two guards hauled them away. The last siren in the sparkly dress looked at Delphine with terror, wondering what dirt Delphine might be about to dredge up on her.

"Nothing is really wrong with her." Delphine shrugged. "She's just not very clever. Which can hardly be considered a crime among some of the present company."

Delphine heard a sharp laugh from somewhere over Reniel's shoulder, but she resisted a satisfied smile.

"Do you think petty gossip is really worth a spot in my Shoal?" Reniel narrowed his eyes.

"*We both know what abilities are valued here, and if it takes going one by one through each person in this room and revealing every secret I've been able to pick up just by sipping while walking around and listening, I'll do it.*"

Reniel stared at her for a long, thoughtful moment. "I will not reinstate your mother's magic—in fact she will be banned from the premises, effective immediately. Which means if you are Claimed, you will never see her again. Is that something you're willing to give up?"

No, *she wanted to scream. She knew she had to play this situation carefully. Her mother had taught her winning the war mattered more than winning a single battle. And she was her mother's legacy.*

"Good," Delphine told him. "If she's gone, I'll be able to prove that Claiming me never had anything to do with a magic necklace. Send her away. I'm not leaving."

The instant Reniel's lips tipped up at the corners, Delphine knew she had won.

49

Delphine was covered in something warm and heavy that hadn't been there when she'd fallen asleep. She shoved away the blanket as she sat up and rubbed her eyes, shaking off the unwelcome dream that had plagued her sleep. Reniel must have come back in the very late hours of the night, which was no doubt normal for the siren, and she was surprised to find he had left her to sleep unbothered.

She tiptoed from the sitting area toward the archway that led into the bedroom and found the man sprawled out on his back across the giant bed. For a moment she thought it foolish that he'd be so willing to sleep in such close proximity to her, given their history. He probably considered the guards on the outside of the room's entrance more than enough of a deterrent, since she was the only viable suspect if he got murdered in his slumber. It was still so tempting.

Her gaze roamed over the sharp features of his sleeping face, down his neck, until they landed on the black key hanging out of the collar of his shirt.

If she just reached out and grabbed it . . .

He would kill her in an instant.

The Obsidian Key would be able to break her Siren's oath. In the harrowing days after Delphine had vowed her oath to Reniel, when she realized how big a mistake she had made, she'd found herself lost in daydreams of him gifting her that key once she redeemed herself. Imagining she would never have to belong to anyone but herself ever again. Lying here now, noting how his mouth was set in a scowl even in his rest, she knew she had been such a naive little girl.

She slowly backed away to head for the front room. She was playing a long game. She was out of the cell, sleeping in his room. She would get that key. She just had to wait for the perfect opportunity—and then she could unlock the tracking ring from her finger and unbind herself from her Siren's oath.

"And where are you going?" a gruff voice said from behind her

Delphine turned and watched as his eyes peeled open. "I was going to the bathroom. Unless you'd like me to ruin your expensive couch?"

"Preferably not," he said dryly, sitting up. "I see you managed to make yourself a tad less disheveled last night. Good. You were beginning to look like a sea witch."

Delphine tensed at the insult to her appearance. "It isn't my fault that weeks of torture and staying in a dungeon took a toll on my beauty routine."

Reniel grunted. "Well, I need you to stay looking presentable now that I've set things into motion with my circle. I have a new wardrobe being delivered for you this morning, in fact."

"You've already begun telling people I'm here?" she asked.

"Better to get ahead of the whispers before the guards at the door start spreading rumors." He smirked. "A good reminder for tonight if you want to stay here: you'll need to behave, pet. I want to control the narrative—don't tell a soul anything other than what we discuss, understood?"

I am not your pet. She asked, tone sharp, "What's tonight?"

Something harsh glinted in his gaze as he stood and grabbed her chin, forcing it down so she had no choice but to look him directly in his eyes. "Tonight I have a very important dinner with my Shoal, and I think it's prudent that you attend. Which means you need to look good."

"I always look good," she said automatically, ripping her chin out of his hold.

"Okay, then you need to look *delicious*." He reached out and brushed a bit of her hair away from her cheek, and it took everything in her not to cringe away. "You should think about growing your hair out again. I liked when it was long."

So had her mother. The first thing Delphine had done when she got to Estrella was chop it all off. It had been short ever since.

"You want me to look . . . delicious. . . ." She resisted the urge to vomit as she said that word. "Are you trying to make someone jealous tonight?"

"No. I just know that before I get to explain my version of events—*the only* version of events—to my peers about why you left, they're going to make their own conclusions among themselves first. I was to make sure there's a clear, visual explanation of why I might have let a traitor back into my life until I can set the record straight."

With that, he stepped away from her and strode across the room to the large wardrobe that took up half the north-facing wall. She didn't press for any more information after that, trying to fight down the acid crawling up her throat as she walked to the bathroom and shut the door. She only needed to get through another week and a half with him. That's when the Blood Moon would be burning in the night sky and Zephyr's Claiming ceremony would distract Reniel enough for her to go through with her plans.

The idea had come to her in the interim between Celeste's visits, after she had learned of Zephyr's ambition to be promoted to Reniel's inner circle at the Claiming. If Zephyr's Siren's oath was broken, Reniel would be too heavily engrossed in the task to realize what she was up to. Delphine had witnessed a Siren's oath being severed once before—which was all she needed to know that both sirens who participated in the ritual would be incapacitated for a few minutes from the amount of magic it took. Less than ten minutes, to be exact.

She would have ten minutes to grab the key around Reniel's neck when he would be too preoccupied to use her Siren's oath to drain her magic and stop her. Part of Delphine worried it was too ludicrous of a plan to work, but another part of her knew she would risk everything to try. The satisfaction of getting to snap that key off Reniel's neck would be worth the risk alone.

A firm knock on the bathroom door brought her out of her thoughts. Before she could say *Come in*, Reniel was already pulling the door open and stepping up behind her, their gazes clashing in the mirror.

"I think you'll like the outfit I picked for you," he told her. "It comes with shiny accessories."

Delphine made herself smile as she turned to face him and the garment bag he was holding up. He unzipped the bag, and she had to swallow the gasp bubbling up in her throat as she saw what was inside.

It was stunning. The one-shoulder dress was made entirely of silvery netting that was strung with opalescent pearls and had strategically placed shells to cover the areas she would want to be more modest. There was a small pouch dangling from the top of the hanger that Reniel reached to open with his empty hand, loosening the bag's drawstrings to pluck out a matching pair of earrings and a shell comb for her hair.

"Put these on."

She took the pieces of jewelry from him and turned back to the mirror, setting the comb on the counter as she fastened the pearl drop earrings into her lobes. She parted her hair slightly off center and scooped up the comb, sliding its glittering prongs into place just above her right ear.

"Exquisite," Reniel murmured as he brushed his fingers across the back of her neck, over the cursed tattoo she had just exposed there.

When she met his gaze in the mirror once more, she nearly rolled her eyes at what she saw. Reniel had always doted on Delphine more than the others when she was young because of the way he thought of her—like a prized trophy. Something pretty to place behind glass for everyone else to see and covet but that no one except him could access.

"I need to get dressed," she told him.

"When you're ready, you can meet me on the terrace for breakfast," he told her.

He set the garment bag on the counter and left her alone to change. She took a deep breath. Just another week and a half. That's it.

She wondered how long it had been for Hannah and Calla—if it was only mere hours that they were without her while she had been here for weeks. A part of her hoped that was the case. Hoped they didn't have to worry about her for too long. Another part of her knew that meant Hannah's promise to come for her was obsolete.

She was going to have to claw her way out of this on her own. For the final time.

50

It took less than five minutes for someone to show up after the dice appeared. The man—no, the *boy*—was an Onyx witch with long navy hair and the Onyx Guild crest pinned to his chest plate. He strode through the forest with purpose, body tense as he searched for the item that called to his magic.

"Looking for this?" Amina asked, tossing the red cube up in the air and catching it leisurely as she stepped from the shadows of the trees.

The witch ground to a halt, whipping out a pair of twin blades at the sight of her, though Amina noted his hands shook a bit where he grasped the blades' hilts. She unfurled a wicked grin, the one she wore anytime she had to be the Valkyrie in front of witches or any other beings that the mask was required for. The boy paled a bit.

"Hand it over, soulstealer," the witch demanded with as much confidence as he could muster.

Amina bared her teeth. "And who are *you* to give *me* demands?

From where I'm standing, I hold your fate in my hands, witch." She tossed the die again to punctuate her words.

"I don't want to fight," he told her, despite the twin blades he still held up between them.

Amina stepped closer to him, and he tensed, fear gleaming in his sable eyes. She almost felt bad for the whelp. He clearly wasn't yet trained—regardless of his weapons and uniform—and she was sure if it weren't for his immortality his heart would have already given out. Unfortunately for him, that made him the perfect target.

"Your affiliation with the Onyx Queen's Guild says otherwise." She traced a single sharp nail over the silver pin on his chest, ignoring how the points of his swords were mere inches from her heart.

"I've only just joined," he rushed out hastily. "My coven suffered from a bad dragon raid last year and we needed the compensation from the queen. I don't care about our rivalry. I don't want to hurt you."

She tilted her head back and laughed. "You couldn't hurt me even if you had been training for the last decade, witch. The egos you and your brethren possess will never cease to amaze me."

The thought of the Onyx Prince and their hasty bargain flitted across her mind for a brief moment.

"Please," he begged, a bead of sweat forming at his temple while his gaze slid to the die.

The longer he went without taking the cursed cube, the worse his magic would make him feel. Amina had seen witches tortured with a newly spawned die many times before, until they were a writhing mess on the ground willing to do anything to make the agony stop.

"I'll give you the die as soon as you give me the information I need," she told him.

The witch only pressed his lips together.

"Okay," she said slowly, narrowing her eyes. "How about you give me the information I need, or I'll rip your heart out?"

"What information?" he questioned cautiously, his body starting to tremble slightly the longer he went without claiming the die.

"There are rumors," Amina began, tone sharp, serious. "About the last Blood Warrior. Have you heard them?"

"Everyone in the Witch Realms has." He nodded. "They said it's a girl—a Siphon. The rumors hailed from the Rouge Realm over the last few days."

"I've heard your fellow Guild members have been scarce around here since. Why?"

He pressed his lips firmly together once more.

"Tell me, witch"—Amina leaned in to place her mouth next to his ear—"do you think my threats aren't serious?"

Amina dug the claws of her right hand into his leather breastplate, enough to scare him into action. As he sliced clumsily through the air with his swords, Amina heard the *whoosh* of Sabine's daggers flying out behind her, cutting right through the witch's wrists, making him drop the twin swords. He screamed in pain, and Amina extracted her hand from his chest and latched on to his neck instead, keeping him upright.

She watched as his eyes widened at the sight of Sabine stepping out of the trees behind her. Lyra was no doubt in the canopy of branches above them, ready to pounce if they needed to.

"Please," he choked out. "I don't know that much. I'm in the lower ranks. All I know is that Queen Lysandra pulled back most of the legions to the inner cities."

"Then why are you still out here?" Amina questioned.

"She left all the new recruits on standby here, at the border. We were given orders not to interact with any"—he swallowed—"*Valkyries.* We haven't even been through more than a month of training."

Amina looked over her shoulder to Sabine.

The queen is preparing for war, Amina thought. The glimmer in Sabine's eyes told Amina she thought the same.

"Poor thing." Amina's voice was saccharine as she turned back to the boy. "Your queen left you to be slaughtered by the big bad Valkyries. Having to follow orders must be terrible."

The boy only stared, and what Amina had just said suddenly dawned on her.

"Wait . . ." She looked down to the red die still in her left hand. "Following the queen's orders means you would have made all your rolls. . . ."

The boy squirmed in her grip now.

"Which means there's no reason for you to have been compelled to find the spawned Witch's Die," Sabine concluded.

"Why would you stay here, then, if you are not yet bound to her demands?" Amina dropped her mask a bit, her tone curious now. "Why wouldn't you all get out of the Witch Realms while you still could if you know what's going on and aren't bound by the magic of your rolls?"

The boy didn't answer, and Amina nearly snarled, tightening her hold on his neck with impatience.

"It would ruin the operation," he gasped out finally.

"What operation?" Amina demanded, loosening her grip a bit so it was easier for him to talk.

"There are these witches, in the Guild, that started a plan to fake everyone's Final Rolls. Usually, the rolls are mandatory when you join, but they've figured out a system to trick the queen. Everyone's known it was only a matter of time before the war started, and none of us want the choice to fight taken away from us. But we have to bide our time or the queen will know."

"Are you saying there are witches in her legions who are in the inner cities without completed rolls as we speak?" Sabine chimed in.

The boy nodded.

"Clever, clever witches," Amina commended him.

"Please let me go," he begged. "I don't know anything else."

Amina did as he asked, immediately releasing her hold on him without warning. He fell to the ground like a rock, clearing his throat roughly as he scrambled back up to his feet.

"You've earned this." She tossed the die at him. "Though I'm not sure it's much of a prize."

He caught the magic cube nimbly, almost sighing in relief as the die landed in his palm. His pallid complexion seemed to brighten as the magic of the cursed die settled into his bones.

"It's not my Final Roll, at least," he muttered to himself.

"Who cares." Sabine waved him off. "Get out of our sights before we change our minds about letting you go."

That comment seemed to make the witch remember whom he was standing in front of, because he quickly bent down to gather his swords from the ground and started to hurry away, never turning his back to them.

Before he could get more than a few feet, however, Amina found herself saying, "Wait."

The witch didn't pause his walking.

"Who were the witches who started this operation? Do you know their names?" She wasn't quite sure why she cared, but something in the back of her mind needled her to get the answer.

The boy hesitated.

"Want knives through your eyes?" Sabine threatened, waving a blade in the air. "I suggest you answer the question."

"I'm not sure who's been helping him," the boy told them. "But I know one of the witches was a beta for some big-shot commander. Caspian Ironside."

Amina sucked in a breath, and the witch finally turned and sprinted away, deep into the shadows of the forest.

51

By the time the group made it to the final stretch of the forest, Caspian and the others had been watching Calla walk for almost four hours without a break. Cass knew the Siphon just enough to tell that the expression on her face was carefully blank, refusing to let any of the guards have the satisfaction of seeing her look uncomfortable. One sideways glance at Gideon sitting on the horse next to him, however, told Cass just how exhausted Calla must be.

Calla had not once looked back at Gideon during the trek, though it was hard for Cass to believe she couldn't feel the prince's stare burning a hole in her back.

As the guards leading the pack ahead of them dispersed for a water break, Cass watched as Calla finally glanced over her shoulder. Gideon tilted his head at the girl in silent question and Calla gave a single nod in answer. The prince's shoulders dropped a bit as some of the concern melted out of his body.

Cass looked away as the pair continued their silent conversation, turning his attention to where Hannah was slumped against their horse's neck, her arms still tied behind her. He felt a sudden surge of relief that the two of them had each other through this entire ordeal. It wasn't that he didn't think he could rely on Calla or Gideon in general—just that the two of them had so much on their shoulders at the moment that they, understandably, couldn't take on any more from anyone else.

"All right, let's get moving again," the leader announced as the guards, who had been out finding water, finally returned to the group.

Only, two of the guards weren't returning as calm as they had left. Instead, they were both utterly disheveled as they paused to catch their breaths and dropped an armful of canteens onto the ground with heavy thuds.

"What in the Hells is wrong with the two of you?" the leader asked.

"A black rabbit," one of them panted. "Chasing us. But it wasn't a rabbit. . . ."

"It was some kind of demon," the other guard explained. "Its eyes were red and—"

Calla rolled her eyes from where she was shifting her weight from foot to foot. "Don't tell me Myrea's guards are scared of a little bunny."

Of course, she and the others knew very well that it *wasn't* just a bunny, but the look on Calla's face said that she was itching for a fight and Cass couldn't blame her. If he didn't have a handkerchief stuffed into his mouth, he probably would've made the same joke.

"Shut the Hells up." The first guard twisted around to bare his teeth at the Siphon.

"We should've gagged *her*," the second guard added.

"Try it," Gideon inserted, his deep voice like the calm before a storm. Caspian knew that voice well and knew the guards should heed the warning laced beneath if they had any sense of self-preservation.

Apparently, they did, because the witches hesitated now, their eyes glossing over a bit as they soaked in the prince's threat.

"Enough," the leader broke in. "Pick up those canteens and get back in line. We don't have time for any more of this nonsense."

"But the—" the first guard continued.

"If you mention anything about a godsforsaken rabbit one more time," the leader threatened them, "I'll leave you both here to find your own way out, understand? You should know better than to invoke the attention of the beings in this forest. Ignore them and be thankful if they choose to ignore you. Now, *move*."

The two guards scrambled to bend down and collect the water containers they had dropped, throwing Calla looks of disdain in turn as they began to hand them out. One of the guards approached Caspian and Hannah with a canteen, relieving both witches of the cloth gags still tied around their faces in order to awkwardly dribble a few gulps of the cool liquid into their mouths. Next, they moved on to Kestrel and Gideon, saving Calla for last.

As the guard stopped before her and leaned in with the canteen, he spoke just loud enough for those close by to hear. "I hope the queen lets us watch as she spills your cursed blood across the palace floors."

Caspian tightened his fists at the heinous words, but Calla didn't respond. She simply tilted her head back and accepted the drink—

And then spewed the liquid right into the guard's face.

Caspian let out a surprised yelp of laughter. The guard was frozen in shock for a moment before he collected himself and went to lunge forward.

The guards' leader grabbed a fistful of the witch's shirt and yanked him away before he could reach Calla. "You got a death wish, boy? She's a *Siphon*." The leader threw the guard to the ground. "You let one little girl rile you up and you can't control yourself. Pathetic."

Calla folded her arms across her chest as the enraged grunt seethed at his leader's feet. The Rouge witch spun on her next.

"You better enjoy the next day of your life, because when our queen gets her hands on you, it will be your last," he spat.

Calla smiled grimly at the man. "It wouldn't be the first time Myrea made an attempt to get rid of me, and as you can see, that didn't work out for her very well, did it?"

The Rouge leader looked like he was about to say something else when a rustling sound snagged his attention. Caspian turned his head to see where the noise had come from, but the forest around them sank into a suspicious quiet.

"Move out," the leader demanded, throwing Calla and the rest of them one final sneer before heading to the front of the group.

As everyone prepared to resume their trek, something caught Caspian's attention in the same direction as the rustling moments before. He squinted into the shadows of the forest a few yards away, but nothing was there. The group started forward, the horse shifting beneath him as if it were uneasy.

The back of his neck began to prick, and he had the unsettling feeling that they were being watched.

"The forest barrier is right ahead," the Rouge leader called out to the group.

Caspian jolted awake at this announcement. He straightened up from where he was slumped against Hannah's back, stretching out his limbs and wiping the little bit of drool from the corner of his mouth. He knew he must have been worn out, since he couldn't even remember drifting off.

"Sorry, Han," he told the little witch as she rolled the ache of his weight out of her shoulders.

"It's all right," she whispered to him. "You need the rest before whatever is about to happen."

"This is such bullshit," Caspian muttered back. "Kestrel is such a Godsdamned prick. If we get out of this, I'm going to kick his ass."

"I just don't understand how he could do this to you and Gideon. He has no loyalty to Calla, I get it, but to betray both of you?" Hannah shook her head. "And how could he not have known to never trust a Witch Queen?"

"His jealousy has poisoned his view of everything," Cass explained. "He was never going to get over Gideon—Calla just happened to be the perfect scapegoat. As for the queen . . . I imagine a good bit of ego was involved there."

"But Gideon and Calla weren't even whatever they are now, when he left."

Cass sighed. "Whatever they are is still not an excuse for what Kestrel's done. But I have no doubt what Gideon has in store for the bastard will be worse than anything I could wish upon Kestrel myself."

Hannah's brows knit as she threw a glance over her shoulder at him. "I'm afraid none of us will make it out of this to even see that justice."

"We're going to get out of this," he assured her, though his voice didn't sound as confident as he was wishing it would.

"I'm afraid I won't be able to keep my promise to Delphine." Hannah's eyes began to fill with tears now, and Caspian brought his hands up to wipe away a stray droplet that fell down her cheek.

"We're going to make it out of this. We're going to get Delphine back. I haven't known Calla for long, but I know she will never stop fighting for either of you. Especially after Ezra. Something changed in her the moment he died—we all witnessed it. I don't know what her power is building up to, but I have a feeling if everyone keeps pushing her to the edge we're soon going to find out. Hopefully, Kestrel is the first to get a taste."

"We're going to fight for you, too, Cass, you know that, right?" Hannah whispered to him.

Caspian gave her a reassured smile. "It's why I'm still here, blondie."

Hannah returned his smile before twisting back around and realizing they were slowing to a halt. They had reached the barrier.

"Once we pass through, we are heading directly to the Storm Gutters." The head guard turned his stallion around to address the group. "The queen has arranged for carriages to take us back to the Rouge Realm. Can't risk anyone in the Onyx territories recognizing such a high-profile member of their court." The latter was directed toward Gideon.

"The second we step into the Onyx Realm, I am granted clemency. The Rouge Queen has no jurisdiction over any Onyx witches as long as we are in our own Realm." Gideon glowered at the man.

"And who's going to enforce that law if no one knows you're there?" The leader grinned smugly. "Besides, would you really take the clemency and leave the rest of your friends to fend for themselves? Run home to Mommy while they're all marched back to the Rouge Realm? Does Lysandra even know you've been harboring one of the most wanted beings in Illustros?"

Gideon's fists clenched for a moment before he raised his palms and let out a massive blast of power toward the front line of Rouge witches, knocking six of them to the ground as if they were made of playing cards. Hannah and Caspian barely had time to tense before three of the guards recovered and seized the prince with their magic.

"Knock him out," the leader ordered. "I'm not dealing with this for the rest of the trip."

Before Gideon could protest, Hannah watched his face pale three shades as one of the Rouge witches manipulated his blood flow away from his brain. The prince held on at least thirty seconds longer than Hannah expected, his eyes wildly looking around for something—no, some*one*—but it was too late. Gideon's body hit the forest floor a second before Calla's.

52

The Storm Gutters were exactly as Hannah had imagined they would be. A place of insidious chaos with twenty-foot obsidian walls surrounding the six alleys that were lined with strips of brick buildings. The Rouge Realm had its Bone Brothels, the Tera Realm had its Venom Dens, and the Onyx Realm had the Storm Gutters. If the Starlight Inn in Estrella was a base for petty gambling, the Storm Gutters were the pinnacle of high-stakes risk.

"Load them into the carriages. Put the Siphon with those two." The head guard pointed between Hannah and Cass. "And I think we should leave the prince with his commander." The leader smirked at his guards. "That ought to be a fun ride."

It didn't surprise Hannah in the slightest that Myrea's guards would have a flair for drama—and putting Gideon and Kestrel together *would* be drama. Whenever Gideon regained consciousness, that is.

The guards came over to assist Hannah and Cass off their horse, shepherding them to one of the five massive carriages waiting near the mouth of the Storm Gutters' entrance. The guards waited for them both to climb inside, their movements made awkward by the fact that their hands were still bound. A minute later, one of the guards heaved Calla's limp body into the cab of the carriage and placed her on the floor at Hannah's and Caspian's feet. The guard slammed the door shut behind them and Hannah heard a small *click* as the lock slid into place.

"Assholes," Cass muttered, then gestured for Hannah to turn around so her back was toward him. "Time to get these restraints off."

It took a minute for Cass to get her knots loosened, since they were back-to-back and he was unable to see what he was doing, but as soon as she could slip her wrists out of the ropes, Hannah returned the favor.

When his hands were finally free, Cass leaned down to scoop Calla up and place her onto the black leather bench opposite the one he and Hannah were perched on. Hannah watched as the Onyx witch gently tucked Calla's arms over her stomach and smoothed away the hair from her face before settling back down in his seat.

The carriage began to roll forward, the *clip-clop*s of the two horses pulling the iron contraption echoed outside. To the Rouge Realm.

Caspian sighed as he leaned his head back against the carriage wall. "We are in such deep shit."

Hannah nodded in agreement and sat back as well. Cass moved to wrap an arm around her shoulder, tucking her into his side as they both yawned in sync.

"Might as well get some rest," he murmured. "It may be the last time we do."

A shiver ran down Hannah's spine at his words, and as she leaned her head on his shoulder and closed her eyes, she hoped that when she woke up this would have all been one long nightmare. Though she had a feeling the real nightmare had yet to begin.

))) ● (((

Kestrel waited anxiously as Gideon's breathing slowly regulated over the past five hours, the sunlight getting more and more dim as the carriage crawled closer to their destination. The commander was sitting pin straight, muscles coiling tighter and tighter the closer the prince came to waking up. When Gideon's eyelids began to flutter, Kestrel held his breath.

Gideon cursed as he blinked his eyes open, sitting up with effort. The prince glanced around a bit, trying to assess where he was, before his eyes finally locked on Kestrel.

"Fucking fantastic," he grunted, heaving himself up to scoot as far away from Kestrel as he could get.

"Good morning to you, too, sunshine," Kestrel said dryly.

"Where the fuck are we?" Gideon demanded. "Where's—"

"I suggest," Kestrel began, his voice carefully even, "you use a nicer tone if you want answers from me."

"Kestrel," Gideon said, his voice deeper, darker, than Kestrel had ever heard it before. Every syllable of his name on the prince's lips dripped with disdain. "*I suggest if you don't want me to rip your throat out for what you've done, you don't agitate me right now.*"

A crack of thunder resounded through the small cabin and a rhythmic patter of rain began beating on the outside of the window.

Kestrel laughed quietly, the sound haunting even to his own ears. "We're on our way to Myrea's palace, I presume. The others are in a separate carriage. The guards are afraid of keeping you and the Siphon too close to each other."

"Use her name or don't speak of her at all," Gideon warned.

The two men glared at each other in silence. Kestrel wasn't sure how long went by as the quiet between them grew more and more hostile while the storm outside brewed into a tempest.

It was Kestrel who broke first. "I didn't mean for any of this to—"

"Yes. You did." Gideon seethed, his jaw flexing with the strain of keeping his rage on a leash. The picture of the ever-composed Onyx Prince. Just as Kestrel had trained him to be. "If you didn't mean for this to happen, you wouldn't have betrayed us. Betrayed *me*. To the Rouge Queen of all people!"

"I couldn't go to Lysandra," Kestrel reasoned. "She would have stripped Caspian and me of our ranks, not to mention find some way to blame this on Ezra failing Myrea's mission, I'm sure. Myrea and Ezra already had a deal. I figured going to her would absolve him of his failure and then we could all go home—"

"At Calliope's expense! At Hannah and Delphine's expense! And

Ezra—" Gideon's words choked off, and Kestrel furrowed his brow.

"Where is Ezra?" Kestrel asked suspiciously. "Why isn't he with you all? He wouldn't have left the girl behind any more than you would have at this point."

"He did leave her—and the rest of us—behind. Just like you did. But unlike you, he didn't do it to betray anyone."

Gideon's tone was hollow, and Kestrel couldn't read whatever emotion the prince was carefully holding at bay.

"Well, at least he got out while he could. Unlike you. You've let that girl lead us straight into—"

Before Kestrel could finish his sentence, Gideon lunged forward and pressed his forearm against Kestrel's throat.

"If you think I'm going to let you blame anyone else but yourself for this turn of events, you've lost your damned mind," Gideon said. Kestrel waited calmly as he watched the obsidian ink of Gideon's irises swallow any hint of silver. "This isn't her fault. This isn't Ezra's fault. This is *your* fault. And I hope one day, when you're burning in Hells for this, your guilt consumes you before the inferno can."

"I can assure you it won't," Kestrel rasped out as he slammed his fist into Gideon's gut, forcing the prince back to the other side of the carriage. "Because let's be honest, Myrea might have double-crossed me and our deal, but I know she's going to let *you* go. Lysandra would rip her apart otherwise. And I will *never* feel guilty for trying to get you home."

"It doesn't really matter what Myrea would or wouldn't do to me, Kestrel! What don't you get about that? Calliope—"

"How the Hells was I supposed to know you would go and get yourself *soul-bonded* to her!" Kestrel finally lost his temper, his teeth bared as he punched the wall of the carriage. "That wasn't the plan! You were supposed to undo your rolls while I made my bargain with Myrea, and then they were supposed to take the girl, and we were supposed to go back and—"

"And what?" Gideon laughed darkly. "Be together? Live happily ever after? You don't know me very well if you think I would *ever* be okay with you doing something like this. What you've done is despicable—"

"*I did it to save you!*" Kestrel leaned forward and pinned Gideon's shoulders back, his face hovering barely an inch from the prince's. "You can hate me all you want, but at least I was trying to keep you alive! What has she done to get you out of this mess? Getting yourself soul-bound to her has all but guaranteed your death!"

"You think I planned for that to happen? Believe me, the whole *bound together* part wasn't even in the realm of possibilities I could have ever imagined. Besides, she is hellsbent on severing the bond. Because Calliope isn't selfish or evil or whatever else you've made up about her in your head." A flash of silver darted through Gideon's eyes when he said the girl's name. "But that's not the point and you know it. I never would have asked you to do this."

"I'm not deluded enough to think you would have approved." Kestrel leaned back. "But being the villain in her story would have been worth being the savior in yours."

Gideon's face went slack with shock for a moment before he shoved himself away from the other witch. "You will *never* be my savior."

Kestrel laughed bitterly, fists clenched at his sides. "I see that now. I realized it the first time I saw you two together, honestly, but I was hoping maybe everything we've shared would be enough to keep you. But nothing is enough, is it? I'll never be enough."

"This isn't about *you*, Kestrel. It's never been about you. It's about what *I* needed. And I didn't need you controlling my life or my thoughts the same way my mother always has."

"And what about *her* is it that you need? Your shared curses? I noticed you still have your numbers, which means something went very wrong."

Gideon said nothing.

"I've seen soul-bonds before, Gideon," Kestrel continued. "I knew it the second that guard cut you and *she* bled that someone screwed up with the Witch Eater."

"It was me who screwed up," Gideon admitted. "How does it feel to hear that? Calliope isn't the reason she and I are bound together with these curses. So you can hold on to whatever grudge you have against her, a grudge she's done nothing to deserve, but you're going to have to come to terms with the fact that I'm not perfect. Despite your training, despite all the plans you and my mother have made up in your heads for my future—I'm not perfect."

Gideon's words grew thicker and thicker as he spoke, his pointed accusations morphing into what sounded like a confession. And it was, in a way. Gideon had always needed to do everything himself, to carry the weight of the world on his shoulders alone. Kestrel had never meant to add to that, but he knew he had expected an exorbitant amount from Gideon not only as his beta, his second-in-command, but as his romantic partner as well. Maybe that's what had driven Gideon away and made him come up with this whole asinine mission in the first place. Kestrel was aware that he couldn't blame Calla forever, but it was much easier to go on hating her than hating himself for being the person who pushed Gideon to his breaking point.

"I don't understand why you didn't just ask for help," Kestrel said quietly.

"When have I ever asked for help, Kestrel?"

"This is different," Kestrel insisted, doubling down. "You swore that you knew what you were doing, but you were keeping secrets. You swore that you weren't the Heartbreak Prince."

"Is that what's important to you right now?" Gideon scoffed. "That I may have lied about such an insignificant detail?"

"It isn't insignificant to *me*."

Gideon laughed now. "Well, fine. I didn't actually know if I was or not. I suspected it was Ezra, and I was wrong. Does that make you feel any better?"

"The girl has the Heartbreak curse, too, then?" Kestrel concluded.

"You've always been good at puzzles."

"You know," Kestrel said, feeling a cruel smile turning up at the corners of his lips, "for someone who has always been afraid to fall in love, you really chose the one person who guarantees you'll have a disastrous end."

"You're assuming I love her."

"Don't you?" Kestrel locked their gazes.

The question hung between them for an excruciating minute before Gideon finally spoke again. "My heart is still in my chest, isn't it?"

"Semantics." Kestrel waved the question away with frustration. "The time and method it takes for the Heartbreak curse to take your heart is arbitrary. The consequences of curses are never black-and-white. Hells, if Myrea decides to rip the girl's heart out when we arrive, she could complete the curse before the sun sets again."

"And whose fault would that be?" Gideon gritted out.

Kestrel punched the bench cushion. "I get it, Gideon! The irony that I did all this to save you and instead it's about to damn you isn't lost on me! But tell me"—Kestrel curled his lips back—"before we get to the Rouge Realm and find out our fates . . . because I'm sure my fate will end with you never speaking to me again . . . what's the secret? What is it that she has that none of the rest of us do?"

Gideon shook his head, his words laced with finality. "I'll never have the answer you're looking for, Kestrel. Maybe it's the tragedy of our shared curses. Maybe the Fates really do have more pull than any of us want to believe. Or maybe they don't, and this convoluted mess is why I found her."

"I don't understand. She was nothing to you a few weeks ago." Kestrel shook his head, eyes pricking with pain.

"Things change, Kestrel. I'm not the same person I was even a day ago, and the sooner you realize that, the sooner you can find peace."

Kestrel swallowed and looked away. When he had been waiting for Gideon to wake up, he'd expected the rage, the fighting. But he hadn't imagined this—this steady finality that hurt worse than any hit or knife he had ever taken. He could feel the cracks in his heart spread with every word Gideon spoke.

"Our breakup was never about *you*, Kestrel," Gideon said. "But now it is. Whatever chasm is between us now—be assured you're the one who dug it."

Kestrel's heart shattered completely.

53

Caspian Ironside's name echoed in Amina's mind all the way to where Meli's cottage sat amid a pasture of grazing griffins on the outer skirt of Valor. Which irritated her to no end.

He was just a pretty witch with a smart mouth, Amina chided herself. *Erase him from your thoughts.*

A smart mouth and an even smarter strategy. Faking the Final Rolls of all the soldiers in the Onyx Queen's Guild to ensure they would have impeccably trained witches to oppose the Witch Queens when the time came . . . it was impressive. Not to mention risky. She wondered if the prince and the commander had been in on the operation as well. It wasn't hard for her to imagine the Onyx Prince being involved in such an endeavor considering his current predicament with the Fates.

A series of quick knocks brought Amina out of her thoughts. Sabine was tapping her foot impatiently as she waited for Meli to answer the door. The noise caught the attention of a griffin cub playing a few feet away, its lion tail swishing curiously as its feathered head tilted at Sabine.

"What are you looking at?" Sabine made a face at the creature.

"Leave the livestock alone, Sabine." Lyra smirked. "It isn't the creature's fault you have to see your ex-girlfriend."

The moment *ex-girlfriend* slipped out of Lyra's mouth, the door in front of them tore open.

"What in the Hells are you doing here?" Meli growled at Sabine as she opened the door.

"I'm here for the charming company and the smell of griffin manure," Sabine told her in a syrupy voice that clearly was on the verge of triggering Meli's urge to punch something. "Let us in."

"No." Meli glowered.

"Meli, we need to talk." Amina stepped forward to shoulder Sabine out of the girl's line of sight. "Privately, please."

"Now you want to talk? How many times have I tried to talk to you after—"

"The breakup, blah, blah, blah." Sabine stood on her tiptoes to shoot a glare over Amina's shoulder. "This is more important than our issues, Meli."

Meli narrowed her eyes, opening her mouth to retort, but the serious look bleeding onto Sabine's expression must have alarmed her. She swallowed whatever words she'd been about to say and stepped back so the three of them could funnel inside. Meli led the trio down a long hall into the main living space and waved a hand toward the green velvet couch in offering.

Meli's cottage looked exactly the same as Amina remembered it from the times she had visited when Sabine and the other Valkyrie were dating. It was quaint, but the natural light that flooded in through the glass back wall made it feel much bigger. The tables and counters were littered with sketches of random objects and people, half-finished paintings piled against the living room walls. Sabine stopped before one of the paintings—a portrait of a girl with gilded hair and verdigris eyes. Amina watched as her friend flinched and looked away.

"What do you three want? Besides to torture me, I mean." Meli broke the silence, crossing her arms over her chest.

"Oh, come on." Sabine rolled her eyes. "If you think a conversation is torture, clearly you've already forgotten what I can do—"

"Why weren't you at your reaping shift today?" Amina asked without preamble, cutting Sabine off before a tangent began.

Meli narrowed her wine-colored eyes before flicking them toward Sabine. "I was sick."

"You were hungover, you mean." Amina smirked, recalling the image of Meli pounding back glasses of ambrosia after running into Sabine at the Reverie.

"Maybe," Meli grumbled. "How is it any of your business where I was or wasn't or why? Besides, it's not like they're short of Reapers these days with the whole witch drought that's currently happening."

"That's just what we'd like to talk to you about, actually," Amina said. "What do you know about that entire situation?"

"What makes you think I know anything?" Meli asked too innocently.

"Meli, don't play games." Sabine shot the other girl a look.

"I thought you liked games, Sabine," Meli countered, bitterness burning in her tone. "That's why you strung me along for so long, isn't it?"

"Gods, we're not going to get anywhere with these two in the same room," Lyra muttered.

"Meli, cut the crap," Amina demanded. "We all know you're the most plugged-in person in our whole damn society."

Meli looked as if she wanted to debate about the topic more, but then she suddenly squeezed her eyes shut and pinched the bridge of her nose. "Ugh, I have a raging migraine. *Fine.* If it will make you get the Hells out of my house—what exactly do you want to know? It's true there haven't been many witches lately. Lysandra pulled most of her Guild back from the borderlines and our Reapers have been having a hard time meeting the new soul quota—which is outrageous, by the way."

Amina nodded. "We know that much. Five hundred souls a month, right?"

"Yes. And it's going to be damn near impossible to do. But we better start getting souls somehow before the queen begins—"

Meli cut herself off abruptly, shaking her head.

"Begins what?" Lyra nudged her.

"I shouldn't say. I don't know if it's even true."

"When has that ever stopped you before?" Sabine lifted her brows.

Meli was about to shoot a venomous retort back to Sabine, Amina was sure, but Lyra cut her off before she got a single insult out of her mouth.

"Meli, this is incredibly important. I think we all know that something big is coming, and if we don't have all the information, we can't prepare for it," Lyra reasoned.

Meli bit her lip, debating for a second before finally sighing. "It was just something I heard last night at the Reverie. I had too much wine and accidentally stumbled into one of the staff powder rooms to, uh . . ."

"Vomit," Sabine supplied.

"Yes," Meli admitted, begrudgingly. "Anyway, when I was cleaning myself up in one of the back powder rooms, two guards came in. They were whispering about the new soul quota and one of them said something about the queen taking the reapings into her own hands if she had to. Then they started whispering about how they were planning to warn their families to get out of the Valkyrie lands 'before it was too late' and that they might even leave Illustros in general before the Fates' War started."

There was a long, heavy pause.

"How many people have you told this to?" Amina demanded, her words coming out almost breathless.

"No one," Meli said.

"Be serious, Meli," Sabine pressed. "This is vital. Who have you told?"

"I *am* serious," Meli swore, glancing at Lyra as if she were looking for help to convince her ex that she was telling the truth. "I haven't spoken to anyone since I left the ball—I've been *sick*—and I'm not even sure if I heard the guards right in the first place."

Amina turned to Lyra. "I am begging you to let us strike sooner rather than later. Maybe even rope your brother into this. People we trust."

"What's going on? What do you know?" Meli demanded.

Amina turned back to the girl and declared, "There's about to be a major soul shortage, and when there is, the Fates' War won't be the only one we have to watch out for. We haven't gotten to the bottom of everything quite yet. But we will. In the meantime, you're going to have to keep your mouth shut."

Meli nodded. "I promise I won't say any—"

Amina shook her head, cutting the girl off midsentence. "We're going to need a little bit more than a promise, Meli. Sorry, but your reputation precedes you a little too much, and this is too big to risk spreading and causing a mass panic before we have a plan in place. If the queen gets word that we know anything about this, she's going to look for someone to blame. And I, for one, refuse to be exiled to that godsforsaken forest again."

"You mean . . . You can't be serious. You want me to take a Blood Oath?" Meli's mouth dropped open.

"Think of it this way." Sabine flipped a piece of her hair over her shoulder as she fixed her ex with a smile. "If you don't take it, we'll know *exactly* who to come back for if word gets out. And then we'll revisit that discussion of torture."

Meli thrust her hand out toward Amina and grumbled, *"Fine."*

"Nope, over here." Sabine beckoned to Meli with a newly unsheathed dagger. "I'm the one with the knives."

Meli gritted her teeth before shifting over to the blond. Sabine took Meli's palm and drew a quick line through it. Bright crimson blood instantly pooled in her hand, and a moment later the cut was healed.

"Swear you will not tell anyone what we spoke of today," Sabine prompted. "Say the oath."

"Testor meo sanguine," Meli recited, and the blood in her hand began bubbling with magic. "I will not speak a word of what we discussed here today to anyone."

They all watched as the blood in Meli's palm turned bright gold and seeped back beneath her skin before her veins pulsed the same gilded color all the way up her arms and straight to her heart—sealing the oath there.

"All right." Amina nodded in satisfaction. "Thank you for your cooperation. And if you hear anything else—"

"You'll be the first to know," Meli assured her.

"Ready?" Amina asked the others, and Lyra headed toward the exit without hesitation. Sabine, however, lingered.

"Meli . . ."

"I'm tired, Sabine," Meli said pointedly.

"We will talk," Sabine vowed. "One day."

Meli didn't respond, but Amina saw a glimmer of hope in her eyes.

Amina waited for Sabine to walk ahead of her before following the blond out.

Amina and the others didn't say a word as they soared through the warm skies. Amina took the silent flight as an opportunity to admire Valor down below. She had always loved the way the city appeared from above—like three overlapping moons dotted with marble-and-gold buildings that looked like stars. She also loved the way the Miroir Mountains glittered on the horizon, the mirrorlike crystals embedded in its peaks casting rainbows into the sky when the sun hit them just right.

As the trio dove in for their landing on the front steps of Lyra's manor, Amina spotted something waiting for them by the front door. Amina snatched the thick envelope from where it was stuck to the entrance, ripping through the Valkyrie Queen's wax seal with a shaky hand. She pulled out the letter and unfolded it with lightning speed, Lyra and Sabine crowding in next to her to read the scrawled text.

Dearest Amina,

Welcome home from exile. I think it's time we get reacquainted. The palace, tonight, at dusk. Leave your pets at home.

Queen Ignia

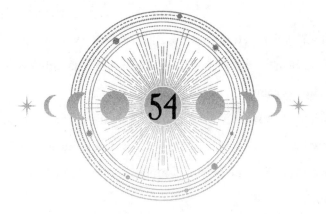

54

The only thing getting Delphine through the dinner party were the six glasses of faery wine she drained during the eight-course meal and the platter of sticky buns sitting in front of her. She'd already sat through an hour of toasts from various members of Reniel's Shoal eulogizing their leader's *incredible enterprise*, followed by a grating barrage of questions on why Delphine thought she deserved to be in their presence. By the time dessert was being served, she had almost lost her will to continue through the night. That's when the sticky buns arrived.

"Your favorite," Reniel said, one corner of his mouth lifting. "I requested them just for you."

Halfway through her first bun Reniel had dismissed himself and the others to mingle in the drawing room next door for after-dinner cocktails. Delphine was grateful for the reprieve from the hostile glares and pointed questions. Now she was working on her fourth bun, icing coating her fingertips, when someone asked her a question.

"What?" she asked with a mouthful of pastry, looking up in surprise, head buzzing a bit from the ambrosia. She thought everyone had left the dining room.

"I asked if those were any good?" A coal-eyed siren watched her display with amusement as he pulled a chair out across from her and sat down. "But the absolute euphoria on your face answered my question."

Delphine swallowed her bite and narrowed her eyes at the man. He looked familiar, but she couldn't quite put her finger on why. His navy hair was combed back handsomely, a striking contrast against his blue skin that was only a shade or two darker than her own. He had a purplish scar cutting through his left eyebrow that curved in a semicircle toward his ear. It somehow made him even more handsome.

"Who are you?" Her words were a tad clumsy. "Have we met before?"

"No one of importance," he answered sincerely.

"I find that hard to believe," she scoffed. "Reniel doesn't hang around people he doesn't consider important or useful in some way."

"Which one are you, then?"

"Useful, obviously." She gestured toward the platter of sticky buns. "I'm here to make sure none of these go to waste."

"You're doing an incredible job." He took a sip from a crystal glass of wine she hadn't noticed in his hand before.

A moment of awkward silence hung between them.

"Are you new to Reniel's Shoal?" she finally asked.

The man's eyebrows jutted up. "You think I'm in his Shoal?"

"Why else would you be here? Isn't this the start of the celebrations for the Blood Moon?" She raised a single brow before taking another large gulp from her drink to wash down the pastry. As she lowered her glass, she caught a glimpse of Celeste and Eros standing on the other side of the room, whispering to each other. She quickly looked away. During the toasts she had felt Celeste's stare on her the entire time—probably confused about how the Hells this turn of events had happened—but Delphine worried that if the sirens confronted her now, she would be too inebriated to hold her tongue.

The man across from her opened his mouth to answer her previous question, but before he could get anything out, Reniel reappeared in the dining room's open archway and said, "Ah, there you are. Are you going to join us, brother?"

Delphine choked on her wine. *"Brother?"*

"I think I'm going to go to bed early, actually," the siren across from her said. "I have a meeting at the Sea King's palace in the morning now that I'm . . . back. Besides, I'm sure you'll have more fun without me."

"It's not even midnight yet," Reniel reasoned.

Reniel's brother shrugged. "Not all of us have your endurance for parties, Reniel."

"Moonlight, would you excuse us for a moment?" Reniel's smile was tight as he prompted her to remove herself from the table.

She did so, taking her goblet with her, but before she could leave the room, Celeste had her cornered.

"What the Hells, Delphine," Celeste hissed, Eros standing over her shoulder with an equally perplexed expression. "How did you manage to get Reniel to let you out of your cell? I was worried sick about you."

"Seems like a waste of your time," Delphine quipped.

Celeste drew back at Delphine's tone. "I'm sorry that I was trying to get a plan together to *rescue you*. Was that also a waste of my time?"

"Depends what the plan is, I suppose." Delphine shrugged. "I managed to get myself out of the cell, as you can see."

Celeste flinched.

This time it was Eros who spoke. "She's drunk, Cel."

"I don't care." Celeste sniffed. "You could have told me you were planning to call on Reniel after we saw you yesterday. I've spent the last several days racking my brain about how to help—what is *that*?"

Delphine followed the girl's line of sight down to the sapphire-adorned ring on her left hand. She tucked her hand into her chest. "I did what I had to do to get out of that dungeon." Delphine gripped the glass in her other hand so tightly she worried it might shatter. "So I'm sure you can get over having to *think* a little harder than usual."

Celeste went very still, the look on her face going from anger to shock to hurt. Delphine knew she needed to shut up now, but she was having a hard time making herself stop.

"I'm out; it's done," Delphine said. "If you still want to make this work, we can meet tomorrow—noon in the formal den. If you don't show, I'll assume you've decided to go in a different direction. Either way works for me."

"Maybe we *will* go in a different direction." Celeste sucked in a shaky breath, and Eros placed a steadying hand on the siren's shoulder. "The tracker ring would hold us back now, anyway. We don't need you."

Delphine's smile was vicious. "Are you trying to convince me of that last part, or yourself?"

"Let's go," Eros ordered Celeste, fixing Delphine with a hostile look as he dragged the other girl from the room. "If she wants to do this by herself, let her."

Delphine stood there as the room tilted for what felt like hours after they had gone.

"Delphine."

She snapped back to the present, turning toward the sound of her name. Reniel beckoned her over to the table.

"What was that about?" He narrowed his eyes.

"Nothing," she muttered, draining the rest of her drink. "They're just upset they've lost their plaything."

"Ah, well." Reniel relaxed a bit. "There hasn't been much for them to do lately with all the preparations for the Blood Moon, and their cohort has been busy prepping for Zephyr's promotion."

At the mention of Zephyr and his promotion, Delphine said, "I need a refill."

A waitress walked into the room as if on cue, a girl with pretty cyan hair, carrying a pitcher. She silently came around to refill Delphine's glass, but when Reniel shifted back from Delphine, he bumped right into the outstretched pitcher. The faery wine spilled all over the white silk tablecloth.

"*Hells,*" Reniel snapped, reaching his hand out to grip the waitress by her bicep with lightning speed. "That tablecloth is worth more than your life. I ought to—"

Delphine hit one of the other wineglasses on the table with her elbow and sent the berry-colored liquid splashing all over the place.

"Oops," Delphine hiccuped.

Reniel's brother locked eyes with hers, a glint of shock shining in them as the waitress held her breath for Reniel's reaction.

"I'm a little tipsy, I think." Delphine forced a giggle as she patted at the swelling stain with a napkin.

Reniel let out a deep sigh and dropped the maid's arm.

"Go get something to clean this up," he barked at the other girl, and she immediately scrambled to leave the room, throwing a quick, grateful glance over her shoulder in Delphine's direction before she disappeared.

"I ought to punish you for this mess, moonlight." Reniel narrowed his eyes at Delphine. "It's like you're begging to have your throat ripped out again."

"I love it when you talk dirty to me," she rasped, keeping her expression as clear as possible.

Reniel rolled his eyes and turned to address his brother once again. "Are you sure you don't want to join us for cards, Bellator?"

Bellator. Why did that name sound so familiar?

"Positive," the siren answered, though his gaze still had not left Delphine.

"What about you, moonlight?" Reniel asked almost reluctantly.

"What about me?" she mumbled.

"I'm sure you have no interest in a card game," he stated plainly.

"You assume correct." She wrapped her arms around herself.

Reniel nodded. "Better that way anyway. It will give me an opportunity to feel out what everyone thinks about your reintroduction tonight."

"I'll be waiting on the edge of my seat for the verdict."

"Don't worry, I'm sure that dress had at least a few of them reconsidering their stance," Reniel drawled in a way that made her want to punch him in the face. "You can head back to our room whenever you're finished here—which I advise should be soon."

Reniel gave one final nod to his brother before disappearing from the room.

"Why did you do that?" Bellator immediately asked. "You're lucky he didn't turn his wrath on you."

"His wrath is nothing I'm not used to." She waved away his question as she stood from the table, her balance not as steady as she wished. "*You* said you were no one of importance."

"In these waters I'm not. And I'm sure if you were to ask my brother, he would say the same thing."

In these waters, she noted. Of course Reniel's brother *would* be just as cryptic as he was, and given the vast expanse of Illustros, and Aetherius as a whole, that means he could be important in a multitude of other places.

"Your name sounds so familiar," she told him, narrowing her eyes. "Bellator. Are you sure— *Wait.*" Recognition finally clicked in her mind. The scar that now marred his face had thrown her off. *"You."*

He looked at her like he was unsurprised at the visceral reaction she was having. "It's been a very long time."

She took a wide step away from the table. "The last time I saw you . . ."

"I wish there had been more I could've done for your mother. I tried to warn you."

She sucked in a breath and spun away from the table, stalking off toward the hallway.

"Wait," Bellator called, following her out. "Where are you going?"

"I'm not really looking to reminisce about the past right now," she informed him. "I'm going to bed. I think you were about to do the same."

"I was," he confirmed as he caught up to her. "It's just . . . I wasn't expecting you to be like this."

"Like *what?*" she snapped, stopping her stride to turn on him. She'd already had to fake nice for one brother; she was not about to bother saving face with the other. "The last time you saw me I was *ten years old.*"

"And just as assertive," he noted with a nod. "But you seemed much more . . . agreeable . . . than you do now. You've grown claws."

"Well, I suggest if you don't want to find my *claws* embedded in your throat, you leave me alone and go back to wherever the Hells you came from."

She started forward once more, but he didn't leave like she hoped he would.

"I find it awfully peculiar that my brother would be with someone so . . . bold. Last I heard you ran away. And now you're back making conversation at dinner parties. What changed?"

Delphine felt a zap run over her nerves. This felt like a test.

"A lot of things have changed," she said innocently as she hooked a left at the end of the hallway. "And why wouldn't he like someone bold? The man is made entirely of pride and audacity himself."

"Reniel doesn't like his prey to fight back," Bellator told her. "His ego is too fragile to survive any direct hits."

Delphine stopped walking again. "Prey? Who says I'm prey?"

He gave her a small, sad smile. "Everyone in this house is prey, darling."

"Does that include you?" She cocked a hand on her hip.

"Yes. Decades of waiting, and my brother finally got one up on me. Now here I am, playing his games, suffering through his dinner parties, same as you."

"It sounds like you have plenty of your own business to worry about," she concluded. "So why don't you stay out of mine?"

He let out a surprised laugh before sobering and narrowing his eyes. "You know what I think?"

She didn't answer him, her stomach becoming increasingly unsettled by how astutely he seemed to be observing her.

"I think my brother has always severely underestimated you."

Delphine's mouth went dry. Reniel was observant about how things looked and the way people perceived him and his power, but he relied on the elite members of his Shoal to keep an eye on everything else.

"And why do you think that?" she gritted out.

He looked like he was about to answer but thought better of it. Instead, he changed the subject. "There were a lot of stories about you, you know. Reniel's young protégée who swore three centuries of life away for taking care of her banished mother. All for your mother to turn around and take a hefty payout for agreeing to never see you again."

Delphine felt like she wasn't breathing.

"That must have been hard."

"She did it because it was best for both of us," Delphine spat. "I couldn't see her again anyway, so why shouldn't she take Reniel's money? She needed to survive. That's why I was sneaking her money in the first place. Her own Shoal had banished her, too. Reniel's connections had made sure she was completely desolate."

"She swore a Siren's oath not to see you ever again, Delphine." Bellator shook his head. "Even if she would have had to wait three centuries until your own oath was paid off to see you again—even if it meant she should starve in that time—that's what she should've done.

The oath she swore was not one with a time limit like yours—hers will guarantee she can *never* see you again."

"Shut up," she snarled. She didn't want to hear this. Her mother had done what she had to do. Three centuries was too long to expect anyone to wait for her.

That's when the memory of Hannah's words slammed through her mind.

I will never *stop looking for you.* Never. *I will search the entire world until I find you again.* Delphine. Delphine, please. *I love* you.

She squeezed her eyes shut. Bellator had ripped open an old wound—one she had spent years sewing up. So many of her sleepless nights had been spent wondering if the only thing her mother had ever thought of her as was a pretty instrument—if, even after Reniel took away her mother's magic, Delphine had been manipulated into joining his Shoal to make sure her mother reached one last goal. All those years spent unlearning the unflinching ability to use herself as a tool for others rather than a real person with substance to offer had nearly broken her down. The first time she had ever felt like a person truly saw *her* was the day she met . . . Hannah. Hannah, who had promised to spend eternity looking for her if that's what it took.

And her own mother hadn't even hesitated at the idea of never laying eyes on her daughter again.

Bellator opened and closed his mouth a few times before finally saying, "I didn't mean to upset you. I just meant to reassure you that many of us have shitty familial ties. We're all in over our heads here. But there are ways out."

"Have *you* found a way out?" she beseeched as she pried her eyes open and recomposed herself, taking a few deep breaths.

"Ah, that's a complicated story. I once had very powerful connections outside the Siren's Sea, and my brother was always a tad jealous. To say the least."

"You don't have those connections anymore?"

"To say the least," he repeated.

"What connections could possibly make Reniel jealous? He knows everyone from the Siren's Sea to the fae courts to the human territories."

Bellator shrugged. "My brother is the sort who thinks one person with proximity to political power is worth ten people without."

"And yet you'd have to pay me to deal with any more royalty." She gave a weak sniff.

"The Sea King, you mean?" He lifted a brow—the one without the scar.

"Worse. Witches," she said before she could stop herself. The faery wine was starting to really sink into her core now.

Something shifted in the man's eyes. "You had a run-in with one of the Witch Queens?"

"Not the queens." Delphine shook her head and immediately regretted it. The room was beginning to tilt a bit. "The witch *princes*. And they were not pleasant. Well, one wasn't. The other one is actually quite charming."

"Oh?" Bellator said.

"You would think being brothers would mean one wouldn't be completely insufferable," she muttered as she tried to start walking again. "Alas, my best friend is attached to them both, so I suppose I'll have to deal with Ezra Black again someday."

"Whoa," Bellator said as he lunged forward to steady her by her arm when putting one foot in front of the other suddenly became too great a task. "I think the wine is finally hitting you. How much did you have?"

"Six glasses? Ten?" she slurred. "I haven't had faery wine in years."

"Clearly." He shook his head, giving her a disapproving look. "Here, I'll help you to your room."

She would have protested, except she couldn't get the words out. And she definitely couldn't walk without his hand steering her. A couple of turns through the halls, and he stopped before a door she didn't recognize.

"This isn't Reniel's room," she told him.

"No," Bellator agreed. "It's an empty guest room. I'm not sure I should leave you in my brother's bed, intoxicated, in case he returns in the late hours of the night equally drunk. Or worse—pissed from losing a hand of cards."

Bellator pushed the door open and walked her inside, helping her gently into the crisply made bed. She wanted to tell him she could handle Reniel and his moods, that she had before, but truthfully, she much preferred the idea of sleeping alone in such a vulnerable state.

Once she was settled beneath the covers, Bellator turned to leave.

"Thank you," she whispered into the dark.

It was silent for a long moment, and she wondered if he was already gone.

Then he spoke once more. "Can I give you some advice?"

She tried to blink open her eyes to look at him, but her lids were too heavy. Instead, she hummed, "Hmm?"

"If you get away again," Bellator told her, his voice softer than the wind blowing outside the room's window, "never come back."

There was a quiet *click* from across the room, and then the darkness finally pulled Delphine under.

55

"Holy Hells," Sabine said for the tenth time.

Lyra narrowed their golden gaze on Amina. "What are we going to do?"

"I suppose I'm going to go meet her at dusk," Amina told them.

"You have the beating heart of her dead lover strapped to your hip," Lyra pointed out dryly, "and you're going to take a meeting with her?"

"What do you suppose I *should* do?" Amina asked sincerely. "Ignore the summons?"

"We should leave!" They threw their hands into the air. "If the guards can warn their families and desert Illustros like Meli told us—then we can warn ours, too, and get out of here. She's already taken six years from you, Amina. Are you going to walk back into that palace and let her take more?"

"Exactly, she's already taken *years* from me, Ly. I'm not going to let her run me out of my home again. I'm not going to let her get away with any of this. We may be the only ones who know the truth—we have to tell people." Amina swallowed, throat tight. "The years I spent in the forest, thinking about the day I would make the queen pay for my exile—all that anger I carried then, the revenge I craved, it was for the three of us. But now? Now this anger is for our people. The Reapers who have lived with the guilt of taking souls they knew weren't ready. All of us who have had to wear the masks of heartless harpies so that the rest of Illustros wouldn't look too closely at our crumbling foundation and prey upon us even more than our own queen already does. It is both a blessing and a curse that the witches are distracted by their own brewing storm right now, because if they weren't and they caught wind of this, their hatred for us would undoubtedly lead them to strike. Because we've fed into a rivalry we didn't need to for centuries. All for that selfish, scheming *bitch*."

After a long pause, Lyra finally squared their shoulders and said, "All right. If you want to take this on—then we'll do it. But where you go, *we* go. We will not be separated this time. I don't care if that note told you to go alone or not. We will not be divided this time."

Sabine chimed in, agreeing, "Either we burn down this monarchy together—or we get banned together."

"What's the plan?" Lyra asked.

"I'm going to go to the palace tonight as she requested," Amina announced. "I'll leave Rovin's heart and my Esprit here with you."

"What are we going to do with them now if we aren't using them?" Sabine questioned.

"Who said we weren't still going to use them?" Amina asked.

When Amina arrived at the palace, it was one minute until dusk. Sabine and Lyra were nowhere to be seen, but Amina could feel their presence in her bones.

Amina walked up the grand steps of the palace, greeted by two doormen at the entrance. They silently pushed open the double doors and waved Amina through, not bothering to look at her as they pulled them shut again behind her. The heavy slam of the doors echoed through the grand castle around her, and Amina almost shivered as she felt the weight of the silence settle over her shoulders. Without all the guests of the Reverie to fill up the space, it looked much larger than she remembered it being the day before.

"Amina," someone to her left called.

Amina turned to find a guard coming down the hall, his face carefully blank as he approached.

"This way," he ordered, beckoning her in the opposite direction of the throne room.

"We aren't meeting in the throne room?" Amina questioned.

"Sound in the throne room carries," the man explained without looking back. "This meeting is private."

Amina steeled her nerves. All signs were pointing to what she had suspected when she saw the summons on the door earlier. The queen had discovered what they took. She wondered if someone had identified them when they were flying away—or if the Wayfarer had betrayed them. She wouldn't put it past him, if the queen had offered him the right price. He was always a wild card.

"Here," the guard in front of her said, and halted next to a large wood door. He knocked once, twice, three times.

"Come in," a haughty voice called from inside. The guard pulled the door open, and Amina stepped inside the dimly lit space, the door behind her clicking shut a second later.

The room was a small library. There were wooden shelves lining every wall, a long track running above them that held a rolling ladder. Piles and piles of books were wedged wherever they could fit. In the middle of the far wall, between two shelves, was a lit fireplace, two chairs sitting near the hearth.

Amina studied the kelpie head mounted above the mantel with distaste. Poor creature.

"You look like you came dressed for a fight," the queen said as she stood from one of the chairs in front of the fire. The glow the flames cast on the woman's usually fawn-colored hair made it look almost auburn.

Amina looked down at her outfit; she was wearing a black mesh bodysuit that hugged her lean curves and tucked in tightly to her black leather trousers. Her laced-up boots crawled all the way up her calves. Only her arms were bare and yet she felt utterly naked without a single weapon strapped to her body, but she had known the Queen's guards wouldn't have allowed her inside if she had shown up with any.

"Were you expecting a fight?" the queen continued.

"Let's see . . ." Amina began, lifting her pointer finger to drag over the spines of the books to her left. "Last time I was in your presence, I was beaten and forced to take a Blood Oath that exiled me to a demonic forest for two years. Excuse me for preparing myself better this time. I don't like repeating history."

The queen didn't smile or banter back like Amina thought she might. Instead she said, "I'm surprised you found a prince's heart as quickly as you did."

"Well, when the Onyx Queen comes knocking on my door seeking revenge on the Valkyrie who killed her foolish son, I'll be sure to give her your address."

"Which son?"

"What?" Amina said with a bit of surprise. That was not the question she had been expecting.

"Which. Son."

"The youngest. Ezra, I believe they called him."

"The Heartbreak Prince is still alive, then. Good."

Amina narrowed her eyes at the instant relief in the queen's eyes. "What do you care for the Heartbreak Prince?"

"That's none of your concern. Now, let's get down to the reason for your visit, shall we?"

Amina braced herself now, straightening her spine so she stood at her full height—not more than half an inch taller than the queen. The queen's pale green eyes flickered with something Amina couldn't quite read, and her alabaster skin was flushed with the heat coming from the hearth or from anticipation—Amina couldn't tell which.

"Why were you at my Reverie last night?" the queen asked.

The expression on Amina's face didn't waver as she answered, "I figured what better way to celebrate my homecoming than a party? So nice of you to plan that, by the way. The wine was splendid."

"Imagine my surprise," the queen continued without missing a beat, "when one of my guards told me they saw you and your little minions launching yourselves out of a window."

"They aren't my minions. They are my partners."

"Do you know why I chose the Neverending Forest as your place of exile?" the queen went on as if Amina had not spoken.

"You were hoping I'd get ripped to shreds by a viperidae?"

"Yes." No hesitation. "But not just that."

"Enlighten me," Amina gritted out.

"There are things looming on the horizon of Illustros that are much bigger than you can imagine."

Try me, she thought.

"I was told you visited the border this morning, so I'm sure you've heard of the current situation with the witches. The last Blood Warrior has been found. And do you know where the poor, cursed being was supposedly spotted?"

Amina said nothing.

The queen smiled with venom as she said, "The Neverending Forest."

"What an odd coincidence," Amina mused.

"I sent you to that forest to be my eyes and ears. I knew if you came across a prince, it would most likely be one of the Onyx Queen's little bastards."

"What do you care of the Onyx Princes?" Amina asked once again. "How do they fit into all this?"

"How about we play a game," the queen said, turning to walk back toward the mantel, where a glass decanter filled with a dark purple liquid sat. She poured the liquid into two small cups and held one out in offering to Amina. "You give me an answer and I'll give you one."

Amina took the glass out of the queen's hand but didn't drink right away, waiting for the other woman to take her own sip first. The queen smiled and threw back half the liquid in her cup, and Amina finally brought the drink to her own lips, taking a small sip. It tasted like elderberries.

"Fine," Amina agreed after another sip.

"Who is the final Blood Warrior? And don't tell me that you do not know. You aren't as good at hiding your reactions as you think."

Amina balled her hands into fists, her long nails digging into her palms. "A girl. A Siphon named Calliope. What importance do the witch princes have?"

"Lysandra did everything in her power to make sure that her first-born would not get the Heartbreak curse, but unfortunately for her, that nasty little curse has never cooperated for any of us."

Any of us?

"It wasn't hard to put together that around the time you returned home with a prince's heart was the same time rumors of the final Blood Warrior began swirling around the Witch Realms. Which means that girl is with the princes. Now, for what reason did you come to my Reverie?"

"I came to—" Amina started before snapping her mouth shut in shock. She had been about to tell the truth. It was like the words wanted to push their way out of their own accord. She frowned down at the glass at her hand. The queen's smile turned wicked.

Amina threw the glass as hard as she could into the fireplace, making the flames roar with ire as the cup shattered into pieces and the Truth Wine splattered on the lit coals.

The queen tilted her head back and laughed. "Truth Wine is my favorite of the fae's inventions. Though it is an acquired taste for most, don't you think?"

Amina knew if she opened her mouth again the truth would spill out. She had to be incredibly careful how she chose her next words.

"I was at your Reverie because I wanted to get revenge on you," she said tightly.

"And did you?" The queen tilted her head.

"Ah, ah, ah. It's my turn," Amina admonished her. The queen tapped her foot with impatience. Amina desperately wanted to ask for the truth about the letter she had found, but considering the queen hadn't brought it up yet, she wondered if perhaps the woman didn't know. So, instead, she asked, "Earlier you said, 'That nasty little curse has never cooperated for any of us'—does that mean you have firsthand experience with the Heartbreak curse?"

The queen scowled now, her lips pressing tighter together. It was Amina's turn to grin.

"What's the matter? Don't like when the Truth Wine is turned against you?"

"Yes. I do have firsthand experience. Did your plan for revenge go through?"

"Not exactly," Amina answered easily, getting into the flow of their little game. "What kind of firsthand experience?"

"I created the Heartbreak curse," the queen declared, and Amina flinched, shocked.

"*What?*"

"Final question: Where is the prince's heart that you stole?"

"Not with me."

"Not a good enough answer. I want the heart."

"And if I tossed it aside the moment it helped me get out of the forest?" Amina posed. "It was only required to fulfill my Blood Oath and release the magic that kept me trapped in the forest. You never said I needed to bring it back."

All carefully spoken truths.

The queen's lips curled back from her teeth. "You foolish girl! Do you know how valuable that could have been against the Onyx Queen? We need every bit of leverage we can get against the witches now that this war is on the brink of beginning."

"Why does leverage against the witches matter?" Amina pressed. "Why can't we mind our own business? It is their mess with the Fates to deal with, not ours."

The queen's eyes narrowed slightly. "What do you know?"

"I know a lot of things."

"That's good." The woman laughed as she reached over to pull a book down from the bookcase to her right. "Because I have an assignment for you, and your vast knowledge of *things* will surely come in handy."

"And if I don't cooperate?" Amina glowered.

Before the queen could answer, the room began to shake slightly, and Amina swallowed thickly as she watched the left wall shift to the side and reveal two guards carrying someone between them.

"If you don't cooperate, I'll sever the head from your friend's body."

Amina was expecting the figure being shoved forward out of the shadows to be either Lyra or Sabine. The last person she was expecting to see was *Meli.*

Amina gaped at Meli's tear-soaked face as the girl's eyes collided with hers.

The queen snapped her fingers, and her guards poised their swords over Meli's neck. "Make your choice."

56

When Delphine finally woke the next morning, her head hurt worse than the mornings after Reniel's torture.

She was never drinking faery wine again.

She crawled from beneath the covers and stretched out her limbs, still wearing the elaborate woven dress from the night before, the little pearls having left divots in her skin. She tiptoed to the door and pulled it open to peek out into the hallway. She sighed in relief to find it empty and stepped out. It only took a few minutes to make her way back to Reniel's suite, but what she found when she stepped inside the room had her wanting to run back down the hall.

"Where the *Hells* have you been?" Reniel growled as soon as he spotted her, cornering her against a wall.

Just over his shoulder Delphine could see the wreckage of his suite; there were chairs thrown on their sides, bedding strewn all over the ground, his outfit from the night before littered in a trail leading toward the bed. She owed Bellator a huge favor for not bringing her here last night.

"I drank too much wine last night and lost my way back," she lied. "I ended up passing out in one of the guest bedrooms."

"You're lying," he said, slamming a fist into the wall next to her head.

She refused to give him the satisfaction of seeing her flinch. "No, I am *not*. Did you miss how many glasses I drank? Believe me, I won't be doing that again."

He narrowed his eyes in on her face, trying to decipher whether or not she was telling the truth, and whatever he found there must have been convincing enough because the tension in his body relaxed ever so slightly.

"Just tell me one thing," he said, speaking deliberately. "Did you sleep with him?"

Delphine's brows knitted together in confusion, her top lip curling in disgust. "I didn't sleep with *anyone*."

"It's just mighty coincidental that you and my brother went off to bed at the same time last night and you weren't here when I came back."

"You think I had sex with *your brother*?" she half-screeched. "First of all, he has a very annoying know-it-all-father aura about him that is a *huge* turnoff. Second of all, do you really believe after working this hard to get back on your good side and suffering through that Godsawful dinner party last night, I would sleep with your own flesh and blood? That isn't the sort of drama I like."

Delphine would be more furious at such an accusation if Reniel wasn't so transparent. This wasn't because Reniel thought Delphine was promiscuous or wanted her himself—it was because he didn't want his brother to have anything he didn't. An incredibly healthy family dynamic to have, she was sure.

"Fine," he said, relenting as he backed away from her a step. "But I don't want you speaking to Bellator anymore."

"Wasn't planning to, anyway." She headed for the bathroom.

"I'll be out until dinner," he informed her, voice tight. "If you leave this room, you are to go nowhere except the dining room or grand room and a guard will be accompanying you the entire time."

She clicked the bathroom door shut behind her.

Delphine wondered if the guard currently trailing her around the palace would be missed if they were murdered. Every step they took on her heels had her resisting the urge to maim them. It was getting closer and closer to noon, and she needed to sneak away, but Reniel's orders to keep her confined to certain rooms were sticking.

As she led the guard through the glass hallways of the palace, she was relieved to notice there weren't many people around since Reniel was out. Shoal members who weren't part of the elites or Reniel's inner circle lived in the far west wing and came and went as they pleased—which meant they were very rarely inside the central house unless there was an occasion. Shoal members who opted to stay with family that belonged to other Shoals after being Claimed resided in the inner villages of the Siren's Sea and were only allowed access to the palace when Reniel was around to give them permission. Their leader didn't trust them to keep what went on inside the crystal walls from their families and the other Shoals—and he was smart to do that considering how many times Delphine had easily collected information from simply being invited to other Shoals' parties.

The elites and inner circle members unfortunately *did* stay in the central palace, and the moment Delphine entered the grand room she regretted it. Several scowling faces turned in her direction from where they lounged as they waited for lunch to be served, and something clicked in her head as she recognized a few. Delphine fixed a taunting smile on her face and approached a trio of sirens, all languidly sipping champagne on the sapphire couch that stretched along the entirety of the massive window on the back wall. Their expressions curdled with disdain as Delphine paused in front of them.

"Hello, Jas, Hayley, Eli. It's been a while." Delphine reached over and snatched the champagne flute from Eli's hand and drained it in one gulp.

Eli stood from the couch, eyes sparking with malice as Delphine tried to hand the glass back. "You insufferable *meretrix*."

Delphine grinned at the sound of being called a harlot in their first language. The language had been lost more and more throughout the last few centuries, and Delphine thought it was such a shame. It was so much prettier to be called *meretrix* than *whore*.

"Don't be jealous, Eli." Delphine shoved the glass into Eli's chest as their friends stood from the couch, braced for a fight. "It's a hideous color on you—just like that dress."

Delphine was being honest about the latter. Eli's green complexion was *not* made to wear maroon.

"No one wants you here." Hayley narrowed her eyes.

"Except Reniel," Delphine purred. "When was the last time he actually remembered any of your names?"

Eli crushed the glass in their hand. The siren had been trying to warm Reniel's bed for as long as Delphine could remember, and from their reaction Delphine was willing to bet they had never succeeded.

"Ten years I left the competition wide open, and you still couldn't snag his attention." Delphine *tsk*ed.

"You always thought you owned this place," Eli snarled. "But things have changed. I don't care what the other elites say—I don't think you deserve to be here anymore."

"Things have changed, yet the scent of desperation coming off you is just as strong as I remember. You're worried about whether I deserve to be here, but perhaps you should ask yourself the same question." Delphine tilted her head. "Better yet—maybe *I'll* ask Reniel that question when he comes to bed tonight. Then he can finally learn your name."

That did it. Eli lunged, but Delphine was already sidestepping out of the way. Hayley and Jas moved into action seconds later, claws aimed at her face. Delphine split a lazy blast of magic between the two of them before spinning around and addressing Eli once more. As the siren tried to attack a second time, the guard who had been keeping track of her threw themselves in the middle to intervene.

"Enough," her chaperone demanded.

None of them listened. Delphine sent another blast of power in the trio's direction, and when the three of them returned it, she dodged, putting half a room of distance between them. The double doors that led to the secondary kitchen on the left of the grand room suddenly opened, and when a waiter walked out with a tray of glasses, she almost laughed.

Delphine waited for the trio's next move—this time from Jas—and as the blast jetted toward her, she sent out a shot of her own magic directly into it. Their blows collided in the center of the room and the swirling tornado of water was redirected right into the waiter. As the sound of shattering glass reverberated around them, a few of the bystanders rushed into the fray. The guard still holding Eli barked a few orders amid the erupting chaos, and while they all were distracted, Delphine slipped out of the room.

It took her a minute to backtrack down the halls, and twice she almost got turned around, but by the time the tolling of the bells announced it was noon, she was only three doors down from the formal den. When she pushed her way inside, Celeste was not waiting for her, but someone else was.

"We need to talk." Eros stood from the couch.

"Where is Celeste?" Delphine asked as she shut the door behind her.

"Celeste didn't know if she wanted to see you today." Eros looked down his nose at her. "Considering what you said to her last night and the fact that you left with Reniel's brother, of all people, I can't really blame her."

"For Hells' sake." Delphine rubbed her temples. "Why does everyone think because some random man left the table at the same time as I did that something had to have happened?"

"Probably because Bellator never really talks to *anyone*. But what does or doesn't happen between you and whoever's brother is none of my concern. Celeste, however, is. You upset her last night."

There was something in his tone that had Delphine's eyes narrowing. "Is something going on between the two of you?"

His expression darkened. "She refuses to give up on the idea that you both are going to leave here together—it's her opportunity to correct the regret she has for not going with you the first time. She can't see things for what they really are—but I can. I remember your ability to hold grudges vividly."

Delphine held her breath as he leaned down until they were eye level. She wondered how he knew she planned to leave them behind, if he was going to turn her in—

"You better keep her none the wiser about how your feelings for her have changed. If you even *think* about telling her you've stopped—"

"*That's* what you're worried about?" She almost laughed in his face.

"Celeste being heartbroken? Wouldn't that work out *better* for you?"

"Not right now. I need her to be optimistic." His hands flexed at his sides with passion. "You didn't see her when you left the first time—and that version of Celeste would not be advantageous to any of us in this situation."

"Done." No hesitation. "I was hoping to see her here and apologize for last night, anyway. I was drunk and Reniel had gotten on my last nerve."

Eros backed off. "I'll relay the message. And I know Celeste didn't want to hear it, but you managing to get Reniel to spin that narrative of you coming back for him was an outstanding move. People are buying it and I suspect that means you will have a front-row seat at the Claiming."

Delphine lifted her chin a bit at the compliment. "What about Zephyr? Has he said anything about the story Reniel's telling everyone? I can't imagine he likes a narrative that makes him look unfavorable in any way."

"I haven't seen Zephyr. He left with Reniel on their expedition this morning. Regardless, he won't go against Reniel. I'm sure he'll take the blow to his ego if it means getting closer to his goal."

"Everything else business as usual? Aside from a few sirens hating my guts now that I'm back."

Eros shrugged. "I expect things to get strange around here over the next week. Between your return and the unpredictable nature of the Claiming ceremony coming up, everyone is on edge. Which is why I want in on whatever your plan is. I know you've been concocting one."

He was right. She said, "Celeste mentioned the Claiming ceremonies had changed. Zephyr is getting promoted at this next one, right?"

"That's Zephyr's plan, anyway." His mouth was set in a hard line now. "Who knows what Reniel is thinking anymore."

"Zephyr getting that promotion will be the opportunity we need," she told him.

He raised one of his split brows, waiting for her to continue.

"If Reniel breaks the Siren's oath on him that night, they'll both be incapacitated and—"

"*Hells,*" he cursed, cutting her off. "You're right. That's it. But how do we escape with that amount of people in the room?"

"You and Celeste are going to slip out right before and shut down the power grid. Then while Reniel and Zephyr are unable to move, and everything is pitch-black, no one will notice we're gone in the chaos."

"And how do we shut that down? I'm sure you remember how cautious Reniel is about anyone getting near the control room without intense supervision. All these years and I've never even seen the inside of it."

"Me neither," she lied. "You're both going to have to wing it. Take out any of the guards posted there. Destroy the entire room. Just make sure the lights go out."

"I'll see if Celeste might have more information on that front," he said, and Delphine didn't bother to correct him—she knew the other girl didn't.

"Great. Are we done here?" She waved a hand between them.

He dipped his chin in confirmation, and she turned back toward the exit.

"Delphine."

She paused, turning her face back halfway. "Yes?"

"This bit we should keep between us, but after the lights are out, it's every being for themselves. Deal?"

She was glad she wasn't facing him, so he couldn't see her satisfied smile. "Deal."

57

More than a week went by before Delphine saw Celeste again. It was two days before the Blood Moon, and Delphine had hardly been allowed to leave Reniel's suite after the scene in the grand room.

For your protection, he had insisted. *I don't want anyone thinking they can get away with attacking you again.*

She was sure if he knew she had snuck off from his guard during the whole ordeal, it would be a very different story. Luckily, she was able to convince her chaperone it would be beneficial for both of them not to say anything about her brief disappearing act—unless he wanted to deal with Reniel's wrath for losing track of her in the first place.

Today, however, Reniel allowed her to fetch her own lunch, since most of the staff were prepping for the Claiming ceremony, and Celeste looked to be doing the same thing. Delphine hadn't spoken to anyone familiar since Eros. Even Bellator had been absent from every single event after the night he'd helped her—something she doubted was coincidental.

"Hello," she greeted Celeste, her voice low. Her newest assigned guard waited outside the door.

"I was just leaving," Celeste told her, pushing off the counter and walking over to place her half-eaten plate of fruit in the sink.

Delphine walked over. "You don't have to leave on my account. I was only coming to grab something quick to eat."

"I don't know if I'm ready to talk to you yet," Celeste confessed.

"Because of what I said at the party?" Delphine asked, swiping a grape off the girl's plate. "A bit dramatic, don't you think?"

"No, I *don't* think it's dramatic to be upset that you continue to throw our past back in my face," Celeste countered, pulling the food out of Delphine's reach. "Especially when I'm trying to make up for it."

Delphine pitied Celeste in this moment. The other girl was trying much too hard, and it was almost hard to watch.

Never soften your heart for someone who's betrayed you. Her mother's voice came back to her. *If someone ever shows you that you are expendable to them once, do not be expendable to them twice—believe them the first time.*

Delphine's resolve tightened back up. "You want to make up for it? Then do your part this time."

Celeste put her plate back down in the sink as she said, "Eros told me your plan. Consider it taken care of. I want you to know I'm all in, Delphine. Whatever it takes. I want to get rid of this wedge between us."

The wedge between us is permanent, she wanted to say. *The splinters have embedded themselves in my heart, and they are not removable by your hands.*

"It's a good place to start," Delphine murmured, and before she could extract herself from the conversation, Celeste grasped her wrist with lightning speed and held her in place.

"For someone who has always sworn they don't belong here," Celeste articulated, "you sure have had no problem fitting back in. Getting into a petty fight with Eli Spring? Hanging on Reniel at parties? Pushing away people who actually care about you? Your mother trained you well, Delphine. It's all been a seamless illusion."

Delphine yanked her arm from the girl's grip now, and the conviction in Celeste's eyes blazed.

"But I saw how your friends fought for you in that forest. I saw how that blond witch screamed your name like you were the last prayer she'd ever let cross her lips. And I know"—Celeste swallowed—"I *know,* your heart is no longer the impenetrable fortress it once was."

With that, Celeste left her alone in the kitchen, staring at the empty space before her in shock. One sentence running through her mind over and over and over again.

Like you were the last prayer she'd ever let cross her lips.

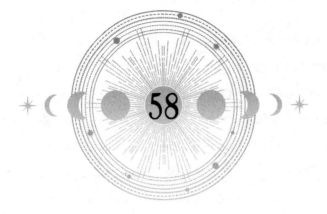

58

When Calla finally came to, her magic was aching in her veins.

"Calla?" someone whispered.

Calla blinked in the dark as she sat up. The seat beneath her was vibrating. That's when she realized she was in a moving carriage. She looked over to where the voice had just come from to find a pair of large violet eyes regarding her with concern.

"Hannah," she whispered back.

"You've been out for a while," Hannah told her. "I was getting worried."

Suddenly the memory of what happened came rushing back to her. She winced a bit as she said, "They knocked Gideon out pretty hard."

Hannah nodded. To the blond's right was a passed-out Caspian, his head tilted back against the wall, mouth hanging open as he slept. In any other circumstance Calla would have giggled at the sight.

"Where are we?" Calla asked as she shifted in her seat to reach over to the small carriage window.

"We crossed into the Rouge Realm about two hours ago," Hannah answered, tone solemn.

Calla peeled back the curtain and peered outside, the breath rushing out of her lungs at what she saw. The familiar peaks and valleys of her homeland were covered in bloodroot trees—the crimson blossoms dripping from their limbs, frozen solid in the winter air. The witch hazel that usually crawled all over the ground was buried under two feet of snow. The familiar red stars hung high in the clear night sky, winking at her.

Welcome back, they said.

The Witch Realms had not changed. But Calla had.

She felt like an entirely new person now than the last time she had been here when she was freshly sixteen, barely able to face the magic inside her, much less use it. Now, almost half a decade later, her magic had never burned so strongly in her veins. The power in her core knew exactly where she was. It thought she was home.

I'm not home. This place isn't home, she told herself.

"I feel weird," Hannah commented, as if she had been reading the thoughts in Calla's head. "Something inside me feels . . . strange."

"Same." Calla flicked her eyes over to Hannah with concern as she dropped the curtain back into place. "But please don't tell me you're about to start raising the dead again."

"I don't *think* so—"

Just then, the carriage dipped forward, the jolting motion cutting off Hannah's sentence as they all bounced a foot in the air and shifted forward. Caspian startled awake.

"What the Hells?" He yawned as they landed with a hard *thud*.

Calla pulled back the curtain again, and the three of them gasped in unison.

The hill they had just crested led down into a place Calla had only seen one other time. They had just entered the Bone Valley. And nestled into the valley's center . . . Myrea's palace.

It wasn't until Calla was standing in front of the Rouge palace's rib cage–shaped gate, craning her head back to take it all the way in, that she felt a flutter of nerves in her stomach. The feeling was gone as fast as it came on. She peeked over her shoulder to search for Gideon. She and the others had managed to retie their bonds just before the carriage had come to a halt, but it had been nice to get some rest without the restraints making them uncomfortable for the entire ride. She was sure Gideon's journey had been uncomfortable for entirely other reasons.

She spotted the prince as he was dragged out of the car, his blue hair a tad disheveled, his eyes wary. He met her gaze almost instantly, his eyes roaming down her body as if checking to make sure she was also still in one piece.

I'm okay, she mouthed at him.

He nodded, but he didn't return the sentiment.

"Myrea wants to see them right away," a guard called as he emerged from the other side of the bone gates.

Calla squeezed her eyes shut at the sound of Myrea's name.

You are not a scared little girl anymore, she told herself. *She will not be able to take anything from you like she did before. You will not let her.*

Calla felt him approaching before he even reached her side.

"I'm here," Gideon murmured.

"Promise me something?" she whispered. "They get out, okay? They're here because Myrea wants *me*. Promise me we will do everything to get them out."

"I'm not losing anyone else," he agreed, reaching out with his bound hands to lightly brush a finger down her arm, over the constellation of dots that matched his. "That includes you."

The moment his skin made contact with hers, the magic in her core began to prowl through her veins with anticipation. She desperately wanted to believe him when he said they weren't going to lose anyone else, but she knew it wasn't something he could guarantee. She also knew that they were either all coming out together or she wasn't coming out at all.

Gideon could feel the turmoil pulsing off Calliope in waves the farther they walked into the palace. On the outside she looked unbothered, her poker face sliding into place the second they walked through the castle's doors. On the inside . . . he could feel anxiety that didn't belong to him slowly slithering up his limbs. It was the first time he had really felt any sort of strong emotion from her side of their bond.

The guards herded their group through the grand foyer toward a set of glittering red doors on the far side of the room. Two more guards who were stationed in front of the entrance gave their guide a single nod before pulling the doors open to the grand throne room. Columns of ivory bones carved into the shape of bloodroot trees lined either side of the room. The marble floor had veins of black and red running through it, the lines snaking their way to the front of the room, where a large throne of skulls was perched atop a dais. Gideon caught a glimpse of Hannah's eyes widening at the sight of the beautiful woman sitting on the throne and wondered if this was the first time the witch had ever seen her queen in person.

It was, unfortunately, not Gideon's first time. Lysandra had always made sure Ezra was occupied the one week a year she visited the Rouge and Terra Realms. Gideon, however, had been dragged along from the time he was born to the age of thirteen when he joined the Guild. He wondered if his familiarity would be an advantage now.

"Two guards per prisoner," the leader barked out to the group. "If a single one of them attempts to use their magic, I want them on the ground and unconscious, understood?"

The guards around them gave a sound of unanimous confirmation and immediately broke out to take their places behind Gideon and the rest of them. Gideon narrowed his eyes at the guard posted next to Calliope. The one she'd spat water on earlier.

The guard leaned down to Calliope's ear, and it took everything in Gideon not to shoot a tornado in the man's direction when he asked her, "How does it feel to be walking to your death sentence?"

Calliope's eyes dropped down for a moment to the man's left arm, before she said, "How does it feel to be nothing more than the queen's lapdog? At least when I die, people will remember who I am."

Gideon smirked a bit as the man straightened himself back up with a scowl.

"Come forward," Myrea's sultry voice thundered out, and Gideon felt a rush of bone-chilling cold run through his veins.

Queen Myrea was perched on her throne of skulls, a vision in a scarlet gown. She had a choker made of small carved bones around her throat that connected to a series of curved ribs wrapping all the way down each of her shoulders and arms like a macabre, skeletal harness. Her ruby crown sat atop her head as always, jewels dripping from the intricate silver circlet onto her forehead, made to look like droplets of blood. The crimson gems glinted in the light of the enormous bone chandelier hanging above them, scattering crimson reflections across the marble floor. The queen's bright auburn hair and pale skin made her dark plum irises striking, and paired with the swaths of vermilion silk that pillowed over the arms of the throne and spilled all the way down the stairs, she was the definition of terrible beauty.

"Well, well, well," Myrea announced as they all came to a halt in front of her dais. "This is quite the entertaining treat."

Gideon could feel how erratic the beating of Calliope's heart was in his own chest as the Rouge Queen narrowed in on her.

"Calliope Rosewood," the queen purred. "Never did I think I'd see you in my palace."

Calliope straightened back her shoulders and lifted her chin up.

"If I recall correctly," Myrea continued, "I told your mother once that she and her wife better thank the Gods I never went looking for you. If I had known that you'd be the one to cause me this much trouble, however, I would have gotten rid of you fifteen years ago instead of that useless wench she married."

Everyone in the room turned to Calliope in shock. She didn't look at a single one of them as rage blazed in her eyes.

"You really are Indra's spitting image, you know. Minus the eyes, of course." Myrea's tone was sickly sweet. Like venom. "Imagine my surprise when a few months ago one of my spies in Estrella brought me news that a Rouge witch named Calla *Rosewood* with hair as wavy as the Celestial Sea and glamoured lilac eyes had been spotted with multiple rolls of sixes. I thought the Fates were surely playing a cruel joke on me."

"That would make two of us," Calliope retorted.

"Indra should have been more clever than to give you her last name." The queen's smile turned cold, but her gaze shifted to Gideon now. "And Gideon Black, how unexpected. Truly *vexing*."

Gideon's patience was wearing thin. "Unexpected? You're the one who roped my brother into your schemes."

"Actually, that was all your mother," Myrea countered. "She's the one who decided to lend me the younger prince to pay back a favor I did her years ago. Which is why this is all just so incredibly ironic."

"What do you mean?" Gideon demanded.

Myrea tipped her head back and laughed. "The Fates are truly masters of comedy. How entertained they must be. I cannot imagine they've been this amused in a millennium."

"The Fates would be masters of *nothing* if you were not their puppet," Calliope said.

Gideon could see the storm forming in Calliope's eyes.

"Puppet?" Myrea mused. "The only one I see on strings around here is *you*. You are the one the Fates want to use in their war. You are the one they have cursed and will continue to curse for their own games. The decisions I make are in spite of the Fates and their plans. Decisions like spilling your blood across this floor before you can fulfill their Godsdamned prophecy and end us all."

"A prophecy *you* agreed to!" Calliope yelled. "You made the decision to curse your own people! The Witch Eater told us—"

"The Witch Eater," the queen scoffed. "They aren't on your side, either, girl. Whatever they told you was for their own agenda."

"We all know what you and your sisters did. Very willingly, I might add." It was Caspian who spoke up now. "You act like we all don't know the nature of your bargain with the Fates."

"And you act like you know what the Wastelands were like before they were turned into the Witch Realms," Myrea snarled. "The earth was barren, everyone desolate and starving after the courtless fae scourged the land with toxic magic. We returned life here; we gave our people magic and made the fae return to their own courts. And now you're all spoiled brats. Raised with power and protection in a Realm *made* for you to thrive in. The decisions my sisters and I had to make would have eaten you all alive."

"Save your spiel for the sheep who willingly serve you," Caspian threw at her. "Doing a single good thing in the past doesn't stanch the evil bleeding from you now."

Myrea bared her teeth at the Onyx witch. "You're lucky you aren't under my jurisdiction, or I'd put a sword through your heart right now."

Caspian's smile was the grimmest Gideon had ever seen it. "Yes, I'm sure Lysandra would hate for you to take that opportunity away from her."

"Enough," Myrea declared. "I don't have time for this nonsense. I want to see the girl's numbers."

The two guards behind Calliope shoved her forward, causing her to almost trip. She looked over her shoulder and glared at them as they pushed her all the way up the dais steps to stand right before the queen.

"Relieve her of her restraints," Myrea told them.

"But she's a—" one of the guards began.

"*Now.*"

The guards carefully unknotted the ropes tied around Calliope's wrists.

"Show me."

Calliope's hands were clenched so tight her knuckles were stark white, but still she moved to yank back the sleeve of her shirt to reveal the four red sixes that were embedded in her arm. There was a single moment when Myrea's eyes landed on the pattern of dots when everything in the room stopped.

Then the queen let out a piercing shriek of anger, and the stillness shattered.

59

Amina gaped at where Meli was kneeling on the ground, blades pressed to the nape of her neck.

"What's it going to be?" Queen Ignia asked.

"What does she have to do with this?" Amina hissed.

"She wasn't my first choice," the queen admitted. "But she was easily obtainable, and one of my spies said you went looking for her at the borders recently. I wanted to get my hands on your coconspirators—what is it you call them? Slayers?—but they're slippery little things, aren't they?"

"Meli is not a part of any of this. She doesn't know anything—"

"Oh, I realized that when she didn't crack after three hours of torture." The queen laughed.

The Blood Oath. Amina looked on Meli with sympathy, but she thanked the Gods they had made her swear the oath before they'd left.

"Besides, it's not about what she *knows*, lovely," the queen divulged. "If her well-being is important to you, then you can cooperate. If not, I can sever the head from her body and find someone else who would be more persuasive. Doesn't your friend have a twin brother somewhere?"

"What is it you want me to do?" Amina questioned through her teeth.

"It's simple, really. I need someone who knows what the final Blood Warrior looks like. I want her brought to me."

"I don't know where she is! Not to mention the last time I saw her I killed the witch she—"

The queen held up a hand, cutting her off. "The details of the drama you caused do not interest me. I'll give you two weeks to bring her to me before I start digging a mass grave for the ones you love."

An enraged sound ripped out of Amina's throat; her claws dug into her palms as her hands balled into fists.

"Your time starts now," the queen said, dismissing her. "And I think I'll keep your little friend just in case you decide not to do what you're told."

As the guards hauled a screaming Meli away, Amina's rage burned so brightly in her belly that she swore she could feel its smoke crawling up her throat. She spun for the exit, pushing past the doors and racing down the hall. She needed to get out of here. Fuck the queen. Fuck the Gods. She was going to shred them all to pieces with her bare hands one day.

When Amina launched herself into the air, a voice shouted her name from her right. Sabine and Lyra, dressed entirely in black, zipped after her.

Sabine's face was drawn in horror. "What happened?"

Amina fluttered her wings to keep her hovering in place as she waited for the two of them to fully reach her. Then she revealed, "Things just got much worse."

)·)·)·●·(·(·(·(

The three of them whirled like tornadoes around Lyra's room as they packed their bags, hurrying to shove changes of clothes and weapons and an array of Lyra's enchanted artifacts into the pouches of their utility belts. The second they decided they were leaving, tonight, they had come to the manor to gather their supplies. When everything was ready, they stood in a circle and took a collective deep breath.

"This is your last chance to back out," Amina told them both.

"We are a unit," Lyra declared. "We're forging a new beginning together."

"We find the last Blood Warrior; we bring her back," Sabine recited. "I've already sent the letter and the proof off to Sydni to help rally other Valkyries. We'll have to hope the word of what the queen has done spreads without us for now."

"About getting the Blood Warrior . . ." Amina chimed in. "I have an amendment to that plan."

The other two tilted their heads at her.

"I doubt the Blood Warrior or her cohorts are where I last saw them, but even if they are, taking her won't be easy. The girl is a witch-Siphon hybrid. I felt her power in that forest. It's untapped at the moment, but when she finally unleashes it . . ."

"You're saying we need her to be cooperative?" Lyra narrowed her eyes.

Amina's eyes sparkled at her friend. "Precisely. And I think I know exactly how we will be able to make that happen."

60

The queen's screech was still ringing in Calla's ears.

"Who is it?" Myrea snarled in Calla's face. "Who are you tied to?"

At the sight of Myrea's visceral rage, a wave of gratitude went through Calla that her bond to Gideon had not yet been severed. Pissing the queen off was quite a thrill.

"Tell me or so help me, girl—"

"Me." Gideon stepped forward, and Calla looked over her shoulder to see a satisfied smile playing on the prince's lips. "Which means if you spill her blood, you spill mine. And then you'll have my mother to deal with."

"You little bitch," Myrea growled in Calla's face. "You may look like Indra, but you're just like Agnes. Ruining my plans because of your foolish little infatuations."

Calla didn't flinch away from the queen's venomous words. In fact, she hoped they were true. Agnes was the only one of her mothers whom she was ever able to really meet, and from the six short years they got to spend together, Calla hoped there *was* something of Agnes in her. Not to mention it was comical that the queen would blame only Calla for her and Gideon's soul-bond.

"You don't understand what you're dealing with," Myrea snapped. "But this is nothing a bond-severing can't fix."

Calla froze. She could hardly believe what she had just heard. A task she had been sure she'd have to search all Illustros to accomplish, and the Rouge queen planned to just hand her the solution. The Fates' musical laughter cut through her mind.

"Bond-severing," she whispered.

"That's right," Myrea said viciously. "Whatever game you're playing will be cut short by tomorrow night. I'll do everything in my power to ensure Lysandra will be present for our little ceremony, too. Won't that be fun, Prince? You and your mother can have a heartwarming reunion." The queen looked to her guards now. "Confiscate all their belongings and take them to their cells."

Calla slashed her gaze to Gideon. If their things were taken . . . the queen was going to find the Fates' Dice. And Heart Reaver. Calla assumed the guards hadn't bothered taking their stuff before because they knew the crew was too outnumbered to do any damage with any weapons they may have had regardless. Not to mention that being bound, forced to walk several miles, and then knocked unconscious had certainly taken too much out of her to even attempt to use Heart Reaver after she'd woken up in the carriage. Enchanted daggers weren't exactly helpful when your opponents could magically control your every movement anyway.

One of the guards yanked Gideon's bag away and then ran his hand over the pockets of the prince's pants and shirt. When the guard brought the items over to the queen, Myrea immediately turned the pack over onto the floor, and Calla winced as the two red-and-black cubes fell onto the marble, bouncing with an echoing *clack ... clack ... clack* down the dais steps.

The room went utterly silent. Cass, Hannah, and Kestrel all watched the scene with bated breath.

"Fates' Dice," Myrea said with a disbelieving sneer, standing from her throne at the sight of the cursed pair of cubes. A guard collected each of them from where they landed and brought them over for the queen to inspect. "The two of you are in a world of trouble."

"You mean more than we are now?" Calla quipped as a guard began running their hands over her pockets, ripping Heart Reaver out of its sheath on her belt. She gave him a scathing glare.

The queen folded the pair of dice into her palm. "Make sure you isolate the girl from the prince. I don't want them refueling each other."

Calla felt the point of a sword in her lower back an instant later.

"Move," ordered the guard who was assigned to her.

"Oh, and, Commander?" the queen called out in a sugary voice. "Excellent work."

Calla watched as every muscle in Kestrel's body tensed up. Good. She hoped he suffered with his guilt for the rest of his life.

Calla and the others were led one by one out of the throne room. They were brought to the west wing of the castle to a large steel door with at least ten different locking mechanisms barring it in place. Once the door was finally opened, Calla saw that there were stairs on the other side. They all made their way down three flights of the damp stone steps to what she assumed was the dungeon. It certainly smelled like it could be one. Dark and slightly humid with a putrid stench that she could only describe as vomit and old blood.

"Put her in the first and the rest of them in the second," the lead guard directed.

Each cell was made of three black stone walls with steel bars running along the front. Calla couldn't see any type of door or hinges, and a moment later she realized why. Two of the guards walked to the wall across from the cells' openings and twisted two black iron valves that made the bars slowly sink into the ground.

Calla was prodded into the first holding, and as soon as she crossed over the threshold the guard quickly lifted the bars back into place. She watched as the others filed into the cell beside hers, Cass and Hannah both flicking their eyes over to her in concern as they passed while Kestrel refused to look in her direction at all. Gideon resisted the entire way. Once they were all secure, the guards hurried out, a few taunting comments the only things they left behind.

"This *sucks*," she heard Caspian's muffled voice ring out on the other side of the wall.

"Calliope?" Gideon called. "Are you all right?"

"No." She laughed bitterly as she flattened her back against the stone and slid down to the ground. "But I'm here."

Calla wrapped her arms around her legs and leaned forward to rest her forehead against her bent knees. She counted her heartbeats in the silence, wondering how the Hells this was going to play out. When she reached two hundred sixty-three beats, a shuffling sound from the back corner of her cell caught her attention. She growled at the thought of having to deal with a colony of rats or other gutter creature, but when she leaned forward to peer closer into the shadows, she knew immediately that it wasn't any kind of rodent.

Calla slowly got back to her feet, heart hammering in her chest as a scream began to crawl up her throat.

"Calliope?" Gideon's voice was drenched in concern. "What's going on, what's wrong?"

Calla took a single step toward the darkness to get a better look at the distinct form of a person she could now see was huddled in the corner. The person moved. Eyes blinking open.

Calla screamed.

"Calliope!" Gideon yelled.

"Watch . . . the noise . . . would you?" the being said, almost too soft for her to hear.

Calla clamped her mouth shut immediately. She took another step forward, her eyes slowly adjusting to see that it was a man, his face covered in dark stubble, long unkempt hair spilling over his wide shoulders. The muscles on his broad frame were so incredibly lean that he looked sickly, and his fair skin clearly hadn't seen the sun in a great deal of time. He might have been handsome, she thought, if he didn't look so gaunt and frail.

Calla reached out carefully with her magic, trying to determine what type of being the poor soul might be. As soon as her magic brushed against his, her breath hitched a little bit.

"Calla!" It was Hannah who screamed her name this time.

"Hold on!" she responded.

"What does she mean *hold on*?" Caspian's distant voice sounded exasperated. "I swear, the way everyone in this group makes me worry has shaved years off my life."

Calla refocused on the man. A Terra witch.

"Who are you?" she asked softly. "Did the guards not know this cell wasn't empty?"

"Probably forgot I was in here," the man answered, his words a little less slow coming out this time.

"How? Don't they feed you every day?"

He huffed a laugh. "I haven't eaten anything in a decade."

She gawked. "How are you *alive*?"

The man sighed and began to unfurl his body. Very slowly he stretched out each of his limbs before shakily pushing himself up from the ground. He had to use the wall for most of his support and was about six inches taller than Calla even with his poor posture.

"My name is Thorne," he told her. "I'm the fifth Blood Warrior."

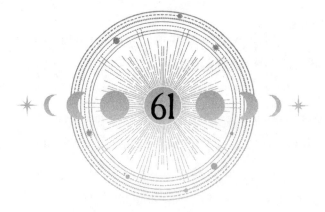

61

Hannah watched as Gideon and Cass pressed their ears up against the wall between their cell and Calla's. By the way Gideon kept pacing and fidgeting with the hoops in his ears, Hannah could tell it was driving him mad that he wasn't able to see or be near Calla.

Hannah glanced over to where Kestrel was leaning back against the wall, arms crossed over his chest as he watched Gideon and Caspian debate on what might be happening in the other cell. The commander's face was completely blank, and it was giving her chills. She wondered what had happened during his and Gideon's ride earlier. She could tell something had changed between the two men—would have been disappointed in Gideon if it hadn't after what Kestrel did to Calla and the rest of them—but she didn't know exactly what kind of terms they were currently on.

Hannah guessed it was somewhere between *dead to each other* and *hope your soul rots in a fiery pit for the rest of eternity.*

"I think I hear something," Cass told Gideon.

"What?" Gideon moved closer to the beta in anticipation.

"Hold on." Cass held up a hand.

They all held their breaths as they waited for whatever Cass had caught on the other side. Well, all of them except Kestrel.

"I hear talking," Cass murmured, pushing back from the wall. "Like she's having a conversation. Poor thing. Didn't last ten minutes in here without her mind making up hallucinations."

Gideon shot the other witch a hard look. "*Or* the reason you hear talking is because there's someone in there *talking to her.*"

Cass looked thoughtful as he said, "That's probably more likely, yeah."

Gideon pinched the bridge of his nose.

"Hey, little witch, are you all right?" Cass asked.

Hannah hadn't realized that she'd even spaced out until Caspian stepped in front of her, a look of concern on his face.

"Oh . . . yes. Sorry, what's happening with Calla?" she asked, but her voice sounded far away.

"Whoa, Han." Gideon stepped up next to his friend, his brows knitted together as his silvery gaze ran over her face. "What's going on? Are you feeling all right?"

"What do you mean?" She tilted her head.

"Hannah, the veins are starting to come back," Caspian told her, hands reaching out to hover next to her shoulders as she swayed a bit on her feet. "Are you going to have another episode?"

"What? I feel . . ."

She was going to say *fine*, but that's not what came out at all. What came out was more of a mush of vowel sounds.

"All right, easy there," Gideon said in a voice that was expertly calm as he and Cass each grabbed an elbow and guided her gently to the floor.

As soon as Hannah was sitting, Cass helped scoot her a few inches back so she could prop herself up against the wall. She felt like that time she and Delphine had drunk an entire bottle of wine on the pink sand coast of Estrella—light-headed and fuzzy but just aware enough to hear what was going on around her.

"What the Hells is wrong with her?" Cass whispered to Gideon.

Before Gideon answered, Kestrel's monotonous tone cut in. "Her magic is overheating."

Gideon tensed up at the sound of Kestrel's voice, but Caspian didn't hesitate to question him. "What does that mean?"

"It means," Kestrel continued, bored, "that her magic must have been dormant for far too long and then it was woken up too fast. Her system is overloading."

"Well, that is just fantastic." Cass sighed. "What do we do?"

"Nothing you can do," Kestrel muttered. "Except wait it out and hope she doesn't unleash it all on us."

"You're the fifth Blood Warrior," Calla repeated in shock.

"Yes," Thorne answered.

"What are you doing here?" she questioned.

"Before my final roll, I made arrangements to head out to the Celestial Sea with a crew of smugglers. The plan was to get my final Witch's Die from them and travel to the first continent to hide out as long as I could, but Myrea sent a unit of guards after me. I managed to solidify my Blood Warrior status before they dragged me here, but since being a Blood Warrior has made me invincible . . ."

"They don't feed you or give you water?" She wrinkled her nose a bit as a pungent smell suddenly hit her nose. "Or let you bathe?"

"I don't really need to eat or drink in this state. I've forgotten what hunger or thirst feels like at this point." He shrugged, the movement wooden. "Who are *you*?"

"My name is Calla . . . I'm the sixth Blood Warrior."

Calla could tell he hadn't expected her to say *that*. She pulled back the sleeve of her shirt to show him the magical red sixes that lined her arm.

"You only have four numbers . . ." Thorne noted. "That means you're here because . . ."

"Myrea wants to murder me? Yeah."

"Why are your numbers red?" Thorne tilted his head in curiosity.

"That's a very long story as well. Short version is that I got myself soul-bonded to the Onyx Prince, who happens to be in the cell next door with our friends."

"Ah, I see." Thorne nodded. "I've finally reached the hallucinatory stage of my isolation. I must say, I didn't think my mind was this creative."

"Believe me," Calla said dryly. "I desperately wish this was all in your imagination and not the very real nightmare that is my life."

"Why did they separate you?" Thorne questioned. "They put the prince and your friends all together, but stuck you in here with me?"

"The bond allows us to recharge each other. Not to mention, I'm sure they didn't want me receiving any magic from anyone else since I'm a . . ." Calla stepped out of the shadows in the back of the cell and moved toward the light that was shining through the bars from the lit torches in the hallway. She pointed to her eyes.

Thorne gave a low whistle. "The Fates picked a Blood Siphon as their final warrior? The Gods truly have elite drafting skills, I'll give them that."

"What did you call me?"

"Blood Siphon. Witches who are blessed with the ability to Siphon each have their own titles—same with any fae or other magic-wielding beings who happen to be Siphons as well. Blood Siphons, Storm Siphons . . . Why are you looking at me like that?"

Blood Siphon. Her magic heated in her veins at the name.

"Did you say *blessed* with the ability to Siphon?" Calla lifted a brow.

"Siphons are incredibly rare, powerful beings. I spent a lot of my younger years on the second continent, Noctum. Siphon abilities are regarded highly there."

"Well, they should give that memo to the beings of Illustros."

"Many in Illustros aren't fond of anyone with more power than them." Thorne snorted. "The Witch Queens haven't helped with that."

Calla nodded. She was about to say something else when someone called her name again. Gideon.

She called back, "There's ... uh ... someone else in here with me. Things have definitely just gotten stranger."

"There's something happening with Hannah!" It was Caspian who spoke this time.

"What's wrong?" Calla asked hastily.

"Kestrel said he thinks it's her magic overheating," Gideon elaborated.

"We can't catch a single break, can we?" Calla huffed. "Is she going to be okay?"

"She's just a little disoriented at the moment," Gideon assured her. "Cass and I are using our wind to try to cool her down."

That was why it was suddenly so drafty.

"Keep her awake," Calla told him. "If she's unconscious it's easier for the necromancy magic to take hold. I do not want to know who or what is buried beneath this palace."

"We'll do everything we can," Gideon assured.

Calla took a deep breath, trying to steady her nerves as her stomach knotted up with the anxiety of being unable to do anything to help Hannah or the others. She looked back over at Thorne and said, "I don't know how we're all going to get out of here . . . but you should come with us."

Thorne smiled at her sadly. "I gave up hoping I'd ever get out of here a long time ago, Six."

Calla rolled her eyes at the nickname, but she didn't bother to say anything more as she settled back down on the ground, laying herself out by the wall and pillowing her arms beneath her cheek. She wanted to tell Thorne that he shouldn't be hopeless, that they could make it out, but she worried that would be a lie. She'd spent all that time trying to avoid being a part of the Fates' War, and yet now she was starting to fear she wouldn't even make it that far. Myrea was going to take her out of the game just when she'd decided to play.

As Calla drifted to sleep, the cool breeze from Gideon's wind from next door settled over her, caressing her skin and combing through the tendrils of her hair. For a moment she imagined she was back in the forest, his hands tangled in her hair at the nape of her neck, telling her they would be okay.

62

Delphine was waiting in the sitting area of Reniel's suite when he returned from planning the final touches for the next day's Claiming ceremony.

"What am I supposed to wear to the Claiming tomorrow night?"

"I've had a dress made for you," he told her. "It should be here in the morning."

She lifted her brows. "Really?"

"It's cutting it close because I was debating if I should have you come—Zephyr didn't think it was a good idea—but there are still a few people who want to see us in action after I told them you were back. I think we should make sure to give them the show they deserve."

She'd give them a show all right.

"Why the Hells does Zephyr not think it's a good idea? What business is it of his?" she said snippily.

"Zephyr is only looking out for me, moonlight. He's become quite the right hand in the last few years, and he's protective," Reniel told her, a smarmy glint in his eye. "Don't be jealous. You could get back there someday."

Delphine fought the urge to chuck a throw pillow at his smug face.

"Get some beauty sleep," Reniel told her as he headed for his bedroom. "You need to look exquisite for tomorrow."

The day had finally come.

Delphine's stomach was in knots. When she woke, Reniel was already gone from the suite, a large garment box left on the table in front of the couch she'd made into her bed for the past couple weeks. This couch was much less comfortable than the old worn-in one she used to sleep on in the apartment she shared with Hannah and Calla, but it still beat the cot in the dungeon or Reniel's bed.

She ignored the box while she got up to bathe and fix her hair, and when she eventually came back for it, she braced herself. She slipped the card out from under the ribbon tied in a big silver bow atop the package and ran the nail of her index finger across the envelope's blue wax seal.

Moonlight,
I look forward to seeing you in this later.
R

Delphine set the card down on the table and pulled the end of one of the ribbons to loosen the bow. She shimmied the lid off and folded back the silk wrapping to reveal the outrageously lavish garment beneath. A gasp fell from her lips when she lifted the dress.

The entire gown looked like it was made of liquid silver and stars. The structured bodice had a deep V cut down the front with the left strap meant to sit on her shoulder and the right to be draped off the side. The material looked like it would fit her body like a second skin, and there was a slit high up the right side of the skirt. At the bottom of the box was a large square jewelry case, and when she pried its lid open, she choked on the bile that crawled up her throat.

Inside, nestled in the plush sapphire cushion, sat a replica of her mother's pearl necklace that Reniel had made her destroy.

She snapped the box closed and threw it as hard as she could against the wall.

Tonight is the last night, she assured herself. *Tonight is the end.*

63

"**G**ideon!" she called in the dark, laughter bubbling up in her throat. She couldn't see anything in the forest that surrounded her except for the looming trees and their large white blossoms. "Gideon, I give up! Where are you?"

She swore the trees turned toward her as she passed by them, their shadows slithering underfoot. Petals fell from the drooping flowers and drifted in the wind that was beginning to pick up around her. Calla heard the haunting sound of a crow cawing in the distance, and she shivered.

"Gideon?" she said, hesitantly this time.

"He isn't here."

Calla froze at the sound of the grating voice. She slowly turned to her left, her breath catching as her eyes landed on the giant gilded mirror standing in the middle of two trees. It wasn't herself she saw reflected in the glass, however.

It was the Witch Eater.

"You," she hissed. "What are you doing here?"

"I wished to see how your progress was coming along," they told her.

"What progress?" she demanded as she stalked closer to the mirror.

They tilted their head at her in curiosity. "I have a riddle for you."

"I'm not interested."

The Witch Eater went on as if Calla had not spoken. "I am something you can lose, but when I am stolen, I am found. I am something you can break, but when I am mended, I am forever bound. What am I?"

Calla's brow furrowed at the puzzle. She turned it over in her head. The answer felt like it should be obvious, but as soon as she thought she found it, it eluded her once more. The Witch Eater grinned like a fiend when Calla was unable to come up with anything, and the sight sent a shot of fear through her body.

She took a large step back from the oculus. "What do you want from me? What game are you playing?"

The Witch Eater nodded. "Now you're asking the right questions."

"What do you—wait." She sucked in a breath as it suddenly hit her. "A heart. The answer to your riddle is a heart."

The glint in the Witch Eater's eyes was approving.

Calla shook her head wildly, her stomach sinking with dread. "I have not completed the curse. I am not in love. You can't take my heart."

"Interesting that that's where your first thoughts go." The Witch Eater's gaze turned knowing. "But you're right. I can't take a heart that's already been stolen."

Calla's mouth went dry. "What are you talking about?"

The Witch Eater laughed, and Calla slammed her hands on the glass.

"What do you want from me?" she repeated, slamming her hands against the mirror once more. "What does that mean?"

"Good luck, Calliope Rosewood."

"No!" she screamed. "Tell me what it means!"

"Sorry, but it's time for you to wake up."

"No," Calla seethed, hitting the glass over and over again with increasing frustration.

"Wake up," the Witch Eater repeated.

This time when Calla hit the mirror, it shattered. One of the sharp edges sliced open her palm, and she let out a cry of pain as she watched her crimson blood spill out and drip onto the ground. When she looked back at the broken reflection, it was no longer the ancient being staring back at her.

It was Gideon, his palm bleeding just like hers. Her eyes traveled up from his hand to his chest—and what she found there made a cry burst from her lips.

There was a gaping hole where his heart should be.

Calla frantically looked down at her own chest, and her breath caught when she found it was ripped open as well.

"Wake up," Gideon told her.

Wake up.

Wake up.

"Wake up." Someone nudged Calla's side with the toe of their boot.

Calla blinked her eyes open slowly, groggy from the short, fitful sleep. She looked around to find Thorne looming above her with a grave expression on his face.

"You've been out for nearly four hours," he told her. "Someone's coming."

Calla pushed herself up from the floor, stretching out her stiff, aching limbs. Down the hall, she could hear the clacking of someone's shoes on the stone. When the person finally came to a stop in front of her cell, the temperature in the room felt like it had dropped twenty degrees.

"You must be Calliope Rosewood," Queen Lysandra said with a wicked smile.

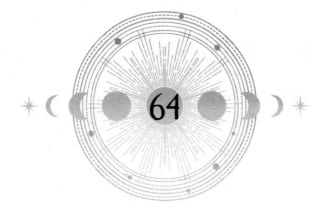

64

The moment Gideon heard the sound of footsteps coming down to the dungeon, he could sense who it was. He had never moved so fast in his life.

"*Mother,*" he growled as he strode forward. "Leave her alone."

Lysandra looked over to him with cool interest. "Gideon, dearest, so lovely to finally see you again. I was expecting you back a month ago. Too bad I didn't know what you were up to; I wouldn't have worried so much."

She was looking as regal as ever; her impeccable sable gown was shining with black diamonds, the scales of the serpent circling her waist like a belt glittering in the dancing firelight. The spikes of the crown atop her head had recently been polished, the glossy obsidian steel shining in the dark, silky strands of her hair, which had been braided through the intricate headpiece to secure it in place. Behind her stood four of Myrea's guards.

"Let me see your arm." Lysandra stepped up to the bars, hand out in demand.

"No," he told her, holding her gaze.

"Don't play with me, boy," she scolded. "You have no idea how much trouble you're costing me. The second we break the bond between you and that little witch, we're going home. And *you two*"—she pointed at where Cass and Kestrel were backing Gideon's flanks—"your parlay on finishing your rolls is over. You'll be lucky if I don't gut you for your part in all this. Kestrel's display of loyalty is the only reason you'll be spared."

Gideon heard Kestrel suck in a breath at his back.

"Now, *show me your arm*." His mother bared her teeth at him, reaching out a hand so fast Gideon didn't have time to jump away. She yanked him forward by his wrist, until the front of his torso was pressed against the steel bars, and clawed the sleeve of his shirt back past his elbow.

When she saw the four sets of red dots marring his skin, she almost choked in shock.

"You fool," she told him. "You've hidden this from me."

"Did you think I would tell you? Do you not remember who you are?" He jerked his arm out of her grasp. She let him.

"I am your *mother*," she spat. "And I expected you to be better than your brat of a brother—who, pray tell, is where?"

"This isn't about Ezra," Gideon said carefully. "He's not the one that stands between you and your plans."

"And neither will you for much longer," she told him, and before he could blink, she reached through the bars and sliced her sharp nails down his bare skin.

Gideon watched as one of the guards who accompanied his mother pulled a few droplets of blood from the wound before it could seal itself back together. The blood floated away from Gideon and hovered above the guard's palm like crimson bubbles.

"What are you doing?" he demanded.

She grinned at him. "Releasing you from this cursed bond. Quite lucky to have the power of a Blood Moon right when we need it, don't you think? I'll come back for you all once the ritual is done."

With that, she turned to the guards and said, "Bring the girl."

Gideon slammed his hands against the bars as they lifted the gate to Calliope's cell, but his own limbs seized up as the guards used their magic on *her* and forced her out of the holding. His mother scowled as she watched the effects of the bond mirror what was happening to Calliope in his own body.

"Calliope," he choked out, ignoring the others' stares.

"Hush, you fool," Lysandra scolded him. "Whatever you feel for her isn't real. It's the insidious magic linking you together."

Gideon scowled. She was so unbelievably wrong.

"Calliope, listen to me," he implored, though he couldn't see where she was. The guards had already pulled her too far down the hall. "Fight. Don't worry about what's happening to me. I want you to *fight*."

Lysandra walked up to the bars, her face inches from his as she told him, "This is your one and only chance. It's me or her. Make your choice wisely, because one of them you won't survive."

With that, his mother turned and strode away.

65

When Delphine entered the grand room, her adrenaline spiked to see the transformation it had gone through for the Claiming ceremony. Every piece of furniture had been cleared away, and there were meticulously drawn runes in the sirens' first language all over the center of the floor. The ceiling in the grand room was made of etched crystal, allowing what little sun could reach these depths to seep in and the moon to cast a faint luminescence at night. Tonight every moon in Illustros would be crimson—even in the finicky Neverending Forest surrounding the sea—and the lights scattered through the room had been set to an ominous scarlet glow for the occasion.

Blood Moons were the only event that lined up no matter the time zone you resided in, and it was strangely comforting to know that wherever Calla and Hannah were right now, they were seeing the same moons.

Delphine stepped beneath the glass ceiling, the surface of her dress glittering silver and red like a burning star. Reniel spotted her then, the slow smile on his face almost . . . hungry, as he watched her make her way over to him. Bellator, who stood to Reniel's right, tipped his glass of wine at her in greeting but didn't meet her eyes.

There were several members from Reniel's Shoal she recognized standing nearby, and they paused their conversations to watch her as she walked by.

"You look exquisite, moonlight," Reniel told her approvingly as his eyes raked her head to toe, only briefly snagging on the detail of the pearl necklace missing from around her neck.

She dipped her chin in acknowledgment. She knew how she looked. "When does everything start?"

"We're just waiting for—ah. Here we go." Reniel lifted his chin at the entrance.

Delphine turned to find Zephyr, Mariana—who was practically hanging off Eros—and Celeste filing into the party. Eros and Celeste didn't glance her way, but Zephyr did.

"Well, well, well," Zephyr taunted as he approached. "How have you been enjoying being Reniel's little pet, *moonlight?*"

"No need to antagonize my date, Zephyr," Reniel scolded the siren. "Save your energy for your challenge."

Zephyr's lips twisted at Reniel's words but he said nothing more as he turned on his heel and stalked off, throwing her one last look of disdain as he went.

"Wine?" Reniel turned to Delphine, glass held out in offer.

Truthfully, she never planned to drink again, but her nerves were beginning to buzz, and she thought one glass to take the edge off couldn't hurt.

"Thank you," she said, reaching for the crystal goblet.

"Now, if you'll excuse me, I have to make sure we're ready to get started soon," Reniel declared before ambling away.

Delphine looked at Bellator, taking a small sip of the wine. "What's your role tonight?"

Bellator didn't say anything for a long moment. Then: "I'm not sure yet."

She opened her mouth to say something else when the sound of clinking glass echoed across the room.

"Welcome, ladies and gentlebeings, to this exhilarating occasion."

Delphine winced as the words conjured up a past memory. She had to force herself to breathe, force her grip to not become a vise around her glass.

"Today is a particularly special Claiming because we are not only welcoming someone new, but one of our own will have the honor of challenging a siren of his choice to prove that he is worthy of being moved into my inner circle. I hope his journey shows you all what redemption can look like when you are a loyal part of this society. Zephyr, step forward for me, if you would."

The crowd buzzed with anticipation as Zephyr moved into the center of the room, chest puffed out. Delphine spotted Mariana watching with glee across the room, hand tucked in the crook of Eros's arm.

Eros flicked his eyes over to Delphine as if he could feel her staring at them. His expression remained emotionless, but something burned in his eyes. She looked away.

"Three years ago, I began these challenges in order to start testing us all, to keep everyone on their toes and ensure only the worthy remained in our ranks. No longer will we Claim sirens who have not proven themselves. No longer will anyone already here remain complacent. If you cannot defend your spot here when nominated, you do not deserve to have it."

Delphine saw Eros extract himself from Mariana across the room, whispering something in the girl's ear before pushing through the crowd.

"In the spirit of this being the first inner-circle member to be initiated since our new traditions have begun, I've decided Zephyr will choose his opponent from a very specific group among us."

Delphine's brow furrowed. She searched for Celeste across the room, and the other girl looked just as confused.

"As you know, some of your fellow Shoal members have had a few . . . lapses in judgment over the years. As a leader I must make sure that there are no discrepancies in our operation that could harm any of you, and I take these indiscretions *very* seriously." Reniel's expression became a mask of mock sincerity as he addressed the hushed crowd. "The punishment for breaking one of our rules or breaking my trust is swearing a Siren's oath of fealty to me—and this Shoal—to prove that you are dedicated to amending your wrongs."

Delphine didn't know why it took her so long to realize what was happening. Why Zephyr's eyes were now trained on her face, grin slowly stretching across his face. She didn't know why she had taken the glass of faery wine, half the contents of which were now churning like poison in her stomach. And above all, she didn't know why the next words out of Reniel's mouth were so surprising. The last couple of weeks she had developed tunnel vision, only thinking about her freedom and not remembering the one fact she knew above all else: cruelty was woven through every inch of Reniel's flesh and bones.

"Zephyr will therefore choose an opponent from one of the oath-sworn in this room, and if he wins his challenge, I will free him from his Siren's oath. If his opponent wins, Zephyr will not only lose his spot in my inner circle, he will swear an oath double the length of the original."

Some of the crowd whispered to themselves at the news, but Delphine noticed instantly that Celeste was frozen while Mariana laughed and clapped in delight beside her. Eros was still nowhere in sight.

"Zephyr, you may now declare the name of your opponent," Reniel told the man.

Zephyr stepped forward, an insidious amount of glee on his face as he said, "Delphine DeLune."

The crystal goblet dropped from her hand and shattered on the floor.

66

Calla must have slept much longer than she assumed, because the light filtering into the palace ballroom through the stained-glass windows was not from the sun but a vermilion moon. Her magic was on edge, thrumming with anticipation in her veins as she faced the two Witch Queens.

I want you to fight, Gideon's voice echoed in her mind.

She balled her hands into fists. She would.

"If only Indra could see what you've become." Myrea *tsk*ed from where she sat atop the dais steps, Lysandra perched by her side.

Calla lifted her chin proudly. "You mean the key to your end? I agree, what a shame she isn't here to witness that."

Myrea's lips pulled back from her teeth. "You talk big for someone whose blood is about to be spilled across my floor."

Calla smirked as she returned, "You talk big for someone who needs ten guards to make sure I don't spill *your* blood across the floor."

Myrea snarled with contempt, but before the Rouge Queen could make another threat, Lysandra chimed in with "Let's see how brave you're feeling in a moment, girl."

The Onyx Queen snapped her fingers, and the witches surrounding Calla all turned toward her in sync.

"Hold her in place. And make it hurt." Lysandra's smile was cruel.

Calla felt her entire body seize up with the force of the witches' magic. She could see the veins in her arms bulge, feel her heart rate double. She strained against their hold, her own magic fighting back, but it was no use—she wasn't breaking free.

"Now for the fun part," Lysandra announced. "Where's my son's blood?"

A guard standing near the dais, the one who had collected Gideon's blood, turned to the Onyx Queen with the scarlet liquid still hovering in his hand. Calla watched as Myrea procured a familiar dagger from the skirts of her gown.

Heart Reaver.

The Rouge Queen handed the ruby-encrusted weapon to Lysandra.

"Now, I must admit I'm curious what you all are doing with Ezra's dagger," Lysandra told Calla as she turned the blade over in her hands, tapping the tip of her index finger over its sharp point. "Did he gift it to you? I had begun to find it peculiar how long his mission was taking in Estrella, so I checked up on him. And do you know what I found?"

Calla couldn't answer, of course. Though she did have a feeling as to what the answer would be.

"I found that he became infatuated with his mark. I'm glad to see, at the very least, that he followed through with his mission. Was the dagger an apology for betraying you, then? Is that why he isn't here? Is that why you've trapped his brother in this heinous bond? You think you can sink your claws into Gideon as revenge, but I think you'll do well to remember only one of us will walk away with Gideon."

I trapped no one, she wanted to scream. *I am not the villain.*

The Onyx Queen dipped Heart Reaver into the orb of Gideon's blood that was still hovering in the guard's hand, making sure the steel of the blade was coated thoroughly before removing it and starting down the steps to Calla.

When Lysandra was right in front of her, Calla could pick out all the small details of the queen's face that belonged to Ezra and Gideon. Her nose, the angle of her cheekbones . . . her lips. But Calla also saw the thing that separated them completely—the insidious gleam in her eyes.

Swathed in the power of the Blood Moon, the Onyx Queen closed her eyes and began to chant. It was an old language, a dialect Calla didn't recognize and definitely not the one the Witch Eater had used to bind her and Gideon together in the first place. When Lysandra was done chanting, the blood on the blade began to change color from bright crimson to an inky black.

When the queen reopened her eyes, she locked her gaze with Calla's and declared, "Sever the bond, sever the power."

Then she plunged the dagger right into Calla's heart.

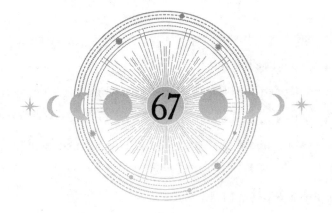

67

"Delphine," Reniel called, tone cloying. "Take your place opposite Zephyr, won't you, moonlight?"

Delphine was frozen. This hadn't been part of the plan. She was supposed to be able to stay by Reniel's side so she could grab the key from his neck when Celeste and Eros shut the power down.

Speaking of Celeste . . . the girl had disappeared.

Did they play me, too?

She felt a hand at her waist suddenly and jumped, turning her head to see Bellator gently guiding her forward as Reniel shifted on his feet with impatience.

"Sometimes to win, you have to take a loss," Bellator grumbled next to her ear.

What the Hells is that supposed to mean?

Delphine's mind was racing too fast to form a retort as Bellator planted her in place, giving her a sharp look she couldn't decipher before returning to his place next to his brother. She refused to lose when she had come this far. Especially to Zephyr. This wouldn't just be a loss; this would be the *end*.

Zephyr stepped into the ring, his pure white irises flashing like a predator waiting to strike at its prey. "Not even warming Reniel's bed could help you, moonlight. You should have learned that from your mother."

Delphine saw red at his words.

"First to cause the other to lose consciousness wins," Reniel announced.

Zephyr poised himself to attack, and Delphine bent down to rip off the bottom of her floor-length gown, making a few people in the crowd snicker.

"This is going to feel *good*," Zephyr taunted.

That's when Reniel's voice boomed through the room. *"Begin!"*

Zephyr didn't hesitate to launch himself at her, unfurling his magic and whipping up a whirlpool around them. Delphine dodged as she sent a jet stream right into his face before reaching out her claws and viciously raking them down the side of his head, nearly tearing off his left ear.

Zephyr's answering scream of pain thundered around them.

He sent another blast of his magic forward, and she held her palms up to catch the violent streams of water before pushing them right back in his direction. The streams of water broke apart into separate tendrils that wrapped around all four of his limbs, holding him just long enough for her wind her arm back and slam it forward into his jaw. His head flew to the side with the powerful *crack* of her fist. Her victory was short-lived, however, his dislocated jawbone healing itself seconds later. The fury that ignited in his eyes made her feel like the water around them was going to start boiling.

He tore his limbs from the clutches of her magic and darted forward to wrap both his hands around her neck. He slammed her to the floor, making her skull crack against the marble, and her vision went blurry, wisps of dark blue blood beginning to swirl around her face as Zephyr straddled her body and pressed his thumbs down over her gills. She clawed at his hands.

"You're a selfish little bitch," Zephyr told her as he leaned over her, his voice dipping so low that only she could hear. "You ran away thinking there would be no consequences for any of the rest of us? Reniel punished us for *years* because of you, making us do things that would give demons nightmares."

"That sounds," she gasped, "like something you should be mad at *him* for."

"I was at first," Zephyr admitted. "Until I realized that there's no beating him. So I might as well join him, right? And none of this would have happened without *you*. You were always his pretty little trophy, the girl who beat the odds. So special, so precious. None of the rest of us even had a chance of earning our way out of our oaths—but you were so close. He was going to break your oath, offer you a spot at his side, and you *threw it all away* like the ungrateful little brat you are."

She couldn't breathe anymore. His fingers pushing down on her gills had stopped all oxygen. She tried to send another stream of water at him, but as it hit his body, he didn't even flinch. Just braced himself against it. She was going to lose. Not just this fight—her last opportunity at freedom. This had all been a setup. Reniel had probably planned to throw her back in the dungeon the second this was over regardless of the outcome.

Sometimes to win, you have to take a loss.

Bellator's words echoed through her mind, and she still couldn't make sense of them. Taking this loss wouldn't help her. She would be unconscious, and Zephyr would win—

That was it.

It took everything inside her to do what she did next. She had never been good at losing, had been trained her entire childhood that losing was unacceptable. But Bellator had given her the key.

She made a show of struggling against his hold a bit more, kicking her legs out and choking. She let her eyelids slowly flutter closed, stilled all her movements, and a moment later Zephyr released his hold.

"And we have our champion," Reniel announced as Zephyr climbed off her.

There was some cheering, some clapping, and Delphine didn't dare move a muscle.

"Someone prepare to hold her when she wakes up," she heard Reniel order beneath his breath, before raising his voice back to the crowd and saying, "Zephyr has earned the removal of his Siren's oath."

She couldn't open her eyes yet to see what was going on, but she heard two heavy sets of feet move to stand next to where she laid. She wasn't sure if Eros and Celeste had ever planned to go through with their part of her scheme, if they had been planning to betray her all along as well, and at this point it didn't matter. The moment Reniel and Zephyr were caught up in breaking the Siren's oath, she was grabbing that damn key from around Reniel's neck and getting the Hells out.

"With my blood," Reniel spoke clear and deliberate from a few feet away. "I hereby absolve you of your Siren's oath, wiping your slate clean."

There was a long moment of silence, and she wondered if she was missing her opportunity already. Before she could open her eyes to peek, however, the gasps of alarm began. And then a scream.

She peeled one of her lids back just as the lights around them began flickering out one by one, and she caught a glimpse of Reniel and Zephyr frozen in front of each other, bloody hands clasped as the magic of breaking the Siren's oath immobilized both of their bodies.

It was her chance.

While everyone above her began shuffling with uncertainty as the power around them began to fluctuate, Delphine slithered over the ground between the men. With every inch closer, her heart thudded faster, until she was sure she would pass out for real.

"*Hey!*" someone called behind her, and she knew. Someone had spotted her.

She didn't even hesitate as she pushed herself off the ground and darted right for Reniel, not bothering to look back to see who had caught her. Thankfully, the pectoral fins on her arms and legs had healed, making her movements much swifter.

As she reached the two men who had made her life a waking nightmare, she smiled, showing them all her teeth. She reached beneath Reniel's shirt and watched in pure ecstasy as the man's eyes bulged when she snapped the Obsidian Key from his neck. The key to her freedom.

Then they were all plunged into darkness.

68

Six minutes. That's how long Calliope was gone before Gideon felt the searing agony go through his chest.

He groaned in pain as blood began to soak through his shirt.

His left arm felt like it was on fire, like the flesh was going to begin melting from his bones. His breathing was labored as he ripped his sleeve back and stared in horror.

His Rolls of Fate were slowly turning back to black. The bond was being severed, and once it was, Calliope would be fair game for his mother to kill.

"Help me break the bars," he grunted at Caspian and Kestrel. Hannah was still disoriented.

"What?" Cass exclaimed, hovering nearby as he watched Gideon struggle against the pain.

"*I have to get to her. Help me break the bars,*" Gideon roared as he wildly reached out with his wind magic, slicing it against the steel in front of him.

Cass didn't hesitate this time as he began to swipe back and forth with his own wind cuts, sawing at the steel bars over and over. Gideon was much slower in his current state, the stabbing pain in his heart and the heat still licking up his arm making it hard for him to concentrate. He glanced back at Kestrel, who was watching him with an inscrutable expression.

"Don't just fucking stand there," Gideon gritted out. "Help. Help or I will *never* forgive you."

"Were you ever going to forgive me anyway?" Kestrel asked, his voice low, serious.

"No," Gideon admitted, his breathing growing more and more laborious. "But if you help, maybe one day I'll learn not to hate you."

Kestrel didn't say anything for a moment, the only sound in the dungeon the grating noise of Cass hacking at the metal over and over again.

"Why her?" Kestrel asked.

Gideon lifted his brows. "Are you fucking *kidding* me? *This is not the time—*"

"Why her?" Kestrel repeated. "You never once risked this much for me. Your position with your mother, your *heart.*"

"I don't know," Gideon said, tone clipped.

"Why. Her?" Kestrel continued, refusing to budge.

"*She's worth the broken heart,*" Gideon finally answered, causing even Caspian to pause what he was doing and look over with wide eyes. "I tried to explain it to you before. She and I started this journey trying to run from our own destinies and gained a purpose, together, instead. The threads that bind us are infinite."

"It's been less than a couple weeks, Gideon." Kestrel's voice was little more than a whisper, but they all heard the unspoken words loud and clear. Gideon had known her less than a couple weeks and he was willing to risk everything, but had laid by Kestrel's side for *years*.

"Hearts cannot tell time," Gideon said. "Someone could mean nothing to you in the dead of winter and everything to you by the blooms of spring."

Kestrel stepped up to Gideon then, until the two witches were toe to toe. "If Ezra wasn't gone and I hadn't gotten us into this situation"—Kestrel waved his hand in the air, his voice shakier than Gideon had ever heard it before—"if she hadn't chosen you and I told you that it's okay if you never love me, that it would be enough if you just warmed my bed—"

"What-ifs don't help anyone, Kestrel," Gideon told him. "But it wouldn't matter anyway. It's not who you're sleeping next to. It's who you're dreaming about."

Kestrel squeezed his eyes shut for one long moment, and when he opened them again, Gideon could see that the commander was going to finally let him go. The breath he released then was almost a sigh of relief.

Gideon turned back, still bracing against the pain, and began swiping at the bars once again. Cass worked tirelessly beside him, and when Kestrel joined, the three of them moved in perfect sync. The bars groaned as the cuts started to dig deeper and deeper into them, but as the pain intensified in Gideon's arm, he knew they were not going to be fast enough.

"Um, guys?" a gentle voice squeaked from behind them.

All three men paused and twisted around to see a now-standing Hannah.

"I think I can help," she said softly.

Gideon and Cass exchanged a look, half-concerned Hannah's way of helping might include zombified corpses rising from the earth again.

"Are you sure?" Caspian stepped toward her. "You don't have to push yourself."

Hannah's face was determined. "I want to help. I don't want to be on the sidelines anymore."

"What do you need?" Cass asked without hesitation, ready to help her any way she asked him to.

"Blood," she said.

Cass didn't bother to think twice as he stepped up to her and used the sharp nail of his index finger to slice a line across the base of his throat, where the skin was thinner just above his clavicle.

Hannah raised a hand and let her magic tug as hard as it could before the wound sealed up, the stream of blood now floating through the air at her will. They all stepped back as they watched her move the blood, wrapping it around one of the half-cut bars. With a small constriction of her hand, the blood began to boil. Gideon, Cass, and Kestrel gaped as the steel melted all the way through.

She moved on to the next as Cass tore a strip off the hem of his shirt to wrap around his palm, protecting him from the heat, and pried the top of the broken post back. Kestrel slammed the heel of his boot into the bottom piece to bend it down and created a space just large enough for her to squeeze out. She dove through the tight gap and rushed over to the valve on the wall that they had seen the guards use to open the cells before. As soon as the steel posts were out of the way, the three Onyx witches rushed out, although Gideon's movements were stiff with pain.

When Cass reached Hannah's side, he tugged on a strand of her hair with brotherly affection. "Good job, little witch."

Hannah beamed.

"Wait!" a voice grunted from the cell next door as they all started toward the exit.

The group paused. Gideon had forgotten Calla said someone was in the cell with her.

"Let me out. *Please*," the man implored, gripping the bars.

"A Terra witch," Caspian noted. "You're the one Calla was talking to. Why are you down here?"

The man shoved his left sleeve up to his elbow, revealing the numbers that lay beneath. Hannah and Cass both gasped.

"My name is Thorne—"

"That's enough for us," Cass commented, and moved to open the bars of the man's cell. "But keep up or you're on your own."

Gideon didn't wait to see what the man decided. He took off down the hall, rushing up the dungeon's steps two at a time, only taking his eyes off the exit door once to check his numbers. Three of them had already turned black.

He burst out of the door, sending a guard standing on the other side flying forward.

"Hey!" someone yelled, but before Gideon could whip out his magic, he heard Caspian behind him say, "Go! We've got it here."

Gideon didn't argue as he dashed through the palace hall toward the throne room, thanking the Gods he had been here enough times to know his way around. When he made it to the entryway, two guards tried to seize him, but he ripped the air from their throats with lightning speed, bringing them down to their knees and squeezing until the lack of oxygen made them pass out.

When he finally entered the throne room, the fire he felt in his chest and arm did not compare to the burning rage he felt at the scene before him. Calliope's body was writhing on the marble floor—a dagger protruding from her chest. Not just any dagger.

Heart Reaver.

Gideon snarled, *"Stop!"*

And everything did.

69

"*T*his is the control room," Reniel told Delphine as they pushed past the guards waiting outside the largest set of doors she had ever seen.

When they stepped inside, she paused in awe and Reniel gave her a satisfied grin.

In the center of the room was an enormous orb of blue light. Not just light—magic. The ball of energy was hovering between two giant circular platforms connected to several pipes on either side of the room. It had been barely more than three months that she'd been here, and she hadn't been adjusting very well without her mother. Never had she had a room all to herself, and there was no one her age to talk to. It had gotten unbearably lonely.

When Reniel had come back from his latest expedition, she had told him as much. Now he was taking time out of his schedule to entertain her, starting with this tour. He said only his inner circle had ever seen the inside of this particular room, that she was special.

"Wow," she whispered.

"This controls everything in the palace. The magic is depleted little by little through those tubes and distributed all over the house to give it power—light, heat, everything. When it starts getting low, members of the Shoal are nominated to donate kernels of their magic to keep it running."

"Can you touch it?" she wondered.

"No," he said swiftly, and when she jumped at his harsh tone, his eyes softened a bit. "If you touch it, it will overload your system with magic, and the power grid could go out."

"Shouldn't there be guards inside, too, then?" she quipped as she took a step back, giving the staticky orb a wide berth.

"If someone touched it, they would most likely perish. And even if they didn't—the power outage would cause those doors to lock." He walked to the door and pointed to the small black bars hanging out of the ceiling in a long row before the door, like teeth. "See these? They'd drop down and trap anyone inside."

Delphine shivered. "I think I'm ready to see whatever is next."

Reniel grinned before waving her over with one hand. "Let's go to the greenhouse. I think you'll enjoy that much more."

70

Everything happened all at once.

Delphine sent a torrent of magic straight toward the ceiling, shattering the crystal above her. Shards scattered through the room and shouts of panic rang out. As the crowd descended into anarchy, Delphine headed straight for the exit she just made. All she had to do was make it out of the sea. Then she would be *free*.

And Eros and Celeste will be trapped forever, a soft voice whispered in her mind. *Does vengeance taste sweet? They kept their promises this time and yet you've damned them for it.*

She didn't know where the voice had come from, or why it felt familiar, but she shook it off. Now was *not* the time to grow a conscience. She kept swimming.

You are not the monster your mother molded you to be.

Delphine hesitated this time. *What if I am? Celeste let me go and then dragged me back. She doesn't deserve my forgiveness!*

Do you think you *would deserve your forgiveness when this is over? Will you let yourself be free of your own guilt? Or will you be trapped by it forever—trading one prison for another?*

Hannah. It was Hannah's voice.

Delphine cursed and turned around.

Finding her way through the inky darkness of the palace was not an easy feat. Sirens were running in every direction, none of them knowing how to process everything that had just happened. Reniel's events were always coordinated down to every last detail; something like this was unprecedented, and it had everyone acting as if it was the end of the world.

A bunch of sheep without a shepherd are utterly useless, she thought.

Delphine had managed to make it out undetected, and as she moved deeper and deeper into the bowels of the palace, she prayed her memory didn't fail her. Another two rights down a long corridor, and then a sharp left and . . . She squinted as she got closer and sighed in relief. She had found the control room.

As she approached, she saw a single guard sprawled out on the ground, throat ripped out. Eros's work, surely. She shoved the man aside with her foot and pulled down on the steel lever of the heavy doors, prying them open with all her might. They made a groaning metallic sound as she moved them both out of her way.

"*Delphine?*" Celeste's anxious voice cried. "Oh, thank the Gods! We're trapped!"

She could just make out where Celeste and Eros were standing on the other side of the iron bars that separated them.

"We've tried everything," Celeste almost sobbed. "We can't break them."

Delphine cursed. She was about to tell them she didn't know what to do when she remembered what she was holding in her hand.

"Stand back, let me try something," she ordered. When she heard them shuffle a few feet away, she took a deep breath and held the key up to one of the bars in front of her. There was no bright light, no magic fanfare. Just like she remembered when Reniel used it to lock her mother's magic away—the key simply slipped into the bar. An instant later the steel prison shattered.

Celeste let out a squeak of relief and launched herself into Delphine's arms. Eros simply watched in tense silence as Delphine cleared her throat and extracted herself from the other girl.

"No time." Delphine shook her head as she waved for them to follow her. "We need to go, it's complete chaos. We have to get out of here *now.*"

The three of them rushed off down the hall, and Delphine let Eros take the lead as they wound their way through the palace to what she hoped was the front entrance. A few adrenaline-charged minutes later and her hopes were confirmed.

Eros had just seized the door handle when a slow clap echoed from behind them. They all whipped around.

"I must say I'm impressed. Never did I think any of you would get past your animosity toward one another to pull something like this off," Reniel said as he stepped into view, the light from the windows that framed the doorway illuminating the foyer enough for them to all be able to see each other as more than silhouettes.

And behind him was Bellator.

"Clearly I didn't torture either of you enough." Reniel scowled at Eros and Celeste.

"Or maybe Zephyr is just a weaker being than we are," Celeste spat back.

"I'm starting to believe that might be the case as well." Reniel huffed a laugh before turning his cruel gaze on Delphine. "I want back what you stole from me."

Delphine laughed bitterly. "And I want back what *you* stole from *me*. This is what you get for being such an arrogant bastard. Inviting people to watch you in your most vulnerable state . . . not a choice I personally would have made."

"Bellator," Reniel ordered. "Take care of the other two. I want to relish draining every ounce of power from this one alone."

Bellator didn't hesitate for a second to send a blast of the most powerful magic Delphine had ever felt into Eros and Celeste. The two sirens went flying sideways, smashing through the closed doors of the study to their left as Bellator pursued them.

"Never in my life have I wanted to hurt someone like I want to hurt you," Reniel lamented as he slammed her back against the door by her neck.

"The feeling . . . is . . . mutual," she choked out.

"Your magic is *mine*." He tightened his vise around her throat. "I will not give you a moment of rest for the next three centuries."

She could feel the tattoo on the back of her neck began to heat as he invoked the magic oath that bound her to him. He could drain every ounce of power she had to give, and when it replenished, he could do it again and again and again. For three hundred years she would be paying this debt. For three hundred years she was supposed to be marked by this man whom she hated more than anyone else in the universe.

She giggled.

A flicker of shock chased by fury went over his face. He tightened his grasp.

She laughed again, this time her entire body shaking with it.

"Stop it, you little—"

She slammed the Obsidian Key into the back of his neck.

"No." His hand dropped away from her as it reached back to clutch where the key was protruding from the nape of his neck, locking away his magic. Forever. *"NO!"* his voice boomed, his knees hitting the floor as his body began spasming with pain.

Delphine lurched forward and snatched the key back out. "That's for my mother. You used her as a ploy to get me to swear an oath to you when I was barely old enough to use my own magic. You made me a puppet for years so you could fuel your own greed." Her hand snapped out and clutched his chin, angling his face up so he'd have to look her in the eyes. "Even now your arrogance astounds me—bringing no more than a single person to back you up because you think you are an infallible God. Well, if you are a God, then I am a Godslayer. Your reign ends today."

Something shattered to her left, and she turned to look for the commotion in the direction of where Eros and Celeste had gone. She needed to help them.

Looking back to Reniel one last time, she said, "I hope I never see your face again. But if I do . . ." Delphine stepped closer to run the back of her hand along the man's cheek. "I hope it's in the depths of the Hells."

Then, before she could stop herself, she plunged her claws into the soft tissue of his throat and tore his trachea out. She didn't linger as she took off for the study where the others had disappeared, worry shooting through her when she found it empty. The only sign of struggle, however, was the giant hole in the exterior window.

She wedged herself through the sharp opening and out to the front side of the palace. Rallying the last kernels of her energy, she launched herself up with two jet streams, flexing the fins running down her forearms and calves as she swam. She moved her arms in broad strokes, one fist still clutching the Obsidian Key as she propelled herself higher and higher. When she finally made it to the edge of the palace's roofline and all there was left between her and freedom was open water, she kicked furiously, scanning the surface line for any sign of Celeste or Eros. Then something suddenly caught her ankle and dragged her back down.

She looked to find Reniel, desperate and furious, his throat leaking blood into the sea around them, clutching her leg. She let out a sound of frustration as she kicked at him, but he only kept dragging her back.

Down.

Down.

Down.

"Let me go!" she screamed, blasting the last bit of power she had left in her body. It didn't even loosen his hold.

He dragged her back another foot.

"No! *No.* I'm going home. *You can't have me anymore!*" she screamed at him, decades of hatred spilling into her voice.

He kept pulling and she was getting tired. So tired. With the last of her strength, she reached down and clawed at his face, thrashing wildly, hoping she gouged his eyes out of his head so he would *let go.*

"I'm going home," she snarled. "I'm going back to Hannah and Calla. *I'm going home.*"

His skin tore beneath her nails and blood poured out of his wounds, but she just kept going and going until someone finally said, "You did it, Delphine. You can stop now. You can leave."

She stopped her movements, her body sagging with exhaustion as she blinked and saw Bellator below, holding on to Reniel's limp, floating body. A sob came from her throat as her chest heaved with effort.

"Why are you letting me go?" she gritted out. "Where are Eros and Celeste?"

Bellator's mouth was a hard line.

"*Why are you letting me go?* I will not switch from being indebted to him to being indebted to you."

"Consider us even," Bellator told her. "You're doing me a favor by taking the key. My brother has become a monster. His aspirations will destroy our entire society if he continues to gain power here." He shook his head, then continued, "Get that key as far from here as possible. Tell *no one* you have it. Not even the other two—who should be waiting for you at the surface now."

Her heart thundered in her chest at his words, the seriousness in his voice.

"We're even," she stated.

He nodded and she began to turn away, to put as much distance between this sea and herself as possible.

"Wait," he called.

She looked back. "*What?*"

"When you see him again . . . tell him I'm sorry. Tell him I hope he found his way without me."

Delphine furrowed her brow in puzzlement. "Tell *who*?"

Bellator didn't answer her this time. He simply dragged his brother back down into the mess below and left her treading water alone.

alla felt like she was lying on the surface of the sun. She swore her flesh must be melting from her bones.

Everyone around her was utterly frozen, the demand from *that* voice stopping everything but their breaths. Heart Reaver was still in her chest. She could feel whatever enchantment Lysandra had put on it like a poison weaseling its way through her veins, her magic, her soul.

"Calliope," Gideon said as he knelt beside her, not hesitating as he reached for Heart Reaver's hilt and yanked it out.

She cried at the instant relief as the burning crawling up her arm dissipated.

"Gideon, what are you *doing*?" his mother hissed.

Gideon paid no attention to the Onyx Queen, however. He simply ran his hands over Calla's face, brushing the sweat-soaked hair out of her eyes as he murmured, "Take some of my energy."

She was so drained from whatever ancient magic had just been forced into her body that she worried *some* of his energy would turn into *all*. She carefully reached out with her inner Siphon and took a morsel of Gideon's magic while the bond sparked to life and replenished all the other kinds of energy her body desperately needed. He leaned back a bit as he offered her his hand, gently pulling her to her feet.

Calla slowly looked around in utter shock. Everyone was truly frozen in their places.

"What's going on?" she whispered to him.

"I'm not sure." He cleared his throat and then called to his mother, "Give us the Fates' Dice back."

As soon as Gideon addressed the room, everyone unfroze at once. That's when the rest of their group came crashing in.

"Who let that fiend out of his cell?" Myrea was off her throne and on her feet next to Lysandra in a flash.

Calla twisted around to see Thorne, looking truly haggard, trying to keep up with Cass and the rest of them.

"You've tried so hard to keep the inevitable from happening," Calla said as she turned back to the queens. "But as I've recently realized—you cannot stop the Fates. They will continue and continue until they get their war. Look at what they've already done here."

"You think you have all the answers," Myrea told her. "But without the Fates' Dice, the two of you cannot complete your rolls. Regular Witch's Dice will be defunct for you now. And if you *are* the final destined Warriors, that means without those dice you will never be able to start the war."

"That's the thing"—Calla laughed bitterly—"you think we *want* to start a war. When really, we just don't want *you* to have any more power than you already do."

"Those dice are long gone to the farthest corners of Illustros and beyond already," Myrea sneered. "As for power . . . " The queen raised her hands, and with a flick of her wrist, every single one of her guards did an about-face toward Calla and Gideon. "You want to play? Let's play."

Myrea conducted the next two heartbeats like someone would a symphony. With a few waves of her hands, the Rouge guards poised themselves to attack.

"Ready?" Gideon asked, sliding his gaze over to Calla's.

"Ready," Calla confirmed, a smirk playing at the edges of her lips.

The room exploded.

The Rouge guards threw out their magic, but Gideon was already summoning a tornado to whip across the circle. Caspian and Kestrel immediately joined the fray, their duet with each other precise. While the two Onyx witches took care of half the guards, Gideon and Calla faced down the others. Calla summoned the bit of Onyx magic that Gideon had let her take and blasted it at a nearby witch who was lunging for her, sending them stumbling back. Calla dodged another lunge, spinning away, when she caught sight of flaxen hair over her shoulder and had to do a double take. Hannah was using her magic.

Calla couldn't help the full-blown grin that was unleashed on her face now as she advanced on another one of the guards, reaching for the exposed skin of his neck. It was the same guard who had been antagonizing her since the incident with the water.

"Come on, leech, you can do better than that, can't you?" he taunted.

Calla glowered. "I'm not a leech."

"Yeah? Then what are you?"

Calla feinted right and then broke left the moment he followed her. She curved to the side and struck, grasping his throat. Her inner Siphon roared to life and sang as it homed in on the blood pulsing through his veins.

"I'm a Blood Siphon," she declared proudly. Then she siphoned enough blood out of his body to make him hit the ground at her feet.

The crimson droplets that she had siphoned from the man were now suspended in the air around her, moving as she shifted her body and hands. In her control. Before she could strike her next opponent, however, she felt a piercing pain in her side and looked down to see blood spreading through her shirt. She whipped her head around to search for Gideon.

"I'm fine," he grunted as he removed the knife stuck in his hip, flipped it around in his palm, and stabbed it through his opponent's throat in one fluid motion.

"*Enough*," Myrea said. "This ends now."

The Rouge Queen stepped off the dais into the battle, heading straight for Calla. The queen raised a hand and seized Calla's body, bending Calla's legs against her will until she was kneeling on the floor. Someone called Gideon's name behind her as his body went down as well.

"You do not get the last word, girl, *I* do. You were never supposed to be here," Myrea growled. "Your mother was never supposed to have you, and now look what's happened! You are a disgrace."

"*You* are a disgrace to any legacy the Witch Realm might have," Calla choked out.

Myrea snarled as she lifted her hand up and began to swing it down—

The woman's arm froze. Myrea curled her lips back from her teeth and looked over to her sister.

"I will not let you risk hurting my son, Myrea," Lysandra told her. "We finish the severing first."

Myrea scowled but didn't argue, and that must have been enough for Lysandra to release the hold on her arm. Myrea twisted around to find where Heart Reaver had been forgotten on the ground. With Calla still frozen in place, Myrea scooped the knife up and shoved it right back into Calla's chest without preamble. The fire began all over again.

Calla gritted her teeth against a yelp of pain as Myrea slackened the magic grip on her body and let her slump to the ground. The enchantment wasted no time working to disintegrate the bond between her and Gideon once more.

"*Stop,*" Gideon demanded, but his voice was hoarse now. Calla looked over to him as he gritted his teeth through the pain and moved toward her.

Cass, Hannah, and Kestrel were taking care of the last of the guards in the background, throwing concerned glances in Calla's direction as she cried out again. Gideon tried to get closer, but Myrea sent over a wave of her magic and kept him in place where he knelt.

"Let her go," he ordered. *"Or—"*

Myrea turned her nose up with a scoff. "Save your breath, prince."

"If you hurt her anymore, I *swear*—"

"Silence," Lysandra ordered Gideon. "Do not make a promise that you cannot keep."

Calla glanced over at the numbers on her arm as they slowly turned back to their original black color. Three down, one left to go.

"Fight," Gideon implored to Calla as he swung his attention back to her.

Calla whimpered. The fire was intensifying, and her chest heaved as she tried to suck in more air. Her eyes fluttered closed.

"No, look at me," he demanded, and something about the way he said it made her eyes blink open. *"Fight.* Right now. You know what your magic is capable of."

"This is our chance to let the bond break," she managed to get out, despite the shakiness of her voice. "Look at what this connection is doing to you. It's dragging you down with me."

"One thing the girl is right about," Lysandra sneered. "Let it go, Gideon."

"I don't care if we keep the bond, Calliope," he told her, ignoring his mother entirely. "That isn't what this is about. You wanted a choice—now you have one. But there is *nothing* they will ever be able to do to make me stop fighting by your side if that's where you want me to be."

Calla sucked in a breath at his words. That was a reckless oath to make in front of the spiteful queens.

"You get to make the decisions," he continued. "But if you think going through with this will change anything I've ever said or felt, you're wrong. They way I feel about you was inevitable long before the soul-bond."

Calla had spent so much of her relationship with Ezra unsure about who she was, what she wanted her future to be, that she'd wasted time and never let herself unleash her full potential with him. With Gideon, she didn't want to make the same mistakes. He was the one who told her she should be comfortable in her own skin, take comfort in her own power, learn how to *use* that power. He was the one who had known exactly who—and what—she was almost from the second they met.

She had made up her mind.

She still didn't know what her future held. Didn't know what the queens were going to do next, or if they would make it out of here at all. What she did know was that the queens didn't think she was a contender in their game of war, but she was about to show them just how strong an opponent she would be.

72

C alla reached deep into her core and pulled at her inner Siphon. She coaxed the magic to spread out to the tips of her fingers and all the way down to her toes. She had no other person to physically connect her Siphon to, no direct energy to pull on, but she knew she didn't need it.

As the last number on her arm began to turn, her back arched off the ground, sweat beading at her temples as she worked to peel herself up slowly. She could feel the final threads of the soul-bond fraying as she managed to rise to her knees. She clumsily swiped at the hair falling over her face, leaving a trail of bright crimson blood smeared across her cheek.

She recalled the demon's oak vision she'd had when she first came to the forest as she got to her feet. She'd never thought she could become someone who was capable of such destructive power. It turned out a lot could change in very little time.

The weapon you've become was sharpened by your own hand, Calliope Rosewood.

She laughed aloud at those words now, a sound that started out a little bit broken, but as she met the queens' gazes it quickly turned into something harsher, darker. It was ironic that the words echoing through her mind in this moment were those of the Fates. She still had every intention of keeping her promise to carry out her vengeance on the Gods—but since the queens insisted on playing Gods with all of them, they would be the first to feel her fury.

Tear the queens to shreds, Ezra had told her. So she would.

"It's time you faced the nightmare you forced me to become."

Calla homed in on her inner Siphon and reached out with her magic. When she was locked onto her target, she *pulled*.

Myrea screeched in horror as Calla drained every ounce of energy the Rouge Queen had on tap. Without a single touch. The queen hit the floor. This was Calla's opportunity.

She reached out to lock onto Myrea's blood this time, but when she pulled, it wasn't the queen's blood that splattered across the floor. It was an unsuspecting guard to her right. His bloodless body hit the ground with a heavy *thud*, cracking the ice on the floor beneath his weight. Calla watched as Myrea's shoulders shook with laughter, and the queen picked herself back up from the ground as if not a single ounce of her energy had just been siphoned away. Another guard dropped to the ground, face gaunt, almost gray.

She was using them to absorb the hits from Calla's magic.

"Go ahead, girl, try again," Myrea taunted. "You'll tire way before you can kill every single witch in this palace under my control."

More guards began piling into the room, alerted by the ruckus, and Calla swallowed thickly as she realized what she was up against. She went to yank the dagger from her chest, but when she tried to touch it, a blue spark zapped her hand.

Gideon was there in seconds, removing the blade a moment before it was too late. Their soul-bond remained intact. The light in the prince's eyes as they stood, together, was almost too bright for her to look at.

"Let's go," he urged her.

"I don't think so," Lysandra interrupted, sending a massive gust of ice-wind through the room.

The floor slicked over with frozen flurries, almost making Calla slip before she could catch herself. A guard came diving in from her left, and she locked her Siphon onto him and ripped half the blood in his body out, painting the ice on the ground in a macabre shade of vermilion. It wasn't enough to fully kill the man, but even being immortal it would take a while to recover. Another guard who had been rushing toward her stopped in their tracks, gaping at the grotesque display in pure terror.

"All of you go," Kestrel barked. "I'll hold them back."

"*Freeze*," Myrea's voice boomed.

Every Rouge witch in the room except for Calla went rigid with the order, the magic of their completed Rolls of Fate binding them to their queen's demand. Every witch including . . . Hannah.

No. Calla sucked in a breath as she spotted how her friend was now locked in a trance.

"I suspected as much," Myrea said, following Calla's gaze to Hannah. "She's *mine* now."

Cass moved into action immediately. He approached Hannah from behind, and with a swiftness Calla cringed at, Cass snapped the blond's neck to render her unconscious before the queen was able to give another order. Hannah's body crumpled, and Caspian scooped her up into his arms before she could hit the ground. Such an injury wouldn't kill an immortal the first time, but if Hannah ever broke the same bones again, her ability to heal would erode away until the damage eventually became permanent.

"Let's go." Gideon grasped Calla's hand and pulled her along behind him as Myrea let out another scream of rage, barking orders at the Rouge witches still under her trance.

Calla skidded to halt at Kestrel's side despite Gideon trying to guide her away, nearly slipping on the icy floor.

"Kestrel—" she began, her voice strained.

"*Go,*" he ordered, his expression turning grave.

She didn't argue, only dipped her chin in acknowledgment and let Gideon lead her after the others. Thorne was doing his best in his condition to keep up with the rest of them, surprising Calla by taking out one of the guards in their pathway to the door. As she and the prince darted through the exit, she felt the power brewing behind her, catching one last glimpse of the storm forming above their heads before ducking completely out of sight. She and Gideon caught up with the group in the grand foyer, and they all dashed out into the night together.

Give them Hells, Kestrel.

"Are we not going to wait for that guy?" Thorne asked innocently as they ran past the spine gate. Caspian beelined for one of the carriages waiting out front.

"We can't." Gideon said, voice gruff with emotion.

Caspian called out for help, and Gideon went over to assist with lifting Hannah into the carriage. After Cass reemerged to begin readying the horses, Calla climbed into the cabin with the others. She moved to sit in the empty space next to Hannah, lifting the other girl's head onto her lap.

"Oh, Hannah," Calla whispered with regret as she ran her fingers lightly over her friend's forehead.

Gideon leaned out of the carriage to say something to Caspian that she couldn't quite make out, but a few seconds later he shut the door and the vehicle lurched forward.

"Do you feel strange?" Gideon asked. "Because I feel absolutely *wired*. Like I could throw up at any moment."

"It's the energy I siphoned from Myrea." Calla nodded, her own body beginning to buzz with the siphoned power. "But I don't feel as sick as I normally do."

"Maybe because I absorbed half the energy from you," Gideon guessed.

"Have you not felt the other times I've siphoned since we got the bond?"

"I didn't think so, at first," Gideon told her. "Maybe because the last couple of times you didn't take nearly as much?"

Thorne cleared his throat as Gideon settled in next to him across from Calla and Hannah's unconscious form. "I'm almost afraid to ask what the Hells just happened."

"Long story." Gideon rubbed his temples as if he had a migraine. "We can explain it when we all get someplace safer."

Thorne nodded and immediately went silent again.

"Where do you think Caspian is leading us?" Calla asked, her knees bouncing ferociously beneath her palms as the energy continued to vibrate in her core. Even Gideon was fidgeting where he sat.

"North," Gideon answered. "To the Dragonwoods."

Calla straightened up. "Delphine—"

"Is still the first priority," Gideon assured. "But we desperately need to regroup, and we can't go back to Estrella. Once was risky enough. The Dragonwoods is the closest neutral territory where the queens won't have such strong connections or spies."

The cabin became silent with the weight of Gideon's revelations, and it wasn't too long until Thorne fell asleep. Calla leaned her head against the carriage wall, letting the vibration of the moving vehicle lull her to a place somewhere between awake and asleep. It was about an hour before she heard Gideon's whisper.

"You chose to keep the bond. After everything . . ."

Calla blinked her eyes fully open and locked her gaze with his. "Yes, I *chose* it."

Gideon's irises flashed silver with hope, but he waited for her to continue.

"You were right," she confessed. "I was being a coward before. I didn't want to face my guilt about how I knew I felt about you once Ezra died. But Ezra was right, too—in the Valley of Souls. He told me guilt is such a stupid reason not to let yourself be happy."

"And now?" Gideon wondered, leaning forward across the space between their benches until his face was right before hers. Their lips almost touching.

"I had this dream . . . when we were down in Myrea's dungeon. I'll tell you about it when we have time. But I think . . ."

Hannah jolted awake.

Calla and Gideon ripped apart, whipping their heads to where the other girl was now sitting up, ramrod straight. Hannah's neck was no longer unnaturally twisted where Cass had snapped the bones to break her out of the queen's trance, but something was still very wrong.

Hannah turned her face to them and a scream lodged in Calla's throat. Her friend's eyes were entirely black—her violet irises and the white around them devoured entirely.

And when Hannah looked at Calla, there was no recognition in her gaze.

73

Delphine burst wildly out of the water of the Siren's Sea and hauled herself up onto the bank. She awkwardly crawled over the earth until she was several feet away, her breathing labored, her muscles aching with strain. Reniel's blood was still caked beneath her fingernails, but in her hand . . . in her hand was the Obsidian Key.

She stood slowly, turning the key and its broken chain over. She swallowed as she thought about Bellator's warning. She couldn't tell anyone she had something so rare. She prayed Eros and Celeste had not seen her use it to get them out of that room.

She looked down at her ruined dress. There was nowhere she could hide the key in the garment. Instead, she bent over to unlace the ribbons of one of the delicate satin slippers she wore and shoved the key inside.

Just as she straightened back up, a voice shouted, *"Delphine!"*

Delphine searched the woods before her to find Celeste sprinting through the trees, Eros right on her heels.

"You made it," Celeste gasped.

"What happened?" Delphine asked them. "Did Bellator help you, too?"

Celeste nodded. "We're just as surprised as you are."

"Did he say why?" Delphine probed.

Celeste shook her head, about to say something more when Eros inserted, "You knew we were going to get trapped."

Celeste's brows knit together at the accusation. "What the Hells are you talking about?"

When Delphine cringed a bit, the girl's words cut off. Celeste's mouth floundered open and closed in disbelief before she took a horrified step back.

"What?" Celeste whispered.

"She knew exactly what was going to happen when we messed with that power source. A built-in security system. You didn't need us to turn the lights out—it was just an opportunity to get rid of us."

"Let me explain," Delphine began, but Celeste's expression was already drenched in betrayal.

"How could you?" Celeste demanded. *"How could you? I only ever wanted to help you."*

"You betrayed me first," Delphine said, but there was no venom in her words. She was too tired. "I was angry. I wanted you to pay. But now . . ."

"Now *what*, Delphine?" Celeste laughed. "You've ruined me. You've ruined *us*!"

"There has not been an *us* since the day you let me go!" Delphine yelled back.

Both girls were breathing heavily, facing off against each other as Eros stood to the side and watched them implode—the outcome Delphine was sure he had been hoping for.

"You don't know me anymore," Delphine told both of them. "You have not known me for a very, very long time. But I will say you were right about one thing."

"And what's that?" Celeste asked, tears shining in her eyes.

"My heart isn't an impenetrable fortress anymore," Delphine proclaimed. "You just aren't the one who unlocked it."

"Go to the Hells, Delphine." Celeste shook her head and swiped the back of her hand across her eyes. "I *never* want to see your face again."

Good, Delphine thought as Celeste turned away. Delphine's eyes flickered over to Eros now. He dipped his chin in a single nod. He knew what she had just done for him—for Celeste. She had cut the other girl loose after all these years.

And what she had said was true—Celeste hadn't been the one who tore down her walls. Now it was time to go find the one who had.

"Good luck," Delphine told them both. "Enjoy your freedom."

She watched as Eros guided Celeste away, toward whatever future the two of them would have to build from scratch together. Delphine tilted her head up toward the vermilion sky, listening to the sound of the trees rustling in the wind. It was time for her to go as well.

Bending down to pull the key back out of her shoe, she twisted it in her hands, taking a deep breath.

Moment of truth.

First, she inserted the teeth at the end of the magic artifact into the ring around her finger. It immediately split in half and fell to the forest floor. She wanted to sob.

As she rubbed the skin where the too-tight band had been fastened around her, something caught her attention. There, on the body of the Obsidian Key, a small line etched itself into the metal. She sucked in a breath and brought the key closer to her face.

Tally marks. Along both sides were tally marks counting each time its magic had been used. One side was already full. She counted them carefully. Fifteen. She flipped the key over in her palm and counted the other side. Eight.

There were only seven uses left.

Use it wisely. Got it.

She braced herself for this next one. She reached behind her, brushing the hair at the nape of her neck to the side, and inserted the key into her skin.

The sensation was odd, like a ripple of shivers vibrating through her body as the key's magic worked to undo the Siren's oath. Then she felt something inside her shatter—*free* her—and a weight lifted off her shoulders as the skin around the key was scorched. She felt something warm run down her cheeks as she pulled the key back out, her body ten times lighter than it had been twenty seconds ago. As her feverish skin began to cool once more, she reached up and brushed her fingertips over her face.

Tears.

I belong to myself again, she thought.

She looked up at the bloodred sky and screamed in victory. The forest seemed to almost preen around her, the branches of the trees bowing to the ground, the breeze kicking up its speed. When she was done, she smiled like a fiend.

It's time to go home.

Epilogue

Digging up a body was not an easy task.

Dirt and blood were caked under Amina's sharp ebony nails, the unforgiving earth chipping away at a few of their tips. The ground was harder than she had expected without any recent rain to soften the surface, but she and the others kept going at a relentless pace until the coffin beneath finally began to emerge.

"Lift it out," Amina directed the others, slipping her hands under the corners of the intricately carved casket and hauling it out of the grave and onto the undisturbed soil beside it.

She held her breath as she lifted the casket's lid. The first thing she noticed was the bed of flowers; not a single blossom wilted around the body. The corpse itself was perfectly preserved as well.

"Here," Lyra offered, yanking the beating heart out of its bag and handing it over to Amina.

Amina ripped a hole in the front of the corpse's shirt and shoved the pulsing organ into its place. Then she moved to unsheathe the long sword at her side and took a deep breath for the next part. She handed the sword over to Sabine.

"Make it quick," she requested.

Sabine turned the blade over in her hands as she announced, "We're going to use my wings instead."

Amina scoffed. "That's ridiculous, Sabine. This is my mess to clean up. It's my idea to summon the soul back. I should be the one to make that sacrifice."

Sabine shook her head. "Amina. We are in this *together*. Truly. You have sacrificed so much already—you're trying to change the lives of our people. Let me show you that you mean just as much to me as you did before. This is my gift."

"I don't need you to *chop off your wings* to know you care for me, Sabine." Amina's stomach churned. "The two of you . . . you came back to this forest with me. That's enough. I'm sorry for the way I acted before. Truly. I was just so . . . lost."

Sabine smiled brightly at Amina's words. "I'm glad you found your way back to us."

Then before Amina or Lyra could stop her, Sabine lifted the sword with both her hands as she summoned her wings, raising the weapon all the way above her head, tip of the blade facing down. With one sickening motion, she impaled the tip through the delicate tendons that attached the appendages to her back. Lyra lurched forward in horror as Sabine fell to the ground. Not a single sound escaped from the Valkyrie's lips. An impressive feat.

Amina cursed as Sabine's left wing hit the ground, blood pouring onto the forest floor from her back.

"Hurry," Sabine panted, pain racking her body. "Do the other."

Lyra and Amina both hesitated for a moment.

"Do the other!" Sabine ordered this time.

Amina sprang forward and swiped the sword from Sabine's limp grip. She wouldn't let Lyra take on the gruesome task—or the guilt that was about to come with it. Amina raised the sword as Lyra helped Sabine straighten up on her knees, making it easier for Amina to swing the sword down and cut clean through the second appendage. It was done. The sacrifice was made.

Lyra helped a nearly unconscious Sabine curl up on the ground, rubbing a hand over the girl's sweat-slicked forehead as her eyes slowly shut.

"Let's finish this," Lyra demanded.

They each grabbed one of the wings and dragged them a few feet away from the coffin and their sleeping friend. Once the feathery appendages were piled atop each other in a mess of mottled white-and-brown down, Amina reached into one of the pockets on her belt and took out a box of matches.

"Ready?" she whispered to Lyra as she struck one of the sticks against its box and ignited a flame.

Lyra nodded.

Bracing themselves, Amina threw the match atop the stack of feathers, reciting an incantation in the old language as an inferno unfurled before them. Billowing clouds of pitch-black smoke began to curl up toward the sky, the flames turning blue as she finished the summoning spell.

"Say the soul's name," Lyra prompted.

When the spirit's name fell from Amina's lips, the blue fire raged higher, nearly twenty feet in the air, and every single feather burned away. Then the blaze completely extinguished an instant later. Left behind was only the thick haze of black smoke, making both Lyra and Amina hack as they fanned the air around them. When nothing happened right away, Amina began to wonder if something had gone wrong, if she hadn't said the incantation correctly or she had said the incorrect surname—but then she saw it.

A faint blue glow hovered in the middle of the charred ring that was left on the ground. A soul.

Amina watched as Lyra's nails elongated, turning from their natural carbon color to the same glowing blue of the spirit. Lyra reached out and embedded their talons into the delicate matter of the soul.

"Hurry." Lyra beckoned Amina over with a gesture of their chin, and Amina stepped past the scarred ground to assist with stretching out the spirit, bringing it to float parallel above the body lying in the casket.

"Now," Amina whispered, and the two of them slowly lowered the soul down to the corpse, reciting the words that would hopefully bind the spirit to its corporeal form.

The two of them held their breaths as they waited for the soul to fully meld with the body. One minute went by. Then two. Then three.

Then: a movement from the chest.

A breath. A heartbeat.

The man's eyes burst open, irises glowing with obsidian flames.

Acknowledgments

Hello friends, I've missed you. I want to start these acknowledgments by saying: sequels are *hard*. There were many months of crying to Taylor Swift songs while eating ice cream and poring over these words to make sure I did Calla justice by letting her feel all the complicated things she feels in this book. All of that to say—here are the people who made the process of writing this book, and getting through the incredible whirlwind that has been this last year, so much easier.

This time I'd like to thank my partner, Isaac, first and foremost. When I didn't know if I was going to be able to do this, you told me every step of the way that I was not only capable but reminded me the only person I need to please is myself, which is a hard thing to remember when you suddenly have so many eyes on your work and eager readers waiting for book two (which still feels not real). You read this book over and over and gave me honest feedback when I needed to hear it. It's so easy to get excited about writing the rest of this series—and my other stories—when you are always so excited to know what's going to happen next. Back before I ever sold a book, when I asked you if I would ever be able to achieve all these dreams, you told me I've had stars in my eyes since the day we met. Never do I want to know a second without you in it. Thanks for never leaving any cracks in the foundation we stand on together.

Thank you to my ever-wonderful agent, Emily Forney, who is the most amazing person in the whole world to be doing this with. I absolutely adore you and I'm always so grateful for your constant support. Thanks for answering my anxious texts and enthusiastically encouraging all of my ideas and for bullying Elba with me.

To my editor, Cassidy Leyendecker—what an adventure we have had! Thanks so much for believing in this book and these characters and for pushing me to take their stories where they soar. I am so grateful for this experience with you and so glad to have had you on the first half of this journey through Illustros. You made my debut into publishing so special, and I am forever and ever thankful.

To my entire team at Hyperion that has worked to make these books special and to my cover artist, Charlie Bowater, for another absolutely stunning cover.

To my archnemesis, Elba. I am so sorry you got pooped on by that seagull in California, but thanks for continuing to come on all of these adventures with me despite the danger of seabirds. I would definitely save you from falling off of a cliff before anyone else, despite the rumors you may have heard. Thanks for telling me I was capable of writing this book and for FaceTiming me every time I had a breakdown about it. I am so so so proud of everything you've accomplished and cannot wait until our books are on a shelf next to each other very soon! You're one of the most talented authors I know, and I can't wait for everyone to fall in love with your words as much as I have. I love you, Luzer.

To Hannah and Alex, what an incredible year it's been with you both. Cheers to many more!

To the greatest sister-in-law ever, Lily, for not only reading this book multiple times, but for giving me the most helpful feedback in the world. Could not be more appreciative of you for your excitement and support and this book genuinely would not be what it is without your notes and enthusiasm. So happy to have another obsessive reader in the family.

Darci, Em, Dee, Gabi, and Raye. Could not be luckier to have the support system I do with all of you. Thanks for being the absolute angels that you are and for screaming about my books far and wide and for always being excited to read the disaster drafts of my stories before they're edited and are basically just my tears on paper. Thanks for keeping all of my book secrets and for loving all my characters. Cannot wait for our next adventures!

To my family for being so supportive through this journey. To Tera for reading this book and giving me such great feedback and enthusiasm—you really got it and that kept me going. To Catalina and Niki for always hyping me up.

To Andrea Hannah and Sheyla Knigge—thanks for keeping me sane, buddies. Andrea, you are the wisest witch I know; also I am like a cat that you have been too kind to that you will never be able to get rid of now, so buckle up, bestie, I'm here to annoy you forever.

To all the booksellers and librarians who have enthusiastically told readers about *A Ruinous Fate*, written recommendation cards for it, posted about it on social, or welcomed me in your stores with such kind enthusiasm—you all are the backbone of the book world and I could not be more grateful for your warm welcome. Thank you for everything you do not just for the authors but the kids!

So thankful for the many people in the book community who have been incredible to me: Hannah Sawyer, Night, Jas, Hayley, Cath, all of my angel agent siblings, Sophie, Kailei, Michelle R., Michelle M., Amber my fellow Cajun girl, Sara, Sam, Catherine C., Tianna, Jessie, Kailin, and so many more. Night—you are an angel and a gift to so many who know you. Thank you for reading like three different versions of this book, for your notes and humor, and for being such a kind soul. Thanks to all the authors I have met throughout the past two years who have become friends and mentors and have been such great companions to know on this roller-coaster ride.

To Rosalynn (Rosalynnarts) for all of the incredible artwork you made for me to promote these books: working with and getting to know you has been such a delight. To my incredibly talented audiobook narrators, Dana and Alex—you both blew me away! Thank you so much for lending your voices to these characters.

To my street team for *A Ruinous Fate*—Matou, Amy, Kris, Nina, Katie, Maddie, Kyla, Kaitlin, Arley, Laura, Teddy, Kate, Rania, and all the others who helped so much—you all went above and beyond, and I am so lucky to have had you all celebrating the release of *ARF* with me!

To anyone I may have forgotten because I'm writing these at three in the morning and haven't slept in two years, add your name here:

And finally, to all the readers who not only read *A Ruinous Fate*, but sent me the kindest messages about the characters, took the most gorgeous photos of the book, made the cleverest videos and edits, and passionately care for this story like I do—I will forever be grateful to you for giving my books a chance. Nothing in my life has been more fulfilling than all of you telling me you felt seen in these characters or that they helped you escape when you needed to most. The ending of book one was very mean, but hopefully you've forgiven me and are ready for the next adventure! I will see you all again soon. All my love.